A Mirror for Larks

by the same author

Dividing Lines

Victor Sage
A Mirror for Larks

First published in Great Britain in 1993 by

Martin Secker & Warburg Limited

Michelin House, 81 Fulham Road, London SW3 6RB

A CIP catalogue record for this book

is available from the British Library

Typeset in 12/14 Perpetua

by Deltatype Ltd, Ellesmere Port, Cheshire

Printed in Great Britain by

Mackays of Chatham plc, Chatham, Kent

To Sharon

who was there at the time

The masses refuse to accept anything from us . . . They think German influence has been decisively negative, and such as to postpone the solution of the problem at least until after the war . . . This has the effect of heaping on to us their contempt, as they said we were not in good faith and hold that the announcement of nationalisation was the nth expedient to draw into our orbit the few mugs who still give us any credit. In brief, the workers consider nationalisation as a mirror to catch larks, and they keep well away from us and the mirror.

Report by Vaccari (head of the Fascist Federation of Commercial
Employees) to the Duce, 20 June 1944

Q   I have a deposition of Master Puddicombe, of the Black Hart Inn. He says you told there of a lunatic fit one night upon the road.

A   I told tales wherever we went, sir. Mirrors for larks, as they say.

John Fowles, *A Maggot* (1985)

Part One

Florence

I had been thinking for some time it would do Zonda good to take a trip. Florence had emptied and filled up and emptied again – her friends from the shop had long since come back from Gozo, and now they had even departed for New York – while financial distress had kept me plugging away all summer long at the racetracks, the trotting, the national lottery, nightly sessions of backgammon, and anything else of a casual nature I could initiate. It had begun to take the promise of a special occasion to tempt her to come racing. In the day, while I was out, she often stayed in bed. When she rose, she painted and decorated listlessly. It struck me again, as I watched her fidget round the kitchen, red-eyed and sweaty from sleep, that she had the air of someone at a loose end.

She poured herself some tea and lit a cigarette, letting the one go cold and the other go out while she treated me to something which began: '*E una storia brutta . . .*' We still had the habit of reading aloud to each other from the newspapers, a practice which stemmed from the time when it had been necessary to cultivate her Italian, and despite the fact that I was in the middle of writing up my form books, a duty as sacred as a young girl's diary, convention prohibited complaint. I knew the article already: it was a reconstruction of the death of her current heroine, Miriam Corte, the supergrass from Padua who had fallen from a balcony in mysterious circumstances. The writer was summing up the many doubts raised by the recent inquest. Zonda had been following the case, and had long ago made up her mind

3

that the woman had been defenestrated, although the official verdict had been suicide. I pointed out to her that the line between *suicidio* and *disgrazia* was a thin one, especially in close-knit communities like Pieve di Cadore, the village near Padua where this incident had taken place.

Zonda sniffed at the implication, but the article was suggesting that they hadn't needed to push her.

' "*Ho paura, mi minacciano, mi sento minacciata.* I'm afraid, they are threatening me, I feel threatened," ' she intoned in a special terrorist contralto, taking quick draws on her rescued cigarette for effect between each phrase. 'She says "*minacciano*" – well, who are *they* then?'

'I'm not saying "they" don't exist . . .' I said, squinting at my own tiny writing.

'Here we are . . . blah-blah-blah . . . "According to one eye-witness, she remained holding on to the edge of the third-floor balcony *for several seconds* . . ." '

'Exactly,' I said. 'It makes my point. She couldn't have been pushed.'

But she was silent, her eyes jerking across the page. 'Mmm . . .' she said.

Every week throughout the heat of August and early September the Italian papers had been full of incomprehensible deaths. With the calm of baroque cherubim, the victims stared out at us from a mass of hysterical print. And each death, so it seemed, uncovered new connections with ever-multiplying cells of terrorists: Prima Linea, Terza Posizione, Autonomia 28 Marzo, etc., etc. 'Terrorismo' had become a special page like 'Culture' or 'Weekend Leisure' and to my disgust it was beginning to threaten the space given to racing in some newspapers. Since the Bologna station bomb of August the second, the whole country appeared to have divided into a set of armed camps, but for a long time no one seemed to know whether *La strage* had been perpetrated by red or black terrorists and while we all argued the huge crater, into which half a railway station and its human contents had been swallowed up, gaped accusingly. Every time I went to the track in Milan, I had to change at Bologna. Every time, my fellow passengers crowded into the corridors to stare down into the rubble over the bunting that sagged between the iron spikes while the train crept past for a furlong or more before picking up speed.

Her side of the bed was stacked high with paperback biographies of the Kray twins, Ian Brady and Myra Hindley, Graham the Poisoner, and the Helen Smith story, which I suspected she was using as a model for this one. Zonda made a bee-line for an outrage, flicking back and forth through its details like a book of wallpaper samples. 'Terrorismo' was merely one chapter in an exotic feuilleton. At Maidstone she had spent months of her young life executing a life-size portrait of the Kray twins.

'Why don't you get on to her dying words in the ambulance?' I said, changing from red to blue biro.

'Raymond, you beast, you've already read it!'

' "*No non mi sono gettata dalla finestra* . . . I didn't throw myself out of the window!' I quoted. 'You should get up earlier.'

'*Que scifo!*' she moaned, getting up to water her plants, and lumping me in with the terrorists. 'The bastards . . . That's it! That fucking witness was fixed . . . Puss Puss . . .'

She stood at the window, the green plastic watering-can in her hand, calling to the white cat on the patch of roof opposite, sporting an old blue and white striped Hawes and Curtis shirt of mine and a pair of pink crêpe pants. She was virtually hairless apart from a haze of blonde strands that caught the light on her legs and arms and under the hairline on either side of her long curved neck. Not a flaxen chestnut, but a short-coupled, flashing chestnut. The hips were tiny, and the legs slightly overfull in the lower calf and ankle, which imperfection, together with a slightly shuffling gait, the ample knees rubbing against one another, made her body the site of a piquant struggle between personal vitality and indifferent breeding.

5

'I agree it's more interesting if they drove her to it,' I said, 'but she grassed. What do you expect? Fair play?'

Zonda dropped the watering-can in the sink with a bang and turned round to face me.

'She was *venti cinqu'anni*, Raymond, that's *all*!'

She was indignant, but at twenty herself it was hard for Zonda to be serious. This was what I found so attractive about her. Her face, even when choking with decency, was highly mobile, the face of a comedienne, who, if she didn't open her mouth, could pass for a glamour-puss; but as soon as the nose began to wrinkle, the lips quiver, and the long teeth show, that impression was immediately replaced by another that began to drive out the glossy magazine model: the actressy comic. Zonda was given to mimicry of uncanny accuracy over short stretches of conversation. After that, her brilliance faded, but she was constantly practising, often without knowing it. In the middle of serious discussions she repeated single words lightly, trying them out for their sound value. The eyes, a steady, distant-sky-at-the-end-of-a-perfect-day-at-the-racetrack-with-your-winnings-in-your-pocket blue, sat large and liquid above the soft bulge of the cheeks. And this was the contradiction of the face, that these eyes always had a serious intent, while the mouth had a fugitive edge of satire and humour, as if it were ready to laugh without an audience, or even the permission of the rest of the features.

She moved back gingerly to the table, straddled her chair, and lit another cigarette. A heated discussion followed, in the course of which I received passing abuse, tactically delivered at intervals in order to interrupt my writing. In return I painted a violent intrusion at the breakfast table by black terrorists, with only myself, my uncle, the submarine commander's sword, and my mother's stubby little pewter-stocked four-ten standing between Zonda and certain incarceration, to say nothing of rape and possible torture, in an insanitary shepherd's hut on the island of Sardinia.

'You are infuriating,' she said.

'Look at the Kronzuckers . . .' I laid down my pen at last, all pretence of writing gone. 'What would you rather I did? Let them take you? I tell you, you've got to have a *go* at these people . . . stand up to them . . .'

'You'd come with us to the hut,' said Zonda, 'but then you'd make a deal with them. They could have me, while you looked for the ransom money. And then you'd bugger off, and never be seen again, you'd *leave* me . . .'

She was only saying this, I pointed out, because she had no answer to my question. We got up and wrestled feebly for a bit. But I wanted to finish my books. Whenever I saw her coming towards me with her pout, and her 'You don't *love* me!' I backed away, not wanting all that mauling and demanding, and of course – good player on the tennis court of the space between us – she anticipated this and stiffened, and there we were, often enough, standing for a long time, in silent struggle by the sink, or leaning motionless against the bathroom door, or swaying as now in the middle of the kitchen. She could see that I was dying for her to put her arms at her sides and behave herself, and the knowledge made her cling more, but in a parodic fashion, creasing up her face and imitating a drowning person about to go down for the third and last time, while she hung on my neck, until I was forced to place my hands lightly on her hips so as not to fall over, and, thence, to titter collusively.

I scanned the results and the form, listening to her next-door humming a Dolly Parton song over the thunder of her bathwater. She was a thousand miles away now. Our friends from both sides stared at us with a mixture of helplessness and resentment, like people on the banks of a suddenly flooded river they can no longer get across. Occasionally they made a gesture of impatience at each other. But most of the time they regarded us with the degree of suspicion usually granted to doorstep occultists. When charged fatuously with the possibility of paternity, I protested its unlikelihood: at fourteen, it might have been *biologically* possible, but I was not precocious enough to have become her father. In vain. Anyway, it wouldn't – it couldn't last, they hinted. But here we were, eighteen months later, Zonda Swift, the vivacious mongrel, and Raymond Bosanquet, the crepuscular thorough-bred, an alliance cemented by flippancy, a shared aversion for sex, which we called 'the fishy thing', the last shekels of my vanished patrimony, and an almost anthropological curiosity about each other's worlds.

It hadn't occurred to me with any real clarity before, but Zonda was turning from Art School into Hostess. The black leather jackets and the dirty, overtight jeans had given way to blouses and discreet silk cravats and napkins on the table; and the lorry-driver Florentine she had begun by acquiring had bloomed – not without wild, briar-like reversions, of course – as the lacquered, rosebud-articulacy of an Italian television programme announcer. What was oddest, however, was not the Italian, but the English side of things: now, after twenty months in Italy, her English veered without control between Maidstone and Sloane Square. This was undoubtedly Julia and myself. And if I had had any influence, I was proud of it. What did it matter, provided she was off the drugs?

So long as it was Dolly Parton, and not the cool, inward moaning of Max Mauldauer, I didn't mind. Personally I loathed Dolly Parton, but I was willing to buy Zonda as many Country and Western records to fantasise in the mirror about being a star to as she liked. Her parents had a lot to thank me for. Champagne and horses were traditional, outdoor forms of dissipation, a whole lot healthier than the quivering pallor of the Maidstone–South London rock band circuit. All she had absorbed from that had been too much Florida Orange Juice, smack, and a slack-mouthed, mumbling style of speech.

On the whole racing types are contemptuous of dope for humans, and although there were social overlaps between my cronies, the Jasper Guinness set, and the junkies that left the steps of Santa Croce littered with old needles , Zonda had so far shown no interest in those sleazier extensions of Chelsea. And she had a defence to her art school friends who visited and queried me:

'Oh, Raymond's *far* too old to be a Sloane . . .'

To my surprise, she even looked like a tall Dolly Parton with blotchy skin as she came out of the bathroom, one hand supporting the pink turban piled on her head.

Casually, I let it drop that I had the tickets for Paris.

'This week*end*!' she shrieked unnecessarily, and fell back with a pleasing access of energy against the doorpost. Then she recovered her part:

'Why *honey*,' she twanged, patting the back of the turban, 'what'n hell's name d'yall 'spect a gal to *wayer*?'

9

Paris

It was a relief to wake up in Gare de Lyon on Saturday morning and check in at my usual little place on the Boulevard St Germain. It felt like being back in civilisation again. After breakfast in the bar with the English-sounding name, le Piccadilly, I took Zonda across the road to see 'La Dame à la Licorne' at Cluny. My favourite panel of this tapestry depicting the purification of the five senses is 'Touch', in which the Lady's lust, personified as a little monkey, is chained to a thing that looks like a garden-roller, so that she is free to caress with innocence the barley-sugar phallus of her smirking unicorn. I said to Zonda it ought to be called 'Having it Both Ways', but she didn't agree with my interpretation as usual and we shouted at each other in Italian, disturbing all the pious Americans waiting patiently with their Leicas on tripods to catch the slightest flush of sun through the lights in the roof.

I was rather disappointed that my build-up had gone astray, but I had learned to be patient. Everything presented a primary challenge to Zonda's own individual taste; nothing could be handed on to her, every phenomenon, however slight, had an invisible label attached to it which had to be removed so that the thing could be properly chosen or rejected: she made constant discoveries for herself: the so-called beautiful was really anaemic, the said-to-be-trivial etc. was frightfully sophisticated, the frightfully sophisticated was an absolute bore. She would stare for a moment, having heard the case made, and then came the drawl and the increasingly confident shake of the head:

11

'No . . . no, I *definitely* don't *like* it . . .' And that appeared to be that. What could be more final? And yet later, at parties, I sometimes overheard her giving an enthusiastic account of that something which was clearly designed to impress the hearer. The thing's stock, at a discount for the period of assimilation, had unexpectedly yielded a premium in the meantime.

We reconnoitred for a dress, and met Julia and Noel for lunch. Julia was in the middle of moving from her little place off République to a *grenier* in the fourth which belonged to an aged aunt of ours. Unfortunately, she had just completed the sale of the duplex that morning, while the other place was not yet ready to move into. She was laughing hysterically about this and could talk of nothing else.

'I'm on the streets,' she said to Zonda. 'I *literally* don't have anywhere to go.'

'So many people misuse this expression "literally",' I said to Noel, just loud enough for them to hear.

Julia stopped.

'Did I say something wrong?' she asked.

'God, Raymond,' said Zonda, blinking earnestly, 'you are *sensitive*, aren't you?' She put a hand out to Julia. 'Don't pay any attention to him . . .'

'What are they talking about?' said canny old Noel, who had no intention of getting involved.

'Oh,' I said in Zonda's direction, 'just knickers and tights . . . you know, girl's things . . .'

Zonda, who was reaching for a cigarette, looked at me threateningly over Julia's shoulder, but it was all too absorbing, the long tale of the wallpaper.

Bridge-building apart, I was tired of lunch being given over to my sister's banalities and I thought she was a bore to cry off the races on Sunday. I agitated at the end of the table, interrupting them, egging Julia on to tell Zonda and Noel the story of Mr Piker, which I enjoyed and hadn't heard for a couple of years. Julia enjoyed it too, secretly, but was ashamed of it and tried to get out of telling it on the grounds of general humanity. But she is so caught up in the Bosanquet myth that it was worth her telling it just to watch the faces of the others.

When she was in London, Julia had been overspending and one day she went to the City office of our bank, in order to do a bit more overspending, as per usual. To her surprise, she was met in the lobby by Mr Piker, a person from Essex, whom she had never seen before. Mr Piker took her into his office, sat her down and gave a long lecture about the state of her account in tones which she described as 'brutish'. She claims to have interrupted Mr Piker once during this speech, to ask in a bewildered fashion: 'But where is nice Mr Silk?' Mr Piker explained that nice Mr Silk was ill, and that he had taken over the handling of Miss Bosanquet's account while he was away. At this point, Julia broke down and began to cry, left the office abruptly without cashing the cheque she badly wanted, and rushed back to her dwelling in Tregunter Road. Unfortunately, she was due to have lunch with our mother, who turned up at this moment, saw her state and learnt of its origin. The next time Julia warily approached the bank, she was greeted by nice Mr Silk who extended her credit facilities handsomely and begged her 'not to worry'. She ventured to ask where Mr Piker was. Mr Silk gave a discreet smile and said that Mr Piker's zeal and ambition had recently been recognised 'by appointment to our subsidiary in Glasgow'.

Julia and I laughed until the tears ran down our cheeks.

'To our branch in the Outer Hebrides!' I said, hooting. Noel and Zonda looked at each other and shrugged.

'Raymond,' said Zonda, 'I can't see anything funny in that. It's disgusting. Bloody well *disgusting*.'

She was indignant, and I could see that this was going to involve fairness, and fairness would lead directly to socialism.

'Oh God,' I said, 'not Piker's rights . . .'

I looked at Julia, who was wiping her eyes and still breaking down into a rain of after-giggles.

'And he was *never* heard of *again* . . .' she said in her tiny voice.

13

'It is not unfunny, you must admit,' I said to Zonda.

'I don't admit anything of the kind.'

'Spoilsport,' I coaxed.

'You're quite right. Zonda is quite right,' said Julia. 'I should never tell that story . . .'

'What possible difference does *that* make?' I said with derision. 'What possible difference can not telling it make? It happened. You're just trying to get yourself off the hook.'

Since Julia had said she was not coming to the Arc, I thought the least we could do was see her for dinner later that night, so she agreed to find us an old-fashioned Parisian restaurant. Then she and Zonda went to look for the dress and some shoes. Zonda told me I was a bore and a bully, and then asked me good-naturedly for the money for the dress, a transition which she accomplished without batting an eyelid. Noel and I spent the rest of the afternoon in fruitless competition on a pin-ball machine in the back of a bar at the Pont St Michel, glaring at the laughing bikini-girl from Acapulco, whose nipples, we were assured, would light up after 5,000 points. The light was bad in the back of the bar. Did I really see a dull flicker from the left-hand bulb? We retired to backgammon at the hotel, which was slightly more rewarding. Later when we were getting ready to go out, Zonda called me in out of the shower. She was lying on the bed smoking and watching the six o'clock news. There had been a bomb somewhere in a synagogue while we were out.

'Look at this . . .' she was saying, staring intensely at the images of shattered debris and police cordons.

'They must have known we were coming,' I called from the door, trying to lighten the tone.

But the TV was making a thing of it, interviewing everyone they could find and calling it a concerted wave of *néo-nazisme*, dragging in Bologna and the Munich Beer Festival bomb, and now this outrage, said the announcer, in the Rue Copernic, no less, *en plein Paris*.

We laughed at the indignation of the French.

14

'Cor,' said Zonda in Maidstone to the announcer, 'you should try living in Italy mate!'

We all liked Julia's restaurant, Julien's in the Faubourg St Denis, and we spent the evening there amusing each other by swapping impressions. I have a tendency to jowls, a solid pack of flesh from chin to neck, and these I can wobble to good effect when doing my only really convincing impressions – of old expatriate queens and Florentine lounge lizards. Julia and I both speak in the same rapid slur whatever the language, which is clearly a family trait, though I had not noticed it until Zonda started imitating it at dinner. We ended up in gales of laughter imitating ourselves whenever we spoke.

Afterwards we strolled down the Rue St Denis for a peep at the *filles de joie* and the roaming herds of their clients and walked over from Châtelet to Noel's sixth-floor place on the Ile St Louis. Zonda was thrilled by the gilt mirrors and kept turning to catch a glimpse of herself as she ran from window to window to look at the lights across at Hôtel de Ville and the St Laurent tower. I pulled her back by the belt.

'We don't want to do a Corte, do we dear?' I whispered. We stayed late in good humour, and eventually crossed back over the river. Zonda was dragging her feet by now, but I wanted to go further down St Germain to our bar for a nightcap.

Judging from the glass all over the road and the crowds – five-deep, fixed and staring at the front, strolling up and down, bored at the back – it was another bomb. Zonda pushed her way through but there was nothing to be seen: no red-blanketed stretchers being slid into the backs of ambulances. No enigmatic forms and people running with drips held high. She struggled and elbowed her way through the press.

'I think they said it was a woman,' she said as she walked away ahead of me.

I looked at the car. It had Dutch registration plates. The engine and front wing on the driver's side were unrecognisable. I caught her up and we stopped for Zonda to hold on to me.

'It could have been us,' she said, tremblingly, in my ear, 'just think, if we'd been a few minutes earlier . . .'

'But we weren't,' I said in the end.

She pulled away and stared down at the clear end of the boulevard, where life was going on as if nothing had happened. And later, when we were lying in bed after a couple of really stiff cognacs, she started going over it, imagining us sitting down at the Piccadilly in the window that had been shattered by the explosion, the same window seat we'd had breakfast in that morning, having not had that last drink at Noel's and stopped to look at the lights. Everything was possible, I said, but not everything was likely, and since it hadn't happened, it couldn't have been *that* likely. She insisted that it was likely for *us* to have been blown to smithereens.

Hadn't she ever heard of degrees of likelihood? No I didn't admit it had ever been more likely than not, and asked her what evidence she had. It had been so close. I pointed out that a miss was a good as a mile where likelihood was concerned.

'It was a good deal closer than a mile,' said Zonda.

'Hypotheses don't count as evidence,' I said, quickly making up a rule, 'and closeness is a hypothesis . . .'

'Raymond, it's just up the fucking *road*. What's hypothetical about that?'

'In terms of probability,' I said, 'we might just as well have been in Sydney, Australia . . .'

'Oh, I don't under*stand* . . .' she groaned, turning on to her stomach and flinging her arms round the pillow.

'Anyway,' I said after a time, 'they didn't blow the bar up, they blew the car up . . .'

But she had gone, the airstream which issued at intervals from between her cracked lips causing a regular flutter in the corner of the pillow-slip.

I saw with pleasure that they were only giving Detroit 8/1 at the course, but I had placed the bet a couple of weeks previously when she had been beaten into third at the Prix Vermeille and the odds had gone to 12/1. Zonda was backing the winner of the Vermeille, Mrs Penny, a class filly, of course, but I couldn't see her taking the Arc somehow, not after her performance in the Benson and Hedges that year at York, which Zonda had been too hungover to watch: the best Piggott could manage on her there had been a fourth. I reminded Zonda of this, but she wasn't interested. All she was really interested in, as she studied the gathering groups of owners and jockeys in the paddock, was Mrs Sangster's egret-plumes and her orange Moroccan silk number.

'*Hideous* gear,' she murmured, 'but such a lot of *mun* . . . ney.'

Noel had Ela Mana Mou, which had beaten Mrs Penny at Ascot in the King George and Queen Elizabeth. This was a reasonable bet, a typical Noel bet, but I didn't think much of it. Longchamp isn't Ascot after all, and I didn't think she'd make it on the heavier ground. In Noel's case I put it down to his education: his inferior public school somewhere in a corner of a damp field in Shropshire had dinned into him the fatal mediocrity of decision that such institutions promote, thus depriving him at the outset, poor Noel, of any really intimate relationship with the future.

If she were going to be with me, I had insisted, Zonda had better have something passable on. To my chagrin, she had refused a hat, but she and Julia had managed to buy a silk shirt-waister in grey with rose-pink facings to go with a pair of strapped, boat-shaped pink things that, she claimed, uniquely accommodated her wide feet, but which were really bought because they were pink. Zonda was just coming out of her pink period. 'The hair', as she referred to it, now no longer pink but slowly recovering via a metallic silver dyeing its natural tone of flashing chestnut, just failed to achieve the shoulder-length which the dress demanded, and still looked a bit thin and darkish at the roots, but she was a presence, even so, as she stared absorbedly at Pat Eddery mumbling to himself and the older jockeys touching their caps to the owners before receiving their last-minute instructions, the full skirt catching with the momentary crack of a sail against her braced legs in a gust of the rather pleasing south-westerly breeze, which, I noted, would drive the horses against the rails in the home straight. I was watching her from inside the little bar as I queued for drinks and for a moment when Noel said something, she looked my way and laughed, reaching like a mime artist to pull out of the corner of her mouth invisible strands of hair that had whipped across her face as she turned. She had opened one too many buttons at the front, of course, but the décolleté was offset by a pink paisley cravat of mine, tied carelessly at the throat, in a knot that had taken the three of us the best part of twenty minutes' consultation and two extra glasses of champagne to arrive at.

It had become obvious in the wind that she was wearing very little beneath the dress. I twisted round the other way to catch some of the punters across the terraces opposite staring at her against the light through the six knobbly plane trees. They were absorbed in marking their papers with last-minute stars and scribbles, some of them diverted by the antics of a loud Algerian who called out the Christian names of the jockeys as they were helped into the saddle, but their eyes sooner or later drifted up and converged at the point where she stood, just above the glossy clattering haunches in front of them, and came to rest there, dreamy and urgent at the same time. A young Dean Martin replica, and three along from him, a large Negro in a dirty, full-length robe of powder-blue, a toothpick jutting two inches from his contemplative mouth, appeared particularly transfixed.

How pleasant to be in the enclosure amongst the owners and trainers. It makes one feel part of the show, I thought, as I watched her shift weight on to her heel and point the toe of the other foot, ballerina-like. What could be more agreeable? The rhetorical question was Sir Kenneth Clarke's in the television programme *Civilisation*, delivered with closed eyes and a little fluttering sigh of pleasure, the façade of San Miniato standing slightly skew-whiff behind him, as he finished a lip-smacking account of a typical afternoon in the life of Lorenzo di Medici.

18

The phrase had caught my ear as a device to render the sensation of excess without the penalties of indulgence, but we all used it so much that year that its point was lost.

Unfortunately the bar was crowded with English people I was rather anxious to avoid. This aversion competed with the desire to get another round in before the surge across to the stands began. I nodded to the inevitable Kempe, and someone called Nigel Tanguy my father had introduced me to while we were having lunch one day in The Boot and Flogger in Borough High Street in the vain hope that I might do something useful in the City, was thrusting purposefully through the crowd towards me, I saw, hoisting his glass just above the sea of shoulders. The waiters had given up being French for the day. One of them kept shouting 'Of course! Of course', his automatic cry audible at a distance through a hail of indeterminate requests:

'Sixteen Bollinger please!'

'Of course! Of course!'

I cruised through on the outside and sped back with tiny mincing steps, so as not to spill any precious drops from the three shallow glasses of gin-sling locked in my interlaced hands, arriving just as the horses were taking their last turn – a moment preserved in an absolute amber of agreeableness, in which the Sangster colours appeared preternaturally bright and one's money as sure as it could ever be of its twelvefold return.

And then, at last, the airport chimes sounded and the young woman's velvety voice was saying: '*Voici le début des opérations pour la deuxième course, le Prix de l'Arc de Triomphe . . .*' It was time to down our drinks and drift, the three of us arm in arm, past the masses of ageing scarlet geraniums along the white railings to the elevators that carried us soothingly amongst miscellaneous sheikhs and silvery Frenchmen and their honey-coloured wives to the top of the stand, just in time to see Freddy Head on Three Troikas emerge below us on to the course and begin the canter down towards the Mill.

*

19

The correct way to leave Longchamp, of course, unless one has a helicopter, is to go early and get a cab from the Suresnes gate, and no doubt if left to his own devices Noel would have done just this. But Zonda and I chose under the circumstances to walk away from the sunset and make for town as the crow flies. After the last bar closed we forced Noel across the hallowed ground, pushing him in front of us, and made a ragged exit on the other side of the course, weaving our way down the tunnel between the limousines filled with impatient members of the French government and their wives, climbing over the turnstile in the little cabin, Zonda sustaining a three-cornered tear in the skirt of her new dress; and the three of us ended up, line-abreast, shuffling in a hypnotised daze through deep leaves along the interminable avenues east of the Bois de Boulogne. Zonda stopped, and the mesmeric swishing came to a halt.

'What about Argument, then? Another couple of strides and she'd have made it . . .'

'Argument is a colt,' I corrected.

'Yes, *wasn't* that amazing?' said Noel. 'Didn't you have a flicker of doubt at that moment?'

'I thought it was more likely than not that we would win,' I said.

'God,' said Zonda, 'getting you to admit anything . . .'

'But just think,' said Noel, 'six thousand pounds!'

'Just *short* of six thousand pounds,' I corrected him.

'I want gold bath taps,' said Zonda decisively, hugging my arm, 'and some new shoes for starters.'

'Ah, yes, that reminds me,' I said to Noel, 'before we go any further . . .'

I sat down on a bench and wrote him a cheque for two thousand, two hundred pounds, a series of small casual loans which had built up over the course of about two years. Noel, whose family are fallen Scottish coal-owners, is cautious with his money, never having had as much as I, and tends to hug to him the allegedly modest returns he gets from his silver investments.

He claimed to have got his fingers burnt in the spring when silver dived from $50 to $10 an ounce. A couple of Americans, apparently, had tried to corner the world market. Since March, he had taken to ringing me up and reminding me what a sacrifice for him a loan was. I was thinking of my creditors back in Italy. What was left wouldn't even begin to interest them, so footling a sum was it. A mere thirty-four thousand francs. It shrank as I contemplated it. Quite the best thing to do with it was stay in Paris a few days and spend it. What could be more agreeable?

Before the taxi-driver had finished telling us it might be better to get out and cross the square on foot, he was paid off and I was in the nearest bar ordering us some drinks. I phoned Julia from the *sous-sol* to tell her we were just across the way and give her the glad tidings. She was watching the demonstration with some friends from her window. She called it, to my disgust, 'the demo'. I told her to book Maxim's. I was longing for a real whole *pâté de foie gras*.

When I went upstairs, the drinks were still fizzing pinkly on the table and the empty taxi was sitting marooned in the same spot, the only change discernible, the fact that its bonnet was now slackly draped with a huge banner, hoisted up on either side of the road by two enthusiastic youths: the red letters flapped their code:

TEL AVIV ANVERS BOLOGNA MUNICH

'What's all that about?' I said.

'Where's Zonda?' said Noel.

I told him I thought she had been with him. The light was failing and the square was still crowded, an acre of dim, pushing bodies, winding back on each other like a queue that had forgotten what it was there for.

'God,' said Noel, 'this is my idea of hell. It even *looks* like a Dante engraving.'

'This is flat,' I remarked, handing him his Campari.

Someone was shouting enthusiastically into a microphone up by the verdigris-covered monument.

'Better try to get across,' I said to Noel as we plunged into the crowd. 'She's bound to make for Julia's place . . .'

When we reached the top of the stairs and pressed Julia's bell, I fully expected to find her inside. But Julia said she hadn't been, so I left the collapsing Noel and went down still panting into the square again, shoving the skull-capped figures out of my way. I was brisk. Several of them shouted at me in what was presumably Hebrew. I got up on to various ledges and low walls at regular intervals to peer over their heads, wheeling my stocky body from one point of vantage to the next in business-like fashion. I tried to recall the last time this had happened. It was getting really quite cold now, and I thought people were beginning to drift away. The speaker was shouting something in French about Giscard, and a cry went up all round me. I saw her at last in the doorway of a bar, nodding and talking animatedly to a young woman with a blood-red bandanna tied across her forehead who was holding a small yelling child in one hand and in the other a placard made out of an orange box in the other on which had been hastily scrawled in black felt-tip: *Les fils et les filles des déportés juifs de la France*. Zonda had her hand on the woman's forearm and was saying something insistently.

I presented myself and she threw her arms around my neck and hugged me tight, glancing at the woman. I smiled, slightly tight-lipped, feeling a little peculiar, and said:

'Hi. Julia's waiting . . .'

'*Tout redevient possible*,' said the woman to Zonda with intensity. '*Tout recommence. Pas question, certes . . . il s'agit d'un alibi idéologique . . .*'

'Raymond,' said Zonda, 'it's really *awful*. She's just been telling me about her mother. They were all rounded up in the Velodrome in 1942 . . .'

'Hello,' I said in the woman's direction. 'Rather anxious to get off to Maxim's . . .'

'He's just won the Arc de Triomphe,' said Zonda apologetically.

22

She turned to me. 'You look pink,' she said. This was for the benefit of her new friend, but I wasn't amused.

'I sincerely *hope* that's not meant to be a political remark,' I said. 'If you're referring to my complexion, it's because I've been running about looking for you . . .'

I took her under the arm, which she immediately lifted slightly and wrenched away, not a crack in her warm smile, to shake hands with her new friend.

'Isn't she nice?' said Zonda, looking back and waving as we walked away. 'We've been having a real heart-to-heart,' she sighed. 'What *bastards* these right-wing terrorists are!'

'Yes darling,' I said. 'You wouldn't know one from another.'

She ignored this.

'She says it's the right's fault because they've been wooing the Arabs for the oil . . .'

I wrinkled up my brow.

'I don't understand that, do you?'

'Such a nice lady,' said Zonda. 'I *liked* her . . .' She looked at me sidelong and took my arm as we reached the foyer of the apartment block. 'There's a serious new wave of anti-Semitism in this country. It's masquerading as anti-Zionism. She was telling me all about Vichy France and this raffle thing – '

'Raffle?' I snorted.

'What are you so cross for, Raymond? I think that was the word she used. Something like that anyhow. And how they were all rounded up on the cycletrack somewhere and how they were all shipped from there to a camp near Drancy and deported to the east, 65,000 of them. Under 3,000 made it back. Her mother never came back. This is the first time since then that Jews have been openly killed in France. She says it's all coming back. They've had this Darquier thing, and some book about Jewish collaborators, and *Holocaust* on TV and now this. She says she's always been a patriot but now she feels a Jew first and a Frenchwoman second . . .'

She stopped because it was obvious that I was being stiff and holding myself away.

'Oh darling, please,' said Zonda, as we stepped out of the lift opposite Julia's door, '*don't* be cross.'

'Want to get going,' I said.

'You *are* cross,' she said triumphantly, as Julia opened the door. 'He's cross,' she repeated as we entered the room.

'Never mind,' said Julia. 'Have some Sancerre. It's *delicious*.'

But Zonda was embracing Noel in the centre of the room and telling him loudly in a baby voice that I was cross with her.

The Grand at Opéra had proved to have suitably aureous bath-taps, and we could take breakfast downstairs in the Café de la Paix: Bloody Marys first thing to tone up the system, and then Buck's Fizz for the breakfast part.

Steady consumption of champagne caused Zonda to heave as soon as she went near food, as it had done in York. She spent most of Monday morning travelling between bed and bathroom, thrilled by the sunken bath, vomiting demurely into its vast expanse of blue porcelain, while I went down to the Arcade opposite the Louvre and bought myself the thinnest gold watch I could find. It had a surprisingly large emerald in the winder, even though it was in fact self-winding. I had it engraved on the back:

DETROIT

ARC DE TRIOMPHE 1980

Zonda thought it 'vulgar'. For the most part she had to content herself with merely looking at the shoes she staggered out to buy, pair after pair – some of which were just strips of leather – heaped around her, because she felt too ill to put them on. Noel and I left her on Monday night sitting with her mouth open, watching an old Clint Eastwood movie dubbed jerkily into French, surrounded by newspapers and shoe boxes, pieces of tissue paper rising from the carpet and floating on every casual draught of air, while we went downstairs *sotto casa* to a rather too fulsome but entertaining *La Bohème*. When we returned, she hadn't moved off the long sofa, the ashtray piled high with ends and crushed packets of MS and the remote-control lying beside her unconscious hand, the thirty-five-inch television on its vaguely medical trolley flickering dutifully in the corner of the room, in the same position in which it had been left by the maid that morning, pushed up flush against the wall.

Meanwhile the feuilleton went on. *Figaro* reported our car-bomb, but couldn't make anything of it. The headlines ran:

MYSTERE DE LA VOITURE PIEGEE

Apparently the St Germain car-bomb had been 'claimed' by some terrorist group, but no one could see the point of it, according to Zonda who was always picking out papers from kiosks and asking me for money I didn't have. A Dutch housewife, a Mrs Carmelia van Puffeln, was the only person to have been injured. She had been sitting in the front seat.

'Ridiculous name,' I said, 'reminds me of pastry . . .'

'Shurrup Raymond,' said Zonda, staring at the photo of the shattered Rover. 'The poor woman had her leg blown off . . .'

'Curious how they "claim responsibility" for things – complete perversion of language, really. You often have two terrorist groups fighting for responsibility . . .'

' 'Very witty,' said Julia. 'You mean as if they were really moral . . .'

I had forgotten this nervous habit of checking my meaning.

'She *had* been in the bar,' said Zonda, reading on, triumphantly. 'She'd been having a drink in that bar . . .'

'It should be "admitted criminality" or "confessed" or something . . .'

'These carrots are absolutely de*lish*,' said Julia. 'They're so clever the French . . .'

'What does "déchiqueté' mean?' said Zonda.

'Lacerated,' said Julia eagerly, fragments of carrot oozing between her teeth.

'Mmm . . .' I said to her. 'This Pouilly-Fuissé's not so good though . . .'

'Oh God Raymond,' said Julia, 'let's change it . . .'

Whenever I frowned, she got into a panic. She might just as well have been still crouching behind the raspberry canes at the Coast Guard house in Norfolk as sitting pretending to be adult at her favourite terrace restaurant in Neuilly.

'That's what happened to the other leg . . .' said Zonda, pursing her lips. Julia had already got up and I stared after her as she pursued the waiter into the kitchen.

'What?'

'What she said.'

'Lacerated?'

'Yes, *that* . . .'

She pushed away the glazed medal of vegetable slices, perfectly centred in an empty hexagon of bone china, and her wine was untouched.

'*Dar*ling,' I said reaching across a hand that hovered about her arm, 'you alright?'

'Fucking sods,' she said.

Julia came back, tense, because her boyfriend Thierry's arrival was imminent. They brought the wine just as he appeared. Zonda perked up instantly and sat him down at her side, dredging up her heavily Italianate French.

I looked round at the terrace which was full of babbling couples and I nudged Julia:

'They *love* it!'

She laughed despite herself at this old family joke. A judge had once said it at home about some disgraceful habit of the proletariat and it stuck in my mind for further embroidery. Julia repeated it. It turned out to have an almost universal application and could be used to impersonate the attitudes of almost any group of people which regarded itself as superior to any other, if spoken sneeringly enough. I myself preferred a reedy, desiccated croak:

'They *lerve* it!'

Thierry was recounting, item by item, in a deadpan sequence the journeys that he had made during the last week in his car. His idea of small-talk was to tell you where he had just come from. Zonda nodded, a giggle frozen on her face, as he went into a lugubrious monologue about his inexorable rise in the world of Fast-Food.

I was listening to this Faustian tale of the Hitburger, however, rather than to Julia whose voice, though it was next to my ear, I could hear only faintly because I was so used to it. After a moment or two, I found its separate sounds almost as hard to concentrate on as the noise of water pouring continuously over a weir. She was talking about Mother's efforts with Pappa's diet. Julia was always going over to Kent. She saw it as her mission in life to mediate between our parents and me, to heal the breach between the owners and the owned. There was a certain amount of self-interest in this, as we both knew, since decisions made in respect of me, the eldest, tended to affect the chances of the other siblings. Any sign of détente, or a slackening of tension in relations, was welcomed, especially by our younger brother Piers, whose future after his one and only job – scratching records for EMI in London – taking perfectly good twelve-inch LPs and scratching a deep groove in them with a needle – looked bleak indeed. I never went back after I left for Italy, unable to face another interview with Pappa.

There were several of these interviews which came back to me unexpectedly at certain moments like scenes out of a film I had seen. The one that kept returning in all its old-masterish darkness and detail was the one after he had had his stroke. Before that, he had been articulate and contemptuous and I had been afraid of him, a thing which it took me years to admit. He accused me of being a profligate and of wasting the money he had settled on me at twenty-one. It was all conventional enough. When was I going to do something useful in life? 'Amount to something' was the phrase he used. Find myself a profession, make some money. But

27

afterwards the scene had a bizarre quality. He couldn't speak any more, because half of his face remained still while he spoke. His mouth tailed off into salivating babble at one side, while the other remained in an expression of fixed resolution. Feeling awful, I found it difficult not to laugh. And indeed, when I first saw him, I heard myself hoot with laughter that seemed to come out, however, as a kind of sob. He tried agitatedly to repeat what was his old speech to me – since I never heard it, I cannot say for sure what variations it might have contained – but nothing came out except a drivelling jumble of words that displaced one another like a pack of cards that have sprung out of the fingers of the shuffler. I looked away through the window of the study across the rose garden that was his pride and joy, the market-garden whose yield was one of the main preoccupations of his retirement, across the meadows that belonged to him, to the parkland, fixing my eyes on two distant Friesian heifers that were rooting peacefully about under some oak trees and understood no more than the trees themselves the fact that they, too, were rented.

'Fuff-fuff . . .' I heard his voice behind me as I stared at this Gainsborough-like abstraction called the view. Would he, or would he not, achieve one of his malingering code-sentences? It seemed likely, if one waited long enough.

But there was a motion, a kind of billowing, beneath all my surface interlacings of prediction, as Pappa fuffed away, struggling to produce some terrifyingly clean, yet wounding judgement of me:

'Fuff-fuff-fuffty . . .' he went. 'Terse back . . .'

And as I listened, the words broke clear of their surrounding haze:

'Terse Coutts fund fuffty not terse . . . not terse . . .'

I stared away from his working features and the stringy hand flecked with brown spots whose fingers clattered unknowingly on the desk amongst his penholders, and the feeling of tension came over me which often accompanies the deciphering of a *Times* crossword clue. I knew what he was trying to say. Of course, it was:

'You will not touch a penny of the Coutts money until you are fifty.'

He sat there with our Huguenot ancestors shelved and bound in half-calf behind him, the legal historians and the explorers, the City men and the dons, their cube-like spines like the wall of a European cemetery, and the news filtered past the double-take of his face – the solemn, stern, immovably patriarchal half, and the other half which was flapping away like the mouth of a foolish adolescent whispering in his friend's ears a remark that is too puerile to be attended to by anyone else – the news, that is, that I was financially up the creek without a paddle.

More likely than not, I thought.

Zonda had seized the opportunity of a male audience, and got on to one of her great themes: the weekend defeat of Ali by Holmes. She had been quite excessively moved by the whole sordid incident of the 'comeback', and gave Thierry her decline-of-the-great-man speech. Maudlin secretions rose in her eyes, overwhelming Thierry who was playfully trying to protest that Holmes was an underrated technician, as she repeated what Holmes had said after the fight as if it contained the key to the mystery of human existence: 'Well, he did his bit.'

'He did his bit!' said Zonda, shaking her head. 'He *did* his *bit* I fucking *ask* you . . .'

Choking, she gave a broken dissertation about the condition of Ali's inner organs, emptying her glass and getting up from the table to render the final moments of the fight, which she had seen on TV. Her lip dropped, her eyes narrowed to slits and she began to shuffle about flat-footedly, rolling away from Holmes's punches into the table next door, which was full of startled computer programmers, some of whom barely managed to snatch their tall glasses of Tavel from the bucking surface and perch them under their chins.

'Ouf . . . ouf . . . *ouf* . . .' said Zonda, looking back at Thierry as

29

her hip barged into the table again, causing another wave of precarious clinking and outraged snatching. Thierry, who had an unexpectedly high-pitched laugh, began to bray and Julia laughed in relief.

Slipping and sliding into the centre of the damp terrace, Zonda placed one hand flat on her bosom, and extended the other arm in impersonation of an invisible male partner. She was like a centaur, two people at once. Muhammad Ali had modulated into her heroine, Billie. I put my head down. I was determined that nothing, not even Billie Holiday, was going to interfere with my *mousse de crevettes*.

'She's absolutely plastered . . .' said Julia in a panic.

I contemplated the air bubbles in the mixture on my spoon.

'Do you think you could accommodate me?' I said.

'But I thought you'd just won at the races?'

We stared ahead of us at the developing cabaret. To the disgust of the terrace, Zonda had snatched up an imaginary mike, and was whining into it, her voice full of exaggerated breaks and catches:

> Momma may *have*
> Poppa *may*-ay have
> But . . . *God* bless the chile
> That's got his own . . .

'Oh hell,' said Julia, 'another restaurant to cross off my list . . .'

'You must have made quite a bit on this property deal,' I said.

'I thought you'd just won at the races,' she repeated.

I shrugged and gave her my serenest smile.

'What, *all* of it?' said Julia. She made a long, horse-face. And then: 'Oh well, I suppose . . .'

I was foolish enough to think she was cracking for a moment, but it was only a resigned identification with how I could have spent close on four thousand pounds in as many days. She was very good like that, Julia, but sometimes a little too sympathetic. The long and short of it was that there would be no loan forthcoming from that quarter.

'I have to live in this town you know,' said Julia, as Thierry shuffled aimlessly round with Zonda, his thumbs hooked in Zonda's belt at the back, the pair of them threatening to trip over on the projecting rustic stones. I glanced at Julia's face with regret. I had not chosen the best of moments. It was better thought of, I decided, as a preliminary approach. The major thrust of the campaign would have to take place, regrettably, on the telephone, later, when things had cooled down a little.

I was still fairly sprightly when we got on the sleeper to go home. It was a grey sort of sprightliness, but I had been finessing all day with regulated intakes of vodka and triple tomato juices and then small glasses of Kronenburg in between. Zonda, who had lain on the sofa until tea-time with cold towels on her forehead which I regularly replaced, groaned and staggered up the platform, her plastic bags full of shoes spinning round like gyroscopes in either hand. She was making a great effort not to cry.

'We're *leaving*,' she said in disbelief through the open window.

'How *dreary*,' I saw Julia say as we moved off, and I wondered for a moment what she was referring to.

'I'll give you a ring,' I said with intent, as I waved to her.

'Oh goodbye Noel darling, do come and see us!' shouted Zonda.

She collapsed into her couchette and wept for a bit, while I inspected the food which the Grand Hotel had made up for us.

'Darling,' I said, holding up slices of charcuterie that swayed with the action of the train and little foil-wrapped cartons of veal in cream and brandy sauce, 'look . . .'

Zonda lit a cigarette in the shadow of the upper bunk and blew a spume of smoke at the ceiling.

'Get that stuff out of my sight,' she said, 'before I'm sick . . .'

'Mortadella, thimbleful of champers . . .' I said. 'Do you good, darling, tee you up, help you to sleep . . .'

'Don't *wanna* sleep,' said Zonda, lying back.

31

'Well, *I'm* going to have some . . .' I said. 'What about a *petit four*, look?'

But she was drawing on her cigarette and staring at the ceiling. Each time the tip glowed pinkly, I could just make out the lighter mass of her face as we rattled out over the points.

'Raymond,' she said after a moment or two, 'what a bore that Thierry is . . .'

'I know,' I said, still combing through the hamper.

'Hope they *don't* come . . .'

'They won't,' I said, folding over some salami and smearing it with mayonnaise. 'Julia won't leave Paris.'

'Noel's fun, isn't he?' she said. 'I really *like* him . . .'

She delivered a halting dissertation on Noel's qualities, which eventually tailed off into silence. I wasn't listening, after a moment or two, because I had begun to explore the tender area of my debts. I grunted in the wrong places and she got indignant, but she was too far gone to get angry with me, rambling sloppily on and on. I gripped the cold champagne bottle, its body slippery with condensation, and carried the thick rim to my lips. My cheeks were full of the liquid when the *contrôleur* slid back the door with a crash and let in a piercing ray of electric light. Zonda had turned on her side, and I saw her beginning to roll back towards me, blinking, when he was gone, just as abruptly, rolling back the thunderous door without a word to crack on its catch and leave us in the double dark. I put a last *petit four* in my mouth, and decided it was not worth venturing out for a few days when we got back. There were too many people on the street who might ask me for money. Better to stay home and finish my review of the Tesio book for *The European Racehorse*. I remembered I had a translation to do for the Commune.

I climbed into the lower bunk, and lay on my back contemplating with gloom my business career. I am a liveryman of the Fishmongers' Company, and after Oxford I got a job in Threadneedle Street in a firm of brokers through someone I met at the annual Doggett's Coat and Badge shindig. The work was dull and I left. Then there was the wine business. I decided after long calculations that there was room in the market for certain makes of Tuscan wine. I went round the *fattorie* of Tuscany, tasting every kind of red wine I could find, taking all my visitors on these trips. I even invited Hornbeam-Whyte over, who was wine correspondent for the *Times* and whom Zonda and I always called 'Twenty-Thousand-A-Year', because he had been heard by Noel on a plane to Venice declaring this gratuitously to a fellow passenger.

Twenty-Thousand-A-Year argued with me over what I had bought, of course. He himself was importing Raboso at the time, which I found unbearable muck and wouldn't touch at any price. He chilled it in the fridge and tried to convince me. No – I preferred these small producers like Artimino at Carmignano and other villages. My backgammon friend Tupper, the antique dealer, came with me and we hired a van. It was cheaper by road. But we chose to come through France and the Massif Central for some reason. The wine, of course, was hardly recognisable when we got to London, so fearfully had its molecules been rearranged. We had to wait six months and by the time it became drinkable, I had lost interest in the whole project. By then I wanted to become a Master of Wine, impressed by the success of Jancis Evans. I enrolled at a course in London and filled my friend's house in Camden Square with encyclopaedias of wine. At night we had quizzes to keep me honed up. Then there was the Clapham Bookshop. I decided to become an antiquarian bookseller and bookdealer. I began collecting books while working as a librarian in the Institute in Florence – first editions of books about Florence – everything I could lay my hands on. Clapham, I thought, since it was rising socially and bourgeoisifying, was a good place for a really first-rate specialist shop. My problem was capital, really. I went on collecting books for several years and storing them in garages all over the city. I even had some hidden in the back of the restaurant underneath the flat in a space which Testucchio had loaned me. From time to time, people vaguely tried to phone up and get rid of my books. I had completely lost interest in this project, which, however, when I was drunk, revived, flamed and burst into burning enthusiasm, and for a day or two afterwards drove me to make feverish calculations on pieces of paper and call up Jeremy at Coutts. But something usually intervened. When Zonda and I had met we used to spend hours sitting up at night seriously discussing business partnerships in the rag trade. I was going to sell the apartment for capital. She, with her flair for materials, would handle the design side, and her friends in the poster shop would help with the outlets. We saw it all, a thriving partnership. Import-Export, to Florence. Knock up the latest London designs, and sell them in Italy with a fabric business on the side. Art fabrics.

But the leitmotiv pressing through this whole evanescent symphony of tedium was the Bloodstock Agency and the Stud-Farm. This was what I had really wanted to do all along.

I had been poring systematically for a number of years over maps of the yards, the boxes, the nature of the flooring, structure and disposition of the buildings, and the general layout of the accommodation at Pompadour, Lamballe, Saint-Lô, Rosières-aux-Salines, Le Pin, Eterpigny, Bois-Roussel, and Viclôt. Pompadour, the stallion centre, interested me the most because it had La Rivière about two and a half miles away, the mares' breeding centre. I visited it. My hunch was correct. La Rivière turned out to be my model establishment, the stables about a hundred years old sited amongst the renovated buildings of the diminutive château – modest, tree-sheltered, discreet, manageable. The stud-farm had about forty brood mares, all fashionable American bloodlines, its twenty-one loose boxes so arranged as to enclose the yard on three sides. North east of Périgueux, smack in the middle of pig-and-truffle country.

La Rivière melted at some indescribable point of mental convergence into the mellow brickwork of Cheveley Park, the home of Isinglass. I bothered to look up the history of the place. The dashing Henry Jermyn had bought it from Sir John Cotton in

1673. Henry who became Earl of St Albans and lover of Henrietta Maria. I ignored discrepancies in the accounts which suggested their relationship was never consummated. What did it matter? Henrietta Maria had been mad about Cheveley. Every year, she always had to have the first melons from the estate. Henry had the gardener send them up to London by the quickest possible route.

It had been run-down. In a terrible state. And while I had wasted myself at Oxford, it had been bought for a song, to my retrospective chagrin, by a meat import/exporter.

I had wasted my patrimony. There was no question about it. In the days when I had had money, I moved from hotel to hotel. Even after Zonda had appeared on the scene we still led a vestige of this life. I had stacks of Harvie and Hudson blue and white striped shirts flown in from London, my shoes and the handmade leather boots I was fitted for every time I went back to London were made by Lobb of St James's (I had my own last), and all my suits and jackets and trousers were made in Jermyn Street. I still paid a visit to Jermyn Street once a year to be fitted for my suits, jackets and trousers, before going up to York. Even when falling drunk, my appearance has always been impeccable. Absorbed in my projects and schemes, I made it a point of honour not to think about money. I was not long in the company of new people before getting up from my chair and obliging them to go to an expensive restaurant, where I insisted on paying the bill. Julia regularly reported to me what people said about me and they usually remarked on my generosity. One of my most frequent remarks was 'It's only money.'

I had managed to support myself for two years by serious, rather grim percentage betting on the Italian tracks. Since I knew the horses so well, I could do this, if I restricted my more quixotic urges to back outsiders out of boredom. In my view they were equally probable and I did not find it difficult to construct schemes of probability-factoring in which they would win or had better chances than the stayers and the hacks. Even so, apart from occasional heights like the Arc, the graph was a steady diminishing curve towards open insolvency. The point of backing them was financial, of course, and the hacks and stayers did not help the long run of one's financial situation. But I told myself I had Zonda now to look after and therefore it behoved me to act like a man with responsibilities in life. It was like a job, the writing up of my form books, which I did religiously at 7.30 every morning, rain or shine, even if my hand was impaired by a hangover. It was an activity, like doing the crossword, which generated its own urgency.

At the back of my mind throughout this period, like a priceless canvas in an attic, had lain the belief that the Trust would come up with something, that my father would not abandon his eldest without a penny. I had the distinct, and pleasurable, sensation that the Trust would cushion me from the ultimate blows whether self-inflicted or the mere work of fortune. Now I knew that this was not the case. There had been repercussions after this interview in the family: a noted coolness on the part of the others, my inferior siblings. This was a blanket decision of Pappa's and affected, naturally, the whole Trust and therefore their arrangements. Whatever dispositions he had made for them, they were not going to get anything after my débâcle.

'Raymond,' said Zonda suddenly, from above. 'You know the Dutch woman?'

'Mrs Van Puffpastry?'

'Well, it wasn't a terrorist brigade at all . . .'

'Who was it?' I asked, taking my cue.

'It was the husband . . .'

'How do you know?' I asked, knowing the answer.

'I read it in *Le Figaro*,' said Zonda.

'With a hangover like yours, I'm astonished you could focus your eyes . . .'

'Well I did, anyway . . .'

'What dedication!' I said, tiresome even to myself, as I closed my eyes in the rocking space.

'Unbelievable cold bastard,' I heard Zonda say, softly. 'They had a drink together, in that bar, and then, on the way back, he gave her the keys and said he was just going for a bit of a walk, would she mind driving and picking him up . . . Then . . . when she turned the key in the ignition . . . Wham!! . . .'

'*Crime passionel* . . . doesn't sound very Dutch though, does it?'

'He deliberately made it look like a terrorist attack . . . the swine . . . but she lived to testify against him . . . How *unspeakable* . . .'

'Well, it proves my point,' I said, yawning.

'What's that?'

'It wasn't very likely we could have been got after all . . .'

This started her off on a brief canter round our possible proximity to the car, but she stopped and lit another cigarette.

'How could *anyone* do a thing like that, do you understand?'

'Ah, they *will* do it,' I heard myself say through another yawn, as the train tilted into a long running curve and my body began to slide down the bed, inch by inch, into the coma it yearned for.

Part Two

Florence

It was Zonda who first leaned over and drew my attention with a slide of the eyes to the figure slumped two places away in absolute stillness. The head, cocked slightly on one side, was supported by the thumb and forefinger of a purplish hand which pincered the bridge of the nose, while in front of him a pair of horn-rimmed spectacles rode untidily over a napkin folded on the damask.

'The tie . . .' she mouthed.

I was familiar with these relics of technological optimism because my history master wore one at school, whereas Zonda was too young, I realised with a pang, ever to have seen one except in a magazine: it was a rare, late 1950s model, a rigid sheet of grey nylon scissored into a polygon and attached to the shirt-collar by means of elastic. The perpetual Windsor knot of these contraptions stubbornly retained the stain of many a meal long after its memory had disappeared, and in order to remain halfway decent they had to be scrubbed down with detergent and water. In this case, there were some unique maintenance problems which took the form of snags in the material irregularly spaced below the knot – a ganglion of plucks, tiny fraying columns of plastic that resembled the sliced sinews in raw scrag-end of lamb. We stared at this object and glanced at each other, Zonda's lips pulling back over her long teeth in an expression of horsey incredulity.

Lunch had been a gamble. It was Sunday afternoon. We had arrived from the station in a cab and dumped the bags inside the door. I led the rush downstairs just in time to catch Sotto Hasa, as we referred in our affected Florentine aspirates to the garden restaurant beneath the apartment. The dining-room, which seemed to be full of businessmen from a conference of some sort, was packed and very noisy. We squeezed in on the long benches opposite one another and while we waited for Zonda's friend Deaf-Aid, the shambling Calabrese with the motor deficiency, to spot us, I was telling Zonda in Italian a story about Britt Ekland that someone had told me in a bar. As I reached the word 'Britt' the spectacles lifted from the cloth in a rapid blur and a voice of senior Irish charm emerged from the heart of the babble:

'So you're Brits are you – Mooney, Gerrard Mooney . . .' A hand swung across the shirt-front of the intervening bullet-headed Indian and fished about demandingly in the air. The fingers were brown with tobacco stains and the nails intermittently black. Zonda was smiling at the tie as my hand slid into a thick, warm, pulsing medium. He drew me urgently towards him.

'Order me a steak,' he said suddenly. 'Would you be so kind? Yes, we'll have a steak . . . er . . . *rapido rapido* . . .'

He released me so that I could wave at Deaf-Aid, who shambled up nodding at us and asking Zonda in his mutant foghorn if we'd had a good trip. Mooney had said 'we' and I was a little puzzled by this, but I translated the request. Deaf-Aid said the steak was off, and all they had at this time was what we were going to have, and then he turned and looked towards the kitchen while he recited the menu with indifference: small pieces of veal, braised gently, and then sautéed in white wine, cream, garlic and lemon juice, with a touch of added egg, and *piselli*. I told Mooney we had this at least once a week and it was excellent. The hook-nosed blue-rinsed creature on the other side of Zonda who looked, her spectacles dangling on two threads and a swathe of yellow daisies nodding across the meadow-green bosom of her dress, pure Golders Green, laughed at this and turned to the plump little Arab by her side who held a dark wooden bead pinched between thumb and forefinger before him on the table cloth –

'Four, tell him four . . .' said Mooney.

'Hmmm . . .' said the woman in perfect South Ken. 'Haven't we any choice?'

I explained the position and the woman clucked. The little fat man twitched his rosary and deftly moved on to another bead, his forefinger tracing over the carved patterns.

Zonda was staring at the piece of Sellotape that was attached to his horn-rimmed spectacles at the junction of frame and sidepiece, while Mooney smiled vaguely and patted the pockets of his houndstooth tweed jacket, looking round with a regretful air as if he had just lost something of minor economic, but major sentimental importance. The Indian sat serenely with his hands in his lap, looking down at them, while Mooney leaned over again and asked, nodding to encourage me as he spoke:

'Are you in business yourself, Mr?'

I glanced at Zonda as I introduced us. The only question in both our minds at that moment was whether this person was wearing a wig or not. The evidence appeared contradictory: at the front the grey hair curled on either side of a central parting into ram's horns so authentically stiff and greasy that their reality was scarcely to be questioned, but at the back a seam was visible, a kind of shelf where the coconut matting of brown met two mauve-pink columns of muscle above the collar. Mooney appeared not to listen to my reply, namely that I owned two and a half horses and was interested in a modest kind of a way in breeding the animals for racing. Behind the square tortoiseshell rims, the watery green eyes were magnified to such a degree by the thick lenses that they reminded me of fish swimming in separate tanks, as they hung and drifted slowly towards something in the centre of the table. The focal point seemed to be Zonda's packet of MS, balanced on which, forming a kind of miniature ziggurat, lay the gold briquet I had given her the previous Christmas, and on top of that a square earring in the shape of an open copy of Dante's *Divina Commedia* which she didn't really like and kept taking off absentmindedly, like gloves, whenever she entered a room. 'We're just a group of simple farming people ourselves . . .' he said and then sighed with sudden weariness, intensifying the pocket-patting. '. . . Trying to bring about a few changes – I beg your pardon young lady, but is it possible that those cigarettes are your own?'

Zonda picked up the top storey of the ziggurat and held it a foot above the lighter and packet. Mooney did not choose to misunderstand but lunged across, one brown half-moon of a fingernail extended, and flipped the packet upwards like a tiddlywink, tipping off the lighter. The cigarette was already bouncing up and down between the rubbery dark-maroon lips, as the voice, expressionless and urgent, went on:

'. . . Changes that are going to revolutionise their methods of seed-sowing. We're developing a new kind of soya bean that will mean that for the first time these *people* out there will have *wurrk* . . .'

He banged the table gently in time to his words as Zonda did the only thing possible, which was to offer the flame to the wildly bouncing unlit end of the cigarette. I smiled at the rest of the simple farming people, and asked where 'out there' was.

'Venezuela mostly,' said Mooney. 'Aha refreshment . . .'

Deaf-Aid arrived with a carafe which he set down in the middle of the table, muttering.

'The shoes!' said Zonda between her teeth, a suppressed giggle yodelling in her voice. The Blue Rinse took out a gold case from the handbag on the bench beside her and snapped open a row of Rothmans King-Size, one of which she let hang limply from the congealed wound of her smile.

'Allow me to introduce my associates . . . Princess . . . Dr Atallah Habib . . . Prime Minister . . .' said Mooney, putting his hand on the sleeve of the Indian. We were nodding at each other through clouds of cigarette smoke, as I poured out the wine. Zonda was urging the shoes again, so I bent down in a fit of coughing for a look. My head swam: the Indian's feet and knees were held demurely together. The shoes were standard-issue black loafers, highly polished by hand with Cherry Blossom which I could actually smell. The Princess's scrawny black-stockinged feet were half out of her high-heels and balanced, resting on their backs. Habib's pedimenta were too far away for me to see. Mooney's, centre-left, were a pair of modified purple winkle-pickers. A drawing pin was visible in the sole of the left-hand shoe where it turned up close to the toe. The socks were a biscuit-coloured yellow, with green diamond patterns at the sides. To my horror, they were ankle socks and stopped before the beginning of the turn-ups of green tweed, exposing an inch or so of puce skin, pocked with a scattering of dead hair follicles.

'Well, *slainte*!' said Mooney across to the others. 'The best of health and good fortune to two charming young English people!'

He lifted his glass and drank. A globule of perspiration sprang out of the parting and began to roll, jinking laterally down through terraced furrows of plum-coloured forehead, like a pin-ball on its way to the bridge of the nose. He picked up the table napkin and wiped it off, while I asked him about his company. The Prime Minister put his hands back in his lap like a little girl and looked at the ceiling with his one good eye, while Mooney explained that his company, The Project-For-The-Americas Investment Corporation, owned substantial tracts of land in the Pequeño Peninsula. The Princess had turned to Zonda and put on her amber-tinted spectacles, the silver chains dependent from the cheeks on each side, and was studying her intently.

'It's actually in Panama,' said Mooney, 'but for business reasons our securities are deposited with the Banco Agno Peccaro of Caracas. Yes, we're over here looking for creative invest-ments . . .' He looked round and laughed, nodding at the others and raising his glass. 'Isn't that true, Prime Minister? We're here to *start the ball rolling*. . . !'

'Is there a lot of money about at the moment?' I said. 'I'm interested to hear it.'

'Ah, you don't want to believe everything you read in the papers, Raymond; no we take the view that the world economic situation at the moment is based on what you might call, for want of a better term, a triangle of mistrust . . .'

'I think that is very well put,' said the Prime Minister.

'You have your three main areas in the world . . .' His hands took the bunched napkin of an earlier customer, the salad salver, and the empty bread basket and placed them in a triangle on the table. He banged the bread basket up and down. 'There's the Western industrial block . . .' He looked up and pointed to the salver. 'Here's OPEC, and here's the developing countries . . .' He picked up the napkin and dropped it again. 'Well, each is boxing his own corner, you see . . . and that's why it's a stalemate at present . . .' He gave the empty bread basket a brief bang. 'The West has technology without capital . . .' The Prime Minister was nodding vigorously, as Mooney transferred his cigarette to his other hand and juggled the salver so that the oil and vinegar sloshed up the sides of the bottles. '. . . OPEC here has capital without technology . . .' Our eyes followed the thick greenish vein on the back of his hand as it moved to the napkin and picked it up again. 'And the Third World has the markets, without either capital or technology . . .' He tossed the napkin down in time to his words and we stared at the crumpled, tomato-stained cloth of the Third World.

'Stalemate!' said Mooney.

The Prime Minister nodded.

'And we are here to do something about it!'

I poured them another splash of house white, wondering who 'we' were.

'The rules have changed and it's time we recognised this,' said Mooney grandiloquently. 'Countries are no longer economically independent of each other – look at the IMF, even they have been borrowing from OPEC recently . . .'

'Getting I would say a dose of their own medicine,' said the Prime Minister. 'I hope the interest rates were as high as the IMF's own!'

I was inclined to argue, thinking I remembered some of my first-year PPE reading from Oxford.

'But Bagehot said that in the middle of the nineteenth century . . .'

'Is that a fact?' said Mooney, ignoring it. He was rising to his theme now. I glanced at the others.

'Money flows everywhere, ladies and gentlemen, without sovereign boundaries or national inhibition. We are all inter-related . . .' He waved his arm in a generous flourish. 'We are . . . the reluctant human family, you might say. Whether we like it or not. This is what the Americans have had to learn, and now that everyone needs oil so badly . . .'

'And oil turns into money . . .' said the Prime Minister.

'So these interrelationships deepen . . . we are living in a different world . . . myself, I believe passionately in invest-ment . . .'

'You're brokers?' I said.

'That tribe of Gadarene swine . . .'

'Well, dealers then,' I said.

'I like to think we have the interests of the Third World at heart,' said Mooney.

'But why Florence?'

'We happen to have some important facilities here . . .' said Mooney. 'But you know, I'm a great believer in the wisdom of the Chinese in this connection. Those old bearded fellas could tell you a thing or two. There's an old Chinese proverb that says it's no use giving fish to a starving man . . .' He paused dramatically, looking along the line. 'What do you give him?'

The Princess and Dr Habib smiled at Mooney, and shook their heads.

'I don't speak Chinese,' said the Princess to Zonda. 'Do you?'

'Well,' said Mooney, 'you don't give him fish, you give him a fishing rod . . .'

The Prime Minister went into ecstasies, screeching like a parrot and rubbing his eye.

'A fishing rod!' he repeated, turning to me and gasping. 'It is good!'

They laughed back along the line and raised their glasses, with the exception of the Princess, who was telling Zonda about how she bought her apartment.

'It was accomplished at the Palm Beach Casino,' she was saying. 'I had nowhere to go except there you see . . . I was homeless when I arrived in Cannes . . . but Mr Quémand, the nice manager of Van Cleef and Arpels, happened to be in the Casino and he made just three phone calls . . . and they brought the pictures from the office in the middle of the night . . . and at dawn . . .' She clapped. '*Voilà, la vente a pu être conclue* . . .'

Zonda stared at her with alarm and blew a final plume of blue smoke above her head, while her eyes followed the progress of Deaf-Aid as he lurched and rolled between the yammering tables, his arms stacked with plates.

'Bloodstock . . .' said Mooney musingly. 'You know, Raymond, I'd like to talk to you about that sometime . . .'

Zonda was smiling up at Deaf-Aid. He looked down at her, as his red-raw hands distributed the plates like someone dealing cards. A smile crested those prognathous features. Zonda wriggled slightly under his roaming stare and made some jokes I couldn't hear.

'Something in the import-export line . . .' Mooney was saying.

She was telling Deaf-Aid about Paris and the Arc and pointing at me, crisping together thumb and forefinger. He turned, his mouth opening silently with delight. I shook my head, and turned out my pockets. His eyes clouded over in sympathy and a hoot came down his nose. He sighed '*Eh . . . si . . .*' to himself, as if this was eternally the way of the world. But he was heading off for the kitchen to tell them the story.

'You're living here, then, are you?' said Mooney with his mouth full.

We all tried not to stare and failed as he dipped his bread into the sauce and brought pieces of meat balanced on the bread into his open mouth, plunging the remains of the bread back into the diminished level of the food, actions performed with a funicular regularity. He paused only to tear off new pieces of bread, while I explained to him that I kept my horses at a stables in Pisa. He picked up his empty glass by the stem and put it down again, and, without thinking about it, I poured him a glass from the carafe standing between us. He put it instantly to his mouth while chewing, and with a haste that suggested he was about to leave at any moment for an urgent appointment.

'Bloodstock . . .' he said again, tilting his plate towards him and polishing it with a piece of bread as if it were a kind of chamois. 'You know my idea. . . ?' He pushed away the plate, stuffing the final bit of bread into his mouth and licking his fingers with zeal. 'Go for the old lines . . .'

'As you know,' said the Princess to Zonda, 'my Cousin Reza is with Sadat and next month he will be proclaimed King of Iran in Cairo . . . Then he will come to visit me in Cannes. He is only twenty. I want to show him the Casino.' She and Habib toyed with distaste at their food, while Zonda lit another cigarette and indicated to me that she needed more wine.

'King of Iran in Cairo,' said Zonda laughing. 'That sounds funny. Aren't the other lot in, you know, whojamaflip, Raymond, who *are* the other lot?'

'Khomeini,' I said.

'Stranger things have happened in history . . .' said the Princess to Zonda. 'You *are* English, aren't you? You above all should know this. Cromwell was replaced by the Kings of England . . .'

'I believe that the government of Taiwan in London has a cabinet meeting every morning,' I said, 'in which they decide matters of national importance after reading the newspapers . . .'

Zonda stuffed part of her napkin into her mouth.

'Exactly,' said the Princess.

'Nor,' I said to Zonda, who was convulsed, 'need I quote to *you* the restoration of the Bourbon kings . . .'

'Go for the old lines . . . Donatello the Second . . .' He waved vaguely, still chewing, and picking with his index finger in the corner of his mouth. 'Tracery . . . and you know . . .' He picked again and changed tack and paused. 'Ah, but I don't know . . . is it Italian stock you're interested in. . . ?'

'Neri di Bicci was Tracery wasn't she?' I said, testing.

He nodded. 'And wasn't there another Tracery mare as well imported at the same time – what was it about 1920 or so? . . .'

'Foliation,' I said, '1918.'

'That's it!' said Mooney, slapping the table and beaming with delight. 'My God, what a memory!' He helped himself to another of Zonda's cigarettes. 'What a memory!' he repeated.

Zonda broke off from saying 'What was it like?' to the Princess and absently clicked the briquet at him as he leaned over, spectacles swimming.

'There's a lot of Tracery blood in Argentina, you know, Raymond . . .' said Mooney. 'Did you know that?'

'That's right,' I said. 'Tracery spent most of his stud career there, didn't he?'

'It's an idea . . . might be worth putting some money into it one of these days . . .'

'Of course that's why they had to import the daughters from England,' I said. 'Because it was too expensive to get the sire . . .' a remark which was meant to suggest the degree of fantasy in such a speculation.

'It was horrible . . .' The Princess had her hand on Zonda's arm. 'Can you imagine? What could we do? I dressed as a peasant. I took my children. I put my jewels here' – she made a stabbing motion at her side with her olive-coloured, blood-red claw – '. . . in my bag, and we walked into that desert . . . They were coming for us, you see . . .'

'Aw . . . horses go everywhere now,' said Mooney. 'It's fantastic . . . I tell you . . . do you know once, I got on a plane at Shannon to go back to Caracas and what do you think a horse was breaking the world record for . . .'

50

'For horse-flight?' I said, looking round passing the joke on. Dr Habib smiled.

'Longest known air trip – Rome to Caracas via Shannon, the Azores, and Gander . . . That was November 1949 and that was an Italian horse, too, Intarsio . . . ended up as a stallion in Chile he did . . .'

'That was a Hurry-On colt . . .' I wrinkled my brows trying to remember.

'No,' he said, holding up a finger in reproof. 'Ingoberta by Cranach.'

'And Ingoberta,' I smiled victoriously, 'was by Hurry-On out of Vice Versa.'

'The man's a masterpiece!' said Mooney along the line. 'Did you hear that, Dr Habib?'

'We thought we would die . . .' said the Princess. 'But the people on the way . . . they gave us food and drink, they knew who we were of course . . .'

There was a cooing noise. Deaf-Aid was back with what looked like the total population of the kitchen for a visitation. He stood slightly in the background while the two others came forward to look at the hero of the Arc, Signor Raymond. I took off the watch and showed it to them, taking care to point out the emerald. They bent over the watch like a crowd of Masaccio thieves, bantering with Zonda and glancing over at me. Deaf-Aid produced another carafe from the folds of his apron and set it absently on the table as he tried to look over their shoulders. In the background I could see two people over by the window waving their arms and vainly trying to attract their attention. The cook who was pear-shaped with a tightly-frizzed grey hair-do wiped her hands and handed it back over the heads of the others, murmuring and nodding. Testucchio made a little sign and whispered behind his hand. They looked round and they were gone in a little group changing places unnecessarily and running for the kitchen like a small bunch of sheep in front of a collie, still with their cooing sounds. Testucchio stood by the kitchen door looking back and counting the numbers.

Zonda was looking very serious as she paused with a cigarette halfway to her mouth, her plate and the Princess's pushed away. She had on her full interviewing manner:

'And what did you *feel* like?' I saw her say to the Princess.

'How do you think I felt?' said the Princess. 'How would you feel if you had lost everything you ever had and were forced to save yourself and your children by walking for two weeks and three days through a burning desert? . . . It was a terrible time . . . Lots of my family thought they could go back to Tehran and just take up where they had left off after the military had taken over . . . they really didn't seem to believe that the Shah would fall . . .'

Zonda was shaking her head. Dr Habib laughed:

'You know, it was their own fault . . . They gave that man a passport . . . The government . . .'

Zonda was looking puzzled.

'The government of Iran,' Habib repeated in his crisp high-pitched voice across the Princess. 'When that madman Khomeini was in Iraq and they had the chance to refuse him entry to the country forever they granted him a passport . . .' He spread his dimpled hands. 'It was like putting your sword in your enemy's hand and baring your neck . . .'

Mooney was talking rapidly to the Prime Minister.

'At a time,' said Habib, 'when they were already driving dogs through the bazaars with placards tied to the rump with slogans on them like "Towards the Great Civilisation" . . .'

'*Darling*,' said Zonda, shooting a hand across to me as I struggled to do up my watchstrap, 'the Princess lost everything, did you hear, isn't it *sad*?'

'Tragic,' I said. 'Have some more vino . . .'

She smiled without seeing me.

'But what *caused* it all. . . ?' she said. 'I don't know anything about it . . .'

'What caused it?' said the Princess, blowing her nose. 'Pooh, the Shah was too liberal . . .'

Beneath her flowered English dress, as she squared her shoulders with contempt, the collar-bones were almost painful to look at.

'You really ask?' said Habib, leaning across the Princess with a smile. 'The Shah changed the calendar . . .'

Zonda thought she was to laugh, and did.

The Princess and Dr Habib looked annoyed.

'You think it is funny?'

'Hysterical,' said Zonda without conviction as she looked from mouth to disapproving mouth. She assumed an equally disapproving expression, I saw with amusement, disapproving of herself, as Habib began to explain that the Islamic calendar dated from the Hijra of Mohammed from Mecca to Medina.

The Princess gave a short laugh downwards.

'It is so *tiresome* to explain,' she said to me, adjusting her belt slightly. The Prime Minister was standing up. We all looked up as he said he was going.

'I'll be in touch', said Mooney. 'We'll be clorsing any day . . .'

'My flight is tomorrow,' said the Prime Minister as he nodded.

Mooney and I slid up the bench until we were opposite each other.

'Any day,' he repeated. 'Yes . . . and then there's the Orsenigo line . . . I went to see him once at the Guanabara stud . . .'

'You mean that de Montel hack . . .' I explained that I was a Tesio man.

'Had a very good career in Brazil, you know,' said Mooney. 'Italian export, sired about thirty-three top-notch colts and fillies . . .'

'I know what you're going to say: "And then there was Escorial" . . .'

'And then there was Escorial . . . who took the Carlos Pellegrini in Buenos Aires, and then won the Venti Cinco Mayo the following year . . . By any standards a good horse, and in the late 1950s he was leading sire in Brazil *and* leading broodmare sire over here . . . The people who organised that one knew what they were doing . . .'

'Who were they?'

'Roberto Seabra got him after the Americans couldn't buy him . . . technicalities . . . they were very keen . . . Ah, there's a lot of room to manoeuvre there,' said Mooney with tired excitement. 'When you think about . . . you know, I think we could do something . . . What d'you think we'd need – a couple of million?'

I stared at his face as he said this, examining the falciform patches of broken capillary that formed the high colour in what were otherwise dark pink cheeks.

As if through a hole in the screen of talk, I heard the Princess say to Zonda:

'So you have not finished your Art School?'

'No. I *have* finished it . . .' Zonda laughed. 'For ever.'

The Princess frowned at her.

'No more Art School. And you are living with this man, who is getting his money by gambling. . . ?'

'Yes . . .'

'Are you *happy* with him?' I saw her say, nodding towards me.

Zonda's reply was not simple, but its clauses and retractions were lost in the hubbub. I tried to lip-read, but Mooney had his hand on my arm.

'Be a specialist business,' he murmured, looking down into his glass. 'Need the right kind of person to look after it . . .'

He looked up and smiled, the green eyes swimming off to the right. The mouth revealed teeth that had never apparently been attended to by a dentist – a panorama of blackened things that leaned against each other. Tree stumps in a wet forest.

'How do you feel about it?' he whispered.

I stared at Zonda, whose fingers were pulling at her earlobe, palpating the infected red pimple where the earring had been.

'And on the fifteenth anniversary in 1976 of the Pahlavi dynasty,' said Habib, 'the Shah – he decided the dating should start from the accession of Cyrus the Great, about a thousand years earlier than the traditional Islamic calendar . . .'

'Christ,' said Zonda, 'must have been a bit confusing for people . . .'

'Confusing!' The Princess laughed mirthlessly, tapping another Rothmans on her case. 'We were already living in 1354, when he did this!'

'Well, what was the point of it?'

'Cyrus is our ancestor,' she said, lighting up. 'You know, Cyrus of Persia.'

'You can imagine how the mullahs felt,' said Habib.

'Oh yes,' said Zonda, and added under her breath: 'If I knew who the fuck they were . . .'

I switched back to Mooney.

'Splosh bureau?' he said, rising to a half-standing position, in which thighs and shins above and below the sagging apex of crooked knees formed the sides of a disappointed isosceles triangle.

I pointed to the scuffed door near the exit, and then on second thoughts I decided to accompany him as I heard Habib starting to explain to Zonda the fundamental tenets of the Islamic faith. Mooney waddled away with broad steps, the feet planted very wide apart, the cigarette held in the hand, with exaggerated care.

It was quiet in the lavatory and we squeezed in side by side. He had transferred the cigarette to his mouth and was breathing out through the incoming curls of silver-coloured smoke supplementary clouds of blue, while the cylinder of ash lengthened and dropped as he talked non-stop, looking up at the small open window in front of us and holding himself in the reverse cupped position.

'Bloody prostate . . . aaah,' he wheezed.

I couldn't tell whether this last exclamation was an indicator of relief or suffering.

'Put yourself in the place of Brazil,' he said, shaking himself.

I had no desire to urinate, so I stood holding myself and staring at the wall with the simulated effort of concentration. A small bird alighted on the window-sill.

55

'At this very moment you owe sixty billion dollars to commercial banks in the West . . . a big consortium headed by Citibank . . . Right? Your foreign debts can only be paid by exports which earn foreign currency. You have no oil. So each time OPEC puts up the price of oil, the chance of your paying your debts recedes, because you've got to have more exports to keep up the payments. You've got three-quarters of your exports servicing these debts. What are you going to do, if you want to prevent a revolution? Because the next thing you know, you'll have the army on your back, riots, and all the rest of the scenario . . .'

'Go to the IMF?' I said. 'The World Bank?'

'Nah . . .' said Mooney, shaking himself again. 'The loans are too long and the interest rates are too high. And there are strings attached. You'd have Albertelli's night visitors like Jamaica did last year . . . you know, *their* people, coming in to check you out . . .'

'I don't know.'

'Well, you've got to *do* something.' He turned to me, and stared hard, as he laid down the rules of the game.

'Find some kind of bridging loan, while I try to increase productivity. Take social measures,' I said.

'Exactly, you'd go to a market like the Eurocurrency market . . . Take the Prime Minister out there . . .'

'Where's he the Prime Minister of by the way?'

'Mauritius.'

'How did he lose his eye?'

'Gored by a bull. Now Mauritius has a debt-service ratio that would make your hair go white and he's absolutely desperate for short-term money, because he's got a coup on his hands if he doesn't do something about the social unrest . . .'

'You mean he *flies to Europe* looking for a bank?' I said disbelievingly.

'That's right,' said Mooney. 'Some of these African johnnies are running around New York right now with the Gross National

56

Product attached to their wrist by a slender chain . . .' he laughed, 'with the CIA running after them . . .'

He wheezed, blowing the ash off the stump of cigarette through his nose, and leaving the last few centimetres of tobacco-less paper, which he continued to give the appearance of smoking, attached to his damson-coloured lower lip.

I looked at the back of the neck. It was definitely not a wig. When you got close, you could see the archaeological remains of hair growth just under the ledge that protruded. The ledge was the result of someone hacking the hair very crudely with a blunt instrument, I decided, and then growth underneath pushing out the top hair.

'We are just about to close a deal that's going to make a lot of difference to some of these people . . .'

The bird stared from the window-ledge as we zipped ourselves up.

'Talking about Italian horses . . .' I said, as we paused to go through the door, 'what do you think of the Tesio lines?'

He paused to tear off the dead stump of cigarette and throw it behind him, spitting, into the urinal. He put his hands in his pockets expansively clenching his fists inside the material and ballooning it out as he swayed back on his heels and contemplated the image of an erect penis etched into the plasterwork behind the door, the tumescent acorn of which was made of revealed brick.

'Federico Tesio . . .' he said, as if listing an article in a popular encyclopaedia. 'Genius. Dormello stud, finest in Italy. Used to disappear into the bushes every time he lost. Fatal attraction to the Isonomy line, which he tried all his life to promote . . . I met him once in the 1940s at those gallops outside Pisa . . . beautiful place . . . You must know it . . .'

'Barbaricina?'

'I don't remember the name . . . but the horses came down along the edge of the pinewoods by the sea . . . he was there, on his shooting stick with the old stop-watch out . . . old man by then, of course . . . but he was still very straight-backed, you know . . .'

'He was a cavalry officer . . .'

'A gentleman,' said Mooney, opening the door and charging vigorously out. 'You could see that at a glance . . .' He turned back and whispered, treading on my foot as we bumped awkwardly together, 'Bit like yourself, Raymond . . . same type, you know . . .'

'I have never been in the army,' I said.

'Fast disappearing,' he said with a sigh.

'I wouldn't call the attraction entirely fatal,' I said as we strolled between the tables, and I stared at Zonda. She looked as if she were receiving an unpleasant dose of medicine from the Iranians. 'I mean look at Turbido . . . that was an Isonomy-line horse.'

'Ah, yes, but what about his dam Tempesta . . . Now if ever I heard of a horse aptly named, it was her . . .' he said. 'They were very erratic that line, you know . . . Turbido as well . . .'

We paused, standing at the table, while he rattled off Tempesta's relatives. Zonda looked up at me with a pained frown.

'It-is-not-a-wig,' I mimed.

'It's all from Coronation,' he said.

'Darling,' said Zonda, reaching across for my hand, as I sat down, 'the Princess was *there* . . . and she wore a real tiara . . .'

'Where?'

'At the Coronation. She met all of the Royals and knows Princess Margaret really well . . .'

The Princess hoisted up the blood-red corners of her lips so that they levelled into a young razor-slash.

'Marvellous people,' she said. 'I particularly liked old Queen Mary while she was alive . . .'

I made a mental note of Mooney's point. I hadn't thought of the full implications of the Isonomy line. But it was perfectly true – Coronation was Isinglass-Sceptre, by Persimmon. And Isinglass was Isonomy-Deadlock.

'My tiara came with me through the desert.' The Princess touched Zonda, who was still in the same position, one arm held across the table the hand palm-upwards inviting me to hold it, the eyes drunkenly pleading. The Princess touched her again more sharply. 'My tiara,' she said with a smile as Zonda finally turned back to her, 'I was saying I have it still . . .'

'Do you wear it for the Casino?' said Zonda, savagely.

'Oh no . . .' the Princess laughed at the idea. 'Did you hear?' she said to Habib.

I looked up. Testucchio was hovering with a tray. The dining-room behind him was empty.

'This mess is all Carter's fault . . .' said Habib. 'It is his policy towards the Arabs which has ruined the Shah's foreign relations with America . . .'

'Sure it was Carter who told the Shah to liberalise Iran . . . you know, get the camp in order . . .' said Mooney.

Dr Habib shook his head.

'This I do *not* believe,' he said angrily.

Testucchio was bending over and telling me that he wanted us all to have a drink with him. I looked at my watch. It was 4.30. I translated his speech.

'Very daycent of him, very daycent indeed . . .' said Mooney.

Testucchio took the brandy bottle off the tray and set it with the glasses on the table. I poured out several shots, not bothering to find out who wanted it or not.

'Well, he had *some* bee in his bonnet,' said Mooney, detaching one of the outside glasses from the tinkling pack and bringing it round in a circular fashion to his place, 'because what was all this flannel about abdication in 1976?'

'It is true that the Shah was *insecure* about Carter . . .' said Habib, raising his voice.

'I think this man wants us to go,' said the Princess to Zonda, nodding at the retreating Testucchio's back. 'He brings us a bribe.'

'It's a mystery why he did this,' said Habib. 'I was an economic adviser to the Hoveyda government and he sacked us all after thirteen years without a word . . .'

'He pretended to be about to abdicate,' said the Princess, 'but this was to win Carter over . . .'

'Government by the treasury,' said Habib, 'that's when I left . . .'

'You and a billion dollars a month in private capital,' said Mooney, laughing and raising his glass.

'I hope Carter is happy now,' said the Princess, bitterly, 'with his friends the Arabs . . .'

Zonda said she didn't understand.

'I thought Iran was an Arab country . . .' she said, lighting another cigarette. 'I thought you were all Arabs . . .'

The Princess drew herself up.

'The Arabs were Semitic,' she said sourly, 'the Jews and the Arabs are both the same – Semites . . . But we Persians . . . we are Aryans, like the Germans, like your Royal Family . . . there are no religious ties or racial ties between us and the Arabs.'

She stood up, smoothing down her skirt and picking up her bag and shawl as we stared up at her.

'We must go now,' she said, as Habib stopped to lift back the bench so that she could step out. 'It has been a pleasure to meet you both . . . Mr Mooney?'

'We'll be clorsing any day now Your Highness . . .' said Mooney, standing.

She turned to Habib.

'We shall be at the Hilton a few days more?' She turned back. 'Yes. You can reach us there.'

'I can ring for a cab?' I rose.

The Princess turned on her heels.

'No, I feel stuffy. I prefer to walk . . . don't you Dr Habib?'

She flung open the door.

'Air,' she said, and stood poised on pin-heels.

Habib was doing the rounds, shaking everybody by the hand.

60

He was level with Mooney's top pocket as they exchanged valedictory murmurs.

I expected a collapse from Mooney, but his manner was unperturbed as he poured out another three fingers of brandy.

'Are we out of cigarettes?' he said, patting his pockets.

Zonda was yawning. I waved for Testucchio to bring the bill.

'I've got lots upstairs,' said Zonda.

'Splosh,' groaned Mooney, rising.

He waddled away, pausing at the entrance to the lavatory. 'One thing,' he said, his voice falling oddly across the empty dining-room, 'I'd keep off the Hurry-On sires . . .'

He disappeared.

I decided it was easier to settle the whole bill and then ask him for his contribution. Zonda was looking much the worse for wear now, after her experience with royalty.

'It is not a wig,' I said as I wrote the cheque.

'It *is*,' said Zonda. 'Of course it is . . .'

'I tell you it isn't. Anyway, we shall decide upstairs at our leisure,' I said.

'Who the fuck *is* he?' said Zonda in an urgent whisper.

I placed the cheque on the tray that Deaf-Aid was holding out.

'Let's find out.'

'Do we *have* to?' said Zonda with a whine.

'Well, you can go to bed.'

'What, with you two jabbering about bloody horses . . . Raymond, I'm really *knackered*.'

'I do wish you wouldn't use that expression,' I said. But I could see she was reconciled. I worked out the amounts on the bill and wrote them on the back of an envelope. We were standing up when Mooney came back.

'They never wanted a challenge. No go in them,' he said, 'anything that came from Coronach.'

He picked up the envelope.

'What's this?' he said, adjusting his spectacles.

He waved it briefly and put it in his pocket.

'Fine,' he said.

'We'll settle up later,' I said.

'Righty-ho,' said Mooney.

Slowly Zonda stood up and took my arm as we crowded towards the door in the corner. Deaf-Aid hovered behind ready to bolt the door. Something made me turn round as soon as we had gone a few steps. My eye caught the movement. A solitary pea was travelling over the carpet behind us. It overtook us, describing a wide arc like a miniature bowl, and rolled to a halt between Mooney's feet.

'They never liked a fight to the finish,' he said as we waited for Zonda's elaborate farewell to Deaf-Aid, blinking at the traffic.

The apartment was my only asset. I had bought it outright with the last of my trust money, staving off my creditors with an account of my affairs which was judiciously exaggerated, aided by perjured testimony from Julia. The building was medieval, and the whole place appeared to have been hewn out of a piece of rock. The stairs were murderously steep, and each step was of a different size and depth; the three near the top, just outside the door, were about an inch and a half wide, so that one could only get a toe-hold when ascending, and a heel-hold when descending. Black mains cables hung in great loops, roughly tacked, against the bulging wall all the way up.

When I bought it, the place had no bathroom. The front room, which Zonda was painting white at the rate of a square inch per day, was entirely bare of furniture, except for an expensive sofa-bed which Zonda had insisted on buying so that we could have visitors, and a large terracotta pot with a bristling plant in it. It looked as if it had been hacked out of rock. It had no corners to speak of, and it echoed as one spoke. The floor was of rough stone, and the whole strongly suggested a cave. On the walls, one could just make out the remains of ancient frescoes which had been ineptly painted over. There was a section of green border on one wall and a purple leg on another, dancing on its own. Cave drawings. We still hadn't decided what to do with these things and we staged long arguments about barbarism and preservation, when we were both rather indifferent. Wires hung out of the walls at intervals which Zonda had tried to paint over discreetly, with limited success. Beginning behind the door and extending halfway along the wall lay a number of bags of cement and various building materials. On top of this heap sat the phone directory for Florence. The phone, which was usually on the floor somewhere, had been barred for non-payment of bills, but with the civilised way the Italians have towards debt, friends could ring in. Occasionally it would ring, and someone would speak feebly of bills etc. After months of negotiation a couple of louts had arrived and built, very slowly, a long narrow room out of bits of the bedroom and the old kitchen which they covered with charming occasional irregularities in blue and white tiles: floor, walls, and ceiling, so that standing in there with a hangover in the morning was like being a pawn in a three-dimensional game of chess. The kitchen, thanks to Zonda, was white, but it still had the huge old stone sink in it because the louts had never returned once they realised that I was not necessarily going to pay.

The bedroom, however, was the nerve centre of our inactivity. This room where Zonda lay for most of the day, sweating and dreaming of peculiar animals, or reading novels I had stolen from the Institute library, was crammed with objects, a sumptuous glowering boudoir which smelt of us. Zonda put loving coat after coat of cobalt on the walls. At her instigation I bought a vast modern Italian bed with elaborate curved head and foot in lacquered brass.

The louts had left a hole in the bedroom wall, so that it gave directly on to the kitchen. Zonda purchased yards of very heavy modern Italian material in rich cream with gold threads running through it, and tiny dark stars that suggested, against the cobalt, when the whole curtain was drawn, the contemplation of deep space. On either side of the bed mounted the books. My copies of *Timeform*, my racing papers, letters from Giuseppe, my trainer in

Pisa, asking for money, letters from the other trainer in Normandy asking for money, and letters from the stable in Derbyshire where Forray had been at one time and which had never been paid – all stacked in ascending order of vituperation. Letters from the British Bloodstock Association, and invoices for subscriptions to the *Sporting Life*, *Lo Cavallo*, *Il Purosangue* etc. Monthly statements from Coutts about the Trust which I never bothered to open for weeks after they arrived and flung on the floor with a gay abandon I never managed to feel. Letters from the Italian bank, letters about the divorce from the Italian judiciary and the lawyers of Francesca, letters about the car accident. A cane basket stacked up to the handle with back copies of *The Times Literary Supplement*, encyclopaedias of wine, unread hardback copies of novels still with their virginal white invoices from Heywood Hill Bookshop, the complete works of my favourite author, a neglected genius in my opinion, Roger Longrigg, spare copies of *The Daughters of Mulberry*, cards from silly people from all over the world, including one from Zonda when she went to Venice for the day with a single red rose rising out of the Grand Canal like a submarine missile in front of San Giorgio and the words 'A kiss for my darling is winging its way ahead of this big wed wose', numerous other cards from silly people all over the world, and my two big blue plastic files into which I wrote my form records in my special system of different-coloured biros.

Zonda's side was relatively simple: stacked high with old shoes, roughly in pairs, in archaeological layers. The ones underneath from the Art School days were all pink or gold, flat shoes, or black 'college' shoes, shoes she had painted and dyed, then above these rose a layer of plainer, more elegant Italian shoes with the change to green the dominant of the whole period, then a brief lick of purple, and they had recently returned to pink, but now a shell-pink, not the acid pink of the old days. In the corner several canvases were stacked, depicting the inside of the same Norfolk fisherman's hut done from different angles, and a blown-up black and white photograph taken by Zonda in a mirror depicting herself coyly pressing the shutter of a camera, which rested on her knee. By the side of the bed, her paperback biographies of millionaires, murderers and criminals, the latest of which she had forgotten to take to Paris – the definitive account of Howard Hughes.

'I'm not so sure about the Coronation line,' I began as we started toiling up the stairs to the apartment. 'I mean, it's all very well quoting all those obscure relatives of Tempesta, but what about Tissot, and Tissot was out of Tempesta's daughter, Tiepoletta . . .'

'You've nothing to hold on to . . .' said Mooney, swaying back against the wall. His hand went out to the electricity cables to steady himself, while he stared at Zonda, blowing.

I left her supporting him, while I leaped up the remaining stairs in twos and opened the door with a flourish.

Visitors usually had to have a period of rest while they got their breath back, before they could converse. Mooney lay back against the kitchen wall, blowing hard, while Zonda slid in behind the kitchen table and demanded coffee.

I flipped the switch on the cassette-player, which had been standing on the kitchen table all the time we had been away, and the fat, silky brass of a Glenn Miller quickstep pumped out of its bakelite mouth, causing its tinny cover to vibrate jarringly.

Mooney inclined his head and held his arms out, crooked at the elbows like a dummy in a clothes shop, as he looked steadily at Zonda. She moved towards him, and they floated off, scraping across the rocky threshold into the front room. Zonda winked at me over his shoulder. Mooney was la-la-ing as they performed some swift turns and half-turns in the shadows. I put the coffee on and poured myself some grappa, listening to the sound of their feet scraping on the uneven stone. He was holding her in an old-fashioned ballroom-dancing way, so that I could see a foot of daylight between them, as they moved lightly back and forth against the glow from the shutters. A scooter roared past down the Via San Gallo and drowned the music. They parted, Zonda and Mooney bowing gravely from the waist.

'Ah, you're light as a feather, so you are . . .' he said, standing still and breathing hard. 'Raymond, come on now, let's see you . . .'

'Coffee?' I said.

'He loathes dancing,' said Zonda.

Mooney was singing in an old man's quavering vibrato:

'He won't dance . . . da . . . da . . . da . . . He won't dance . . . How does that go now?'

Zonda sang it, fulsomely, leaning against the fridge door.

'Are you married?' I asked Mooney.

His wife, Mamie, lived in Florida. He had five children, scattered all over the place, he said.

'The diaspora . . .' He sat down heavily and took the cigarette Zonda was offering him. '. . . The Mooney diaspora . . .'

'Nice place,' he said, looking round. Zonda was watering her plants.

I put the grappa bottle in the middle of the table.

'Come and look at the estate,' I said.

He looked doubtful for a moment.

'Splosh?' I said, and his face brightened.

We had a lot to talk about. It was clear to me he knew something about horses.

'And Turbido, after all,' I said, 'was not a bad horse on his day.'

'Does the squawk box work?'

I was rather anxious that he not think it didn't work because of debt. I looked at Zonda watering her plants with myopic care, and said no, it had only recently been fitted. He nodded and patrolled the room. There was a fault with it, I said, it only rang in. At that moment, it rang and Zonda ran to it.

'Well, you have to look at the whole thing . . .' he said, as we strolled past the kneeling Zonda, who was looking up at the ceiling and laughing, her face suffused with light and well-being, as she told the Paris story to someone that sounded like Tamsin from the range of jokes. 'It's the final lack of acceleration in that particular line . . . I mean look at Jacopo da Sellaio . . . Italian

Derby, 1932 . . . Tesio had to watch him beaten into second by Fenolo . . . coming out of the turn, they were . . . and what did the mare do. . . ? She just stared . . . It's that sort of thing . . . But do you know, Tissot and Toulouse-Lautrec are still covering mares to this day and you could pick something up in this line . . .'

'I just feel so *ill* . . .' Zonda was saying.

We sat down at the kitchen table. I poured the coffee into the tiny blue cups with blue stripes. I could see he wanted a cigarette, and I went into the front room and lifted up Zonda's bag to her, a question on my face. She nodded, saying to whoever it was: 'Raymond's here darling, trying to pinch my cigarettes . . .' She put her hand over the receiver. 'Tamsin sends her love . . .'

'Of course,' I said, disbursing a cigarette and then taking the rest back to the kitchen. She knelt staring at the wall, the unlit cigarette between her fingers, her voice booming and cackling.

'Toulouse-Lautrec,' I said, pouring him some grappa, 'now there's an interesting horse, especially on the distaff side . . .'

He looked at me, as I flicked the briquet alight.

'What distaff side?' he said.

'You know, Fausta . . . Catnip . . .'

'Raymond,' he said, 'I'd like to put something to you . . . to *both* of you . . .' he amended, as Zonda slid groaning round the corner and dropped into one of the folding slatted white kitchen chairs. 'You see, I'm in need of a bit of help . . .' He looked from one to the other of us. 'I can see you both speak the lingo and I could do with some translation help from time to time . . . Can you type at all? Either of you?'

'What's it all about?' I said, staring solemnly at Zonda, who bit her lip.

'It's this way,' said Mooney. 'My company has this big deal that's just about to clorse . . . Now, I can see that you're two young people of resource . . .' He repeated the phrase. 'And you know with these sort of things there's sometimes a bit of running about to do . . . I'm not as young as I was . . . and the long and the short of it is, really, is there a chance at all you could give me a hand over these few days? . . .'

'What are the terms?' said Zonda, sipping her coffee.

'Naturally you'll have a share of the profits and I'll provide you with a written note to that effect . . . Can you drive, by the way?'

I looked across at Zonda and told him I could drive. I did not tell him about the Golf, becalmed in the garage, after my accident.

'Well, it's just a little help, typing, driving, translating, that sort of thing . . .' he said, 'just during this very busy period . . .'

'What kind of money is involved?' I asked.

'Could be a hundred thousand dollars. Are you interested?'

'For how long?' I said.

'Well, that depends. Naturally I can't say at the moment when we'll actually clorse. But any day now we'll be putting together the country list and working on the details.' He smiled. 'But I take it you wouldn't object to that . . . I'd look upon it as a personal favour,' he said meaningfully.

I poured some more grappa. Zonda yawned and said she was going to bed.

Mooney stood up.

'Now that is a pity,' he said.

'It's so tiring meeting royalty,' said Zonda.

'Ah, the Princess . . .' said Mooney with a knowing look. 'Sure, she is indeed a woman of presence . . .'

Zonda pulled a face.

'Horrid,' she said, and yawned.

'She liked you, do you know that?' said Mooney. 'I could tell . . . and quite right she was, too, for you're a charming young . . .'

Zonda yawned and slid off along the wall towards the bedroom.

'I can't type,' she said, turning with closed eyes, 'or drive.'

'But you can trans*late*, darling,' I said.

She muttered, opened the door, closed it and the muttering

continued undiminished while we listened to her, through the aperture in the kitchen wall, crossing the room. The shoes kicked off with two bangs as I filled us up.

'What is this deal you keep talking about?' I asked.

'*Slainte*,' he raised his brandy glass and sloshed the grappa around in it. 'Well . . .'

'I assume she's going to lend you some money,' I said by way of an opener.

'Now there you'd be wrong . . .' said Mooney. 'She's only bringing in the Venezuelans. It's not her, it's Habib actually, who's the important figure there . . .'

'You mean they're looking for money?'

'They'll get their cut . . .'

'I knew she was horrid,' said Zonda from the bedroom. 'She's not even *rich* . . .'

'But I thought Iranians . . .'

'Everybody has to borrow sometime, you know,' said Mooney patiently. 'That's how bankers get rich. No, she and Habib are just selling information and putting people in touch with one another . . . and very grateful I am too, because he's done a very good job in bringing these Venezuelans in.'

There was a rebellious crash of springs as she fell on to the bed.

'Now we'll get some peace and quiet,' I said.

'Do you know money at all?' he asked.

'Not much.'

'Well, it's this type of a way. My company is putting together a deal with a B and three between the lenders in Zurich.'

'A billion dollars?'

'The Eurodollar and petrodollar markets are geared right up at the moment,' he explained, 'and now is the time to do this when there's so much money sloshing about in the old system, you see. The dollars have got to be recycled, and there are people over here absolutely desperate to borrow them. It's fantastic. The market's never been like this before and it's bound to blow soon and the game will be over. You see, that's why we've got to be in, *now*, Raymond. Then you can buy all the . . .' He waved his arm. 'All the stud-farms you want . . .'

'How does it work?'

He was really revving up now, and I was beginning to feel tired as he explained. He took out a piece of grubby paper and we sat there in the dusk staring at the scribbles with which he accompanied his explanation.

'Basically, it's just a form of arbitrage.'

'Arbitrage?'

I admitted I didn't know, but it rankled.

'It's simply the principle of buying and selling simultaneously in different markets to take advantage of the difference in prices.'

I got the bottle, hovering with it on the other side of the table while he began talking through his cigarette, screwing up his eyes and describing a circle several times above the paper with the biro before committing the point to the paper.

'Suppose you have, say, a New York banker who knows that the sterling cable rate in NY is 2.395, *with* me?'

'With you,' I said firmly, topping him up.

'But he is told that in London dollar cables are being quoted at 2.39. He then sells sterling cables in New York for 2.395 while the London bank he's dealing with sells dollar cables for 2.39 to get the sterling to cover the sale . . .'

'What's the profit?'

'A one half-cent per pound spread, say about . . .' His false teeth clinked against the rim of the glass as he drank. '500 dollars per 100,000 pounds.'

'This is because you always have discrepancies between markets?'

'In this case, they only last as long as the deal you've done – I mean, the sale of sterling depresses sterling in NY . . .'

'And the sale of dollars in London depresses dollars.'

'So your opportunity for arbitrage is gone.'

'It automatically irons itself out.'

'That's correct. Supply and demand, you see . . . or you might have a three-point arbitrage between, say, New York, London, and Toronto, to take advantage of a discrepancy between the price of sterling in New York and Toronto.'

'So if you send your money in a circle . . .'

'You pick up the spread, that's right, but again it won't last long because if you trade much, you yourself will bring about the relative adjustments in the different markets and there won't be any more opportunity for arbitrage.'

'Sounds fun,' I said.

He looked at me severely over his spectacles:

'This is not so interesting in itself, it's just the principle.'

'And this assumes you've got the money on tap,' I said.

'That's right, it's a spot exchange of funds.'

He laid down the pencil and crossed his arms one over the other.

'But the more common way is to arbitrage against future rates. Here's how your investor makes a profit by a simple set of transactions.' He began to write on the pad, waving his other arm. 'Come round here, now, Raymond, so you can see – now, first, he makes a loan for two years at, say, six per cent . . .' He wrote '$\times(1.06)(1.06)$' in his strange backward-sloping hand. 'Then, he raises the funds for the loan . . .'

'He hasn't any money at all?' I heard myself ask.

He looked up and grinned through the smoke, not understanding my question.

'Not a cent,' he said briskly. 'Now he could borrow the money for one year at three per cent and renew the loan at the end of the year at seven per cent. So he repays $\times(1+b_1)(1+b_2)$ on his borrowing. Net result? Average cost of funds – five per cent. Cost of loan . . .' He moaned through his smoke as he wrote it all out, underlining enthusiastically the figures and dashing them off with a flourish. 'Six per cent. So – profit equals . . .'

'One per cent.'

He took a slug of grappa and looked at me unseeingly.

'I know what you're going to say,' he said.

I wasn't going to say anything, overcome as I was by this effortless, gleaming sum.

'You are going to say supposing the rates are such that our man can't borrow that cheaply, supposing funds are only at four per cent. Well, he reverses the procedure – he borrows long and lends short – say he borrows for two years at four per cent and he lends short – one year at three and the next at seven per cent.' He wrote '$k_2 = 0.04$ and $b_2 = 3$ & 7 per cent.' 'Result? The same, a one per cent profit.'

The biro flourished again.

'Get the idea?' he said, picking up the tumbler of grappa and pursing his lips as he held it up in anticipation. He paused. 'Now, what we have set up is a three-strand country loan. Brazil, Mauritius and Venezuela . . .'

'Those are the borrowers . . .'

'Those are the borrowers. And they are going to deposit their notes through us.'

'And the lenders?'

'The lenders are clients of the Handelsbank in Zurich.'

'You mean you don't know who they are?'

'We know who we're dealing with. That's all that matters . . .'

'You don't know them?'

'What d'you mean? I don't know them from Adam's off-side ox, but we can do business with them. We have a representative in Zurich. Mr Drakulič, who is handling that whole end of things.'

'OK . . .' I let him have his point.

'The Handelsbank tells us it is ready to deposit in our fiduciary bank the money at a certain rate of interest, on certain terms . . . right?'

'OK . . .'

'The individual country quota is worked out and the rates of interest and the schedules of payment are arranged – differently for each country – in such a way that the rates are quite different for different borrowers. Each borrower does not know what the other borrower's lending rate is.'

'Why not?'

'Well, it's obvious. They would then all want the lowest rate and the longest time. Lend short and borrow long is the banker's rule everywhere . . . and some of the people might get a bit difficult to deal with, especially these Venezuelans. You haven't any Venezuelan interests have you, now, Raymond. . . ?' He turned and laughed. 'You wouldn't tell me if you had, would you?'

'His father is Fray Bentos,' said Zonda from the bedroom.

'Argentina . . .' said Mooney. 'Altogether different, a civilised country.'

'That was years ago. He's retired now,' I protested. 'Go on . . . go on . . .'

'Well, the capital is loaned and split three ways in separate deals with the borrowers and their notes are deposited with the performing bank for Zurich to pick up. Zurich are cautious people, but happy to make country loans because everybody believes at the moment that countries can't go bust, and it's true in a sense . . .'

'So your company is standing in the middle.'

'Exactly, lending and borrowing at the same time.'

'So your profit is the difference between the lending and borrowing rates.'

'Not just a pretty face, I can see . . . That's right, we discount the notes of the borrowers against the loan, which we arrange as part of the front end of the deal, so they will pay, say, a year's interest with the deposit of the note . . .'

'A year's interest on how much?'

'In the case of Brazil, the deal is for five hundred million dollars . . .'

'And the rate?'

He laughed, and wagged his finger:

'That would be telling, now, would it not?'

'Well, what *sort* of rate is common. . . ?'

'It all depends on what the Interbank rates are on the dollar at the time of closing . . . and how long the loan is . . .'

'Just roughly . . .'

'Well at something over nine per cent a year's interest will amount to about 45 million dollars from that strand alone. And a percentage of all parts of the transaction will land in our lap . . .'

'What percentage?'

He was modest, almost coy:

'Well, let's say for the sake of argument we fixed the Brazil notes at say ⅝ of one per cent higher than the Interbank rate on that day, and the spread amounts to, I don't know, say 750 thousand dollars . . . we estimate, at the end of the day from the three strands if all goes according to plan, we will be looking at something between one and a half and two million gross.'

'I don't understand. Why don't these Brazilians or whoever they are go direct to Zurich? Or Zurich to them? You know, cut out the middle man.'

He tilted his greasy horns like an animal about to charge.

'We make – we *create* – the markets, Raymond . . . Because we are prepared to leg it around and do the work on the ground to put these people in touch with one another . . . You might say it's the price of information. We get ourselves into the position where they need us to pull off the deal, because we're the only people who are talking to all parties at once, you see.'

'So you are the only person who can see the whole thing?'

'That's right. The banks are only interested in security. Once the loan is secured, it's an asset on their books.'

I laughed:

'But who guarantees?'

'You mean the lender of last resort? That I can't tell you. I can't even tell if there is one in the current atmosphere. Bisig represents Ickle. Ickle represents either himself, whom he keeps referring to as "my client", or some other unknown source . . .'

He raised his arm and I looked along the crumpled tweed at a shadowy queue of lenders, one behind the other, vanishing off into the distance.

'I have my ideas . . .' he said. 'But I'm not saying anything. The essence of the whole thing is the way that banks communicate with one another. The deal is worked out and approved, and then the notes are exchanged simultaneously on a certain day with penalties for non-performance by any party. It takes two seconds for the money to cross the Western Hemisphere, if you're in the same time zone. But once the notes have been exchanged, they can't be called back . . . it's completely irrevocable, and anyway, with the current way money travels, the money has vanished immediately and is already being loaned out elsewhere . . .'

He rose, groaning.

'Splosh,' he said. He paused at the door of the bathroom. 'It's all part of the deregulation of finance that's happening at the present . . .'

He put his cigarette in his mouth, and adjusted his glasses.

'Flip,' he said, crossing his limp hands one over the other.

'Raymond,' said Zonda, sleepily, as soon as the door had closed.

'Doll,' I said.

'Come here a minute,' she said. I pulled the curtain aside: she lay in state, a fine film of sweat over her face.

'Lovely tie, but he hasn't got a lot of the old street cred, has he? Darling, come *here*. I want to . . .' She patted the coverlet beneath her, twice, with a flopping hand.

I poured another couple of grappas and dosed up the two cups with black coffee. I could hear him groaning to himself in the bathroom.

'He seems to know something about horses,' I said, staying where I was.

'That's all you *ever* think about. What's he been talking about in there?'

'I thought you could hear everything,' I said.

'I can, but I want to know what *you* think.'

'I don't think anything. It's all rather amusing.'

'Well, *I* don't like him.'

75

'Oh, *darling*,' I mocked. 'He's brought a little *fun* into our dull lives . . .'

She turned over.

'He smells funny,' she said, 'as if he's got a cancer.'

'Who?' said Mooney, as he closed the bathroom door. I dropped the curtain.

'A friend of ours,' I said. 'More coffee?' I gestured at the two glasses of grappa.

He rubbed his hands, listing slightly to the left and paying excessive attention to the chair as he sat.

We sat in the almost dark, with the night folding round the kitchen window. I could just make out his face and some light from somewhere caught the oily liquid in the two glasses before us on the table. Outside, on the roof across the tiny yard, the dim form of the white cat lay curled at the base of the chimney.

'Well?' he said.

I told him I'd like to help him.

'I feel it's a worthy cause,' I said.

We shook hands far too long, as he laughed and put his head on one side to look at me.

'Let's *do* it, then, Raymond,' he said, giving my hand one last enthusiastic little shake.

He lit a cigarette from the packet and we drank to the stud-farm and the generations of classic winners to come.

'And to the brilliants . . .' I said, pouring some more grappa.

'And the stouts . . .' he said, clinking me, 'if they're winners, eh?'

We drank another to the stouts.

'And one for the roughs? Never underestimate the roughs,' he said. 'That's where the staying power comes from.'

'You wouldn't like to write that down, would you?' I said.

'What?'

'That you will pay me one hundred thousand dollars for my services . . .'

'Certainly, I will, certainly . . .'

76

'Oh well,' I said, 'I can't be bothered now.'

'We shall be seeing plenty of each other, I hope, in the next few days. There'll be time for that. But in the meantime . . .' He raised his glass. 'We have a gentleman's agreement . . .' He coughed and took the cigarette from his lip, shaking his head at the vehemence of the sudden fit. 'I'll tell you . . .' He tried again and went off into another spasm. 'I'll tell you . . .' he said and coughed again, searching for the final one. 'I'll tell you something else about that Dormello stud. The colours . . .'

'What, the St Andrew's cross?'

'No,' he shouted through another unbelievable rain of secondary coughs. 'No damme . . . Here's another, you see . . .' He went on talking to an imaginary third person of Irish descent. 'Would you look at that now?' He turned to me. 'The St Andrew's cross is in the way of a *white* cross over a *white* background.'

'And the Dormello cross was a red cross on a white background.'

He took another cigarette and lit it.

'Right, my man, and do you know what cross that is?'

I didn't.

'St Patrick's.' He laughed. 'So it is.'

A spume of smoke fled across the kitchen and annihilated itself against the window. I poured the last few drops of grappa into his glass.

'If we want further refreshment,' I said, 'we shall now have to go forth and seek it.'

'Ah ha!' he said, getting to his feet. 'A little trip is necessary . . .' He fished in his pockets, taking out of the inside of his jacket a shiny, plum-coloured wallet which bulged with papers. He peered at it, myopically, and I switched on the light. He handed me a piece of paper which was tightly folded into four, and shuffled off into the bathroom.

I undid the tight, dirty folds and spread the sheet out on the table. It was a piece of plain notepaper, with a telephone number scribbled in pencil on it, and underneath the words 'Minsky – an alternative?' The heading was scribbled in pencil: PEQUEÑO INVESTMENTS LTD

Incorporated in the Isle of Man, British Isles,
Reg. No. 12004 87 High Street, Ramsey, Isle of Man

Directors	*Representative Office*
Captain J. R. O'Meally	66 Cumberland Road
Michael Casey	Ballsbridge
Gerrard Mooney	Dublin
Irving J. Glucksman	EIRE
Donald Divine	Tel 668962/6688093
Kevin Mooney Jr	Telex 426043 (IMAG)
Michael Ryan	
Shane Donnelly	

'I want you to see if you can find me a jobbing printer and get this made up,' he said. 'I want it tomorrow.'

'Tomorrow?' I laughed. 'You must be joking. This is Florence. Even in London . . .'

'You know what hangs on this. Tomorrow.'

'But tomorrow's Monday, I don't even know where . . .'

'Get him to do a couple of thousand . . .' He waved vaguely. 'And some cards . . .'

He was finishing doing up his trousers. Hoisting at himself.

'It's not possible . . .' I said, 'in one day.'

He stopped hoisting.

'Nothing is impossible. I want you to put one hundred per cent into this . . .'

'It is most unlikely . . .' I said.

'Now you're talking,' he said. I opened the door. The stairwell was just a pitch-black hole. We stood, our shoulders touching in the narrow space, and stared down into it.

'But I thought you were called "The Project-For-The-Americas Investment Corporation?"

'It's all right. I've got some of *them*, back in the room . . .'

78

I put a light on. Our voices boomed in the confined space. Now the top six stairs, the deformed ones, were illuminated by the feeble bulb and then fell away into blackness. He wobbled, his heels precariously placed in the narrow ledges, and caught my shoulder.

'Woah,' he said.

We were a long time coming down.

'How did you get into this business?' I asked.

'What, mountaineering?' He gripped my shoulder and I felt him laughing.

'Finance.'

'Oh,' he said, 'I've knocked about a bit, you know . . . Free-lancing . . . Argentina . . . specialising in Latin American port-folios. Worked for Geneva for a bit in the Mutual Funds business in the seventies . . . Bahamas . . . you get to know people,' he said stopping. 'Do you know what one of my first jobs was, Raymond?' He stood near me in the darkness. I heard him fumbling.

'Hang on,' he said. The match struck and flared up. He was lighting a gnarled cigarette stump with a large box of kitchen matches. We were back in the dark, going down step by step. 'I built the special concrete bunker they put Nearco in during the war in Newmarket, you know . . .' He paused and the cigarette stump glowed. 'To protect him from the bombs . . . What do you think of that, eh? He was at stud, and a real old stamper with his fillies and mares, too . . . And I was in the construction trade at the time and we got this call . . . would we come down and do this special job. . . ? He was at stud there till 1945, safe as houses . . .'

I opened the door. The street was empty, lit by faint moonlight.

'That's better . . . let the dog see the rabbit, I say . . .'

We walked out into the Via San Gallo.

'Which way are we going?' I said.

He stood and looked around. He pointed to the lower end of the street, the cigarette stump sulking on his bottom lip.

'Oh yes, I've knocked about a bit . . .' he said, as we began to walk. 'I used to work with a fella called Seymour Lazard. Friend of Bernie Cornfeld's. There was a character for you! Seymour used to call himself the only hippie arbitrageur in the world. Always had a stable of girls around with him. A bit like Nearco, Seymour was . . . Do you know, it was Seymour actually financed the defence of the Mormon Will in the Howard Hughes case? He thought it was a safe bet. He told me it cost him 250,000 dollars maximum, and he was hoping for an eight-figure return . . .'

'What happened?' I asked.

'Well Seymour spent weeks in Europe lining up handwriting experts. All the American ones had said it was a fraud. In the end they threw it out, said it was a forgery. There's no such thing as a safe bet . . .'

'Aren't you assuming that, with your deal?'

'Speculation in loans is not the same thing. The banker's money all belongs to other people. Gambling's a mug's game. The money belongs to you.'

We had come to the end of the street.

'Where are we going now?' I asked.

'It's called the Ricasoli Something.' said Mooney.

'The Residenza,' I said, wheeling. 'I know it.'

I was rather anxious to get him delivered now. It was chilly in the street.

'Just point me in the right direction,' he said.

'No, no, not at all,' I said. 'It's not far now . . .'

'Did you say something about Toulouse-Lautrec?' he asked.

'I don't remember,' I said.

We had come in sight of the Residenza Ricasoli.

'Do you know he was the grandsire of this year's Epsom Derby winner? Henbit?'

I didn't know. I was shivering.

'Chilly, all of a sudden. Well, it just goes to show. The old lines are the best . . . Cavaliere D'Arpino sired Morston . . . Donatello the Second . . . with Crepello . . . that won the Derby . . .'

'And Nearco . . .' I said, 'sired Nimbus and Dante . . .'

He stared down at me with sudden fierceness from the semicircular steps of the Residenza.

'We'll go for the old lines,' he said, and turned away towards the closed door.

I spent too much of the next day hanging round at a small printer's I had remembered out by the old Florence goods station. There had been a time when I could come back from the track at Milan on the Rome Express and get off at this station. But now it was only used for goods trains. There was a restaurant out there which was one of Zonda's and my favourites, and nearby was a paper factory and small printer's. I had no intention of confiding to Mooney that I had paid altogether a total of 250,000 lire for 500 sheets of heavy grade watermarked linen paper, embossed in blue *relievo*.

At first the man had thrown up his hands and looked at me as though I was mad. I told him how desperately urgent it all was and he was very curious as to why. In the end, between two rocking walls of tightly bundled paper, we got down to business and he agreed to produce the sheets for an extra consideration. On an impulse, I added my own name to the list of the firm's directors. As I went off to pay the telephone bill and lay some bets down at the Piazza della Repubblica, I trod with a lighter tread.

When I got back, the factory and the shop were closed. I went from the front to the back and peered in through all the windows. A dog was barking inside somewhere. As I went to the front of the factory, I heard it running alongside of me on the other side of the wall. I stood in front of the building, out on the road near the railway bridge, and stared at its façade, as if it might give me some clue. I thought if he were in an upper storey, he could see me and let me in. It was very windy. A man was hanging out of the second-floor window of a low-rise block of flats, staring at me. I took the number down off the front of the shop. When I rang, I got his wife. No, he wasn't at home. She was surprised to learn he wasn't at his work. I could hear that. Could she think of anywhere

where he might have gone? She couldn't think of anything except to ask at the garage. I walked back along the road, past the paper factory. I went back inside the yard to check that he hadn't come back. The dog barked, then his face and paws appeared between two pots of geraniums on the window-sill at the back. He was a German shepherd, an Alsatian with long hair. I went on to the garage just before the bridge. There was no one on the forecourt, so I walked into the small shop at the back. Two legs were sticking out from under a small ten-hundredweight truck. The youth told me that he had never heard of Signor Gaspari. He got up after lying back abruptly and fixing something under the truck and went off through a door at the back of the workshop. There were raised voices. A middle-aged Italian came out in greasy overalls and asked me what I wanted with Signor Gaspari. I explained to him that I was here to pick up an order. He wrote an address down. He waddled to the front of the shop wiping his hands on a cloth and wrote slowly with his tongue hanging out under his moustache and then handed it to me. He told me that Signor Gaspari had gone into town and I could find him there. It was an address in the Via Forlani.

When I arrived, it was a laundry under an arch. I showed the ladies the address and they waved me through the piles of washing into a small yard full of partly dismantled antique furniture and wood shavings. Gaspari was sitting on a kissing seat jammed between two mirrors, a wood plane on his knees, arguing with another man in a dark blue shirt with a grey blazer with shiny buttons, standing in a narrow corridor inside the building on the other side of the yard. He told me he couldn't do it. I looked at him. He put the plane down, and said that it was impossible. I wanted my money back. The other man said he was going, and left. We hardly noticed him. Gaspari kept saying that he hadn't had time. If I would like to go back with him. Or could I come again later? It was half-past six. I insisted that he must do it. I must have the paper as arranged. He eventually agreed to get his car out and go back to the paper factory, where he tried to sell me a stamp which impressed itself on the paper. He said it would be much cheaper. I said I didn't want the stamp. I wanted the paper embossed. I would come back at eight. At eight when I arrived, it was sitting in its carton in the front of the shop on a table. The cards would be done tomorrow he said.

When I reached Apartment 60 in the Residenza Ricasoli, it was a quarter to nine. I found Mooney in his shirt-sleeves, red-faced and sweating, trying to stab a tin of Fray Bentos steak-and-kidney pudding with a camping knife. Every time he attacked it small geysers of gravy welled up through lesions in the top of the tin. On the draining-board lay a range of other instruments smeared with the same mud-stains.

I tapped the carton.

'There you are,' I said. 'But I can't get the cards till the morning.'

'Can you help me with this thing at all Raymond?' he said.

'The paper,' I said.

'Blood sugar you see,' he said. 'I have to have something.'

Another thin arc of mud rose from the tin and spattered on to some papers on the table. He sat down shakily in a wicker chair, and began to mop his face.

On the draining-board, I found the tin-opener. I fitted it on to the tin, and drove a clean cut round the edge with a few turns of the wheel. The lid lifted as I worked. I brought the open tin over to him in the chair together with a fork which I rinsed. He said it was marvellous and began to eat it.

I looked around the room. A cigarette was sending a grey ribbon of smoke up to the ceiling. The elegant proportions of the Residenza's apartment suite, its marble floor, light wickerwork furniture and discreet flowered-cotton sofa, were almost obscured by heaps of different papers and lengths of multi-coloured telexes in concertina-like strips. Cartons of files and unopened tins of cheap food were distributed amongst them at random.

He held the tin under his chin and scooped the food up into his mouth with the fork. From the back, I could see his head ducking regularly. He groaned.

I flopped on the sofa. While he was eating, I craned round to read a memorandum which was lying on top of one of the piles of papers. It was from a financial consultant, dated a week previously, and signed by one I. Drakulič. It read:


```
To Americas Investment Project Co.

To Attention: Mr Gerrard Mooney
c/o Mr Kohlhammer
Bahnhofstr. 13
Zurich

Ref: Baron Andre de Van de Velde
Re: Loan to Govt Brazil
Code: Drakulex 1092

We are pleased to inform that we can arrange a long-term
loan to Govt Brazil on the following terms and conditions:

        Amount: up to 50 million US dollars
        Interest: 9% to 9.25 per annum, payable annually in
                  arrears
        Emission: 100% - return 5% - net 95%
        Term: 20 years + 1 day
        Guarantee: 1CC 290/322 promissory notes - Central
                   Bank of Brazil.



Our procedure requires that you submit to this office three
letters in hard copy as follows:
(1) Hard copy appointing Window On The World Consulting Ltd,
President I. Drakulic, to negotiate exclusively with lenders,
for loan to Brazil. Also assure accredited capital will not
be utilized for purchase of gold, silver, diamonds, and war
equipments.
(2) Hard copy from Ministry of Finance or Central Bank,
expressing irrevocable acceptance of funds. This letter also
to designate bank for commitment of funds.
(3) Hard copy from Central Bank - irrevocable and unconditior
commitment to pay 5% flat of amount borrowed at time of closi
Loan will be made through bank to bank transaction.
```

```
After receipt of these copies, lender (lender's bank) will
notify designated bank of availability of funds for subject
loan and give instructions for closing.
We look forward to your information whether offer is of
interest or not,

Best regards,
```

I put down the telex and went over to the window. The
apartment wasn't far away across the rooftops. Had I been able to
see it, I should have seen the white cat, prisoner on its tiny patch
of roof, lying in the shadow of the chimney or dragging round the
piece of raw lights which the brute who lived below us threw up
for him from time to time.

'What's emission?' I said. 'It sounds faintly obscene . . .'

He stopped eating and groaning. He explained it was the up-
front part of the deal.

'It's less than a year's interest, but we have to cover
ourselves . . .'

'What happens to that money?'

'Most of it is passed on to the lenders as part of the up-front
end of their terms . . . Didn't you say your people were Fray
Bentos, Raymond?'

'My father was General Manager of their Argentine operation'.

'Well, give him my compliments . . .' He got up and took the
tin into the kitchen, where I heard him throw it into the waste
bin. The fork clattered in the sink and he came out picking his
teeth. He sat down at the table and stubbed out the cigarette that
was smoking in the ashtray.

'God! that's better,' he said, lighting another. 'Damn phone's
been going all day . . . Do you know, Raymond, I once spent
seventeen hours on the telephone almost continuously . . . it must
be a world record . . .'

'Must have been quite a deal,' I said. 'What were you
negotiating?'

'Divorce. She was in California, and I for my sins was in
Tennessee . . .'

'Don't they have lawyers for that sort of thing?'

'This was before all that started . . . We went through every possession we ever had and every item of every bank account, statements . . . etc., working out the terms of the settlement . . . And then . . .' he started laughing, 'we never got divorced in the end . . .'

'Why not?'

'*Far* too expensive . . .' he said. 'Do you know, the taxes alone would have broke the pair of us . . . So we went into business together instead . . . A charity for Catholic victims of alcoholism which Mamie runs . . . and the IRS can't touch us . . . By the way, Raymond, do you know anywhere to eat that's, you know, a cut above?'

I suggested Da Noi. He said it sounded grand. The Baron would like that.

He got up.

'Splosh,' he said. 'Book us a table, would you?'

He put his head round the doorpost.

'Oh, invite your charming friend . . . What was her name again? . . . Don't tell me . . . Zelda . . .'

'Zonda . . .'

'Ah, yes, I knew it was some sort of old-fashioned name . . .'

I booked a table at Da Noi. Da Noi is too small to accommodate late bookings, but I persuaded them. Then I rang Zonda.

'Doll,' I said.

'Where are you?'

'Just across the road – in the Ricasoli . . .'

'With – your funny man? Seamus?'

'Yes. Listen, get your glad rags on. We're going to Da Noi. It'll be fun. There's a real live Baron coming . . .'

'But I haven't got anything to *wear*. . . !'

'Never mind that. Do something with a handkerchief . . .'

'Bloody *cheek* . . .' The receiver bulged with her soft protests.

'Doll? Are you all right?' I asked. 'What have you been doing?'

'Painting. What have *you*?'

'Never mind. I'll tell you when you come . . .'

'Raymond. There's a name for that, you know . . .'

'Half an hour?'

'At *least* . . .'

'Darling, do try to put your best foot forward . . .'

I put the phone down to a snarl of obscenities.

Mooney was coming back into the room, sniffing and hitching up his green houndstooth trousers like a cheap comic about to begin his Cagney impression.

'Everything OK?'

He put his hand on my shoulder while I told him it was all done. I caught a strong whiff of camphor, apples and tobacco, all rolled into one. The odour issued from his suit, his mouth, the lank horns of grey hair that he had plastered with water which was dripping now from his white-furred earlobes. His ears were like the inside of a poppy. He stared at me with his cracked smile.

'You're wet,' I heard myself say.

'You're a fine young man,' he said, his green-marbled pupils floating a little behind wet spectacles. The hand gripped my shoulder. He was breathing heavily. I could hear each individual wheeze in the labyrinth of tubes.

'Time for a snifter?' he said.

I followed him into the kitchen, saying something about the Pretty Polly line.

He opened the fridge and stared into it. It contained nothing, except a knife lying across one of the shelves, soiled with something I didn't care to look at, and a bottle of Gordon's gin. He took the knife out and threw it into the sink.

'Dossa Dossi,' he said. 'Now you are talking. She was a long lanky streak of a thing, inbred three to four on Pretty Polly, unless I'm very much mistaken . . . A chestnut,' he said, holding the gin bottle up to the light, 'a golden chestnut, was she not?'

'Nearer to flaxen,' I said.

'In between the two . . .' He grinned. 'I'm not going to argue . . .'

'I'm rather impressed with this line . . .' I began.

'Let me see,' he said, 'what have we got?'

'Ice?'

He opened the ice-box like a robot.

'She was by that Irish Derby winner, Spike Island . . . an iron constitution she had . . .'

I pointed out that, though he was imported, Spike Island was himself out of Spearmint.

We had progressed no further with the drinks, but the Pretty Polly line was unfolding fairly well, when the phone went.

'But . . . do you see my point?' I said, following him eagerly into the living-room.

'Oh yes,' said Mooney. 'Yes? . . . Yes? . . . Show him up, yes, indeed . . . *rapido rapido* . . .'

He sat down at the table and stared at me distractedly.

There was a knock at the door and someone so tall was coming into the room that he had to duck to enter.

Mooney bounded across from behind the table, his hand out.

'Good of you to come, Baron . . .' he said over the Baron's shoulder, a slight falter in his voice as he realised there was someone else too in the shadow of the landing outside the door.

The Baron straightened up into a drooping S.

'Gerrard,' he said. He allowed his bony hand to be shaken.

Behind him, equally tall and ducking, a long-legged black woman in an apricot dress that buttoned all the way up the front, her hair sculptured in infinitesimally tight long dreadlocks, hawked in on wobbling black heels. I saw with disappointment that she had enormous feet that ran up into slender ankles and no calves at all to speak of. Round her shoulders lay a headless fox with three tails dangling.

Mooney brought the two of them over to the window where I was standing. The Baron's clothes hung on his scrawny frame, his trousers flapping over shiny shoes apparently cleaning them as he walked.

'Baron Van de Velde,' said Mooney, 'this is my nephew Raymond, who is just on a brief visit to me here . . .'

My hand shot out.

'Delighted?' I suggested.

The Baron inclined his head to look down at me and offered me his hand. Then he swung aside and we all turned to the black woman, who stretched the cracked pink lipstick across her mouth and looked down at her shoes.

'Désirée,' said the Baron, 'is the niece of an old friend of mine, President Mobutu of Zaïre . . .'

Sunshine crossed Désirée's face. She shook her head.

'He has many nieces,' she said in her deep voice, 'many different nieces . . . *beaucoup* . . .'

Her hand was cold and dry.

We stared at each other, the niece and the nephew.

'I haven't much time,' said the Baron to Mooney, in his light French accent. 'We must go back to Zurich tomorrow. I called to know . . .'

'To know. . . ?' Mooney shoved us all somehow into an untidy heap in the centre of the room, extracting the Baron by a gentle pinch of the upper arm, and leaving Désirée and me looking politely past each other.

'To know if arrangements are proceeding smoothly, Gerrard. Drakulič has telexed you?'

I felt weak. Offering Désirée a seat on the cane chair opposite, I almost fell into a low armchair of dark corduroy and tubular steel. Désirée sat on the edge of the chair and threw apart the skirts of her dress like butterfly wings. I lay opposite, looking along satin columns of thigh. Her tall crossed shins seemed dented and discoloured all the way up to the knee.

Mooney was explaining something about diversification. It was a daisy-chain, he said. Things had developed since Drakulič had been in touch. They were about to go into closing during this coming week. The possibilities had become almost unlimited, he said. It was a major deal with major countries involved besides Brazil now. Mauritius and Venezuela, too.

The Baron began by nodding and saying '*Absolument*' or '*D'accord*' to every second word that Mooney uttered, but as Mooney went on, warming to his theme, he began to look disappointed and fell increasingly silent.

'But . . . is this wise?' I heard him say. He looked over towards me.

'It's all right, Baron,' said Mooney, 'I have no secrets at all from Raymond. He's helping me right now with some typing and small matters . . .'

Désirée looked over at me and raised one eyebrow. Her bottom lip, which was cracked in deep red fissures beneath the lipstick, appeared huge. With pinched finger and thumb, she made a delicate motion as if tipping a little of something out of an invisible jar. Then she fished in her leather bag, and took out a single, enormously long cigarette.

'Have you been to Zaïre?' she said, the cigarette dangling unlit from her hand, as if she were a child concealing it.

'Raymond,' said Mooney, extracting himself from his sales pitch, 'would you mind doing the honours? Gin's on the draining-board and there's some orange in the cabinet . . .'

I looked into the bottoms of beer-stained UPIM tumblers and listened as I fiddled at the sink. There was no washing-up liquid.

'We are waiting on Glucksman at the moment . . . who'll be hand-delivering some papers and then we'll be going into clorsing . . .'

The Baron began to raise some objections:

'Isn't this diversification going to affect the time factors involved, Gerrard . . . It makes everything just that much more complicated to arrange. . . ?'

'Oh,' said Mooney, 'never you fear, Baron, that'll all be slotted in quite neatly when the time comes . . .'

'What does Mr Bisig say to this?'

'As far as I can see it's the more the merrier.'

The Baron began to laugh.

'Don't leave it too long, Gerrard . . . The American elections are forthcoming and I have an idea there won't be so much money around then . . . these new economic ideas mean interest rates will be very high . . .'

Mooney spluttered theatrically:

'D'ye think we'll still be hanging round here in November? I shall be wanting me Bahamian holiday . . .'

'Quite so,' said the Baron with a thin smile. 'But it would not do to be greedy after all the patient good work we have put in . . .'

'Rest assured,' said Mooney heartily, 'everything's under control, Baron . . .'

'Well I am just a messenger,' said the Baron unconvincingly. 'I have no technical competence in these matters . . . but I meet a lot of people . . . What's the performing bank, by the way?'

'Well, we're looking into this. We have several possibilities, Baron. There's the Savings and Industrial Bank in Livorno . . .'

'*Whose?*' said the Baron immediately. 'Have I heard of him? Don't pick anything too small, Gerrard, it sounds far too small to handle the kind of . . .'

I handed round the drinks. Désirée gave me a broad smile as I put the grubby iceless gin-and-orange into her hand. The cigarette poked up out of the palm of her hand. The Baron immediately put his drink down on the table and never touched it again.

'Thank you so very much,' he said. He was shaking his head.

'I think the young lady requires a light,' I said.

'Livorno – that's Signor Esclapon,' said the Baron. He bent slightly and without looking down pressed the lighter with his thumb so that the flame almost ran up the wide nostrils of Désirée. 'I am surprised, Gerrard.'

'I know what you're thinking – that he's undercapitalised – but you know Baron, money moves a lot faster now – things have changed a lot since '73 . . .'

'How impolite we are,' said the Baron into the hole which this remark had caused, 'talking about business all the time . . . Raymond, what is your calling?'

'Italian thoroughbreds,' I said.

Mooney, from the kitchen door: 'He's of the turf, turfy, Baron . . .'

I explained to the Baron that I was the Italian correspondent for *The European Racehorse*, and that I owned several horses.

He laughed.

'You are quite an expert then, but I know nothing about racing . . . I did most of my riding in Zaïre . . .'

Désirée flashed him a great smile, and murmured with pleasure at the name, little gushings of grey smoke coming from her nose and mouth in profile as she turned.

'Zaïre . . . isn't that the place where the President made a speech telling the Civil Service to "steal cleverly". . . ?' I said.

Désirée turned to the Baron, a deeply puzzled expression on her face, and repeated the words without sound.

'*Yibana mayele*,' said the Baron to her with a sigh.

Her face lit up and she nodded, opening her mouth in silent laughter.

'*Haricots pour les enfants*,' said Désirée with a giggle that made her chair vibrate.

'Where does it all go?' I asked.

Mooney was laughing.

'It's like Brazil,' he said. 'D'ye know what the current status-symbol is there, since they started going bankrupt in a serious way?'

I shook my head.

'A government-paid butler.'

I turned to Désirée.

'Is Zaïre full of butlers?'

She asked the Baron what I was saying.

'*Naturellement, chez le Citoyen Mobutu il y a beaucoup de serviteurs* . . .' said Désirée.

'An unfortunate misinterpretation of President Mobutu's words, which has been turned by the unscrupulous gutter Press of the Western nations into a repeated slur on the Zaïrean national character . . .' said the Baron.

'I read it in the *New York Times* . . . Hardly the gutter Press . . .'

'Sure, the Baron means he was having them on, Raymond, you know . . .' said Mooney, clapping a hand on my shoulder. 'A little joke?'

He turned away to pick his burnt-out cigarette out of the ashtray on the table, and relit it.

But the Baron was flurrying again. He sighed deeply as he referred to the problems of Zaïre. He knew several members of the board of Société Générale de Belgique, good people, who were doing all they could. They had rescheduled the foreign debt, not once but many times. It was escalating all the time. It now stood at the beginning of the year at four billion dollars.

'They've got a lot of paper with private banks in Europe and America . . .' said Mooney. 'Maybe half a B . . .' He laughed, turning half to me. 'I keep telling the Baron they should come in with us . . .'

'No, no, Gerrard . . .' said the Baron with disbelief in his voice. 'I am a member of the Belgian State Committee for Public Assistance to Zaïre . . . It would not be . . . mmm . . .' He clicked his fingers.

'Compatible?' I suggested.

'*Voilà, le mot juste* . . .' said the Baron with a smile.

'Ah, come on now, you're a great fixer, André . . .' said Mooney. 'Look at those shares you've got in the brewery.'

Désirée was pulling at the Baron's arm, and demanding a translation of the conversation into French. He spoke a few sentences, and broke off, shrugged, and waved his arm.

'*Trafic* . . . *détournement* . . .' he said.

Zonda did not actually knock at the door, because the man delivering the telegram for Mooney was already doing that when she reached the top of the stairs. Nor was her entrance noticed by

93

anyone except Désirée and myself. Mooney left the door ajar while he turned away and ripped open the envelope, and then waddled towards the ringing onyx and brass imitation 1920s telephone on the table. It was Potter's office, from the Isle of Man. The Baron had gone into the kitchen and I could hear him running the tap. Zonda advanced across the parquet, heels clopping, and instantly the physical aspects of the room began to change, as I saw her looking about. Zonda had a way of raking the physical environment with her eyes. And as soon as she did this, I found that I started sketching in things where there had been a blank before. This usually occurred with servants, or anyone in a menial position. When alone, I didn't notice them. I merely took account of what they did. My eyes looked along the waiter's arm to what he was holding, not at the inference written on his passive features of a strained biography. His struggles with his mistress or his motorcycle or his piles. When Zonda was present, without her saying anything in particular, I began to notice things, objects and tiny details I had no ability to notice when alone. I saw generalised brushstrokes that corresponded to what people did. She on the other hand lived in a world of materials and blemishes, of colours that did or didn't go with one another, of tiny brass pins that disgusted her. Everything that she and everyone else wore repelled or excited her and she radiated intense curiosity about everything and everybody in the room. I could feel her interest humming like an electrical gadget as she took my arm and I moved forward to introduce her.

The Baron appeared in the doorway and started talking to Mooney, who was standing with his back to us, feet planted wide apart, one hand supported on the desk by a spread of fingertips, saying to the person on the other end:

'Within the next seven banking days ... seven ... Audrey, have you got that?'

As we moved forward, the Baron's neck moved out of his collar as he stretched to say something audible to Mooney above the noise of the phone. I noticed that he had had surgery of a quite radical nature in the region of the Adam's apple. At the same time, he saw us out of the corner of his eye and broke off, striding over to join the introductions. My eyes were glued to the double row of suture marks peeping above his collar.

The Baron snapped open his briefcase, and handed me a fat photocopied document.

'You can take this, if you are interested, I have another copy . . .'

I glanced down at it. It was a section of the 1979 World Bank report on Zaïre's economic situation.

'Last year,' he said, 'we in Brussels lent them three point eight billion Belgian francs in public assistance . . .'

'And yet no one's declared them in default . . .' said Mooney with a laugh, 'because it suits everybody else to keep the debt running . . .'

'You know, Gerrard, it's much more complicated than that . . .' said Baron Van de Velde. 'The stability of the world banking system is threatened by defaults of this nature. Mexico has been about to go for a long time, but the Americans will never let it . . .'

'It has been estimated that two-thirds of the Civil Service does not exist . . . Do you know, there are more non-existent people in Zaïre than anywhere else in the world?' said Mooney. He dived into his inside pocket. 'Look at this . . . Mobutu admitted it in a speech last year . . .'

He took out a battered clipping, and slapped the marked paragraph with the back of his hand.

'We are going to get rid of the fake teachers and the imaginary schools . . . imaginary schools! I tell you, these fellows are coining it over there . . . Look at all those shares you've got in Bralma, Baron . . .'

'I didn't know they were selling off Hinduism,' I said.

'Not Brahma – Bralma. It's a Congolese brewery,' said Mooney. 'What's the name of it?'

'Brasseries, Limonaderies, et Malteries Africaines,' said the Baron. 'Unfortunately, it was Zaïrianised . . .'

'Zaïrianisation,' said the Baron. 'A national tragedy . . .'

Mooney laughed, sarcastically.

'But retrocession, when they handed all those businesses they nationalised back, was OK, wasn't it, Baron? The so-called 1969 Investment Code . . .'

'It's true,' said the Baron, ever the diplomat. 'It was a liberal measure which had the effect of saving the economy . . . attracting foreign investment. It had the effect of giving everybody in the country the right to have a foreign bank account . . .'

'God these curtains . . .' said Zonda. '*Que caaaaatso!*' She smiled in an imitation of the Queen, put out a limp hand and said to Désirée: 'Hello, I've never met an African before . . .' and then covered herself in laughter and confusion by wheeling to the Baron and saying: 'That sounds awful . . .'

'That sounds worse,' I said.

The Baron introduced himself perfunctorily as 'a pleasure'. We stood in silence, smiling.

'Are you here for the art?' said Zonda, looking at Désirée's shoes, 'or the shopping?' She looked at me. 'Raymond, is there a drink?' Back at Désirée: 'Would *you* like a. . . ?' and she tipped back an imaginary glass. She was conspiratorial.

'We're just talking about Zaïre,' I said.

'Where is Zaïre?' said Zonda, looking challengingly at the Baron.

'About in the middle,' I said. 'Used to be the Congo . . .'

'Christ, this is hard work,' said Zonda.

'The Baron's just been telling us it's the most bankrupt country in the world . . .' I said as I made off to fetch the gin. The telephone receiver lay silently on the table, still connected with Potter's secretary Audrey, I assumed, in the Isle of Man. Mooney was in the bathroom.

'Kinshasa, beautiful . . .' said Désirée, nodding slowly. 'Beautiful city . . .'

'Ah, Kinshasa,' said Zonda, as if remembering a visit she

96

had once made. 'That was where Ali had the George Foreman fight . . .'

I came back from the kitchen with two tiny spirit glasses, which I found in the cupboard. Obviously left behind by a German travelling salesman. They had red and yellow coats of arms on them and 'Gebr. Muller o HG, Weingut Iphofen/ Franken' written in italic lettering. I handed them to Zonda and Désirée, brimful of Gordon's with a dash of orange.

Désirée picked up her own empty glass and looked quizzically at the Baron, holding the two. At this point we all wobbled off into French, with loud undisguised asides between Zonda and myself in Italian.

The Baron took the glasses off Désirée and poured one into the other and set them on the table without a word, developing his dissertation on the nature of Zaïrean corruption. He continued in his benevolent lovable Rathbonian fashion (the Baron had a face like a soft hatchet) to attribute the continued bankruptcy and ineffectiveness of foreign aid from the West to the national penchant for petty swindling, or, as he put it, '*trouver une solution Zaïroise*' to all questions.

Zonda asked Désirée where she lived. Désirée said: '*Ça dépend . . .*' Then she put up one finger and began ticking off, prefacing each place by '*parfois à*', 'Kinshasa . . . Savigny . . . Paris . . . Brussels . . .'

'It's a nightmare,' said the Baron. 'There's corruption everywhere – in importing, exporting, the Department of Justice, even the Post Office . . . Do you know one can't even make a telephone call without the operator intervening and threatening to cut one off unless he gets a commission . . .'

'Donatello. . . ? Botticelli . . . ? Michelangelo. . . ?' Zonda was saying to Désirée, who nodded or shook her head as they counted simultaneously on their fingers.

'. . . *Fausse factures*,' said the Baron, in a run of descending scale, '*fraudes fiscales, dépassement de la marge bénéficiaire . . .*'

'Audrey . . . you still there?' said Mooney into the telephone,

97

cradling the receiver in his collar-bone while he hoisted himself a few times. 'Here's the consortium . . . Bank of America . . . European American Bank . . . Bank of Montreal . . .'

They were all shouting softly. Out of the window I could see the lights of a helicopter moving across the sky. I began just under my breath reciting the names of horses according to a staccato rhythm which irresistibly suggested itself:

'Darkie . . . Dark Ronald . . .' I said, nodding at the Baron, 'Cicero . . . Burne Jones . . . Miss Matty . . . Via Via!' I finished with a flourish at the top of the scale, and a snigger of mental castanets.

'*Exactement*,' said the Baron with a curt nod. '*Et puis . . .*'

The frail fugue staggered on, breaking up all around me as something alien intruded. It was the person in the apartment next door hitting the wall with slow, insistent knocks.

The Baron simpered. He looked at his watch.

'Are we making so much noise?' he said.

'Wachovia . . .' said Mooney, 'W . . A . . . that's right . . . C for Carol . . .'

'I have a table booked for 9.30,' I said to the Baron. 'My uncle and I were hoping you would join us . . .'

The Baron would be delighted. Désirée had embarked on a long tale of how the Zaïrean foreign minister had been ousted with the help of witches. As Mooney came off the phone and made for the lavatory, the Baron took the opportunity of crowding him into the kitchen.

Désirée was in full swing. I decided to refresh the drinks.

'I'm sure you'll appreciate, Gerrard, that it's important that everything should be completely impeccable . . . and they have asked me downstairs to remind you . . .' He turned as I came in. 'I am only conveying a message, of course, but I would be relieved myself if you could attend to this . . . My goodwill, you understand . . .'

'Baron,' I heard Mooney say, 'it *shall* be done . . . I'll do it on the way downstairs as we go out . . .'

Mooney came out of the kitchen.

'You people go on,' he said, turning to include the Baron. 'Raymond and I just have to go down and send a couple of telexes and we'll be over there with you in two shakes of a lamb's tail . . .'

I could hear Désirée's *outre-mer* French all the way down the staircase floating up through the central stairwell as we clattered down the marble explaining how everyone in Kinshasa uses witchdoctors to protect their families. Even the President had been obliged to install some in the Prime Minister's bedroom to protect him. In the street, we parted and Zonda looked behind at me once. Mooney and I were hurrying to the end of the street and had almost reached it, when I heard her footsteps behind us running. Zonda.

'Raymond!' she said. 'Don't just go off like that . . . I haven't any money, don't you understand, I haven't a cent . . .' The other two were standing in the middle of the road. Désirée had risen on tip-toe and was looking at something in the Baron's eye. I dug in my pocket, while I watched them over her shoulder. Her thumb was over his eyebrow, the other hand held under his chin. Her heels rose out of her shoes and in the light from the hotel lobby sculpted knots of muscle appeared high-up towards the back of the knee.

'For Christ's sake,' said Zonda, 'what am I going to do with them. . . ?'

Mooney had disappeared.

'I don't know,' I said, pulling out a fistful of mixed notes and small change. 'Just keep them talking till we get back . . .'

Zonda caught my sleeve. I heard Désirée's deep giggle behind her.

'Raymond,' she said, 'don't be long, *please* . . .'

'Half an hour,' said Mooney from the corner.

'Get a couple of G and Ts . . .' I said, by way of assurance, 'and remember I'm his nephew . . .' I stuck my thumb back over my shoulder at the place where Mooney had been standing a moment before.

She faltered, stuffing the money into her plastic carrier-bag, and then turned and started trudging away down the centre of the street towards them.

Mooney dictated at the same pace throughout. He began with formal telexes to Zurich of the terse, urgent, telegraphic type I expected, which reported the use of a property called the 'Cumberland Plateau Ranch' as collateral security for the opening of trading accounts with various banks and financial institutions. Everything referred to was in the past definite, had already been negotiated by telephone, and the tone of these missives merely invited confirmation.

The next phase contained more elaborate flourishes and was concerned with actually establishing the collateral security. Here there were telexes within telexes which contained requests to the recipient to forward the text of the following, in order to save time, to such and such a bank or financial institution. These turned out to be rousing redescriptions of the prospective investments by the company in 'large ranchlands in the United States for the production of soya beans, grain, cattle and timber (lumber) for their exports in Europe and the Far East.' Mooney was seeking to arrange with Mr Daniel P. Kelly, Vice President of the European American Bank (Code reference 'Princess' and Our Reference 'Stella Futura') for a Mr Irving Glucksman, a director of The Project-For-The-Americas Investment Corporation, who happened to be passing through New York, to collect by hand 'your written reply and acceptance of our proposal so that we may go into closing next week'. The telex offered to place promissory notes of 1.078 million dollars payable annually in arrears for a twenty-year term and requested the issue of promissory notes by the bank (Paris international format) in corresponding sums and maturity dates, agreeing finally to a 'wash transaction' whereby the amounts required to meet the promissory notes could be offset against the cash earned by the collateral account.

The final set, which were concerned with the imminent purchase of the Cumberland Plateau, seemed devoid of main verbs altogether and were enormously long and rambling. Belting away on the ancient high-action machine, I didn't have the time to find out whether this was caused by the increased delicacy of the task or the fact that he was falling asleep. The concertina ribbon of telex paper with its green border marked Amm. ne PT TELEGRAMMA had dropped to the floor, and it was just beginning to mount up round our feet, folding back on itself like fugitive toilet paper, when the Post Office clerk, a sallow young man, looked over meaningfully once or twice and rattled his keys.

Mooney broke off his dictation:

'What do you have on you Raymond?'

I felt in my pockets, and reported about twenty thousand lire.

Mooney pulled his fingers repeatedly towards the palm of his hand and back in an unmistakable wagging motion. I laid the money by the side of the telex machine on the bench and we carried on the next transmission:

214240

WAGNER GOLD AND TREUMANN LPA

2100 CENTRAL TRUST CENTRE
CINCINNATI
OHIO

ATT. MR RORY MACALLUM JUNIOR
REF CUMBERLAND RANCH

FOLLOWING UPON LENGTHY NEGOTIATIONS THROUGH OUR AGENT MR CLYDE WELLCOMBE, WITH YOUR CLIENT MR JAMES CONRAN CONCERNING THE PURCHASE OF THE CUMBERLAND PLATEAU RANCH IN TENNESSEE, DURING THE PAST WEEK WE HAVE CONTINUED THE DISCUSSIONS THROUGH MR

WELLCOMBE AND HAVE BROUGHT THEM TO A FINAL STAGE DIRECTLY WITH MR CONRAN. OUR ASSOCIATE, THE PROJECT-FOR-THE-AMERICAS INVESTMENT CORPORATION LTD, IS A NEW COMPANY REGISTERED IN THE BRITISH CHANNEL ISLANDS IN JUNE 1979 TO INVEST IN THE PURCHASE OF US RANCHLANDS AND THE PRODUCTION OF US FARM AND FOREST CROPS FOR EXPORT TO ITS CUSTOMERS IN EUROPE AND THE FAR EAST ALSO TO DEVELOP ENERGY RESOURCES IN THE USA. THE COMPANY HAS AMPLE FUNDS AT ITS DISPOSAL FOR THIS PURPOSE. ON BEHALF OF THE ASSOCIATE COMPANY WE HEREBY CONFIRM THE ACCEPTANCE OF MR JAMES CONRAN'S OFFER FOR THE SALE OF THE PROPERTY WITH THE FOLLOWING AMENDMENTS:

THE PURCHASE OF THE TOTAL SHAREHOLDING OF THE COMPANY OWNING THE CUMBERLAND PLATEAU RANCH IN TENNESSEE CONTAINING 480,000 ACRES OR THEREABOUTS FREE AND CLEAR OF LIABILITIES AND WITH FREE POSSESSION, WITH THE EXCEPTION OF A LIMITED NUMBER OF SQUATTERS, AS A GOING CONCERN WITH THE PRESENT EQUIPMENT THERE-ON FOR THE CASH PRICE OF 24,000,000 (TWENTY-FOUR MILLION) US DOLLARS. MR JAMES CONRAN TO REMAIN PRESIDENT OF THE COMPANY WITH A SHAREHOLDING TO BE AGREED AND TO ENJOY THE FOLLOWING PARTICIPATION IN THE PROFITS OF:

THE DEVELOPMENT OF THE GAS AND OIL RESOURCES IF ANY: 40 (FORTY) % (60% BEING FOR THE ACOUNT OF THE COMPANY) THE DEVELOPMENT OF THE EXISTING COAL RESOURCES: 40% (60% BEING FOR THE ACCOUNT OF THE COMPANY)

THE DEVELOPMENT AND SALE OF THE MINERAL RESOURCES: 25 (TWENTY-FIVE) % OF THE ANNUAL AUDITED PROFITS TO MR CONRAN AND 10 (TEN) % OF THE ANNUAL AUDITED PROFITS FROM THE SALE OF THE EXISTING TIMBER TO MR CONRAN.

100% OF THE PROFITS FROM THE AGRICULTURE AND CATTLE DEVELOPMENT SHALL BE FOR THE ACCOUNT OF THE LAND-OWNING COMPANY, IN WHICH MR CONRAN WOULD PARTICI-

PATE THROUGH HIS SHAREHOLDING IN THE COMPANY. THE
PROJECT-FOR-THE-AMERICAS INVESTMENT CORPORATION
WISHES TO KEEP OPEN FOR THE PRESENT THE OFFER OF THE
PURCHASE OF THE SHARES BY MEANS OF A CASH PAYMENT OF
4,800,000 (FOUR MILLION EIGHT HUNDRED THOUSAND) US
DOLLARS PROVIDING THE BALANCE OF THE PURCHASE PRICE BY
WAY OF A MORTGAGE OF THE PROPERTY TO MR JAMES CONRAN
FOR 19,200,000 (NINETEEN MILLION TWO HUNDRED THOUSAND)

At this point the Post Office clerk came over and began
indicating that he was closing. There was a lot of watch-tapping.
Mooney took the young man by the arm and began to croon in his
ear, waving me up from the telex machine and into the fray.

'Major transaction . . .' he was saying, 'vital to get these things
off *rapido rapido*, you see . . .'

The man began to protest.

'Something in it for you, you see . . .' said Mooney, waving ten
of the twenty thousand.

The young man pointed to the clock (or was it the device of the
Italian Post Office?) in order to assert his unwillingness to enter
into any transaction. Mooney added the other ten, pressing it into
his hand and then when that was withdrawn looking for
somewhere in his waistcoat, a shirt pocket, settling eventually for
the trousers pocket, rolling the notes round carelessly as if they
were so much waste paper and thrusting them into the pocket.
The young man walked to the door and flung it open, rattling his
keys, the notes still poking out of his trouser pocket.

He was not to be moved.

I persuaded him to allow the ones we had completed to go, and
retrieved the money by leaning over and plucking it out of his
pocket, explaining that my friend was trying to pay for the telexes
all along. He was just a little impatient, that was all.

Mooney was spluttering 'major transaction' etc.

On the way back to Da Noi, Mooney tried to cheer himself up

with a digression about post offices – in particular, the Zaïrean Post Office, which he had just spent some time studying.

'They don't put it in boxes there, you see Raymond,' he said, 'the clerk just leaves it in a heap on the floor . . . When you open your box, it's always empty . . .' We passed a moonlit Piazza della Signoria. 'Naturally, at this point the clerk comes over: Hello Sir, he says, can I help you? which you can translate roughly as "How much are you going to give me for your mail?" . . . Either that, or the people behind the counter will hand you your mail, Raymond, but it's empty . . . With all due solemnity, you know . . .'

He placed his hand on my shoulder.

'They'll hand you some package which is just a ragged mass of string and cardboard which had contained books, medicine, tobacco or something of the like . . .'

I was not really listening. I was trying to get him on to the telexes via the role of the Baron.

'Do you know the President has over 100 billion Belgian francs in his private fortune, which at current rates probably adds up to about three to five times the national budget – and enough to pay back the national debt?'

I asked if he got this information from the Baron.

'Went out there last spring to stay with him – fact-finding mission for the company,' said Mooney. 'Shameless they are . . . shameless . . .'

'I gather it didn't go well . . .'

'What, for our sort of line in finance? Too small. And the Japs are in there . . . SODIMIZA . . . you know . . .'

'You mean there's large-scale Japanese sodomy in Zaïre?'

His face was poker-straight.

'Mining company.'

'I gather it didn't go well . . . the trip . . .'

'Well, most of the debt is to American creditors,' said Mooney, 'but we thought the operation was a bit small-scale for what we were looking for . . .'

I asked him what the role of the Baron was in the present deal.

'Well, he's an essential contact with Zurich, you see . . . very distinguished man . . . member of the Yale Club and all that . . . He's really a good friend of Ickle and Bisig . . .'

'He didn't seem to like the diversification of the deal . . .'

Mooney paused and spat into the Arno.

'He's a bit of an old-fashioned fella. But it doesn't do to let the grass grow, you know. That's the art of the whole thing . . .'

When we reached Da Noi, it was in darkness.

On the way back across the river, in the cab, Mooney was not inclined to discuss the Cumberland Plateau deal and, as we passed through the town, the talk veered to Michelangelo and the prevalence of carpic bridle in the horses that came out of that line, including Navarro.

'Bah,' said Mooney, getting down at the Residenza in a cloud of smoke. 'It was only a minor ligament. We'll be seeing you in the morning, ten o'clock sharp, then, Raymond. We have a busy schedule tomorrow . . .'

'And then she came and said: "Little Suitcases." She came to our table and said: "I have Little Suitcases." '

I knew about the Little Suitcases. The woman at Da Noi was Swedish and this was her little joke. You had to let her have her little joke, for this was what she called her pasta.

'Very good they are, too,' I said.

Zonda was bubbling, when I slipped wearily in between the sheets. She had obviously had a good time with Désirée and the Baron, which meant, inevitably, that she had done a marvellous selling job.

'I *hate* but absolutely *hate* her, but he's really . . .'

'Really rather *sweet!*' I chorused.

'He's invited me to go to Africa on a safari,' said Zonda with satisfaction.

'Who paid?' I asked with interest.

'They did, of course,' said Zonda. 'You left me with hardly a cent . . .'

105

I apologised for my unchivalrous behaviour, and then began in my turn to narrate the scene at the Post Office, my voice rising with genuine excitement as I thought of the telexes I had typed.

'*Millions* in it,' I said sleepily, 'millions.'

'But Raymond, you don't know anything about it. They're crooks.'

'What does it matter?' I said. 'It's worth the risk. If I keep him in my sight, and pay a few bills, there's at least a hundred thousand in it for us. Darling, it's romantic . . .'

'But he's a tramp, Raymond,' said Zonda, sitting up in bed and beginning to thump the sheets. 'He is *obviously* a tramp.'

'People are not always what they appear to be . . .' I said seriously. 'I am willing to admit that these operations are just brass plates and so on, but supposing it *works*. Just think, whether it's fraudulent or not – and it's not been proven that it *is* fraudulent – it's simply a question of probability – there must be a chance that he could pull it off. And if there's just an outside chance – let's say a hundred to one – then it's worth investing a few days and a bit of money in, don't you think?'

'Speculation . . . bullshit, Raymond,' said Zonda. 'You are willing to speculate with our lives, aren't you, for the sake of this caper? What about me?'

'You're the one who's speculating, not me,' I told her.

'How on earth do you make that one out? I haven't got a cent to my name. How can I possibly be speculating in anything?'

'You are speculating in your own future,' I said.

'What do you mean?' She rolled round in the bed. 'Don't be absurd, Raymond!'

'I mean, Doll, that you are taking the calculated risk that nothing untoward will happen to you.'

'Raymond, that's called living . . .'

'That's as may be, but it's still a form of speculation. Do you have insurance?'

'Have *you* ever thought about insurance?' she asked in a nasal mock.

'I'm serious. Supposing for example I run my car over the President of the Swiss National Bank . . .'

We both realised what an unfortunate analogy this was.

'*You* already have run somebody bloody down,' she reminded me.

'Alright, let us suppose that *you* run your car over him . . .' I beat a hasty retreat.

'I can't drive. I don't have a car. How could I?'

'No . . . this is just supposing.'

'Alright.'

'When he sues you for a million Swiss francs, how are you going to cover yourself?'

'I can't afford to buy myself a drink, as you well know, Raymond dear, let alone pay insurance premiums.'

'Alright, but let's suppose you *have* got a policy . . .'

'Alright, but . . .' She knew something was coming.

'It probably doesn't have anything in it about Swiss bank chairmen.'

'I don't understand.'

'Just listen a moment . . . therefore even if you *have* got an insurance policy that covers you for the ordinary risks, *that* sort of risk isn't included . . . therefore you are speculating in the sense that you are uncovered against any potential chance of loss or gain . . .'

'Acts of God? But I thought they were natural disasters and things?'

'Yes, well we're all speculating madly against *them*. But no, that's exactly my point. Being a Swiss bank chairman is not a natural disaster. In any sense.'

'Disaster for the Third bloody World, innit?'

'No, but you see the point. It's a natural fact or whatever.'

'Is that what you call it?'

'Concede?' I said in the chess tone.

'But I'm a pedestrian!'

'Pedestrianism,' I said, 'a particularly dangerous form of speculation . . .'

'I stay in most of the time.'

'Even as a . . .'

'Domestic prisoner . . .' she shot back, 'and . . . interior dec . . .'

But she had seen the point about falling off the ladder.

'You're not going to get me that way!'

'Stayer inner . . . you are still speculating . . .'

'I lie in bed . . . sleeping and breathing . . .'

'Fires . . . earthquakes . . . burglaries . . . sudden pulmonary embolisms . . . you are speculating against these risks by not having any cover. Therefore *you* are the one who is gambling, not me.'

'But I'm not doing *anything*!'

'Precisely. It's not doing anything that is the basis of the speculation in your case.'

She sniffed and slid down in the bed.

'I always knew you were an insurance salesman . . .'

'In principle you are indistinguishable from those New York widows who invest only in American Telephone and Telegraph Common Stock and are wholly uncovered against changes in the future of that company . . . a wild-eyed speculator . . .'

'I'd *love* to be a New York widow and all you said . . . with all that lolly . . .' she said, kicking a leg free of the clothes and pointing her toes at the ceiling. She stopped with a sigh and crumpled back against the pillows, curling and tucking herself up.

'Anyway, I don't *like* him,' she said in a little girl's voice. 'He *smells* . . .'

'I'll get him cleaned up, don't worry . . .'

'Look Raymond, I want you to promise me something . . .'

'Millions in it, do you hear, millions I tell you . . .'

'Raymond . . .'

'How do you explain all these contacts he has then . . .'

'I want you to promise me that you will ask somebody who *knows* what this is all about . . . promise? . . .'

'I can't ask Jeremy at Coutts,' I protested. 'For one thing, if I

108

tell him I'm associated with Pequeño Investments and Pequeño Investments turns out to be irregular, then he won't let me have any more money . . .'

'Well, so what . . . you can always sell this place . . .'

'But what about Rag Doll Ltd and The Clapham Wine Bar. . . ?' I asked.

She was silent.

'Look,' she said, 'go and see Avvocato Lanzieri tomorrow, and ask his advice?'

This wasn't a bad idea. Avvocato Lanzieri had been particularly helpful over my divorce.

'Anyway,' said Zonda, 'I'm going to Africa . . . Raymond, take me on safari . . .'

There were other reasons why I didn't want to see Avvocato Lanzieri. He was handling the possible appearance I would have to make in court over the accident with the Golf, and I didn't particularly want to discuss this matter.

'This is not the kind of thing you want to advertise to people in banking,' I said.

'But you must *know* . . .'

'Why?' I asked again. 'I don't follow your argument. Why do I want to know? The only thing that matters to me is whether this thing comes off or not. If it comes off then we shall be rich, and all we will have done is hang around for a few days with a character . . .'

' – who is boring and smelly – '

'And if it doesn't come off – well, as the song says, it's just one of those things . . . it's just a question of probability . . .'

'That's the last thing that enters into it . . . and meanwhile we have to live our lives somehow I suppose . . .'

'Remember Bill Gauguin . . .'

This was an allusion to a running argument we had had. One day Zonda had found a photocopy of something left over from my Oxford days sticking out of a heap of my *Timeform* and racing papers – an essay in some philosophical journal called 'Moral

Luck'. Intrigued by the title, she had begun to read it only to find it laughably incomprehensible, and one of those sessions began in which she read out bits of the offending piece in ever more satirical tones while I tried to explain and defend it, snatching it from her and counter-declaiming from it in tones of high seriousness. She was particularly exercised by the case of an alternative version of Gauguin.

'Let us call him Gauguin! What the fuck's that supposed to mean . . .'

'Bill Gauguin,' I said. 'Yes?'

'Either he is Gauguin or he isn't, isn't he?'

'No Doll, this is *Bill* – not whatever his name is . . .'

'You don't know . . .'

'Neither do you . . .' I said, getting the encyclopaedia out. 'Here we are: Eugene Henri Paul (1848–1903). I'm afraid I was never at Art School . . . anyway it's irrelevant . . . The point is Bill had responsibilities to other people and that he chose to go to Tahiti and pursue another life, gambling that he was going to become a great painter . . . What would justify his action, that's the point.'

'Success . . .'

'Correct. But if he *fails* then he has no basis for acting as he did . . .'

'Either this is obvious or I'm . . .'

'No basis even for thinking in the first place that he was justified in acting as he did . . .'

'Well, if you think you're an artist, you've got to make the sacrifice haven't you, otherwise you'll never know properly.'

'But the point is it's luck as to whether Bill turns out to be a great painter or not . . .'

'Rubbish . . .'

'Well, supposing the ship sinks on the way to Tahiti . . .'

'Come on Raymond, that's cheating . . . it's got nothing to do with . . .'

'What, with painting?'

'Yes . . .' she smiled.

'It still affects his decision, doesn't it?'

'Well, yes, but that's only an – I mean an . . .'

'External factor?'

'Yes. Now he'll never know whether he was right or not . . . It doesn't prove he was wrong . . . This is stoooopid.'

'Well, what it shows is that some luck enters all our decisions including moral ones like deciding to turn your back on your nearest and dearest in order to pursue some activity the outcome of which you are not fully in a position to ascertain . . .'

'Mer mer mer . . .' said Zonda, putting out her tongue. 'So there!'

'Yes, but his family would forgive him if the ship went down, but . . .'

'Not if he turned out to be a lousy painter . . .'

'Well, let's suppose he does succeed. Isn't it luck that he turns out the way he said he thought he might turn out?'

'He didn't say he thought he might. He *knew* he would . . .'

'What is he, God?'

'Don't be stupid Raymond. He just believes in himself as an artist that's all . . .'

'Alright, let's admit that he could know in some sense. It's *still* luck that he turns out to have known.'

'No, no, he knew all along . . .'

'How? He only knew that he knew after the event.'

'I've told you – he believed in his own talent and he made the decision on that basis.'

'You mean he assessed the likelihood of his turning out to be a great painter and decided on that basis?'

'Yes – I – I mean no!'

'There's no difference between that and gambling!'

'It's not the same thing at all. When you put it that way, it just sounds stupid. You're twisting.'

'Well, let's call this kind of luck intrinsic luck because it's to do with him, and the other sort – the sort when the ship goes down –*extrinsic* . . .'

But she had started to get angry.

'Let's say that both sorts of luck are necessary for Bill Gauguin to be justified in his decision.'

'No Raymond. You just make everything sound so neat and fucking clever all the time. But it's all just mechanical. It's just stupid! People aren't bloody robots. They have such things as inner lives, you know. Their lives mean something! Of course a guy knows whether he's got talent or not!'

'But he can know only afterwards . . .'

'Alright, he *believes*. Know . . . believe . . . You're just playing with words . . . He doesn't *believe* he's got talent *afterwards*, does he? He believes *then*, when he has to make his decision, doesn't he?'

'But that's exactly what I'm saying. It's his luck that he happens to be the kind of guy that makes that decision on that evidence. I mean some other guy might judge the same degree of talent differently and not want to risk anything on it . . . It's all risk management, you see . . .'

'As far as I'm concerned, the choice he makes and the belief that he has talent are two different things. Look Raymond, either people are responsible to each other or they aren't. And if they aren't they're shits in my book. It's as simple as that . . .'

'You believe in the rectangle don't you?'

'I don't know what you're talking about!'

'You believe that all times of your life are of equal concern to a person. Do it all at once and fill it in. The moral rectangle!'

'Stop telling me what I believe and what I don't believe!'

'Well, if you don't accept that luck affects moral decisions and that it is impossible to make the moral decisions except by reference to a future state of one's actions which cannot be known, then you must believe in some kind of moral symmetry between the occasions which bears no relation to the passage of time and the relative states of ignorance and knowledge which time's whirligig in all its emptiness brings in. I mean, are you perhaps a believer in the incomprehensible grace of a non-Pelagian God, for example?'

'If things don't turn out successfully, you try something else. But you don't stop living, Raymond, while you attempt them like your bloody stupid Bill Gauguin did . . .'

'Well alright, take the example of Anna Karenina . . .'

'Oh God, showing off again, Raymond! You know damn well I haven't read it . . .'

'I don't know anything of the kind! You just want the moral choice to be immune from luck, a safe place at the end of the day . . .'

'Well, what do *you* want then?'

'I believe luck to be immune from morality.'

'Oh *don't* start all that again,' said Zonda, thumping round in the bed. 'All that stuff about gambling. It just means you haven't any common sense, that's all . . .'

'But . . . *don't you see* . . .' I said, imitating our friend Freddie, 'he's going for the big one . . . What has common sense got to do with it. . . ? What has anything as banal and one-dimensionally lower-middle as "common sense" got to do with it. . . ? What is common sense – this mythical sixth sense, anyway – define it,' I said, pulling the sudden challenge, which I knew she would resist.

'I'm not going to talk about it. You're just so *stoooooopid* . . .' said Zonda from under the sheets. 'You just haven't got *any* intuition whatsoever . . .'

'I suppose intuition and common sense are the same thing, are they?' I asked in my best sarcastic Bernard Williams tone, ready, if an admission came or did not come, to launch into demolishing strings of absurd consequences.

'Oh fuck *off*,' said Zonda with serious violence.

Conversation tottered on along ritual lines for a bit, but I could see that her dog-eared copy of *Dune* had made its appearance round the outside of the sheet and that was a signal that she wasn't prepared to talk any more.

'You're out of your depth, Raymond,' she said.

'I know, but I can swim . . .'

'All I've ever seen you do,' she said, turning back to me for emphasis, 'is make a lot of noise and splash about in the fucking shallows.'

'How cruel,' I said suddenly, my eyes misting over. 'What an unpleasant, *fishwifely* thing to say!'

'Oh darling,' said Zonda with a sudden, exquisite, *delicious* bout of remorse, 'I didn't *mean* it!'

She rolled over and wrapped soft arms around me, kissing me on the cheek, saying 'Oh you poor little *thing*' over and over again, half-giggling with the pathos of it all.

'And how un*true*!' I said, indignantly.

I was in serious danger of carrying this too far, I thought, but she was too tired to wince back and begin again. Her mood had changed and she stroked me constantly, her lips hissing softly close to my ear, as she fell back into sleep.

Montegufone

Julian turned and – rather unnecessarily, I thought, since we were silent anyway, staring idly at the monstrous copy of the Palazzo Vecchio created by Osbert Sitwell – put his finger to his lips. I had come out to Montegufone with them, taking the day off from Mooney on Zonda's advice, and we had played cards and various other games of chance all day long. I had decided that Julian was the person I should talk to, because he had a sense of humour. Or maybe I should talk to Lanzieri as well, but Julian first.

We sat and stared at their two heads as Zonda and Julian's Dino descended the narrow rock stairs in front of our table, subtracting themselves in jerks from the square of our vision – hemmed in as it was with oleanders and box hedges of yew, but still yielding from time to time insect shapes in the thick air of late afternoon. The large table was littered with bottles of mineral water and the curious sulphurous wine of the region had gone to my head, thickening my perception and filling gaps in conversation with aimless rattles and sudden affecting gusts of wind that no one else seemed to notice.

Julian tilted his chair back from the table and sat with the elbows of his pearl jacket aligned with its arms, the manicured fingers gripping the ends to contain a sudden burst of suppressed laughter. A few blonde strands lifted in the breeze and his still Grecian profile cracked into a Chelsea snigger.

'Sort of Irish Gatsby . . . he said, fluting.

I did my Robin impression, the ex-Institute director, wheezing plumply with collapsed 'rs' and a high breathy little whisper.

'Sort of awfully shabby little fellow . . . came up to me . . .'

'God, it's such a long time since I saw him,' said Julian, digressing into Robin just when I didn't want him to. 'I wonder how he and Bentley are doing.' Julian and I were at school together – he was a year above me – and when I worked at the Institute, I actually lived with Robin and Bentley for a time and he was a frequent dinner guest, together with Dino and Tony Weston-Lewis and some of Harold Acton's entourage.

'What's your opinion?' I asked.

I had finished writing down the columns of names and the arrows between lenders and borrowers.

Julian took a sip.

'Well all the background is perfectly accurate. Everything your friend Mooney has told you checks out with what I know about the current situation. The Euromarkets are geared right up at the moment. From say '74 until last year these markets have been recycling OPEC funds and everybody is very keen on this at the moment. Since about '73 when the last price hike took place, the Euromarket has been expanding by about 25 per cent per annum.'

'Pretty fierce, isn't it?'

'Mmm. Problem is now it's clear the markets can't handle the rapid build-up of producers' money.'

'So what's going to happen?'

'Well that's where your friends come in. Or rather that's where, if her role is correctly reported, your Principessa comes in. The Arabs have started going outside the markets . . .'

'And there are no controls on this process?'

'Central banks talk a lot about controls, but they've shirked the whole issue . . . now they have a problem . . . Obviously they don't want to impede the capacity of the markets to recycle such vast amounts of petrodollars. But at the same time, think of trying to control the principal currencies in which these deals are taking place. The Euromarkets allow the creation of vast amounts of dollars, deutschmarks, or whatever, outside the direct control of central banks.'

'And meanwhile all this stuff has to be recycled . . .'

'That's right. It's got to go somewhere. Since the first price hike until the end of last year, the markets lent a net £640 billion to various borrowers. That's all they had the capacity to handle . . .'

'To whom?' I asked. 'The Third World?'

'Oh, no, Western Europe, America of course . . . other Arab nations . . . the majority of that. Non-OPEC developing countries took only about $150 billion.'

'But that in itself is a massive debt . . .'

'Not in itself. But it does have to be serviced. Debt-servicing obligations of non-oil-producing developing countries on medium- and long-term public external debt rose between '74 and last year from £8.7 billion to $30 billion. People are coming and borrowing short-term to pay long-term debts, and they can do this because the extent of liquidity is so great that the banks can't even get the spreads . . .'

'So when he says this is the time to do this kind of deal. . . ?'

'He is absolutely correct.'

'So what do you think of the deal?'

Julian sipped cautiously at his drink.

'What do you mean, what do I think of it?'

'Well, you know, is it probable?'

'What are you asking me?' said Julian, rather shrilly I thought. 'Whether it is a legal or a fraudulent transaction? Or whether it can be done, pulled off?'

'Let us assume it is a legal transaction,' I said.

'Judging by your man and his general demeanour, I'd say it was preposterous.'

'Why?'

'Well, people just simply don't scramble about like that . . .'

'Are you sure? Why not?'

117

'I'm not sure, but I would say that Mr Mooney didn't really know what he was doing. I'd say he was making it up as he went along . . .'

'What *ever* makes you say that?'

To my astonishment, Julian missed my tone. He went wading on:

'He's just not kosher. I never met anyone like him in all my years in the bank. It's a small world. People tend to know, or at least be able to "recognise" each other.'

So much for expert knowledge. I had to get him off this:

'Julian, if this is what you mean by preposterous, I don't want to know about it. Let me be the judge of that. Alright, let us assume it is fraud. What kind of fraud is it? If I could find out that, I might be able to gauge what the chances are of its success.'

'Difficult to say . . .' said Julian musingly. 'Five or so types of fraud, really, that's all . . . He's bound to be doing one of only a few things, if he's perpetrating a fraud . . .'

He leant forward and looked at the table napkin with its diagram and scrawls of names, ticking off the rest of the possibilities on his fingers.

'You see, he could be paying dividends out of capital, or borrowing . . . that seems possible . . . or he could be dealing in company stock on inside knowledge . . . you know, using company funds for non-competitive purchases from insider interests . . . That doesn't seem likely . . .'

'But that's all stock exchange stuff . . . I mean . . .'

'True . . . or then again, he could also be just altering the companies' books . . .'

I wasn't very impressed with this.

'Isn't there anything *else*. . . ?'

'Not a lot . . . fraud's awfully boring, really,' said Julian. 'It's just the variations that are interesting, but often if they're good, as I say they're hard to spot . . .'

'Might it be legal?'

We laughed at the idea.

'Well, what he's told you so far could be got out of an elementary economics textbook,' said Julian, 'and doesn't mean much, really . . . I mean all this arbitrage stuff . . .'

He looked at the paper.

'I'd say he was certainly parlaying into fraudulent collateral . . .'

'What do you mean?'

'Well, from what you've told me, the Cumberland Plateau deal is secured against Brazilian promissory notes which haven't yet themselves been secured. But I think he's probably persuaded some South American bureaucrats to let him have all the stamps and signatures to some useless piece of land or something . . . Have you checked this Pequeño Peninsula story?'

I hadn't.

'It sounds as if he had a perfectly simple deal with Brazil for 500 million, which is not impossible . . . but he's decided to complicate the whole thing no end by dragging in these other countries . . . Now the sums of money are, frankly, *impossible*. No bank could take them . . .'

'He calls it "getting these little ones out of the way" . . .'

'Yes.'

'Well, the Baron didn't like this at all. I could see instantly that he'd got cold cold feet . . . However, by Friday Glucksman will be here hand-delivering the ranch papers from New York. . .'

Julian was looking at me curiously.

'D'you know Raymond, in all the years we've known each other, my dear boy, I've never known you so excited about anything . . .'

I heard myself speaking, my remarks still echoing the tones of Mooney himself, a kind of weary evangelism.

'You were always the very soul of *sangfroid*,' said Julian. 'Perhaps it's Zonda that's done this to you . . .'

'Oh no, Zonda's against it . . .'

It occurred to me that Julian was suspicious of Zonda. They got on too well. There was just a little too much eagerness to compensate for distaste on both sides that passed for theatrical affection. It was a class distaste on Julian's part, I decided.

'It will end in tears,' said Julian. 'Of course . . .'

'But what a *vision* . . .' I heard myself saying. 'Think of it Julian, if he could pull it off, against all the odds . . .'

'Do you have any idea what the odds are. . . ?'

'Well, what you've been telling me about how banks will see through all this flannel . . .'

'Well, unless they've got a tame bank . . . and they're just planning to run off with the proceeds . . .' said Julian. 'But how much are you going to invest, that's what it really boils down to . . . How much have you invested already?'

Julian had always been interested in one thing. How much was I *actually* worth? It was a question he had asked a lot in Florence. I knew from my other friends and aquaintances. He knew my family and could make educated guesses as to what Pappa was worth. It wasn't that. It was what I was doing with the money that interested him. We went to the races together quite often and Julian was really quite cautious. He maintained his apartment in Florence and Dino who was training to be a local government officer on his investments. I could never force him to back outsiders, though he liked a flutter. We made up a foursome and played a lot of cards and Rummikub together after Zonda arrived on the scene. Julian and Zonda teamed up together against Dino and myself quite a lot. It was a question of class fastidiousness on Julian's part and class fascination on Zonda's which made an ideal social combination. Against his will, Zonda won Julian over on almost every occasion, because of her warmth and quickness and her ability to mimic everyone and everything like a child, an ability which he didn't have and which amused him greatly.

'So you don't know what the odds are and you're not telling what you've put in to the thing?'

'All I need is to know what is going on.'

'Well, it *smells* like a scam of some description . . .'

'Julian, even I can tell that . . . but there's *millions* in it . . . we could all be rich . . .'

'You don't know the lending and borrowing rates . . .'

'I don't know anything more than I've told you.'

Julian was musing again.

'Well, I mean, it's true that this whole thing does depend on the way in which banks communicate with one another . . . There has to be a point where everyone is committed and if any "mistakes" are made at this closing stage – which they inevitably are – then a lot of money can go adrift . . . and it may be just this, that he's creaming off a lot . . . with those sort of sums, he's bound to . . . I don't know . . . the problem is you don't have enough information, Raymond, to judge . . .'

I picked up my winnings from Rummikub and wiped on my forefinger a smear of aioli from the big bowl in the centre of the table.

Zonda and Dino began to appear up the stairs again, back from their walk.

Julian looked.

'You certainly have begun to mix with some pretty unsavoury people,' he said. 'Bit of the old rough trade, eh?'

I ignored this remark, which I took to apply to Zonda. If Zonda was rough trade, what was Dino I wondered.

'So you can't really tell me anything?' I said.

'Well it's my duty to tell you Raymond – for the sake of your family – not to get mixed up in this thing. If I were you . . .'

By a stroke of intuition or desperation, I struck in at this moment.

'Julian,' I broke in, 'by the way, d'you think you could let me have a couple of grand on account . . .'

We had loaned each other money in the past and I had been helpful to Julian before he met Dino because he used to spend quite a lot of money on cruising in the parks. Sometimes he used to have cash-flow problems in those days. Now that Dino was around, he seemed to have put his investments – as he once explained to me – on another footing. I think what this meant was that an aunt had died and left him some, though to be fair Julian was capable of making his money work for him.

He looked quizzically.

'Not for this thing, nothing to do with it . . .'

To my surprise, he agreed.

Zonda had her arm through Dino's as they sauntered across the terrace, and he was getting the treatment. Looking much less sulky than he was, I saw, when they had set out. The intensity of Zonda's attention was irresistible, legendary amongst her friends who called it 'getting the infra-red'. So much so that when it was withdrawn, the world seemed a barren, empty, cold place. Dino was basking under the sunlamp at the moment, and enjoying every moment of it as she poked and prodded his ego into life, cajoling, waggling her arm in his and squeezing it as she threw back her head and laughed, eyes shining, aware, I saw, of her simple leverage. I felt in a sunny mood as I watched her extended finger steal out and touch the dark tip of Dino's Sicilian nose.

Pisa

When Zonda and I arrived at the Ricasoli, there was a scene of some tension unfolding on the threshold of the foyer. The *Padrone*, surrounded by his staff, who looked for all the world as if they were posing for an official photograph, was engaged in repelling a charm offensive mounted by Mooney and his aide-roped-in-for- the-nonce, a large moon-faced fellow guest, Signor Pipo Bini. Adjusting his spectacles repeatedly, Mooney sprayed the ear of Signor Bini with ever more refined tactical lines which the latter relayed as best he could – head whipping to face each speaker, brow furrowing deeply – as he tried to sort out one voice from the other in the soft cacophony of protest around him on every side.

We stood and listened to this burr of muted anguish from the corner of the street. Curiously, various threads were audible. It seemed that Signor Mooney was unable to deal with his telephone bill at the moment, he regretted, but he was very pressed for time. He had an appointment in Pisa, for which he was already in danger of being late. He would, of course, deal with this matter just as soon as he had a moment to spare but he was due in Pisa – he swung his arm round in a stylish curve and pulled back his shirt cuff with a stubby index finger to glance at his watch – in two hours, to meet a distinguished business colleague – one of the directors of his company – off an aeroplane.

I stepped forward, but Zonda grabbed my arm.

'Raymond, don't,' she pleaded, turning me towards her. 'Leave him to it.'

123

But I was at the foot of the marble steps of the Residenza. Mooney's eyes lit up.

'Raymond,' he called, advancing halfway down the steps, 'you're the angel of Providence itself, so you are.'

The manager had begun to hint that it would be necessary for him to take steps, but I managed to calm him down by referring to myself as a director of the board of Pequeño Investments and, taking the manager to one side, leaving Signor Bini on the other, I explained that it would be my pleasure to vouch for Signor Mooney, who was *persona da noi favorevolmente conoscuita* and, as I was sure he had become aware by now, a distinguished financier involved in some vitally important transactions which could make quite a lot of difference to the prosperity of Northern Italy. The manager smiled with mock-shyness and the bill for eighty thousand lire, which was drooping languidly from his scissor-like fingers, swivelled towards me. Signor Bini had collapsed in an armchair behind us and was staring at his shoes. I resisted the urge to brush some dandruff from Mooney's right shoulder and relieved the manager of the bill. I fingered with regret my Montegufone winnings at backgammon and Rummikub, winnings which I had been hoping to reinvest in a little outing at the track. They would have to be 'invested' in the telephone bill. Zonda left us to it, sharply contemptuous, and went back to the apartment to finish her painting.

At Pisa airport, we waited in the lounge. Mooney had groaned all the way there, and had gone to the lavatory four times on the train. The plane was late and we were on our third gin and tonic. These diuretics seemed to go straight through him. He sploshed and drank by turns, but nothing dissipated his anxiety as he peered out of the passenger lounge windows at the empty sky.

To take his mind off the wait, I tried to engage in helpful conversation. What was Irving doing here, apart from bringing him some cash to pay his hotel bills and meals?

'Irving will have passed through New York, and if he's picked up the ranch papers from the bank, as arranged, then we can start the ball rolling over here . . .'

'The Cumberland Plateau Ranch?'

Mooney looked at me humorously. He had forgotten for a moment that I had typed the telexes at the post office.

'And what are we doing at Livorno?' I pressed.

'The only reason for travelling anywhere at all at my time of life,' said Mooney, his eyes following the jet as it staggered above the shimmering mirage of the runway, 'is to find a bank. We have a contact there.'

Irving Glucksman greeted Mooney with a weary smile. He looked as if he had flown personally, with his own tiny wings of gauze beating against the trade winds, halfway round the globe. Mooney recycled his line about the angel of providence. I found myself liking the look of Irving's graveyard full of teeth, his grey-green molars, which gave a faint *memento mori* quality to his smile. His ape-fringe (another wig?), his silver-metallic suit, creased from hours in jumbo-jets, and his Gucci shoes, his bulging briefcase into which he had thrust carelessly a pair of silk pyjamas so that a glimpse protruded under the lock, all gave him the air of a dishevelled Mercury, to whom all experience was merely the prospective leg of a journey.

'Italians,' he said, gently, helplessly, looking round the airport lounge.

But Mooney was brisk. 'Well, what about Cumberland Plateau?'

'Into every life a little rain must fall . . .' said Irving, lifting up his briefcase.

Mooney was revving up as he led the way out of the airport. 'Let's do it, then, Man, let's do it!'

What we were supposed to do was not clear to me, but Irving headed for the car hire.

Livorno

All the way down to Livorno, the talk from the back seat was about spreads and lending officers and closing, the car thick with smoke as Irving passed the papers to Mooney and briefed him about the Cumberland Plateau. I drew up as instructed opposite the Savings and Industrial Bank. Mooney led the way in. Signor Esclapon came to meet us and showed us into his office. He wanted to know who I was but Mooney forestalled the question that was forming itself on his lips by introducing me as 'our financial consultant and member of the Board'.

The interview itself was unexpectedly fraught. We were shown into an 'office' which was merely four frosted-glass screens hoisted on metal poles, like an old-fashioned pissoir, above and below which were spaces which communicated all sounds quite clearly to the rest of the bank, and throughout the whole thing I imagined all the clerks and tellers smiling to each other behind the counters as Mooney boomed away confidentially. Esclapon's English was good. Mooney gave him an orotund opener about their trading arrangements with the USA. Esclapon got somebody to go and look up Pequeño Investments in the Companies' Register. They were over here to close an important business deal with the Third World, Mooney continued, and they required a current trading account, into which they would be putting several thousands of millions of lire in the coming weeks. Mooney made the mistake of asking Esclapon if he were the agent for a bigger bank. The clerk put his head round the door and told

Esclapon they couldn't find Pequeño Investments. Mooney seemed to be having some trouble with his teeth at this moment and salivated a lot as he went on to describe vaguely the chain of borrowing and lending for which the collateral represented by his company's acquisition of the Cumberland Plateau Ranch, Tennessee, formed a support. He made a gesture that was just short of snapping his fingers and Irving dug in his briefcase and produced the Cumberland Plateau papers. The upshot was that the company would like to open the account and immediately be able to draw upon a sum of let's say up to $10,000.

Esclapon looked the papers over, raising and lowering his thin black eyebrows. He put some intricate questions regarding the matter of the collateral which were answered smoothly by Irving. Mooney, apart from the excess of saliva, was as inscrutable as ever. Esclapon was only too pleased for them to open an account, but he seemed to stick at the question of access to ten thousand dollars. Mooney told him to try the register again under 'The Project-For-The-Americas Investment Corporation Ltd', because there were, in effect, two companies here. Esclapon went out and came back, saying that it was alright, and that he now needed to see some identification. He looked up and smiled at Mooney when he handed over his passport.

'I'm afraid this has expired, Signor.'

Mooney stared at it. He laughed.

'Well I'm . . .' he looked at Irving. 'Curious how you forget these little things sometimes . . .'

He looked at Esclapon over the desk.

'Do you know,' he said with a slight clack of the false teeth, 'I hadn't even noticed. I'm very glad you pointed it out to me.'

Esclapon inclined his head almost imperceptibly. He indicated that he was only too pleased for Pequeño Investments under their registered title to open an account. As to the question of access to ten thousand dollars, it was not the kind of thing he could arrange without notice. There would naturally be some delay while the bank inspected all the accreditation. Meanwhile if we would like to fill out some application forms. Mooney tutted theatrically. In the meantime, Irving and I handed over our passports and Esclapon wrote down all the details from them. Outside, in the car, they conferred.

'But I thought he was our contact,' said Mooney, turning on Irving.

Irving didn't know what had gone wrong.

The banks would soon be closing.

A large man, built like a second-row forward, emerged from the Savings and Industrial Bank and limped briskly over to the car. He tapped on the window.

'Signore, signore!'

'Shall I let him in?' I asked.

'No,' said Irving. 'Let's get out.'

So we stood on either side of the car, talking over the roof. The man introduced himself as De Negris. He said they would do better at the Banco di Roma, where his brother-in-law worked. De Negris offered to show them where it was and do the introductions. He had been a reserve driver for Ferrari in the 1976 Monte Carlo Rally. An injured cartilage had finally put him out of racing. Now he limped and worked in a bank. I was driving, small-talking, and translating for the two in the back as we hurtled round the back streets of Livorno, following his instructions. Irving tried to ask him about their friends in New York, but he knew nothing. Mooney started on his Pequeño Investments pitch, but De Negris cut him short.

'I know about your deal, Signor Mooney,' he said in English. 'I hear everything at the bank.'

Ettore, the brother-in-law at the Banco di Roma, was rather more accommodating. In manner, at least. In terms of ready cash, Mooney and Irving got no more out of him than they had out of Esclapon, and an advance of ten thousand pounds was equally unforthcoming on production of the ranch papers. But we at least established that the bank had good connections with other banks in Europe and could act as an intermediary if necessary. He had several in mind. The one that seemed to him perhaps most suitable was the Societé Générale de Monaco, whose manager, a M. Henri Münzen, was a colleague with whom he – meaning, he explained shyly, not he himself personally we were to understand – had cooperated successfully on several past occasions in the matter of large financial transactions. However, this would take several days to arrange. Mooney fumed with impatience, as they came out of the bank.

'We haven't got a bank,' said Irving. 'You wanna know why?'

Dutifully, I asked why.

'Because we haven't got a politician.'

Vaguely they looked around the Piazza for someone to bribe, Mooney appearing in visibly better spirits at the thought. After the Banco di Roma, De Negris seemed to be a permanent member of staff now, and drove everywhere with us. He even checked in at the hotel with us.

Most of the Grand Hotel was closed up for the winter. In order to reach our rooms we had to wait while a flunkey unhooked a velvet and gilt hawser and traverse behind him cavernous areas of uninhabited landing, our steps forming a series of ragged crashes over the glacial marble. The rest of the time until evening was spent looking for telex machines. Mooney clearly didn't feel that things were right unless he had transmitted one of his long, semi-intelligible messages. We went to three Livorno tourist offices and he managed to send one to Michael Casey in the Isle of Man complaining about the Company registration, urging him at the close to 'stand by closing funds required short-term arrangements'.

When we got back I phoned Zonda.

'Raymond,' she said. 'Where are you? I've had an *awful* experience.'

'I'm in the Grand Hotel, Livorno. What's happened?'

'Well, this sinister man arrived downstairs at the door, asking for Mooney. He was wearing a Homburg, like they do in films, you know. I told him you were all in Pisa, and I offered him some coffee. Do you know what he said?'

130

I didn't.

'He said . . .'

And I knew I was going to get one of Zonda's impressions as her voice dived into the lower register, and she started croaking:

'I have done many of these deals with gold. They have come and taken away my furniture . . . evereezeeng . . . Zese daisy-chain are reesky zings . . . But you tell Mister Mooney somessing from Mordechai . . . Mordechai weel be keeling of Mooney . . . *keel*ing . . .'

'What happened then?'

'Well, he left.'

'Good Lord, it's just like the movies.'

'Seriously, Raymond, when are you coming back? I really think we should drop all this.'

'Well, I can't drop it just now . . . Things are moving . . . We're in Livorno with Irving and De Negris . . .'

'Who are these people?'

'Well, Irving's part of the set-up. But De Negris just seems to have walked in off the street . . .'

'Just leave them, Raymond, *please*, and come home. He's obviously a crook.'

'Doll, I can't leave just now. There's millions in this. Do you hear me, *millions*. It's the real thing. We can retire for ever to wherever you want in the world and drink champagne for the rest of our lives and gad about . . .'

'Raymond, I don't want that, just now. I just want *you* – home in one piece. Don't you understand?'

'I'll be home tomorrow. I promise.'

'Besides, I haven't got any money. I can't even buy any food.'

'I'll bring some,' I said vaguely, looking for an exit. 'OK? Bye now . . .'

'My legs hurt,' said Zonda.

'Ah ha . . .'

'And I've got some more trouble . . . downstairs . . .'

'What sort of trouble?'

131

'Well, bleeding . . .'

'Make sure you go to the doctor first thing in the morning . . .'

'That's a fat lot of help . . .' she wailed indignantly. 'I want you *here* . . .'

'I promise I'll be there tomorrow. OK?'

'Just make sure you do,' said Zonda, 'and no more of this silliness.'

How on earth had someone called Mordechai got our address at San Gallo? It seemed a million years since we were in Paris at the Arc, and yet how long actually was it? I looked at my gold watch, the material proof that we made that trip. I had won the Arc on Sunday October 5th and it was now October 15th. I descended a stair or two from my room, and paused at the turn of the staircase. Floating up the cold stairwell, I could hear the sound of their voices somewhere through an open door, arguing about the American elections. I looked dizzily into the stairwell. I was used to a certain amount of boredom at the tracks of course, but much of that was heightened by expectation and alleviated by casual acquaintances. This was different. I gripped the brass rail of the stair. It felt real enough under my hand, but it was far too cold. So cold that the pads of my fingers left thin elliptical patches of steam on the brass. We were all encased, even Zonda, in an ever-expanding noumenal bubble through the walls of which, like fish-eye lenses, distorted landscapes were becoming more and more visible.

When I got back to his room, Mooney was on the telephone. Irving was smoking and looking at some papers. De Negris just tapped his foot and smoked. He picked up papers and put them down again.

'Yes, Michael,' Mooney was saying, 'you haven't got yourself organised on this thing, have you? I mean . . .' He paused and looked across at us, 'it was a major embarrassment to my colleagues and I today in trying to negotiate with Italian bankers that the Company was not even properly registered. I mean . . .' he grew plaintive, 'how d'you think we look, eh?' He paused while Casey defended himself at the other end, picking out of the ashtray a cigarette whose peaceful silver-grey column, in the sudden movement, produced two perfect blue Lorenz attractors. I watched the two cylindrical pipes of heavy smoke rolling slower and slower as they approached the ceiling.

'Well, if they can't be produced that quickly – and I don't see why not Michael, it's a brainless operation – then we'll be needing you over here with the papers to deliver them by hand as soon as possible. Because we're on the move, my boyo, I can tell you . . .'

'Let's go eat, Gerrard,' said Irving without looking up.

I looked at my watch. It was nine o'clock. The room was full of beer bottles.

Mooney waved across.

'Light at the end of the old tunnel, Irving, me lad,' he said, his eyes wandering over the litter of cigarette stubs in cups and saucers on the table. He patted his pockets.

'I just have one or two more calls.'

'Why don't we go down?' I said to Irving.

'Yes go on. I'll join you in a minute or two,' said Mooney, dialling with the end of his pencil, and reversing the dial movement like a secretary. De Negris said he was hungry and came with us.

Irving's eyes were dropping, I noticed as we sat in the deserted dining-room.

A waiter glided up. All he had left, he regretted, was *Conchiglia alla paesana.*

'What are they?' Irving asked. 'Scallops done some peasant way?'

De Negris and I laughed.

'Ever hopeful, these Americans,' I said.

'Just pasta,' said De Negris. 'Not fish.'

'OK. So we'll order anyway and see,' said Irving to the waiter.

While we were waiting I asked where he and Mooney had met. He raised his eyes, murmuring while he lit his cigarette.

'Bahamas,' he said, 'long story. Remember the Hughes thing?'

De Negris and I looked at each other.

'Sort of,' I said. 'Didn't the Mormons have to do some kind of a midnight flit?'

'Early morning,' said Irving. 'They had to get the dying Howard on a stretcher down the fire escape and hide him in someone's bedroom while the cops searched the place . . . Then they got him away by boat.'

'I remember,' said De Negris. 'They brought him from Acapulco. The Mexicans didn't want him no more . . .'

'Right. Well, guess who tipped them off he was there?' Irving nodded and pointed to the ceiling. 'Him. We'll get him to tell us about it when he comes down . . .'

'And you?'

'Both in the hotel at the time,' said Irving. 'Gerrard was arbitraging for Bernie Cornfeld with Seymour Lazard and I was wrapping up some other little piece of real estate business . . .' He looked up. 'Hey, talk of the devil,' he said, raising his voice from the confidential whisper it had assumed. 'Get through OK for tomorrow, Gerrard?'

Mooney's cigarette was hanging over the end of his lip and his face looked grey, mottled with little vermilion streaks running from under the eyes to the jowls. He clacked his teeth heartily.

'Aye, the lady and the gentleman will be awaiting us in the morning at their suite in the Hilton. So now we can relax for a while.'

He rubbed his hands.

'You look drawn,' I said.

'Overdrawn,' said Mooney with a sigh as he sat down and scanned the menu.

'There's no baked beans, if that's what you're looking for,' said Irving. He turned to me. 'Always looking for junk food,' he said. 'Just like Howard Hughes.'

Mooney grunted and poured himself some Chianti.

'That is the only thing we have in common,' he said.

'Why were they after him?' I asked.

'Who?'

'Just talking about the Bahamas thing, Gerrard,' said Irving.

'Now don't start on that old business,' said Mooney. 'What have you ordered?'

We told him. He shook his head.

'Well I want something a little more substantial than that after a day's work.'

'I hear you tipped them off Hughes was there,' I said.

He looked over his glasses at Irving, who shrugged.

'He asked where we met, Gerrard,' he said.

'Not so, not so, Raymond,' said Mooney. 'It was Vesco. Bob Vesco that did that . . . I merely, well, passed some information along the line . . . In fact,' he laughed, 'Irving there is modestly concealing his own crucial role in the affair . . . whose room did they put him in, eh?' he taunted across the table.

'But I thought Vesco was supposed to be somewhere else,' I said. 'Costa Rica?'

'No, he was actually in the Bahamas at that time. You see, it was this type of a way. It was common knowledge in the Islands that Vesco had taken control of the local Casino empire and he was afraid that Hughes was moving in on his territory. Now we were there trying to salvage something for Cornfeld from Vesco and we actually had a deal going – quite a good one – which involved arbitraging some of the ITT proceeds which were in dispute between the two of them and things had reached a very critical stage, when I actually caught sight of one of them, Hughes's barber . . .'

'That's right,' said Irving. 'The guy was on a retainer. He went everywhere with them, on red alert to cut Hughes's hair . . . the most underemployed man in the West . . .'

'Hughes had hair down to his ass at the post-mortem . . .' said Mooney. 'Anyway this guy, Bob was his name, was a very lonely fella without his wife and children and always waiting to cut Howard's hair, so he used to sneak down into the bar he was so bored, you see, and I recognised him . . . It was lucky really

135

because you'd never catch one of the Mormons doing that . . .
Well, then I had a problem, because we didn't want anything
disturbing Vesco at that time, so I just passed the word along to
one of Vesco's people . . .'

'Vesco had the local scene all wrapped up and he tipped off the
local police that Hughes was up in the penthouse and . . . hey
presto . . .' said Irving.

'But why shouldn't he be there?' I asked.

'Oh, he didn't have a passport . . .' said Mooney. 'Hughes
never bothered his head with papers of any kind . . . he never
needed to . . . always flew in his own plane everywhere . . .'

'I see . . . so the aides had to move him . . . How did they know
the police were coming?'

'That's where *he* comes in,' said Mooney, lifting his glass and
pointing it at Irving with a laugh.

'I had been talking to this cop, I didn't know he was one of
Vesco's people, the night before and he let it drop . . .' said Irving.
'So we knew there was going to be a raid.'

'There was a lot of rumours flying around at the time . . .' said
Mooney. 'So anyway Irving tipped them off . . .'

'Why did you do that?' I asked.

'Well, I didn't want Hughes there either . . .' said Irving.
'Nobody did. It was nice and peaceful before they arrived . . .'

'But I thought he wasn't capable of even going to the toilet . . .'

'Yes, but no one knew what his real state was then,' said
Mooney. 'Everybody thought this was the beginning of the end
for their little patch, you see Raymond, when he moved into
town.'

'So how did Irving come to hide him?'

'Well the cleaners already had all the bed linen off the beds and
these couple of Mormons just came down the outside fire escape
with him and had to make a run for it inside the hotel. I just
happened to be coming back to my room to pick up my things
and this guy ran up and asked me if this was my room, and I said
yes, and then the next thing he waved them in, and in they came,

two guys with the stretcher and one running with the drip alongside . . .'

But De Negris was saying something to Mooney about the Vatican bank, and Irving stopped and pricked up his ears.

'Tell you another time . . .' he said under his breath.

'I know this from the bank in Livorno,' said De Negris, in a whisper. 'The chain of command runs from Milan to Lugano, through the Banco del Gottardo at Lugano to Cisalpine Overseas in Nassau, OK?'

This was far more interesting. Heads bent forward.

'On the one side of the balance sheet it shows the borrowing of 200 million dollars from Banco Ambrosiano in Milano. On the other side of its balance sheet there are 183 million dollars assets, described as unspecified financings. Where have they gone? Spirited away? Well on the Board of the Nassau Bank, guess who sits? – Calvi, the Prussian, and Marcinkus, Chairman of IOR. Now IOR owns Suprafin, Suprafin secretly bought up fifteen per cent of Banco Ambrosiano's shares between 1974 and 1977. Where did these shares go? – They were dispatched along the chain to the Banco del Gottardo, on buying orders placed by Cisalpine in Nassau on behalf of a number of shell companies in Panama and Liechtenstein . . .'

'I don't understand,' said Irving. 'Isn't IOR a Vatican firm . . . Oh, I get it . . .' A slow smile dawned on his features. He looked across to Mooney.

'I don't,' I said.

'Well, it's like a one-two in soccer, Raymond,' said Mooney.

'Fraid I played rugger . . .'

'You know – a give-and-go . . . The Vatican passes the ball to Cisalpine and Cisalpine passes it back on the rebound. But naturally they're *both on the same team*!'

De Negris was nodding as Irving finished off:

'In other words, the Banco Ambrosiano is lending the money to Cisalpine to buy control of itself. *Non e vero?*'

De Negris nodded.

The waiter looked over Mooney's shoulder.

'I am afraid Signore we are closed now.'

He came round and doled out our three plates of dull pasta shells. Mooney started spluttering.

'I'll have a steak . . . and some peas . . . ridiculous . . . major representatives . . . major countries . . .'

I looked at my watch. It was nearly ten o'clock. We all got up and went with the waiter to the kitchen, where De Negris was shoved in front to interview the cook who was taking off her apron. The exchange began abrasively with Mooney standing behind us, waving his arms and shouting the usual *rapido rapido*, but gradually the lady seemed to abate her hostility. She had a heart-shaped face, a perpetual expression of condescension that played around the lips, and a broad squat figure. Mooney was blowing smoke over our shoulders into the kitchen, and in the end she grew impatient and threw us all out. I asked the waiter what he thought this meant, and he said that Mooney would get his steak. He was a lucky man.

Back at the table I asked them who Mordechai was.

'Ah, Mordy has called, has he?' said Mooney. 'That is good.'

I told them he seemed to have frightened my friend Zonda. Mooney tucked his serviette under his chin like a huge white bib. He looked more corpse-like than ever, more than ever like a dying tramp invited to a charity dinner. He raised his bushy eyebrows and took another swig of Chianti.

'Good Lord, Mordy, do you hear that Irving, such a gentle little man. Very good chess player, isn't he?'

'The last time I saw Mordechai,' said Irving, 'was in Mexico City in 1975. He had Conchita with him . . .'

'Ah,' said Mooney as the steak appeared. 'No peas?'

'But he threatened to kill you.'

'Who, Mordechai? Just a form of expression, excitability.'

'You wanna know what I really think?' Irving suddenly reverted to the argument I had heard floating up the stairs. 'The Iraqis have got Iran by the balls . . .'

He held these imaginary objects in his hand, and began to close it.

'And this permits Washington to gently squeeze . . .'

'You mean they sponsored the invasion?' I asked.

Irving extended a triumphantly knuckled fist over the tablecloth and shook it:

'They have a fucking election to win, Gerrard!'

Mooney was looking sceptical.

'Look at the way the State Department's been licking Saddam Hussein's ass. Look at the encouragement for the Egyptians, the Jordanians, the Moroccans, the Sudanese – all of these support the Iraqi war effort . . .'

I splashed some more Chianti while Mooney still shook his head:

'I believe anything of Carter,' he said, 'but not that . . . he's surely not that smart . . .'

'What is he supposed to be doing?' I asked.

'He hopes that Iran will be weakened by the war into negotiating a settlement to the hostage crisis . . .'

'But why should they?' I asked.

'Because,' Mooney explained, 'to fight the war they have to have spares – am I right?' He glanced at Irving who was nodding, '– purchased by the Shah, but embargoed by the US, if you remember?'

'You hear what Ed Muskie said the other day?' said Irving to Mooney. 'He said he was opposed to the "dismemberment" of Iran, while at the same time he's transferring US military material to Egypt to replace Soviet-made Egyptian stores which the Egyptians are giving to Iraq – I tell you it's obvious . . . this war's a set-up . . .'

'It may be obvious, but it won't work,' said Mooney. 'Khomeini's told them what he'll accept and he's going to stick to that . . .'

Conversation got round to the failure of the American rescue attempt on Tehran. What had actually happened in Desert One?

Mooney told a story about the commander advising one of the helicopter pilots, who was worried that he didn't have enough fuel to get back to the carrier across the southern desert of Iran, to siphon it out of the C-130's tank.

'Kicked up so much dust as he went to do it, he ran smack dab into the C-130 and, bump, up they all went in flames . . . What a goddam crew, eh?'

Irving told a story about Chargin' Charlie Beckwith, the good ole boy who had led the expedition, meeting with Jimmy Carter afterwards. He assumed a Georgia accent, weeping crocodile tears as he portrayed the two men hugging and kissing each other tearfully for the honour of their country:

'You know Mr President, my boys and I usen t'thank you were kinda soft, but now we've met you, we think you're *tougher'n woodpeckers lips*!'

Irving then took a book on whether the hostages would be out by the end of Carter's presidency.

'Because he sure as hell is not going to make a second term,' he said.

'Not if his brother has anything to do with it!' said Mooney, laughing into his plate.

'Yeah, if Teddy Kennedy didn't cook Carter's goose in the spring with all that shenanigans over the nomination, this goddam Billygate, has,' said Irving. 'That jerk just has to be on the Republican payroll.'

I left the table and went to my room. I didn't know anything about the American elections, and I didn't particularly want to reveal this fact. Besides, I had rather wanted to get Mooney on to the merits of Fred Darling's set-up at Beckhampton. I wondered if Mooney had forgotten, when he was making his pronouncements about Coronach's line, that Darling had trained Coronach.

I lay on the bed and knew I was not going to sleep. The relationship between Irving and Mooney was difficult to fathom. They were both getting on. Showing signs of wear and tear. They clearly, despite flannelling protests to the contrary, didn't know each other very well. Irving was the Henchman, and Mooney the Figurehead, but occasionally one caught a glimpse of something else at work. Irving's openness, his bagman role, gave way to something a bit harder every now and again, as if he were letting Mooney do this thing, nursing him through it even. I needed to try and strike up a relationship with Irving. He was a much steadier source of information than Mooney, but also if I were to make myself indispensable, I would need to be indispensable to him as well, not just to Mooney, since he was the one with the line back to all the arrangements in America, and I had the strong but indefinable sense that their interests were not, ultimately, identical. If I could get Irving, perhaps, to acknowledge me as Gerrard's 'minder' while we travelled about Italy, then my final 'cut' would also be that much securer.

Florence

When we got back to Florence the next day, we booked Irving and Mooney into the Hotel Metropole. Irving settled up in the morning at Livorno and we went down to see Ettore before we left, so that Mooney could sign some more documents. Then we went to the Ricasoli, where Irving settled up the disputed bill there as well. From the Ricasoli, we went straight to the Hilton, and were shown up to one of the top suites. Mooney had asked for Dr Hahib, and he was out on the landing as we stepped with the flunkey out of the lift. He greeted Mooney with both his hands held out.

The Principessa was fuming on a calf-leather sofa in the long penthouse sitting-room. She waved a letter she had received from the State Department.

'Can you imagine, a man who had been the ally of the Americans for thirty years. And that . . . man . . . Carter would not allow him into the United States, because he was afraid it might prejudice his relationships with the terrorists in Iran. Can you imagine the humiliation we all felt? Because Carter wants to be able to win the next election by saying: "Look how I got the hostages out and brought them home! Aren't I worthy to be President *again*?!" '

The Rothmans King-Size came out. She was warming to her theme.

'Oh yes, I know how the shallow minds of the Americans work. To do this he will dishonour any agreement, betray any cause. Just to get into that White House again . . . The Shah was shunted, a dying man, around the world from pillar to post, from country to country. That Torrijos in Panama, he was simply trying to keep the Shah quiet on the island for the Americans. He was in their pay . . .'

'Didn't they have a beautiful place there? Contadora?' said Irving guardedly.

'But they were prisoners. Whenever the Siabhanou bathed, the guards were watching her . . .' She shuddered. 'Ugh, the lecherous brutes . . .'

'But didn't she have a habit of bathing topless every morning, Your Highness?' said Irving, who couldn't help but be stung by her remarks about his shallow American mind.

'Who told you that?' she cried. 'It is a lie!'

'It was written in an article in the popular Press, Your Highness,' I said, trying to come to the rescue. 'I read it myself.'

'Which paper?' she leapt to her feet. 'I will sue them to the ends of the earth!'

We couldn't remember the name of the paper.

'They were innocent people,' she cried. 'My cousin and his wife, they knew nothing of Panama. The whole world had turned against him. Nobody wanted to know. Only Anwar Sadat in Egypt would take him . . . Hawking his frail body round the world on a stretcher, just imagine it, a dying man . . .'

'Just like Howard Hughes,' I remarked to Irving under my breath.

'Right,' hissed Irving. 'We've got our own Shah. What do we need another one for?'

Mooney interrupted, easing his way through some preliminaries and then announcing that he had arranged for Münzen to receive the Venezuelan promissory notes.

The Princess and Habib looked at each other.

'Why have you chosen such a small bank, Mr Mooney?' she asked.

'The Project-For-The-Americas Investment Corp.,' said

Mooney, whose face in the shadow had turned the colour of a boiled aubergine as he bent to light a cigarette, 'has been dealing with our trusted colleague, Monsieur Münzen, for years now . . .'

'Of course we should not dream of doubting the honesty of anyone you recommend, Mr Mooney,' said the Principessa, breaking in, 'but the question is really can such a bank handle such a transfer of funds?'

'We are confident, Your Highness.'

And so it went on. They conferred constantly, asking a stream of questions concerning the length of repayment schedules, amortisation, the borrowing rate, while Mooney sweated and fumed smoke at them, referring them before they had finished speaking to Irving, who dug in his briefcase and produced documents and figures.

'Of course you realise that we shall have to go back to . . . our clients with these details,' said Habib with a smile. He had reached another bead in his rosary, and his fingers let the whole chain hang by this new bead, hitching it every now and again with a faint click and rattle as he spoke. 'If they approve the thing on principle, then we shall recommend that they send representatives to Monte Carlo . . .'

'If you recommend it, they'll approve it, Your Highness, I am sure of that,' said Mooney, his eyes on Habib, but flattering the Principessa.

'But it may take some time to arrange,' said Habib.

'How much time?' said Irving.

My mind was wandering. I realised that I was hungry. It was mid-afternoon and all I had inside me was some Peroni beer, which we had stopped for on the way.

Habib shrugged.

'We're very anxious, you understand, to go into closing as soon as possible . . . everything is already lined up on our side . . .' said Mooney.

Habib shrugged again.

'The Princess and I are spending this week in Florence. We

145

shall be contactable here. It is to be hoped we can obtain an answer in that time . . .'

'It is natural for our people to want adequate safeguards when they are moving so much money . . .' said the Principessa.

We all stood up again and shook hands, and when we left the apartment, Habib came out with us on to the landing.

'Much appreciated, Dr Habib,' said Mooney, automatically unflattering the Princess now. 'Without you, this whole operation would be unthinkable . . .'

Habib bowed slightly.

'There is just one thing,' he said. 'I have told the Princess of your offer, and she seems to feel your percentage will be too high for our clients . . .'

There was a storm of blustering and hissing from Mooney and Irving.

'Perhaps you would like to think this over before our next meeting. Naturally, we should be disappointed if this facility could not finally be arranged . . .'

In the lift they were quietly optimistic, murmuring in front of the flunkey that it had been a useful meeting, as the bottom of my stomach dropped away and the indicator skipped along from floor to illuminated floor.

Mooney clapped me on the shoulder.

'Another stage completed, Raymond my boy,' he said heartily as we stepped out of the lift doors. He turned back towards Irving, his tone changing almost immediately as the doors slid to on the gloved braided figure.

'But did you hear that little joking Jesus peloothering about his cut, there?'

'They always slip the real point in at the last minute,' said Irving, gleefully. 'Did you notice how he came out of earshot of the Principessa before letting us have the sting in the tail? Do you think there's something extra in it for him?'

'For sure,' said Mooney. 'What do you think, Raymond?'

I said they seemed very suspicious.

'Not a bit of it,' said Mooney. 'They will recommend this deal to the Venezuelans by the end of the week, you mark my words.'

Irving agreed they were keen.

When I got back to the apartment, I ran up the steep, irregular stairs under the rocky roof, that always reminded me of the Cheddar Gorge, a gallery in between caves, and shouted for Zonda. I felt a sudden surge of energy. I was dying to tell her about everything.

There was a note on the table in the kitchen saying that she had gone to the doctors, asking me to water the plants. I stood for a moment in the front room. The stepladder still stood in the middle of the room, but she had finished. The difficult patch in the corner had been covered over. The paint tray was over in the corner of the room, and the brushes, meticulously washed, were arranged side by side, in order of size, on top of the tin, whose lid had been carefully, tightly shut.

I showered and changed my clothes completely. The cat was nowhere to be seen, but a large piece of meat lay rotting in full sunlight in the middle of the roof.

I took the Gabriele out of its case and sat at the kitchen table. It occurred to me, as I slipped a sheet of paper under the roller, that I wasn't very far ahead of the game, if I was about to type what I was about to type.

I typed:

```
To: Raymond Bosanquet, 110 Via San Gallo, Florence
We hereby irrevocably
```

I had got no further than this word, when Zonda fell in through the door of the apartment. I looked up as she strode through the builders' mess towards me. Her face was wet and red and slightly bulbous with weeping. Something impelled me to carry on typing.

147

'Hello darling,' I said, as she crashed into the bedroom and flopped on to the bed. I carried on:

confirm the payment of one hundred thousand pounds
or dollar equivalent at your option to you immediately
upon the closing of the transaction with the Bank of
America or [and here I listed all the banks that I had

heard mentioned in the last day or so] on which our
group is engaged in consideration for the kind assistance
you have given towards the conclusion of these businesses.

> For and on behalf of:
> Pequeño Investments
> & The Project-For-The-Americas Investment Corp.
> Ltd.

16.10.80.

I got up from the typewriter.

'Hello darling,' I repeated.

'Bafftud,' said the muffled voice. She was lying face-down on the bed. Her skirt had rucked up and a couple of blue veins stood out behind her knees.

I sat down on the edge of the bed and put my hand on her back. Instantly, she turned on her side and held out her arms to me, her face blurred, red and sticky in patches, the lips drawn up into a soft snarl.

I handed her the document.

'Pretty good, eh?'

She looked at it, then at me, and rolled back over, the shoulders beginning to shake.

'I thought I'd get this into his hand and signed before anything else happened . . .'

'*Scifo!*' she cried violently, thumping the bedspread, as I got up. '*Scifo scifo se devi stare qui . . .*'

'Yes, but I've got to keep with him . . . especially now, when things are hotting up . . .'

'*Dove va?*'

'I don't know. Probably Monte Carlo . . .'

'*Quando ritornera?*'

'I don't know. Why don't you come? We could do the Casino . . .'

She rolled over, shaking her head and weeping loudly.

'I'll ring,' I said, as I picked up the typewriter and let myself out with a clink.

When I got down into the street, it struck me that I hadn't asked why she was crying. I glanced up for some reason at the windows of the apartment. She was looking through the shutters, her elbows on the sill. Kleenex, the grocer opposite, had come to the front of his shop to look.

'What's the matter? What are you crying about?' I shouted.

'Fucking bastard . . .'

I shrugged in my best Italian manner, partly for Kleenex.

'I've got to have *tests* . . .'

'What for?'

'Raymond,' said Zonda, 'I have to go into *hospital* . . .'

My legs began to run underneath me. I turned, and then turned back. I lifted up the typewriter in an awkward gesture of farewell.

'Call you this evening,' I mouthed.

She was shaking her head and clenching her fists and even her friend the grocer thought that was a bit operatic, throwing his arms up and turning his back on both of us.

Pisa

After searching for an hour, I found Irving in a corner of the Metropole roofgarden. Their table was a small shambles behind a tree. There were four empty champagne bottles on the tablecloth, in between which, on the paper oversheet, weaved a crazy dance of figures. Cigarette ash gave the usual patchy grey aspect to what had been sparkling damask, and an ashtray had been upturned on the floor. Several hardly-smoked cigarettes had been stubbed into the various plant pots which stood around the table, and looked as if they were vainly trying to grow out of the soil. Two waiters were hovering nearby with evident distaste.

Sitting down at the table was like entering a special sealed room in a spaceship which was travelling across the galaxy to some unknown, infinitely far-off destination. I was still out of breath, but I felt the slight wrench of time-loss as my elbows touched the soiled tablecloth, rather like those few seconds when the lift has touched the bottom of the shaft, but the brakes are still operating to let it finally settle flush into its resting-point.

Irving was sitting at the table with a young man in a black leather jacket and dark glasses, powder-blue Sta-Prest slacks and a mop of greased black hair combed back off his forehead which caught the light in whirls and loops like the tracks of a marshalling yard seen from above. Where had I seen this version of the young Dean Martin before? Irving's head was resting somewhere on the edge of the table.

'Ah Raymond,' he said, looking up, 'Gerrard's on the phone.'

'In his room?'

'Yes.'

'Oh no he isn't,' I said, 'I just looked in there . . .'

'Splosh, then . . .' said Irving. 'Raymond, I want you to meet Don Divine, a member of our outfit, who's just got in to town.'

Don turned his glasses towards me and smiled into what I thought must be empty air for him. I smiled back, unconvinced. Don's face was the colour of old mahogany and he was sweating through his ten o'clock shadow.

'Hey,' said Don, to himself.

'Raymond,' said Irving, 'I wonder if you could do me a favour?'

'Well, depends on . . .'

'I'm going to have to check out of the hotel, unexpectedly tonight, and I'll have to fly back to New York in the morning. I can get a connecting flight from Pisa to London . . .'

'Will I drive you?'

'Yes.'

I looked around the empty roofgarden, and then off into the twinkling darkness.

'I can't think why I shouldn't,' I said. I looked at Don, who nodded and said 'Yep.'

'It's OK,' said Irving. 'Don's going to look after Gerrard, aren't you Don?'

Don sneered.

'Real close,' he said, nodding again to himself.

'Don's family hail originally from Israel,' said Irving.

'Napoli,' corrected Don sharply. 'Based in Fiesole at the moment.'

Irving shrugged.

In the carpark, I looked at Irving over the roof.

'Don isn't a banker, Don is a thug.'

'Don is here to look after Gerrard's interests, while I'm away . . .'

'He looks like a thug.' I sounded like Zonda.

'Don is a member of the Board of Pequeño Investments, a

business partner . . .' He looked around as we headed out towards Pisa, and sighed. 'Florence, city of bankers,' he said, 'where it all started. Ironic to think of it being owned by the government of West Germany . . .'

'What?'

'Well, in part at least. There's also the Italian Treasury, the cities of Rome, Turin, and Don's home, Naples, the autostrada company, Alfa Romeo, and FINSIDER the steel combine . . . in fact, a large chunk of Italy is not financed by Italy at all any more . . .'

'How come?'

'Well. Italy's growth in the Sixties was about ten per cent a year and they all started borrowing Eurodollars, billions of them in all, all on a ten- to fifteen-year basis at around eight per cent . . .'

'From West Germany?'

'No, no, commercial loans from banks in Western Europe. Yeah, they cleaned up on the wops. Front-end percentage on each deal was around three per cent of the face value of the loan, so that amounted to 30 million dollars for every billion floated, then year after year around eight per cent interest, when they could buy the money at five per cent . . .'

'So what happened?'

'Well, all these commercial loans started falling due about five years ago, and you know what the banks' line was? "Let the Common Market take care of Italy." '

'So . . .'

'So West Germany stepped in, but only short-term. Around 3B . . .'

'So what's going to happen?'

'Oh, I expect OPEC will put it in, they're about the only people who can, although if Italy defaults it could be the collapse of the whole show . . .'

'The whole show?'

'Yes, the whole of the International Banking System. You see,

153

the question that worries bankers, and has worried them since the oil crisis of '73, is really this: when you're lending to countries, and they go into default, who is going to guarantee you? Some of these debts are so colossal that no single organisation could handle them, not even Chase, or Citibank, say . . . So it's in everyone's interest to roll the debts over because if one of 'em bellies up, well, we all go . . .'

'But what about the IMF, for example?'

'Are you kidding? The IMF is borrowing from OPEC, that's what I'm saying . . . the whole bananas is one great big daisy-chain . . .'

'Irving,' I said, as we passed a truck on the hard shoulder of the road.

'Yes.'

'Can you tell me in simple language what Mooney's deal is all about?'

'Yes, if it's going to help . . .'

'Well, hasn't it struck you I have an interest in it?'

'Of course, I just assumed that Gerrard was . . .'

'Paying me?'

'That's right. Going to pay you would perhaps be more accurate, because – as I'm sure you're painfully aware by now – Gerrard never has any cash on him . . .'

'Why not?'

'Oh I don't know,' said Irving. 'First of all, he's a pretty unstructured guy, and second of all, he's superstitious . . .'

'Chaotic, you can say that again . . .'

'But don't underestimate him,' said Irving. 'Never underestimate Gerrard Mooney. He's a crackerjack mind when it comes to dealing . . .'

'Is that why Don's there?'

'Don is there, simply to help Gerrard with the security aspects while I'm out in New York.'

'OK, the deal?'

'Well, the deal is elaborate, very elaborate. Gerrard is putting together Eurodollar and petrodollar loans from Zurich banks for investment in Brazil, Venezuela, and Mauritius. We've come out of the arbitrage tunnel of the last few years and it's possible to get the spreads. There's a couple of years' work gone into this . . .'

'Hence, the Baron at the one end, and the Iranian Princess on the other?'

'Right,' said Irving.

'OK,' I said, 'so Zurich – but ultimately, American banks – are the lenders . . . ?'

'Right,' said Irving. 'Now, Gerrard is acting as broker, he's the man in the middle, because he is going simultaneously to lend these borrowings to Brazil and the other countries at the higher rate of interest . . . with a big front end . . .'

'If this thing goes wrong, aren't there going to be a lot of very angry people looking for Mr Mooney . . . ?'

Irving paused and reached for a Lucky Strike. It was his last. He crumpled up the packet and threw it into the night.

'Well, there might be a certain amount of misunderstanding there, I suppose. But if you're in banking, somebody's always out looking for you with a meat cleaver wrapped in a velvet bag. You know, this whole situation is just like what happened in the Twenties . . .'

I was blank. But he had to be humoured.

'I mean that banks are recycling Arab oil money to the Third World to pay for imported oil. In the Twenties, the bankers sold German bonds to the American public to enable Germany to pay war reparations to France and England, so that they in their turn could pay their war debts to the US Treasury.'

I murmured interogatively, suspending what little interest I had in the conversation to overtake a truck. Irving lit a cigarette.

'It was the House of Morgan then,' he said. 'In 1924, the State Department pressured them to sell German bonds in the American market . . .'

'OK, so what have the State Department to do with the current situation?' I asked.

'They're running it. See, Congress passed a piece of legislation back in March called the Depository Institutions Deregulation and Monetary Control Act . . .'

'Quite a mouthful . . .'

'Eighty-five pages.' Irving looked down at his suit and brushed some of the ash from his silver trousers. 'But just as an all-party house Senate Committee was about to pass the whole thing, the Fed got six crucial lines added. There couldn't have been more than a dozen Congressmen who knew about this, but it was a very important inset for the whole current scene . . .'

'Double Dutch to me Irving, I'm afraid. What's the point of it?'

'It gives the Fed the right to buy securities of foreign Governments. That's why US banks are still lending to Mexico, because they all know there's a bail-out from the Fed.'

'I still don't understand what the Federal Reserve have to gain . . . ?'

'Money, just like the Twenties. It's recycling. Anyway, Paul Volcker put them up to the inset and when I tell you Volcker's Chase Manhattan . . .'

'Aha,' I said, 'Rockefeller was helping the Shah, wasn't he?'

'That is true,' said Irving, 'and now he is also helping recycle the Iran revolution's petrodollars to the Third World.'

'Do the Europeans know about this amendment?' I asked.

'Sure,' Irving laughed. 'Especially if they happen to be Swiss!'

I laughed with him. I judged it was time to move him over, while he was still warm:

'So what's Mooney's background?'

Irving laughed.

'What *is* this Raymond? I don't think anybody really knows . . . He's been everywhere . . . I think the family used to have some money in the old days, but Gerrard started out as a teller with the Bank of Ireland . . . Then he went out to Venezuela . . . tried some ranching, raising beef and that sort of thing . . . gave it up and worked in New York at the World Bank, somebody must have pulled a few wires there, come to think of it . . .' Irving was pulling on his chin, trying to remember. 'Yeah, he did some deals out there in Venezuela . . . Then he met Mame, and they went down to Florida, had a lot of kids . . . Yessiree, Mame Mooney, quite a lady . . . and boy did she threaten to sting Gerrard for the alimony . . .' Irving whistled. 'You know the song Rita Hayworth used to sing in the movies "Put the Blame on Mame" – well, that's Mame alright . . .'

'Is that why he's doing this deal?'

'Oh yeah, sure, but not altogether. Gerrard'd get the spondulicks, as he calls 'em, he'd get the loot from somewhere OK . . .'

'Well, why is he doing it then?'

'Gerrard's a romantic.'

'Maybe that's why he doesn't like Venezuelans . . .' I mused. 'I bet they're not going to get a bean out of this . . .'

'That's just it. They'll get plenty soya beans . . .' Irving laughed. ' . . . plenty soya beans . . . Gerrard'll probably offer to recycle the soya . . . No, I'm serious . . . Gerrard is an old-fashioned romantic. He kind of likes the look of a complicated deal, and he enjoys the process of bringing it off . . . y'know, it's the creative aspect he goes for . . .'

I giggled profanely:

'You mean he's greedy, Irving?' I looked sideways at him. 'Irving, I'm going to ask you a peculiar question . . .'

Irving shrugged.

'Hey,' he said, 'so what? Can I have a cigarette before you start getting weird?'

'Sure, go ahead . . .'

He reached into the glove compartment and brought out a packet of MS, which he ripped open fiercely.

'Do you believe in this deal?'

'What sort of question's that, Ray?'

'I mean, do you really believe it can work?'

'Look, Ray, I'm a businessman. Of course it can work . . .'

'No, that's not quite what I mean . . . I put it badly. What I mean is, d'you think it *will* work? . . .'

157

'Hell, what d'ya think I'm greasing the seats of all these planes and automobiles for? I mean, do you really think . . .'

'No. That's not quite what I mean either. It's . . . is it a reality, or is it some kind of fantasy of Mooney's?'

'That's a hell of a dumb sonofabitch thing to say!'

I could see that I had touched some sort of nerve, here, almost without meaning to. Irving was angry. He wound down the window and hurled out his half-smoked cigarette with a sweep of the arm.

I was thinking of Zonda. It was a calculated risk, but I needed to know.

'What I mean is, Irving . . .'

'I know what you mean, the hell with what you fucking mean!'

He lit another cigarette. We were silent. I could feel his anger in the way his legs were pushing hard against the moulded, carpet-covered recess in front of him.

I drove through the outskirts of Pisa. A red light shone steadily at some roadworks. We crept towards it.

'I'm sorry, Irving.'

He took a huge drag on his cigarette, curling a brown forefinger around the white cylinder for depth. I thought I knew exactly how he felt, all of a sudden, and I had a painful premonition that he was going to say precisely what he did say, seconds before he said it.

'You don't ask me questions like that, OK?'

'OK.'

'So just drive, OK?'

'OK.'

But I could feel the anger draining out of him now.

'We're all in this together . . .' I said.

'You haven't been in it *five goddam minutes* for Chrissakes . . .'

But I could tell he was relenting in full flow now.

'Do you really think Don can look after him?' I asked softly.

He sighed at once.

'Yeah,' he said, 'you're right there . . .'

158

'Irving,' I said urgently, 'look, why don't you let me take over? I can drive him wherever he needs to go. All you need to do is transfer some of the funds you've given to Don into my account.'

He looked at me.

'Oh come on,' I laughed. 'There's hardly any money involved. What have you arranged with Don? Five grand? Just put it into my account, and I'll see to everything. I mean, just look at Don, he's got about as much credibility as Al Capone . . .'

'Al Capone had plenty credibility . . . he had politicians eating right out of his hand . . .'

'Exactly, that's my point, I mean, Don couldn't get a donkey to eat carrots out of his hand . . .'

'Don's not as dumb as you think. He used to be with Richard Helms . . .'

This was interesting. An ex-CIA man.

'Look Irving, I can call on a certain amount of credit with Coutts in London. I've got fluent Italian, French and quite good German. I know my way round Northern Italy . . .'

He was thinking.

'Gerrard sure has taken a shine to you. He thinks you're his long-lost goddam son . . .'

This was it. I saw my chance, painting a more detailed picture of my credentials for undertaking this job, imagining a few successfully organised meetings in different countries, regular meals, and a sedate watch on the alcohol consumption. The whole thing was a quietly humming machine which moved inexorably towards closing date.

We nosed into the air terminal carpark. Irving was still thinking it over.

'Here's the number of my account, if you want to have it to hand . . .'

Irving took it, but I think he was rattled.

'Just leave the security aspect to Don,' I said. 'And I'll look after Gerrard's personal needs . . .' I had better start calling him this, if I was to get anywhere.

'We are talking,' said Irving, 'as if I'm not coming back . . .'

'I agree. This whole thing has a slightly funereal air . . . Don't you think it should be a *little* more festive?'

Irving laughed, his tension easing.

'All I'm doing is checking out the IMF conference. The Mauritian Prime Minister is bound to be there touting for money, and I just want to make sure he comes in with us . . . I'll be back . . .'

'But you want to rest easy in your bed . . .'

Irving got out of the car. I went round the back like a taxi-driver and got his briefcase out of the boot.

'Well?'

'You know,' said Irving, 'for an Englishman, you're a pretty pushy sonofabitch . . . more like an American . . .'

'What about it?'

'Let's see how you go,' said Irving.

I bit my lip. I felt like a child who's lost his pocket money.

'You know Irving,' I said, as he moved off, 'that's the second time I've been called a bastard today.'

Irving vaguely waved his hand, at hip level, somewhere behind him.

As I drove back, I didn't know whether to check the Metropole or go to the apartment and see what was happening with Zonda. I thought in the end I'd look in at the Metropole, because whatever was happening with Zonda's tests, she would be asleep, whereas the Metropole might just about have had enough of Mooney. But there was no scene. Everything appeared to be very quiet. Don and Mooney were in the middle of a game of cards, which had plainly been interrupted by a phone call. The cards were face-down on the table. Don was leafing through a magazine about cars and Mooney was holding the receiver with a creased look.

'Go down and *see* the bank?' he was saying. 'But I never heard of such a thing. Does she not believe it exists or something?'

'Oh yeah,' said Don to me as I waved at him.

'But we want to go into *clorsing* next week,' said Mooney, nodding at me and waving at me to sit down. 'We don't want to be running about like this . . . it's ridiculous, things like this are not done . . . in the professional . . . ?

I leaned forward to Don.

'Has Irving said anything to you about money, Don?'

Don looked up.

'You know, cash-flow for this . . .'

I made a gesture to the noble ceiling.

'Nope,' said Don.

'Professional world of banking . . .' said Mooney, 'surely . . . surely . . . of course, I do see that point of view but if you could just tell her that Mr Münzen has the best possible credentials and these can be provided for the Committee's scrutiny . . .'

'Well, who's paying for the rooms here?'

Don was vague.

'Don't worry bout a thing . . . kiddo,' he said, 'just quit bustin' your ass worrying . . .'

'But you can do that through your *own* bank . . .' said Mooney desperately.

There was a silence. Mooney put his hand over the receiver.

'Holy Mother of God,' he said. 'These people are so suspicious . . .'

He listened again to the voice droning on the other end.

'But surely there has to be *some* trust in this world . . .'

The voice sounded as if it was speeding up.

'Yes . . . yes . . . of course . . .' said Mooney, mopping his greasy forehead with a brown handkerchief and staring into the tumbler of whisky on the table. He adjusted its position minutely as he said: 'Of course, Dr Habib, I do apprec*iate* . . . Yes, we'll surely be seeing what we can do about this matter . . .'

He rang off, and took a slug at the whisky.

'This boyo Habib really takes the biscuit,' he said, and continued, as if no one was in the room: 'Of course, it's not him. It's her . . .' He brightened. 'Well, it looks like we'll all be taking a little trip to Monte Carlo . . . Raymond, my lad, stranger in camp, let's wet your whistle . . . and forget for a while the vagaries of the oriental mind . . .'

I looked at my watch. It was a quarter to four.

'Little nightcap,' said Mooney, motioning to Don to fetch me a drink, never ceasing to sketch something in pencil on the paper in front of him.

'Here you go, kid,' said Don as he handed me a paper cup full of neat whisky. 'All we got . . .'

We drank to success. I was conscious of the IOU I had typed, nestling in my inside pocket, but it didn't quite seem the right occasion to spring this on Mooney, especially with Don looking on.

'So what time's reveille?' said Mooney.

''Bout eight, I guess,' said Don.

'What time do you want me in the morning?' I asked.

'Nine o'clock,' said Mooney, briskly and efficiently. 'Up here . . . I want you to type up the text of some telexes tomorrow . . . '

I put down the paper cup and made my excuses. It was obvious they were going to settle down to some more nightcaps and some more poker.

Zonda murmured when I slipped my cold knees into the backs of hers. I flung my arm carelessly over the escarpment of her hip-bone. She was awake.

'What are the tests for?' I asked, nuzzling her back.

'What?'

I repeated my question. It was her 'I am mortally offended' tone.

'I don't know,' said Zonda, '*do* I?'

This always was difficult to reply to, so I was silent for a moment.

'Anyway, where have *you* been, when I needed you?'

'Pisa. What did they *say* the tests were for?'

'You know what they're like. What you bin' doing at Pisa?'

'Seeing someone off. You mean they didn't tell you anything at all?'

'Who?'

'*Them*, doctors . . . Lanzieri and company . . .'

'No. Who at Pisa . . . ?'

'Oh, Irving . . .' I said.

The bed seemed to be floating through the dark, and only her back was stable. A life-raft of skinny, curved gristle as we swept round the bend, in a smooth rush, towards the falls of sleep.

'What a bore the whole thing is,' I said about nothing.

The bangs were very deep, and muffled and seemed to come from below. It was stiflingly hot. I sat up and reached for my watch. We had overslept. It was two o'clock in the afternoon, and someone was trying to knock down the door of the apartment.

I pulled back the crooked spring bolt that always gave me trouble, and the door began to grate on the bits of cement underneath it, dragging itself back with a shriek as Mooney, battered suitcase in hand, marched in past me. As he passed, my sleepy nostrils took in a wall of rich aroma, mainly, however, the acrid smell of real burning, not just cigarettes. He stood by the stepladder, smelling.

'Signor Bosanquet?'

I hadn't noticed, but there was a carabiniere standing in the shadows of the cave-like staircase.

'Do you realise, this could jeopardise the whole thing?' said Mooney, putting the suitcase down and patting his pockets.

Zonda had left a cigarette stub on one of the rungs of the stepladder and he picked it up and put it in his mouth.

I looked at the carabiniere who slowly emerged from the darkness and came into the centre of the room. Mooney was already sitting on one of the sacks of cement, balancing the telephone on the other.

The policeman and I conferred. It seemed that Don had managed to set fire to a room at the Metropole. Don was being

163

held at the police station because he had taken a swing at a fireman. Was it true that I was Signor Mooney's nephew?'

'*Si, il Banco Crédit Suisse a Chiasso . . . rapido . . . rapido . . .*' said Mooney.

I explained that Mr Mooney's Italian was sometimes a little inaccurate. I was just a friend.

'*Ah, capito . . .*' said the policeman, looking round with a mixture of indifference and relief. Every now and then he stared cautiously at Mooney, who sat on one of the sacks, idly swinging his leg and kicking the other sack, while dialling. Little puffs of cement began to rise in the air and cruise about, a fine dust of motes in the sunbeams that were falling in through the shutters.

I dressed and made sure my chequebook was in my pocket. I went over and picked up the suitcase.

Zonda was looking over the sheet.

'Wha . . . ?'

'Visitors. Got to go out,' I said.

Her head settled down again.

While Mooney and the carabiniere and I rattled down the stairs and off to the police station, I tried to get out of him what had happened at the Metropole.

'Poor Don,' he said. 'A trusted friend and associate, but terribly accident-prone. Neglected to put out a cigarette that was still in his hand when he went to sleep.'

When we got to the station, there was a mêlée of people typing and walking quickly to and fro.

I turned to Mooney.

'Have you got a passport, or not?'

'Raymond my boy, I have indeed.'

And he produced the same dog-eared card from his inner pocket that he had tendered to Esclapon in Livorno. It declared him to be a citizen of the Republic of Ireland and to have been born in 1923, at Swords, Dublin. It had expired two months previously.

After hours of vouching for everyone and everything and

signing cheques, I paid a final cheque to the Metropole for 200,000 lire, which represented a deposit on the damage, and we brought Don and the battered suitcase back through the afternoon streets. Don was looking cool with his little shoulder-bag, glancing all round at the girls and the closed shops, and muttering to himself little bits of encouragement and deeply incomprehensible exclamations. Mooney walked stiffly by my side, the sweat glistening in his grey hair. I changed hands with the suitcase.

'So what's the situation?'

'What, what?' he turned. 'Ah! I was miles away. You know, we once spent the summer in Cork when I was a child. Do you happen to know Cork at all?'

I didn't know Cork at all.

'The situation is that we have to go to Monte Carlo toot sweet.' He looked around. 'The system of drainage in Cork is most inadequate I remember. Perhaps they have improved it now. And you know, even here in this fine city, from time to time, one comes across a ripe smell or two.'

'We have to take Habib and the Princess?'

'They will be accompanying us, yes. It is most important to keep their confidence, and I gather that they urgently want to see Henri Münzen's bank. We need to hire two cars and De Negris can come over from Livorno to drive one and I hope that you'll be at our disposal for the other . . .'

'This is Giotto's Campanile,' I said, as we rounded the square.

'Yes, yes,' said Mooney, adjusting his spectacles and staring at the pizza parlour across the road from the slender white tower. He marched straight towards it.

'Those look good, by Jupiter.'

I stood by his side as he watched the obliging young man wrap two of them up. I gave him the money.

'Very civil of you, Raymond,' said Mooney as he stared down at the vermilion slab. Don had already eaten his and was letting his hands dangle from the wrists as he screwed up the paper and let it drop into the gutter. I led the way into the Via Cavour, turning back to see if they were following. Mooney had a smear of tomato on his cheek and his lips were bunched in a rapid, a very rapid chewing motion, as he transferred his mouth's burden from one cheek to another.

I dropped back when the pavement widened at San Marco and we stood waiting for the lights to change, braving the horde of motorcyclists on the filter road who were revving up ready to charge.

'What's in this for you?' I said to Mooney.

'Ah, that is a question now.'

'Seriously?'

'The chance to eat these beautiful confections of other countries . . .'

'But *why* are you doing it . . . ?' I shouted as the lights changed on the main road and we began to cross.

The motorcyclists broke out into a storm of throttling up. On the other side, it was Indian file again on the narrow pavement. I didn't really care at that point. Zonda was still lying in bed, I thought, not knowing what was approaching. I was thinking of the wobbly way she rode a bicycle, the almost lunatic weavings to perform the simplest directional change. I had a vivid memory of riding behind her and laughing insanely as she seriously stood up on the pedals to gain more speed, sinking into the camber of the road and dangerously brushing the pavement at one side and then veering out into the road in a semicircle at the other, straight into the path of the buses that snorted behind her. We rode that day to the Arno, a trickle in the smelly mud, and pushed our cycles up the bank through the long stretch of gardens to the weir and sat in the blazing heat dangling our legs down the gently sloping concrete embankment. I wanted to climb down. I did funny walks up and down the stone like a music hall artist, but she was looking at the families and doing imitations of the Italian mothers and the way that they treated their little sons, the way they spoke to them in a kind of harsh caress. It was all as clear as day, a kind of film whose projector could only be triggered by inconsequential moments like this. And then we cycled home. I heard myself trying to keep the projector turning as I became aware of the noise of the motorcycles passing me in zooms of sound. What did we . . . do then? We rode home and had a . . . no stopped for a drink and Zonda went to sleep as soon as we got into the cool kitchen sighing and dying with the heat, arms and legs out on the bed like a starfish, deep baritone giggles for a bit, and then silence. I sat in the kitchen and brought her a drink of orange juice which stood by the side of the bed untouched for two or three days. Soon after we met, I said aloud to myself in the noise of the traffic.

The real Zonda was still in bed when we let ourselves in. I was still looking for an opportunity to grill Mooney, but he was already on the phone, sitting on the sacks of cement as if he had never left them. I made some coffee as I listened to him. Don sat on the floor with his back to the wall, knees up, his sneakers placed so flat and square in front of him they looked silly and vulnerable, like a person's face when they take off their glasses. He was chewing something and looking at the tops of his knees, brushing the material of his trousers with his thumb and squinting closely at them. Every time there was a squeal or a shout in the Via San Gallo or the noise of a drill somewhere he looked up at the shutters and had to go over to see. I went in and looked at Zonda while the coffee was on. She was all sweaty and gaga, awake, but uncaring.

'Madame Seghay?' Mooney was saying. 'Mooney . . . very well, yes, thank you, and yourself and Mr Wylmer? Mr Piech? Good, your health is everything, is it not? Now, I am calling about an arrangement I wonder if you would be interested in making. We have a first-class private Zurich bank who will take from us AU in twelve point five kilo bars delivery at Kloten free airport . . .'

'Wha?' said Zonda.

'We're back, Doll,' I said, stroking her head while I tried to listen to Mooney's polite ramblings.

'Well,' he said, 'it would be I suppose the second Zurich fix on the day of delivery . . . Discount, but of course . . .'

Zonda's eyes were trying to fix on the source of the sound, but they kept closing over the effort of the rolling pupils.

'Payment?' said Mooney. 'I should think the usual bank-confirmed purchase order. Would that be acceptable to you, Mme Seghay?'

I stepped into the front room. Don looked at me abstractedly over his knees.

'Like to go out and get some cans of beer and some Alka-Seltzer, Don?' I threw him the keys.

'Sure,' said Don very rapidly, almost before I had finished speaking, springing to his feet, catching the keys, his eyes exaggeratedly on them as if they were a ball approaching in the outfield, and bouncing round the stepladder to the door. Just like that. All in one.

Mooney had placed his green battered address book flat on top of one of the sacks and was smoothing the pages down with his palm and staring at a crack in the wall as he talked.

'A mutually convenient regular delivery date could be arranged. This is, you understand, the small shipment. The larger arrangement will be taking place sometime later . . .'

I smelt the coffee and heard a croaking from Zonda at the same time. I took the coffee in to Mooney and handed him the typed IOU as he put the phone down. He had already started dialling another call.

'We'll need to type out the text of a telex to confirm that arrangement for the gold,' he said, looking at the paper. 'What's this . . .' And his lips began to move in silent reading and his head moved to one side and then the other like a newsreader's. He took the coffee in his hand, and, balancing it on a plateau of cement, placed the paper on top of his address book.

'But of course, Raymond, my boy, I shall sign this little beauty with pleasure. Ah . . . ye . . . es . . .' he sighed as his biro flourished away at the top of the paper.

'A very efficient young man you are, Raymond . . .' I couldn't really tell if this was a pointed remark or not, whether it referred to the contents or the fact of the IOU, nor did I care much as I pocketed it.

'Was that gold bullion you were ordering?' I asked.

'It was indeed,' said Mooney, sucking up his coffee from the rim of the cup.

'What role does that have in the affair?'

'It's handy collateral for any short-term bridging loans we may have to organise in the next few days . . .'

'I see that you've given them the telephone number here . . . ?'

'Indeed, I hope you don't mind, but we have to have a stable base over the next forty-eight hours. Between you and me and the gate-post,' he said, putting his hand into my jacket pocket and drawing out a packet of Camels, 'I wish we were not having to make this unfortunate trip to Monte Carlo . . .'

With astounding timing the telephone rang.

Mooney picked it up, and started describing Pequeño Investments. I could hear a loud Italian voice.

'It's for young Zonda,' said Mooney, holding it out for me.

It was the dulcet tones of Anglophile Claudia, one of Zonda's new pickups. Claudia had a moustache and wore thick English tweeds and hacking jackets, even in the high summer. I suspected her of swimming on the other side of the river. I put the phone down on one of the cement sacks.

'I hope that this won't take long,' said Mooney. 'We have a lot to do, you know, Raymond . . .'

Zonda came padding out of the bedroom in a nightshirt that was cut right up to the thighs. Her face was puffy and pale and her eyes were red and half-shut.

'*Pronto*,' she said, turning in a half-circle away from us, and then shrieked piercingly and began to laugh. 'But darling, no, that's just one of Raymond's friends . . .' She had her Tunbridge Wells imitation on. Zonda's voice oscillated wildly when she got out of bed. Some mornings she was Chip, with her Cockney

169

twang, or, subtler, her South London, or Maidstone twang, and some mornings she was more like an army officer's wife just come back from a bridge session at the Club. When she rose from the sheets she always looked severe, as if deciding what persona to wear, and often she only rose to the sound of the telephone ringing, so that if you were there you could see her throwing on a manner like the nearest loose garment.

'*Quando?* Well, what *time* is it? But Claudia darling I don't believe it. Half-past *five* . . .'

She was pawing at the ground with her bare feet and giggling.

'He *didn't* . . . I *don't* believe you . . . you're making it up . . .'

Mooney and I took coffee and cigarettes through into the kitchen. She turned and looked after us.

'That's nothing . . . this place is chock-a-block with people . . . Yes . . . I don't know . . . some of Raymond's banking friends . . .'

Mooney and I sat at the table and lit a couple of Camels.

'She won't be long,' I said, 'and then she'll probably go out . . .'

Mooney was scribbling.

'I have a very important call to make to America,' he said. 'Two calls . . . telexes to send to Newtrier . . .'

But I was thinking about my bank. I needed rather badly to get hold of Jeremy at Coutts. I could see that my whole financial position was going to suddenly worsen in the short term, as they said. Besides, if we were going to Monte Carlo . . .

'Darling,' said Zonda, she was clinging to me and poking her nose under my collar-bone, 'Claudia's coming for supper . . .'

'Fine,' I said blandly.

Don was breathing more heavily than I would have expected. His arms were full of cans which he let slip with a crash on to the surface of the kitchen table.

Zonda turned to look with pouting distaste. Mooney winced slightly but carried on with his important scribbling. Don fiddled in his pocket.

'Yup,' he said, 'Seltzer too . . .'

'Oh,' said Zonda, snatching up the Seltzer and moving to the sink, '*just* what I need . . .'

'Thank you Don . . .' I said to her.

'Thank you Don,' she repeated as she ran a tap into the tumbler she was tilting.

'*Okay* . . .' said Don, easing a can out of the twelve-pack and sliding a long dirty nail under the ring at the top.

Zonda stood the tumbler on the draining board and dropped two Seltzers in with a chime.

'Oh *don't* . . .' she put her hands over her ears as Don's nail began to bend backwards.

I reviewed my options. Maybe I would have to sell the horses. Trouble was their feed bills were so great that there'd be nothing left for me after the sale. The stables would have the lot. But Jeremy didn't *know* the feed bills hadn't been paid. Of *course* Jeremy knew the feed bills hadn't been paid. Jeremy knew me . . .

Mooney was on the phone again, a can of beer unopened in his hand.

'I'm at Raymond's. All calls to here now . . . Yes, you have the number? Right. Little bit of a contretemps with our Iranian friends . . .'

Zonda came with me into the bedroom, grimacing and swivelling her eyes at Don, as she stood on tiptoe to pass him.

'I don't like that one . . .' she said in my ear.

I was grave, as Mooney explained the situation to Irving.

'I'd like to speak to Irving,' I said to Mooney round the corner, 'when you're ready . . .'

I held Zonda in my arms and kissed her.

'Come to Monte Carlo,' I said. 'We can play the Casino like we did last time, remember how much you won . . .'

Zonda sighed.

'I *caaaaaaaaant* . . .' she wailed. 'Gorra have *tests* . . .'

I smiled.

'Put them off . . .'

'You just don't care, do you?' said Zonda, pushing backwards, and we got into one of our mock-wrestling matches – she giggling and saying 'no' through her teeth and pretending to be really serious, and being so as well, but not quite as much, and I breathing heavily into her neck and saying 'oh *dar*ling . . . oh *dar*ling' over and over again.

We fell on the bed, and rolled apart.

'Get . . . off . . .' said Zonda and lay still with her eyes closed.

I lay looking at the ceiling. Even if we only got a hundred thousand, it would stave off all my debts. And the stud. I imagined it on a cold February morning. Cheveley Park sitting in its coronal of mist. Zonda still asleep as I stole to the window and looked across the kitchen garden to where the distant stables pushed up their red tiles.

'The gables of the stables,' I said aloud.

Zonda laughed and looked sideways across the sheet.

'What are you talking about?'

I produced the IOU and held it high, so that she had to reach up for it. I could hear her breath being expelled, and just as her fingers reached higher and touched it, the soft vein in the neck suddenly swelling, I lifted it half an inch. She fell back with a groan.

'No more . . .'

'Man's reach should be always beyond his grasp.'

Instantly, she was Chip, the ignorant Cockney sparrow.

'What you *on* abaht?'

I gave her the paper. She held it on to her breast, squinting down over a double chin, and then held it out to me without looking.

'You're *mad*,' she said, in the voice that took portions of reality like old, unpleasantly-smelling parcels and dumped them in a remote spot.

I could hear Mooney calling. He was holding out the telephone to me. As I put it to my ear, I saw that Zonda had gone into the kitchen. She was bending with a jug, watering the huge scraggy plant by the window. Her buttocks were exposed between the tails of the shirt. Don was there, but from where I was I could only see his hands fiddling about on the kitchen table.

'Irving?'

'Raymond, I hear you've had quite a party with Gerrard already?'

'I wouldn't put it as strongly as that . . .'

'Complications?'

'Not too bad. Just a few domestic arrangements.'

'So I hear. I know what you're thinking, that'll cost . . .'

'That's true . . .'

'On the other hand, Raymond, you're in this for something. I am willing to bet you've made some sort of arrangement with Gerrard already.'

'Yes, but you were going to have to send him expenses anyway. Why don't you just transfer them to my account and I can use them as you would have done?'

There was a silence.

'Do you want the number?' I was trying to see what Don was doing, but Mooney's waddling figure was in the way. He was off for a splosh.

'OK,' said Irving. 'Let's say four grand to your London account . . .'

I gave him the number.

'I'd better know a bit more about what's going on, hadn't I . . . ?'

'Ask Mooney . . .'

'I mean about what's supposed to be going on . . .'

Irving laughed.

'What's the difference, Raymond? You must tell me one of these days!'

I saw Claudia arrive. She blew me a moustachoid kiss. There was a lot of shrieking and kissing. She put down her purse and headscarf on the table so that I couldn't see Don's hands any more. I turned to face the shutters.

'Bravo. Very good, Irving . . .'

'As I have said to Gerrard,' said Irving in his serious voice, 'everything's OK this end. Mauritius are definitely interested. Mooney will tell you, but Michael Casey will be coming over to see you, he's one of our partners in the Isle of Man. He'll probably want a plane from Monte Carlo to Frankfurt. He'll have a letter to take to the bank . . .'

'You mean I should get him an air ticket?'

'A *plane*, Raymond. The letter will be a letter of confirmation from Münzen's bank to the Frankfurt bank . . .'

'Confirmation of what?'

'Confirmation that the money is there and waiting for transfer . . .'

'You mean the Brazilian money?'

'Hell, hasn't Gerrard briefed you at *all*?'

'Fraid not, we've been a bit too busy for that . . .'

'Well, Raymond, I've got to get back to the Sheraton. Keep Brazil and Mauritius sweet. Do your stuff with those Iranians now.'

And he rang off.

I was now a member of staff, a fully paid-up associate. This called for a drink. Lots of drinks.

I went out to get some provisions and wine, leaving Mooney in the bathroom, and Zonda standing in the kitchen telling Don and Claudia about the brute next door and the cat he imprisoned on his patch of roof. She was barrelling away in Italian, and just called out to me 'Ciao, darling' without looking.

I went down and checked on some of the bets I had laid. Not very satisfactory. There was a horse called Catnip I was interested in, brother to Scapa Flow, out of Nogara, but it had been pulled up. Italian ways are often very crude, breaking horses' legs with hammers and all that sort of thing, so it might have genuinely been unwell. In the Piazza della Repubblica, I bumped into Ettore and Marco and one or two other cronies, and I was beginning to feel quite depressurised. Ettore was the partner of my trainer in Pisa and I owed him, on the face of it, quite a lot of money, but it was all very pleasant and we still laid bets off for one another from time to time. We sat on high stools in Antinori's and bought a couple of bottles of their house champagne. He'd had a bad fall recently while taking the horses out and shattered his pelvis. The doctors had told him he must never get up on a horse again. That's what they had told him when it happened before, and the pelvis had cracked. Rosella was very *disappointed*, he said with a wink. Marco laughed a dry, solemn laugh, and nodded.

'What, completely?'

'Well,' said Ettore, 'Raimundo, we have to wait and see, but . . .'

His shoulders hunched and his face assumed an attitude of comic despair.

'Doctors told me they make a temporary arrangement and we wait to see if *pistolino* make a glorious resurrection, but . . .'

'Nothing?'

He shook his head.

'It's only women, but I love to ride.'

'To ride horses,' said Marco solemnly to me.

Ettore punched him:

'Hey . . . stop that . . . of *course* to ride horses . . .'

I wanted to talk to Ettore about Forray and how he was getting on. I was rather proud of the name, which was an anagram of Raymond and Forguon Blindé, the French mother. Zonda had designed some colours in turquoise and royal blue quartering which I thought hideous, but they had the virtue of being distinctive. So far you didn't need to distinguish Forray, however, because he was always in the back four every time he ran.

I asked them back. On the way, Marco said easily that Sergio in Milan had asked him to mention that he would like some of my account paid off. I owed Sergio about half a million lire, a debt which had slowly accumulated over about three or four years. Usually he was happy if I paid for his business trips to London. Marco acted as a sort of unofficial debt collector from time to time, nudging my elbow like this. But Marco was very keen on learning backgammon, and I could usually reduce the debt by teaching him how to play. Solemnly, he stands on the doorstep and you know what he wants. So you ask him to stay for the weekend, and get the backgammon set out. Open the beer, brew the coffee, and start playing for a few days. But recently, Marco had been in Florida and after he came back I noticed his backgammon had improved a great deal. He now played the aggressive American way, and there didn't seem much chance of doing this any more.

I mentioned my forthcoming trip to Monte Carlo. I thought I could see to it after I came back if Sergio could wait a bit.

I put a step on, forcing Ettore with his pelvic troubles and his stick to hobble at speed. I thought Zonda could distract Marco a little, if I could just get them to the house. Especially, if he knew I was going away. I knew Zonda had her troubles down there, but fortunately he didn't, so even if he did try while I was away, he was in for a pretty thin time of it, ho ho. I was feeling quite cheerful, still, when we got back.

You could hear the racket all the way up the stairs, and when I finally opened the door, I had to push against a row of bodies on the other side.

'Oh, just a mo . . .' someone that sounded suspiciously like Ponsonby said. Two fingers appeared round the edge of the wood, and whitened, visibly, between the quick of the nail and the first joint.

'. . . and everywhere the *smell* . . .' somebody was saying, '. . . a sort of vague compound of shit and fruit going off . . .' They were obviously talking about India.

The hand dragged the door open wide and Julian came into view holding up a glass of something very fastidiously and spouting at full spittle-spattling throttle at someone behind the door.

'*Hell*ooo . . .' I sang to everyone and no one as I pushed a way through, clutching my parcel under my chin. I looked around. I had completely forgotten we were supposed to be having a party. Zonda was over with a group of people at the stepladder. Don was staring at the side of her head with his mouth open. Eddie, the tall pornographic painter with the voice of velvet, was staring shyly up at the ceiling, as Zonda boasted to him about her decorating, while a huge Italian girl in bulging tigerskins and fluorescent pink lipstick, Eddie's latest by the look of it, was looking quickly from Zonda to Eddie with an expression of distaste that could have been mistaken for interest only by the most unwary.

I pressed through the throng with Ettore and Marco smiling and nodding in tow. The kitchen table was full of bottles and paper cups.

'Raymond daaarling,' said Philomena, from the boutique, pressing some large, sharp metal jewellery into my shirtfront. 'We were just talking about you . . .'

'Philomena,' I said, turning slightly, anxious to get another look at her hands that were so old and freckled and tired and horny and gave her game of twenty-seven-year-old freshness such a ghoulish twist, 'you were discussing Salvatore's latest outburst, and comparing it with Dinkie's notes about Alberto's latest threat to beat her up, weren't you?'

Dinkie, the adenoidal Australian from the wool shop, put her head round the bedroom door.

'I *heard* that Raymond,' she said, 'and if Dinkie wasn't so busy trying to get liddle Em'ly off in here, she'd pop you one right on the . . . ah *there* there, lid . . . dul . . . bundle . . .' she turned back.

I introduced Ettore and Marco to Claudia and Philomena and Dinkie and pushed towards the stepladder, leaving them to open the new bottles. So far I couldn't see Mooney anywhere. There was a crowd from the British Council on the cement bags, having a learned conversation about Rupert books, and the phone, which was ringing, had fallen down between the sacks somewhere and was out of sight.

'But didn't Mr Bear have *check* trousers and Rupert have *plain* ones . . .' said Edgar, an immensely tall cultural attaché who looked like a giraffe with the gripes.

I pushed between them and scrabbled behind the sacks.

'No, no, I distinctly remember them,' I could hear Ponsonby saying. 'They were mustard-yellow check . . .'

I dragged out the receiver, pulling the cord between the sacks, and knelt on the gritty floor.

The dark silence in my ear was broken by long distance bleeping.

'Mr Mooney?'

'This is an associate,' I said, realising that the voice on the other end had broken.

'Can you get him . . . it's *real* urgent . . .'

'Well, I'm not quite sure . . . can I take a message . . .'

'. . . For Chrissakes never *mind* . . .' sobbed the voice. 'I probably won't be around by the time you get a-hold of him, these guys are on my back here . . . tell him, will yer?'

'Who are you?'

'Just tell him, Clyde rang, d'you hear me, Clyde Wellcombe rang . . . just tell him the heat's on over Cumberland Plateau . . . I can't hear ya . . .'

'All right Clyde, can you say more?' I said, staring at every detail of an upturned cup that seemed very close.

'Well . . . I don't know whether this thing's gonna work out . . . after all, I've had to go to some kinda funny outlets for finance . . . some of our friends in Cleveland, Ohio, tell him, are coming down to see me here . . . ho *Christ*, I'm scared . . .' said Clyde in a small strangulated cry. 'I've put everything out on this deal, my whole livelihood is at stake, everything, do you hear me, sir . . .'

'I hear you, Clyde . . .'

'It's taken me twenty years . . .' Clyde began to sob again. 'twenty god-damn years to build up . . . this . . .'

'How did you get our number, Clyde?' I shouted.

'Mr Mooney called earlier . . . asked me to call back if there was any news . . . Look you guys have just *got* to get that money

178

through here, do you understand . . . If that money doesn't come right now, why, my ass is just so much . . .' He tailed off, whispering with grief.

I laid the receiver down on the floor and went over to Zonda. The whole knot of people by the stepladder, their drinks resting on its steps like a bar-counter, was doubled up in various attitudes of hysterical laughter. Zonda was puce, a tear trickling out of the tightly shut corner of each eye, and having trouble with her breathing, her arms waving limply in tiny circles.

'Where's Mooney?' I said in what I thought was a lull.

Zonda stamped softly, her eyes pebble-like.

I took her by the arms and shook her urgently.

'Darling . . . where . . . is . . . Moo . . . ney?'

'. . . bathroom set . . .' said Eddie, and there was an instant redoubling of hysteria.

'. . . children's *bicycle* . . .' said Zonda, and they stiffened again.

I'd seen this game before. They were imitating the programme Sale of the Century on English television in which greedy people, progressively whipped up by an auctioneer-like compère who talks faster and faster throughout the programme, attempt to remember a number of consumer goods which have recently passed before their eyes. It was one of Zonda's favourite things to do at parties. I turned round, and caught sight of Mooney's dirty brown suit. He was kneeling on the floor by the paper cup talking decisively into the telephone.

'Now Clyde,' I could hear Mooney saying in a soothing but firm brogue, 'take hold, there's a good man, brace up now, we'll have the spondulicks over there for you in two shakes of a lamb's tail, do you hear me now, we're going to clorse very soon . . . No I can't say when to the day at the moment . . . there's still a little bit of fluidity in the situation, but it is most important that you keep a calm head on your shoulders at this stage . . . Do you hear me now? . . .'

He rang off. The noise was so great we had to kneel and place our lips against the other's ear, and shout.

'What is wrong with Clyde?' I shouted.

'Bathroom,' said Mooney, pointedly.

We stood in the long tiled room. Papers were strewn all round the toilet seat and all along the edge of the bath.

'Pity we can't move the telephone in here,' said Mooney.

'What's the matter with Clyde?'

'Clyde is a real estate agent from Massachusetts, who is helping to handle the purchase of the Cumberland Plateau Ranch for us. He's our man on the spot, and he's had to raise money quickly and very short-term, but when we clorse, as I just told him this minute on the phone, he'll be buying three real estate businesses . . .'

'Who are "our friends from Cleveland"?'

'Pequeño Investments is a legit company. It has nothing to do with such people . . .'

'They're the Mafia, aren't they?'

'We are bankers, not criminals . . .'

'But what's going to happen to him?'

'He's going to become rich, that's what's going to happen to Clyde . . .'

'Or dead,' I said.

'Nonsense, there's no need to talk like that. There's a lot of work to be done, Raymond. I need to talk to Irving and . . . we need some typing done. You can get rid of these people.'

'They are some of our dearest friends . . .' I said in my mock-pompous voice.

Someone was banging urgently on the door. I could see the bolt beginning to dig into the wood of the door frame, causing a split. The louts had not done a very good job on the second-fixings.

'Let's get a drink anyway,' I said, opening the door.

Dinkie was standing on the step, holding little Emily by the hand. They pushed urgently by.

'What's this, a bloody office?'

Mooney was bending over the bath gathering up his papers.

180

'There you are my liddle dinkum doll,' said Dinkie to Emily. 'Go to it.'

She caught Mooney by the waist and started to do the conga with him, while Emily hoisted up her white organdie skirts and sat sniffing and staring at him.

'No time to work. Time to *play*,' said Dinkie.

I poured Mooney and myself some whisky from the fridge, and we made a space at the kitchen table. He looked really quite ill, I thought. He had lit a cigarette and plucked it from his dry lips between brown fingers. The lip had a strip torn from it and was starting to bleed.

'Ah, will you look at that now?' he said.

Purple shades of broken capillaries ran from the greasy grey temple down the cheeks to the nose. He coughed violently all of a sudden, spitting into his hand and then lurching to the sink and running the hand under the tap. I handed him one of Zonda's big soft turquoise tissues that matched something or other we had never purchased. She had come home with four gross of these things once. It seemed that physical reality was against him. He was serious as he buried his face in the tissue and coughed for his life. The cigarette with its strips of blood already dried on its yellow, moist rim of paper was giving off a steady column of white smoke as it burnt into the white, Formica table top a dark brown, cone-shaped mark. I looked at the heap of papers and I saw this mark repeated on the edges of several of them. I stared at the back of his brown, stained suit and over it appeared the hideously ugly face of the white cat by the chimney stack on the roof opposite. The noise had gone into a blur, and it was suddenly as if one could hear in a kind of pocket of insulated air around the table. I picked up one of the telexes and stared at it. It was an order to Kevin Mooney Jr at the Bank of Ireland to forward a loan of three and a quarter million pounds sterling to the bank in the Isle of Man. I looked back at the figure still bent over the sink, and I drank some whisky from the cup.

'What's this?' I asked in a low voice that was perfectly audible.

I riffled through the papers and came across a letter to an estate agent in Dublin concerning the purchase of a property near Swords, a country club, house and surrounding lands, called Turvey. It struck me that the great majority of Mooney's telexes and letters were from, not to him.

'What is Turvey?' I asked, the question pitched out, again, to the air in general.

He collapsed back in his chair and fussed with the cigarette, wiping ineffectually at the groove it had burnt in the table, while he held the dog-end upwards with its long bent cylinder of ash. He tipped the ash with one flick on to the floor and put the dog-end with the tip glowing pink between his sore lips. He adjusted his horn-rimmed spectacles.

'What has Turvey got to do with all this?' I repeated patiently.

He took a deep swig from the plastic cup.

'Ah, that's better. What was it you were saying just now, Raymond?'

I held up the telex.

'Ah, Turvey,' he sighed, 'the gem of gems . . . a sweet little spot, so it is . . .'

I felt Zonda's arms slide round my neck as he spoke; her soft hot cheek brushed against mine and her hair fell partly over my face, so that I couldn't breathe. I pushed her away, and she staggered into the sink.

'That's not nice,' she said laughing.

'Used to belong to my family,' said Mooney in the same, musing tone. 'Topsy Turvey was always the Mooney place and we'll make it great again, Raymond, my lad, a major stud-farm.'

Zonda was back and the curtain of hair fell over my face again. This time I parted some strands and watched him through the gap, feeling her sway against me and then holding her, while he spoke, as she swayed away again.

'You and Zonda can come and manage it for me. The Turvey Stables and the Turvey Export and Cold Store Company Limited, major exporter of beef and horsemeat to Europe . . .'

'Oh darling,' said Zonda, 'are we going to . . . live somewhere else . . . have a drink of your . . . wicksey-in-the-cup . . . yes . . . ?'

'It's as good as bought already,' said Mooney, stabbing the dead dog-end very precisely into the piled-up ashtray.

I looked around for the Italians, who had been hovering near the door for some time, murmuring to one another with gentle smiles, but they had gone.

'Where . . . d'you gettat tie from?' said Zonda to Mooney. I got up and let her flop into my chair.

'Tie?' said Mooney, his hand going up to his open collar.

'Yes,' said Zonda eloquently, 'tie, tie . . .'

'Horsemeat to Europe, bit like coals to Newcastle isn't it?' I ventured over the top.

'I think it's great, it's 'spired, 's *wonnnn*erful . . .' said Zonda, in her fake French. 'Dinkie darling . . .' she shrieked.

'Packaging and flash-freezing, and absolutely top-quality Irish stud meat . . . major exporter . . . to say nothing of the Turvey Moss Peat Company, that's a very lucrative little number too, y'know . . .'

'Look at this, Dinkie,' said Zonda. 'Look at his tie . . .'

'I hate to disillusion yer, doll, but the man hasn't . . .'

Zonda reached forward.

'No *this* tie . . .'

She lifted the long serpent out of Mooney's pocket, still noosed with its massive, sprouting Windsor knot.

'Good God,' said Dinkie. 'Hey, Phil . . .'

Philomena poked her head round the kitchen doorframe.

'My *God*,' she whined like one in pleasure. 'How *heav* . . . en . . . ly . . .'

'Where did you get it?' said Zonda.

'This tie,' said Mooney, 'I believe my wife bought it for me on O'Connell Street in 1957 . . .'

Philomena was giving out little squeaks as it was passed to her.

' 's the coming thing . . .' said Zonda with a wink.

'Zonda darling,' said Philomena. 'What a *good* idea.'

'Alberto would just love it,' said Dinkie, as little Emily began to screech somewhere.

'But I just *love* the idea of dressing *all* these Italian men in those things, you know, can't you just *see* them in great baggy suits and . . .'

Zonda swung an arm.

'And *shoes* . . .' she said with a hiccup, 'toecaps . . .'

I got up and wandered away, leaving Mooney in the midst of the harpies offering his Nazionali round. Development of this creative idea was already under way. I looked back from the door. Zonda was pouring out more whisky with her back to the others. She was fuelling up, otherwise she knew, obscurely, she would go, fade, disappear. I thought I detected a trace of marijuana in her behaviour, but I couldn't quite understand where she'd got it from.

Chelsea Freddie, in his white flannels and his impeccable blue and white Viyella shirt, was telling a lot of people behind the door something urgent about India. I took them all a bottle of some wine I found on the floor and filled up their plastic cups.

'. . . absolutely *pitch*-dark,' he was saying, '. . . and these thundering great juggernauts *without* lights bearing down – well, I mean you couldn't tell whether – or what – or whatever – but anyway there we were – I mean by grace and good fortune . . .' He raised his eyes to the ceiling, 'they all seemed to be going the other way . . . and you know we passed an ox-cart on the other side of the road . . . thought nothing of it because Fali my friend was telling me about the Parsee scrambled eggs – an absolutely de*lic*ious – ravishing – *only* thing I could eat – all the rest – well I just shudder really when I think of it, my God, yes – anyway one of these things just – didn't *see* it you see because no lights – just ran the ox-cart down – eighty miles an hour – driver and everything – naturally we stopped and – oh terrible mess, nothing left really – the driver of the lorry came running up as we stood there in the dark – he'd stopped about half a mile away – and d'you know he apologised to us for having to see all

184

this mess . . . completely different attitude, you see . . . towards human life . . .'

'Ah,' said someone called Sidney, 'there you get your Hinduism you see . . .'

'Marvellously easy now for people to borrow and postpone repayment . . . I think Dee Hock's doing us all a service . . .' said someone else called Sandra to Chelsea Freddie's liquid-eyed Calabrian. 'No I mean it . . . time itself has changed its nature . . .'

'What are you driving at? I don't quite follow,' said Edgar, holding his cigarette upwards at an angle of forty-five degrees and giving it a quick, delicate double-puff.

'Who?' said Sandra.

Freddie expelled, with impatience.

'Well,' said Edgar, dribbling a luxurious syrupy cloud of white smoke out of the corner of his mouth, 'Hinduism and Dee Hock, I don't quite . . .'

'No,' said Sandra, 'I was just talking about the coming revolution . . .'

'Hullo, some pretty heavy stuff over here chaps,' said Doug the guitar teacher. 'Where is this Hindu revolution, I thought they were non-violent types, the Hindus . . . ?'

'Credit-cards,' I said.

'I see,' said Doug.

He specialised in this rather downcast timing. Edgar, the dominant-double-puffer and he had worked this one out to a fine art. I looked at them, imagining them jiggling together with the shutters closed on very hot Sunday afternoons.

'No,' said Sandra, dragging them round, 'I mean it's already happened, for God's sake, we all get these letters now from machines pretending to be people – they get nice with us if we pay – and nasty if we don't and it's painless and everybody saves *time* . . . banks don't have to employ an extra teller to run this vast empire of people within the credit circle . . .'

'And credit cards are only a *stage* . . .' said Sidney.

'And credit cards are only a stage,' sang Sandra in canon, 'because you'll have EFT.'

'ATMs,' said Sidney.

'OLTTs.'

'And POSTs . . .'

'New York already has EFT – Electronic Funds Transfer . . .'

'And with the help of Automatic Teller Machines and on-line teller terminals . . .'

'*Love* it . . . ! On-line teller terminals . . . !' said Doug.

'You can bypass *people* altogether,' said Sandra.

For some reason, I could smell parsley, or was it basil? I looked round. Don was smiling at me through the slats of the stepladder.

'Doug,' I asked, 'do you and Edgar *jiggle* on very hot Sunday afternoons?'

'Oh Raymond please,' said Edgar, blowing out an artistic plume. 'Why do you *always* have to be so unpleasant?'

'But . . . *don't you see* . . .' said Freddie, dancing up and down with excitement.

How many times since we were at school together had I heard him say that. But . . . DON'T YOU SEE . . . and always it would be something completely worthless that was about to emerge from his impatiently bubbling lips, as he looked with a beady eye towards anyone who would listen. I looked away towards Don, who smiled again through the slats. What on earth was the matter with him?

'But *don't* you *see* . . . the possibilities for surveillance are increased en*or*mously . . .'

'The thing is that this scene creates a whole new *reality*,' said Sandra. 'Got a match darling? No, you see, this credit circle . . .'

'The global village, McLuhan was really right, you know . . .' said Sidney, looking across at me.

'Absolutely,' I said, doing my imitation of John Snagge. 'But what *about* surveillance . . . ?'

'Yes,' screamed Freddie, 'thank you Raymond – what I was about to say was – I mean – it's all been discussed by the American Senate Judiciary Committee donkeys years ago in seventy-six – you see they did this sort of war-game thing – whatever – supposing they were the Kremlin what system would they design – yes – that would be most effective for the surveillance of the Russian people – that was their hypothetical problem – or whatever – and they all had to . . .'

'Go away and form groups . . .' said Edgar, doing hundreds of little tiny smoke rings and looking at them as if they were offering him an obscure invitation.

'Who were "they"?' said Sandra.

Freddie threw up his hands.

'Experts – whatever . . . But anyway – do you know what the result was – what the best sytem was? . . .'

I went over to the stepladder.

'Don, you've got to come and listen to this,' I said grabbing his arm. 'After all you're an expert . . .'

'Hey,' said Don, adjusting his shades, 'sure am, and it's a cool little lady you've got there . . .' He nodded to the kitchen.

I led him like a sheep into the corner.

'Don used to be with the CIA,' I announced.

'Hey,' said Don, letting out a single giggle. 'Who told you that? You're not supposed to know that, man . . . Hey, that's confidential . . .'

'It's true,' said Freddie.

'What is?' I asked.

'EFT,' said Freddie, 'best method . . .'

Don was holding himself as still as a board.

'Hey paranoia you can really smell-it-you-can-hear-it every time you turn on . . .' He shimmied to himself. 'If you really-wanna-wear-it . . .' he added to himself.

I just recognised the outlines of 'At the Hop'.

'Bop bop bop . . .' I said, and clicked my fingers.

'Hey, man, that's *it* . . .'

'You're absolutely right,' said Sandra.

'They've been doing it for years in South Africa,' said Freddie. 'Do you know that the last time I was . . .'

187

'Freddie is always popping over to Jo'burg for the cut-price rough stuff, aren't you Fred?' said Edgar.

'Diamonds, or boys?' said Doug.

'You *beasts* . . .' said Freddie in a high, squeaky voice, 'you've been gossiping about me . . . But really it's true,' he insisted in his reasonable tone. 'When I was there last November . . .'

I led the jeering.

'Raymond, since when have *you* been a liberal . . . Anyway, I was saying . . . if you pay for your hotel or a rented car – or whatever – with a credit card, and you always do because it's *so* much easier when you're travelling – then they've *got* you . . .'

Don was doing the twist, softly, at my side.

'What sort of operations have you been on . . . er Don?' said Sandra.

Don was sniggering and talking very rapidly to himself in a whisper.

'All over the whole *wide* world . . . yes *maam* . . . On Don . . .'

'Were you a plunger?' said Freddie.

'Plumber, isn't it?' said Sandra. 'I thought it was a plumber . . .'

'Yes, you're quite right my dear,' said Sidney, nodding. 'Plumber, quite right . . . White House plumbers . . .'

Gravely, Don pursed his lips, while they waited for an account of the Watergate affair from the inside. I could see them queuing up, and then, who *did* kill Kennedy, really, from the inside.

But Don had begun to imitate a police-siren with considerable accuracy, complete with Doppler effect.

'What were we saying?' said Sandra.

I led Don away, back to the stepladder and poured him a drink.

'Yes, the surgeons had to go in from behind – above – here – ' Ettore was saying in Italian to Eddie, who sucked his lips with imagined pain. '. . . Well, yes, I have a temporary arrangement, but I must wait to see if anything . . . you know . . . happens . . .' Eddie looked down nervously, sideways, and gave a few small chuckles, as if there was a small but deadly insect approaching Ettore's head, a spider shinning down a web that hung over his scalp. 'They told me . . .' said Ettore, 'I could have another thing whereby you press a button *here* . . .' He pointed to his diaphragm. 'And . . .' he whistled, 'up she comes . . .' Eddie, who was chortling affectionately, blowing tiny kisses at his huge tigerskin-clad consort, looked interested all of a sudden.

'I *say*,' he said. 'What, *any* time you like . . .'

'Any *time*,' said Ettore.

Eddie twitched his ancient dark-brown corduroys with delight.

'Do you know,' he said in a very low voice to the girl, 'that's such a *mar*vellous coincidence, you see, because of my book, don't you think?'

'Oh *yes* . . .' Her pale face was raw with pink make-up which had created a greasy second skin. 'Eddie's book is so good . . .'

'What is this book?' I asked, as I was meant to.

'My pop-up penis book,' said Eddie, with a weary sigh. 'I've been having *such* a lot of trouble getting them to . . .'

'Pop up?'

'Exactly.'

Ettore was looking puzzled.

'I spent three or four mornings last week with them all over the floor.'

'It is hard,' said Hilaria earnestly, 'very hard for Eddie when the . . .' and here she giggled and dug through his Harvie and Hudson shirt with her elbow, 'the pops don't *pop*!'

'Perhaps it's not hard enough,' I said and instantly regretted it, for Ettore's face had cleared and his hand strayed instinctively to the crook of his elbow, at a point just below the bicep. He clenched his fist and folded the arm back twice in rapid succession.

Hilaria looked away, sweating.

'By the way.' Eddie had bent his huge, walnut-coloured head. 'I'm having a party and you and Zonda must come.'

'What is it this time – spacemen?'

'I keep telling you, Raymond, it *wasn't* spacemen, it was aliens from outer space.'

189

'Well, *I* was a spaceman.'

'But Zonda certainly wasn't and she looked absolutely charming. No, you see, you wouldn't *see* anything if it were spacemen, everyone would be wearing their suits . . . Mind you,' he went off into an ecstatic piece of teeth-sucking, as if he were just finishing off an apple-pie, 'I *love* the idea of those *transparent* suits . . .'

'What is it this time – seedy side of the Renaissance?'

'No, that's the Venice carnival party, Raymond, you're *so* awkward sometimes . . . No, this time, I had a choice, didn't I darling . . . between "Aztecs and Atahualpa" which *I* think would be fun and plenty of scope for drag, but Hilaria preferred "Holograms" which I *must* say I'm just a *little* bit doubtful about still . . .'

Eddie was looking as if something bad had got into his mouth.

'You can't *see* much with Holograms . . .' He sighed, 'and the whole point is to get a subject that's really er*otic* . . .'

'What about "stud-farm"?' I suggested, wondering what was going on in the kitchen.

'Yes,' said Hilaria brightening. 'You could come as a bull.' She laughed indulgently and slipped an arm through Eddie's Norfolk tweed.

'Anyway,' said Eddie, clinging sadly to the arm, 'it could be the last.'

'Oh?'

He turned away and whispered:

'Had a letter this morning from my mother. Looks as if my Trust Fund's sort of running dry. Oh dear, it means *another* trip to Hampshire.'

'Holograms are a bore,' I said, looking straight at Hilaria. 'You can count me out if you're doing Holograms.'

Eddie pursed his lips and gave another of his sidelong pseudo-shy, would-be gazelle smiles.

'Ye . . . es, I know whatchoo mean . . .' Hilaria began to protest in her dark chocolate voice, her mouth forming an 'O', a pink vortex in whirlpool of sweating pancake. Eddie bent and whispered behind his hand:

'Only been together a week . . . Isn't she *marvellous* . . .'

'You guys got a john?' said Don.

'What are you two whispering?' said Hilaria in a traditional sort of way. 'You little boys.'

'You guys got a john?' said Don, wandering off towards the kitchen.

'I'm doing an eight-foot canvas of Hilaria as Juno,' said Eddie, cosily, to Hilaria. 'Her biceps are an absolute *dream*, aren't they darling?'

'I have to stand for hours with a spear,' said Hilaria, delighted the subject had finally been broached.

'You're *very* patient Hilaria, darling.'

She had taken the paint brush off one of Zonda's tins and assumed the position obscene.

'Britannia,' I said.

'No, *Juno* . . . see it is very hard . . .'

I took them over to the serious group at the door.

'Well, I understand it's really extensive,' Sandra was saying in her deep summer-pudding voice. 'Oh hello Raymond, d'you know something?'

'What?' I asked.

'Julian and I *both* had shares in the Vatican lavatory firm.' She laughed breathlessly.

'What, Ceramica Pozzi?'

She nodded.

'Can you believe it? And we've both got rid of them.'

'Why?'

'Sindona's bought the firm off the Vatican bank.'

'Biggest scandal Italy's ever known,' said Sidney, nodding and looking to his wife for a cue. 'They say . . .'

'They *say* . . .' said Sandra, 'that the Vatican's involved and everything . . .'

'All the government,' said Edgar. 'God this country's so *corrupt* . . .'

'Isn't it something to do with Freemasons – or whatever?' said Freddie.

'That's right,' said Sandra. 'The cabinet is just a vast Masonic lodge apparently.'

I was looking into the kitchen. I could see the smoke from Mooney's Nazionali swirling under the shade. Dinkie had the sleeping Little Emily tucked under her arm like a parcel and Philomena was holding Bingo, the grovelling beige-coloured miniature ant-eater that she referred to as her dog. They looked ready for departure. Zonda and Don were nowhere to be seen.

'I say, Raymond,' said Edgar, 'who's that tramp fellow in your kitchen, do we know him?' It was not clear to whom he referred.

'Yes, Irish chappie,' said Freddie, 'or Scottish or whatever?'

I glared at them.

'He's just somebody Zonda and I met *sotto casa*,' I said.

'He smells,' said Edgar, wrinkling his nose.

'I know,' I said very quickly and evenly.

'He says he's a businessman,' said Doug.

'But he looks like a navvy,' said Edgar. 'He has a navvy's hands.'

'Is he here for long?' said Doug.

I shrugged.

'You'd better ask him,' I said.

'No *fear*,' said Doug, laughing. 'Good God Raymond . . .'

But Edgar was whispering, sprightly, and putting a finger to his lips.

'Let me just have a *look* at him . . .'

He ran with tiptoeing steps. I could hear his cream suit-trousers brushing against Zonda's rough white wall as he crept up to the kitchen doorway and stood just outside the circle of light, wrinkling his nose. He put his arms akimbo for a moment, and then came tiptoeing back.

'Hmm,' he said. 'Yes, yes I . . . hmn . . .'

192

'I can see that he might be one of those sort of respectable *turfy* Irishmen,' said Doug.

'I don't think he's respectable at all,' I said.

'Well,' said Freddie, 'Raymond's used to bad company, aren't you Raymond, all those wide boys at the tracks, hmm?'

'I never bet,' said Edgar.

'Well, I have a flutter on the big races,' said Sandra, pouring oil on troubled waters.

'Is he *staying* here?' said Edgar.

'For the moment, yes,' I said.

'What about the sidekick?'

'Him too.'

'Better watch out for your silver, Raymond,' said Sandra.

I heard the grand sounds of Dinkie and Philomena's departure coming from the kitchen. They were calling for Zonda, who swayed round the corner from the bedroom. The procession came down the steps towards us, and then halted in the middle of the group. Emily blinked and transferred from one side of Dinkie's neck to another, while Sandra tried to look at her to say goodbye. Exhausted whimpers propelled Dinkie to the door. Zonda clung to them, tearfully.

'Remember what I said to you,' she said.

'Don't *worry*, darling,' said Philomena to Zonda. 'Take a leaf out of Bingo's book. When *his* little botty bled, he was *awfully* brave, weren't you darling?'

They were all crowding to the door now. Claudia was clinging to Zonda, and Zonda was wiping the tears from her eyes, and laughing.

This was obviously going to take ages, so I wandered back towards the kitchen. I looked into the bedroom on the way. Marco, Ettore and Don were all sitting on my side of the bed, their feet straying in the litter of my *Timeform* and my form records and my neat stacks of racing papers. They had the bedside lamp on behind them, which threw up a salmon glow on to the cobalt walls of the bedroom. Someone had taken down the large square bedroom mirror with the bamboo frame and they were sharing it on their knees, all looking intently into its depths. I leaned against the doorjamb. Don looked up and grinned. He had a razorblade in his hand. Ettore and Marco were sitting side by side like two small boys and Ettore lifted his elbow high and pushed it slowly into Marco's ribs. Marco moved up slightly. Don was emptying out a small packet of stuff that looked like cement on to the surface of the mirror. He took the razorblade and made two small inroads into the pile and then delicately combed off the tops of the three miniature slag-heaps so they equalised with the others. Where the dust obscured his tracks, he cleared them carefully. Ettore and Marco were looking at each other in the mirror and pointing. Ettore, whose features looked as if they had been driven to one side of his face with a hammer-blow, said something out of the corner of his mouth and whistled and their laughter began to jog the mirror.

'Hey you guys,' said Don, 'quit goofin' will ya!'

He straightened up.

'OK,' he said, 'who's gonna take the first line?'

The two Italians looked at each other, and demurred.

Don took from the pocket of his jacket a white tube that had been fashioned out of the top end of a Tampax holder.

'C'*mon* guys?'

He sighed, and laid the tube on the mirror.

'You try to give the guys a good time . . .' he said, flipping his two hands over and holding them like a juggler ready to receive an invisible ball.

'Me, me, me . . .' said Zonda, rushing in and kneeling in front of them all.

'Take it *easy*,' said Don. 'You'll mess up the whole *fucking* . . .'

'Sorry, sorry,' said Zonda, bouncing up and down on her heels. 'May I?'

'What about it Ray?' said Don.

'Don't ask *him*,' said Zonda, taking the tube and inserting it into her nostril. 'He's horrid.'

'Ray?' said Don.

'I don't approve,' I said, shrugging.

Zonda isolated her left index finger and with all the boredom of an air hostess demonstrating a lifejacket, flattened her left nostril, pushing the tube into the tiny white heap on the mirror. A single slow breath, and the tube moved through the heap like a vacuum cleaner, the grains vanishing systematically into the end until the mirror was clean.

She sat back on her haunches shaking her head and squeezing the bridge of her nose between thumb and index finger. The tube dropped to the floor.

'Mmm . . .'

'Hey, goddam . . .' said Don, pointing at the tube. 'Fucking *dames* . . .'

Zonda was laughing.

'Look at you three,' she said in a high-pitched tinkling fashion, her voice like brittle china. 'Can't get your little toy now can you, eh?'

They sat looking at the two fragile heaps of powder on the mirror, unable to move for fear of disturbing them.

'Aw cmon, baby,' said Don with a snigger. 'Reach us it.'

Zonda shook her head very slowly from side to side.

'Ray?'

I went forward and bent to pick up the tube.

Zonda grabbed my arm.

'*Dar*ling,' I said.

'No, don't let them,' said Zonda. 'Whatever happened to femin – ever happened to the spider woman?'

I picked up the tube and handed it back to Don.

'Hey, why don't you turn on Ray? These guys sure ain't gonna take any trips. They're *chicken*, ain't ya guys, huh?'

'I don't take drugs,' said Marco quietly, and removed the mirror to one side so that he could stand up. '*Amico*,' he said to Ettore, a question in his voice.

Ettore pushed the mirror so that it slid across Don's lap and began to tilt as he stood up. Zonda laughed as neat little heaps of grains skittered like snowdrifts across the surface of the mirror.

'Thanks a *lot* . . .' said Don, catching it and levelling it out. 'Chicken shit.'

I looked round.

'Raymond, thank you for a *lovely* party,' said Sandra, holding out a gloved hand.

'Most enjoyable,' said Sidney.

They peered past me into the bedroom.

'Where is she?'

I was still holding the gloved hand, idly fingering the relief-stitching on the back of it, when the rest of the stragglers came and stood round the doorway.

Zonda danced out between the two Italians, her eyes brimming.

'Oh,' she said, 'you're *leaving*.' I let go of the gloved hand.

'It *is* four thirteen,' I said.

She threw her arms about Sandra's neck.

'I hear you're going to Monte Carlo,' said Edgar, peering round the corner into the kitchen at Mooney.

Zonda was talking in a muffled voice into the material of Sandra's dress:

'. . . wish you weren't going, because there's so much to talk about and when shall I *ever* see you again . . .'

'Yes,' I said to Edgar, 'Zonda doesn't want to come . . .'

'Doesn't want to *come*,' said Sandra, pushing her away and looking under her lowered eyebrows. 'What's this, doesn't want to come?'

'England again,' I said to Sidney, edging into the centre of the doorway so that Don would be properly concealed.

'Yes,' he sighed. 'Back to dear old blighty. I envy you two, I really do,' he said. 'I think Sandra and I will come out here when we retire . . .'

'You're so over*wrought*, darling, what *is* the matter?'

'She's just tired,' I said. The immortal line.

'Where's my bag?' said Sandra.

'On your arm,' I said.

'Oh, so it is,' she said. 'D'you know sometimes I . . .'

'Must be getting old,' said Sidney.

'Hurry up please it's time,' I said.

'Ha very witty Raymond,' said Freddie from the back, standing on tiptoe to squeak over the heads of the others.

Zonda turned on me ferociously.

'Sometimes you are *so rude* . . .' she said. 'They're *leaving*, don't you understand, I may never *see* them again . . .'

'Don't be silly darling,' said Sandra.

'I say, that's a bit much,' said Sidney. 'Never.'

'It's only T. S. Eliot,' I said, catching her by the elbows and looking into her red-rimmed eyes. 'A quotation?'

Suddenly I wanted to get a brush and sweep the whole stammering, stuttering crowd of them, as they huddled together like so many chickens, out through the door and down the stairs.

'Come on you good people,' I said loudly, 'I really want to get my head down . . .'

A ripple went through the mob and they started to move away in an indistinguishable mass of trousers and skirts, suits, gingham check arms rubbing against one another, and I could hear quite clearly the rustling mass of their garments, someone's watch scraped the wall, and the drop of their feet, relaxed by drink, clopping and clattering softly one after the other, irregularly, like many muffled cricket balls rolling down a staircase.

At last, we had begun to make some progress.

I thought of them as one large dying organism, the fringes of which kept reactivating themselves. They seemed to have an insatiable capacity for introducing leading conversations as they stood on the threshold. In this spirit I actually pushed them out through the door on to the landing.

'Hey,' said someone, 'steady *on* . . .'

Their feet thundered on the stairs. I could hear them:

'*I'm* going that way . . .'

'What, towards the Porta Romana?'

'Anyone else for oltr'Arno?'

'Stop *pushing* you'll . . .' said Edgar.

'Is there a light?' said Sandra.

'What's the hold-up?' said Sidney.

I knew what the hold-up was. There wasn't a light and they were all trapped on the stairs in the dark, because they couldn't see how to open the bottom door on to the street. It had a Byzantine bolt, that had to be twisted before it was drawn back. I yawned and left them. They would find their way eventually.

In the kitchen Mooney was asleep with his head on his chest. His legs were folded one over the other and I could see the punch-punch of his blood beating as the toe of his winkle-picker rose and fell. He farted and gave a sigh, raising his head with closed eyes and licking his lips as if he had a nasty taste in his mouth. Before him on the table lay an array of paper cups, their bottoms all stained with Chianti, and the ashtray, which was heaped high with a fine dust of ash, interspersed with lipstick-covered tips and Mooney's own soggy ends of Nazionali. I threw it in the bin and opened the window to let out the staleness. The flush in the sky was beginning to compete with the electric light. Zonda gave out a giggle in the bedroom and I heard her voice and then Don's rise and twine rapidly together. I opened the refrigerator and stared at its gleaming empty shelves. I took the last bottle of champagne out of the door.

'But is there an orange?' I said aloud.

I found two wrinkled specimens and crushed them into four tumblers and then sat and eased off the champagne cork with a 'plurp'. I took two of the fizzing tumblers and stood in the doorway of the bedroom.

'Breakfast,' I said.

Don was sitting on the edge of the bed. Zonda was standing over him, one hand on his shoulder, the other ruffling through his greasy hair.

'He's got fleas,' said Zonda.

'Hey,' said Don, 'watch your step little lady.'

'Sorry it's warm,' I said, handing them the glasses. 'There's no ice left.'

'Keep *still*,' said Zonda sharply to Don.

His hands rose to hold her round the waist.

'I can't,' he said with mock-helplessness, 'with you pushing me down on the bed all the goddamn . . .'

He looked across and grinned at me.

'I'll put them here,' I said, indicating the bedside table.

'Just *feel* these muscles,' said Zonda to me. 'Just come and feel them.'

'No thanks,' I said.

'And guess what,' said Zonda, writhing away backwards and whispering. 'He's got a *gun*.'

'How did you know that?' said Don.

'A real gun.'

'Where?' I asked.

'In his bag,' said Zonda, high-kicking twice.

'Hey,' said Don, 'you bin through my things?'

'So ya berra watch aht, *guy* . . .' said Zonda in Brixtonese.

'He's an American,' I said to Zonda. 'They all have guns, didn't you know?'

'I'm still going to fuck this one,' said Zonda, her eyes shining like glowworms, 'if you go and leave me.'

'I rather think you're not in any condition to do that sort of thing,' I said. Zonda froze, and closed her eyes.

Don dropped his mouth and looked from one to the other of us.

'Whatsamarrer, hon?' he said.

'Anyone for backgammon?' I said, archly.

Don flopped backwards on to the bed, the bulge in his Sta-Prest trousers looking enormous.

'You'll have to teach me,' he said to Zonda.

'You absolute bitch,' said Zonda to me. 'Yes, let's play . . .'

199

'Bring your gun,' I said to Don.

To my surprise, he did. We sat and played three games of backgammon on the kitchen table while Zonda watched, the gun lying between us next to the board. It was a Rossi .38 Special with a blue steel barrel and chamber and a curved wooden butt. Unloaded. Mooney looked as if he were pretending to sleep at the end of the table, but the full glass of Buck's Fizz had only one or two bubbles in it now.

'For cash?' I said to Don after a couple of games. 'Just to raise the interest?'

I looked across at Zonda who was idly spinning the gun in circles on the shiny surface of the table.

'Darling, don't do that . . .'

'It's not loaded,' said Zonda, defiantly.

'I don't care,' I said.

I beat him easily, taking in three thousand lire.

'Cards perhaps?'

'Hey, yeah, poker,' said Don, 'I can't get the hang of this stuff, but poker . . . you wanna play poker?'

It was curious, this habit of asking himself rhetorical questions all the time. Don was better at five-card stud. He played with animal cunning, lifting the corners of his cards and all that sort of thing. Zonda was hopeless at cards. She always lost her count. I won again, raking in the money theatrically with two hands, even though it was only a matter of five thousand lire. Don whistled through his teeth and every now and again burst out like a tone-deaf Dean Martin:

'Luck! Be my lady tooooniiiight . . .'

It grew softer and softer until he only repeated it under his breath.

Zonda was fading visibly, mouth opening, lips turned outwards as they relaxed, revealing tiny striations of purple where the skin had chapped and been pulled off in strips.

She was pale, almost greenish, in the mixture of electric light and full dawn. She rose from the table in a trance.

'Night . . .' she said, and trailed away towards the bedroom. Don and I looked after her.

'Night hon,' he said.

Her toes turned in as she dragged her turquoise espadrilles over the kitchen tiles and she rolled visibly from side to side with each step. At the doorway of the bedroom she kicked one of them off, lolled bumping round the doorjamb, and disappeared.

Immediately Don put in to borrow some chips. I refused the loan, saying that there wasn't much point in my winning the chips if I had to give them back to him. We had given Zonda some chips from time to time, he said. That was different, I said.

'They are *my* chips,' I said. 'I own them.'

'Then the game is over,' he said standing up.

'Wait,' I said. I jumped up and searched through the kitchen and brought back the Rummikub pieces. I won them one by one, grumbling all the time that I had to pit my real pile against his stack of plastic.

'Have you got any more?' he asked.

Without a word I got up and searched the house. At length, I found a box of tiddlywinks I bought for Zonda which had fallen down behind the fridge.

'Now we've got enough to play good poker. And I'm gonna whup ya,' said Don. 'Head to head.'

'We'll see,' I said.

On his deal, I had a pair of tens. But he had an ace and made a sizeable bet. I called.

On the next face-up cards, I had an eight and he had a nine. Quickly, he put down the deck and looked at his spare card. I knew then that he didn't have another ace, simply because he wouldn't have forgotten an ace. He probably held a nine or an eight, reminded by the cards we had just drawn.

He bet. I raised. He called. I felt even more confident now that he held nines. He must have a pair or he wouldn't have called, but I was almost certain he didn't have aces because he would have

201

raised again. Not once had he tried to tempt me by soft play. He had to have nines, I decided.

He dealt. I had a three. He got one of my tens, which may have made him think I had eights, not tens.

He bet rather heavily.

I pushed my whole stack forward.

He looked at me nervously.

'How much did you bet?' he said.

'More than you can call,' I said.

'Count it,' he said, looking at his meagre stack of chips.

'You count it,' I said. 'Look, if you call I win everything. So just push out your chips.'

He grinned at me.

'I could have aces,' he said.

'If you do, we'll count the bet,' I said. If he had aces, I thought, he would not be hesitating.

'I can beat eights,' he said.

'Not if you don't call my raise,' I said. I glanced at my watch. 'It's now or never.'

'I'm going to call you,' he said. He pushed out his columns of red and yellow chips.

'My tens beat your nines,' I said, flipping my face-down card over and reaching for the pot.

'You're a lucky bastard,' he said.

'It's not *all* luck,' I said, looking at him over a pile of lire notes, dollars, Rummikub pieces, and tiddlywinks.

He looked me in the eye. 'You're not only a lucky bastard. You're one arrogant son-of-a-bitch!' He looked over at Mooney. 'What are we gonna do now?'

'A gentleman,' I said, shuffling the cards Vegas-fashion, 'is never bored.'

'Well, I ain't no gentleman,' he said, picking up the Rossi and breaking open the cylinder. 'Got a rag?'

'Exactly,' I said, under my breath.

'Got a rag?' said Don. 'What you say?'

202

'Behind you,' I said. 'I think Zonda has some under the sink.'

He laid the gun down on the table and twisted round. Mooney gave a jump and another sigh at the end of the table.

I picked up the Rossi and swung the cylinder in with a wave of the arm. I pointed it at Don's head.

Like a slow-motion overarm bowler, he was bringing the chamois down on to the table, expelling his breath.

'Heh,' he said, 'knock it off, will ya?'

I was pointing the gun at his face.

He grabbed, flicking up the chamois.

'I am a liveryman of the Ancient Order of Fishmongers,' I announced. 'I have the freedom of the City of London and if convicted of homicide I have the right to be hung by a silken cord from the centre of Blackfriars Bridge . . .'

I pulled the trigger as the smelly leather flopped over my vision.

'C'*mon*,' he muttered wrenching the gun away from me. 'I wanna *clean* it.'

I pulled the chamois off my face.

'Asshole,' said Don, breaking it open again. 'Don't you ever try that again.'

'I was quite good at school,' I said. 'A marksman in the OTC.'

'*School?*' said Don, showing the gap between his teeth. 'This *is*n't *school*, Raymond. It was point-blank range and you missed. Where I come from you don't get another chance.'

'D'you play chess?' I asked. 'Billiards?'

'Nope. Wassamarrer with you anyway?'

'I'm just trying to find something else I can honourably defeat you at.'

'Oh I get it,' said Don with a full grin. 'Sore cause I was foolin' around with Zonda, huh?'

'I know,' I said, 'let's find out who *would* have died.'

'Well, you heard what she said in there, man,' said Don, patting his duck's arse and rolling on his real behind like a mannequin. 'I do believe I'm gonna get me some *tail* . . .'

'You haven't even the courage for *that* . . .' I said, primly.

'What you talking about?'

'With or without,' I said indicating the pistol he was rubbing, 'I don't mind. I suppose without might be less inconvenient.'

'What you mean . . . this?' He held the gun up.

'The laws of probability give us each a one in six chance,' I said. 'It's quite simple . . . and no one suffers, unless you'd *like* to play it that way . . .'

'What, Russian Roulette?' said Don.

'You may choose,' I said, leaning forward, my hands clasped across my belly, 'since you are the guest . . . seeing that you are masochistically inclined, which is interesting. A masochistic coke-head, an interesting type I haven't encountered before.'

'That wasn't coke,' said Don. 'It was smack.' He grinned again, showing that big gap between his front teeth: 'Smack's a whole lot more accurate.'

'That settles it,' I said, briskly, like a zealous scoutmaster. 'Whoever wins get the girl. Pistols. I think we can just about manage thirty paces . . .'

'Raybaby, *I'm* the one that's supposed to be stoned, remember . . . Jeez, you must have a contact high.'

'I've got my grandfather's duelling pistols somewhere . . . under the bed, I think. I don't think we ever unpacked them . . .' I reached over and opened the fridge, wobbling back on to my chair with the almost empty bottle of Marc held by the neck. 'The condemned are entitled to a last drink.' I poured out a couple of slugs. 'And incidentally, don't call me "Raybaby".'

I stood up.

'Bring the gun,' I said, wandering off past the bedroom into the black hole of the front room. Somebody had switched off the light. I put it on and stared round at the little heaps of cigarette ash and fallen paper cups that indicated where each group had been. I could hear the babel again as I looked across the expanse of fetid air. I lurched into the stepladder and knocked off a shower of items on my way to the shutters. I threw them open and turned round with my back to the window. Don was still sitting at the end of a long square corridor of shadow.

'*Bring* the bloody *gun*,' I said, my voice echoing in the empty room.

Don was bent over the table. He blew into the Rossi's barrel.

'Bloody,' said his deep voice, and he blew again. 'Is that a swear word?'

The telephone gave out one long deafening ring. It was authoritative. Lying on the floor with the lead indefinitely extended, it looked like an animal straining at the leash to come towards me.

I ran to it and picked up the receiver. There was a hissing noise, then a galaxy of tinkles like stars in a black firmament.

'Mooney?' said the faint, but very harsh voice of a woman. 'Is that Mr Mooney?'

'This is an associate,' I said. 'Mr Mooney is indisposed at the moment . . .'

'This is Dodie Maxwell? . . . United States Eurodollar Recyling Programme?'

'Yes?'

'Would you give Mr Mooney a message?'

'Assuredly,' I heard myself say.

'What's that you said?'

'I said "Yes",' I said, poking my finger into the side of one of the cement sacks.

'I don't like this line . . . There's something on this line . . .'

I listened. I heard her saying to someone else: 'I think there's something on the line . . . I think they've got something on the line . . .' Then she came a little clearer and the hissing stopped.

'OK . . .' she said to someone not me. 'Hello, hello . . . is that the person I was speaking with just now? Hello . . . ?'

'Yes . . .'

'Could you give me your name?'

'Bosanquet.'

'Look Mr . . . Bosanquet? Could you tell Mr Mooney that we

have spoken with Mr Drakulič and right now we have a facility here for eight hundred million dollars . . .'

'Eight hundred million,' I repeated, looking up as Mooney took the receiver abruptly out of my hand.

'It's for you,' I said, lying down on my back beside him on the floor. I looked up at his sweating face as he nodded animatedly at the wall as if she was there in the room:

'But of course, Miss Maxwell, hard copy tomorrow when I've just made one or two final adjustments . . . penalty for non-performance . . . clorsing hasn't been finally arranged yet, but I think we'll be going into that within the week . . . yes . . .'

I stared at the freckled hand placed flat on the cement-strewn floor near my eyes. The nails were long and yellow and where the wrist emerged from the frayed grey wristband of the shirtsleeves, there was a bunch of wiry red hairs. I fell asleep looking at the stubby fingers as if each were a small separate animal.

When I woke, Mooney was stretched out, stiff, like a comic cadaver beside the phone, propped up against the sacks, his papers beside him. The bedroom door was closed, an un-precedented thing, and also pointless because one could see through from the kitchen into the bedroom via the small window near the lavatory wall. When I looked through this, I could see Zonda's pale, creased forehead and a hand beside her head, palm upwards in the position of a child warding off a threat. Don lay on his stomach, his arms wrapped around the pillow, head resting on one of his arms. His back was covered. I went into the bathroom and closed the door. It was freezing cold, but I took everything off. The phone started to ring as I stepped into the shower. Mooney must have woken instantly, because it scarcely had time to complete its one long tone before I could dimly hear his voice full of its usual combination of urgency and reassurance. I wondered, as the water ran down the sides of my hair, spilling over my chest and shoulders and filling my ears, who was calling.

We hadn't ordered the Princess's limousine to Monte Carlo, or made any of the arrangements as yet. Since it was off-season, it wasn't going to be difficult to get a car. (But a limousine?) I decided that I had probably better take that in hand. It was more likely that we would get one than we wouldn't, but it needed seeing to. Deaf-Aid downstairs knew several garages, who could do us a deal of some sort. Plus De Negris was supposed to be coming from Livorno with the other car, according to Mooney.

I stepped out of the shower with the radio skittering on about the American hostages in Tehran and the scandal of the Vatican Bank. The chaos of the kitchen was disgusting. The gun lay wrapped in the chamois on the table. Lying by the side of the inlaid backgammon set, it looked like an archaeological find, something from some remote and violent era of civilisation. I had, I remembered, used up all the orange juice. Don hadn't taken me very seriously, and he had been right, I thought. I put the coffee on and opened the bedroom door. Don was wrapped in one of Zonda's big turquoise bathtowels. They stirred as I poked in the cupboard for some clean clothes. I was suddenly very angry for a moment with my socks, and threw them hither and thither in a frenzy.

'What are you looking for?' said Zonda.

Don sighed and settled.

I chose not to answer.

'*Caro*,' said Zonda opening her eyes and looking at the ceiling, '*che voi?*'

'You haven't seen my clean shirts, have you, the ones I brought back from the lavanderia?'

'*Le ho messo nell'armadio?*'

'Which cupboard?'

'*Quello*,' she said, waving a limp arm and shutting her eyes again.

'Do you want coffee?' I asked.

'Milky coffee,' said Zonda.

'And Don?'

'Sure thing,' said Don. 'Make it black for me.'

Torn between administration and retribution, but conscious of the bathtowel, I got dressed in the kitchen. I wear very long dark socks because my sister Julia once said to me that what she found particularly hideous in men was the inch or so of white flesh that regularly appeared between the elasticated top of the sock, and the end of the trouser. Under the towel, these socks swept up my legs like tights. All I had on. I waltzed out of the bedroom, feeling like a butler in a Turkish bath. They laughed. I had other things on my mind, however, and all this was registered in a kind of abstract blur. I heard them discussing the Eurythmics 'Sweet Dreams Are Made of This'. Don hadn't heard of it. Zonda got her friends to send her The Police, and Culture Club and the latest UB40 albums, and I was forced to listen to this stuff. Our records were thus a mixture of South London reggae and punk rock, and collections of grand opera. I even had some seventy-eights of Richard Tauber. But it was Ann Ziegler and Webster Booth I put on now, rather too loudly, as I moved the trash on the table to make a space for the four cups. 'We'll Gather Lilacs in the Spring Again' I thought just right for this merry winter's morning. The hissing, cracked recording from the BBC archives accompanied me as I poured the coffee and took it into them.

Zonda made a face.

'God,' she said, 'what have you got on?'

'Very tuneful,' I said.

Don was rolling a Marlboro in between his fingers and tapping the end of his knee, raised beneath the bedclothes. I saw that he still had his underpants on.

Zonda began to jig from side to side in the bed, almost upsetting their coffee.

'Hey,' she said, in her Chip voice. 'Guv?'

'Are you addressing me, by any chance?' I asked.

Zonda dug Don in the ribs.

'Hear that?' she said. 'Fackin' English Upper Clorssse . . .'

'Crazy man . . .' said Don.

'It's not crazy,' said Zonda. 'It's how he talks, inn'it Raymond? Innit, you *cunt*?'

'Hey . . .' said Don, mildly.

'Vass how we tork dahn in Sarf Lannen, innit Ray?'

'I'm afraid I wouldn't know,' I said. 'As far as I'm concerned to move across the Thames is to move into the outer darkness, to become as one benighted . . .'

I drifted out and took Mooney his coffee. Zonda was beginning to explain, switching for the purpose to the voice of a brigadier's wife just back from an afternoon's golf, the nature of my noble family tree.

'There's not a trace of real, what one would call, *snobbery* about him . . .' she was saying as I exited.

Mooney sat up and took his coffee and we sat together on the step. A terrible odour oozed from the region of his shoes.

'You smell awful, if you don't mind my saying,' I said.

'Yes . . .' he said vaguely, as he slurped at his bowl of coffee. 'We've a busy day, today, Raymond. We'll be wanting to set off soon now . . .'

'I've got some clothes I can lend you, actually,' I said, looking at his size. 'I think we're about the same . . .'

I got up.

'Come with me,' I said.

'I'm expecting a call,' he said, 'from Irving.'

'That's all right,' I told him, 'I'll look after that, while you change . . .'

I took him up to the bathroom and took out some clothes from the cupboard. A pair of grey corduroy trousers, a tweed jacket, and a pair of long brown woollen stockings. Tactfully, I threw in a pair of my special white baggy underpants too. He was saying something about the dollar exchange rate as I closed the door on him. I heard the thunder of his piss, as I opened the door again.

'Sorry,' I said. 'It's best if you let the shower run for a few minutes before stepping into it.'

'Thank you,' he said, without turning round.

While he was in there, there were three phone calls. Each time, he came out in whatever he had on and stood on the top of the step between the kitchen and living-room, listening for a moment. Then he went back in. His body was white and pear-shaped, as he stood in my baggy underpants and my special extra-long dark-brown socks. He had a scar running vertically down the middle of his belly, disappearing without signs of diminution into the underpants. He kept his spectacles on, even thought they were soaked with drops of water and steam. The Elastoplast had turned from a streaked pink to grey. Two of the calls were from people ringing to say thank you for the party. Zonda came running to answer Philomena, covering herself in my navy blue naval officer's dressing-gown. There was the usual playing with whatever was in sight, while she giggled her careful lubricative remarks. Zonda was working herself up to asking Philomena for a job in the boutique, although it sounded about as imbecile, I thought, as inane, as anything could be.

'Better get up,' I said as she went back. 'There's quite a lot to do today.'

She pulled a face and came over to me. She had a large red spot on her cheek.

'What's the matter?'

'Nothing,' I said, easing myself up on to my toes and down again, as she lunged and clung to me. Her breath smelt.

She pulled another face, and ran clumsily, toes turning in, back into the bedroom. Her legs needed shaving I noted. The door banged shut behind her.

The next call was from Steve, one of my informal bookmakers. He wondered if I wanted to go to Il Trotto. Il Trotto, I told him, was the absolute pits. He agreed, but said that he didn't have time to go to Milan today, which was the only full meeting. He reminded me that I owed him half a million lire, and asked if I could pay enough to let him have a reasonably entertaining time at the trotting.

'People who go to the trotting don't *deserve* to be paid,' I said, with a fair degree of desperation, since to pay Steve was the last thing I had counted on that day.

'Raymond, you're stalling,' said Steve.

I admitted this, and began to haggle, as he expected me to.

'How much do you *absolutely* need?' I asked.

'How much can you afford?' Steve asked cautiously.

In the end I beat him down to one hundred and twenty thousand, and arranged to meet him at Repubblica. I looked at my watch. It was approaching noon. Mooney had put on my corduroy trousers during this conversation, his face covered in shaving soap, his spectacles spattled with little flecks of it.

'Hurry up, everyone,' I said in a loud hearty voice. 'Chop, chop. It's nearly time for lunch!'

I thought that if I finished that translation of the ineffably boring piece about the change in regular bus routes for the Commune, we could probably all go to lunch. Besides, I was beginning to need a drink very badly.

I sat at the kitchen table. The table was so crammed that things began to fall off the end as I pushed up to make room for my typewriter and papers. In twenty minutes I had the thing typed, but couldn't quite make sense of one phrase, which I had rendered as 'taking up and alighting points' – this clearly wasn't good enough. The phone rang. This time it was indeed Irving, who was making final arrangements to meet us in Monte Carlo. He told me that Michael Casey would also be turning up and asked if I had made arrangements for the aeroplane.

'Not yet,' I said. 'Things have been a little fluid here.'

'I see. Well, you'd better take charge of that, because Gerrard won't do anything on his own account.'

'First things first. I'm *dressing* him at the moment.'

I turned, and he was standing on the top step again, but this time he had a jacket on too. I hardly recognised my own clothes, as I gave him the receiver.

I went back to pondering the problem. 'Alighting . . . setting down points' I wondered. It offended me profoundly that there didn't seem to be an English equivalent for these phrases in Italian. You couldn't say 'taking-up points' either. What about embarkation and disembarkation-stages? No, because that repeated the phrase. Embarkation and alighting? No, that mixed up two different kinds of mood, active and passive. I tried it out to Zonda, talking across Mooney, who was busy on the phone. He kept saying: 'That's interesting . . . that's interesting . . .'

In the end, I typed in 'taking-up and alighting points'. Zonda suggested 'hovering and vomiting points' from the bedroom, but that is, I said, because she was feeling simultaneously sick and guilty about the housework.

I wanted a minute word with Irving about Don, but thought I had best discharge some of my duties first.

As I had anticipated, she and Don wanted to stay in bed.

'I'll clear up,' she said vaguely.

She made a production, as the Americans say, out of Mooney's new clothing, adjusting his tie and all that sort of thing, and we set out. I delivered the translation, while giving Mooney some guidebook information about the town. He was urgent to find a telex machine, so we set out for the Italian tourist office, where I knew they had one. On the way, he kept remembering calls he had to make, so we went into a couple of bars where he shuttled back and forth in the dark crowded interiors between toilet and telephone. I drank several glasses of not very good champagne while he pushed his way through the crowd of fastidious Italians, all grasping their sandwiches in paper napkins, endlessly checking to see if their fingers were touching the food.

The Arno was brown and swollen. Great triangular chunks of ice floated in its surging waters. There was a fine rain coming down over the town as we made our way down by the side of the Ponte Vecchio past all the closed jewelry shops and boutiques. We only had plastic macs and the wind was cutting as we came over the bridge. Taking-up and setting-down points, I was thinking. We could have done with a few of those. Conversation was difficult. You had to shout at your own shoulder and hope your words would carry to the other person. Mooney, wearing my clothes, his pockets stuffed full of papers that kept threatening to blow away in the whipping gusts of wind, looked like a solid ghost, a hologram of a person, a kind of super-robot that could perform every human function, even walk through the slush and rain at my side and go grey with pallor and have his teeth chatter, his lips chap, and his eyelids coat with sleet.

In the Commune office Mooney wanted to dictate the text of the message to me, but we had to wait because my hands were too cold. We sat on two tubular chairs and I made pleasantries with the girls. One was called Rosa and came from Romagna and the other was a Calabrese called Maria Domenica. They let us pay for the use of the telex machine. We had coffee in the back room, while Mooney scribbled and then dictated to me a telex to one Eamon Costello in the Isle of Man and another to the unfortunate Clyde Wellcombe. They were identical:

WE ARE NOW CLOSING PROCEDURES FOR TWO MAJOR TRANS-ACTIONS WISH TO EXECUTE THE CONTRACT FOR THE PUR-CHASE OF THE CUMBERLAND TENNESSEE RANCH WEEKEND IN MONTE CARLO AND WE WILL REQUIRE YOUR PRESENCE IN EUROPE FOR THIS PURPOSE. REGARDS. THE PROJECT-FOR-THE-AMERICAS INVESTMENT CORPORATION.

At the bank, I took out two hundred thousand lire. Mooney sat on a chair in the reception area and kept staring at his battered pocket-book, turning the pages over, as if he was weighing up who to telex or telegram or telephone next. The bank teller asked me if I wanted to know what was in my account, but I didn't. I knew there wasn't anything in my account. I telephoned Julia to get a loan, but she wasn't in. Meanwhile I could see Mooney in the next booth yapping away to someone, no doubt on long-distance. The girls had paid me for the translation, so at least we could have lunch. I wanted to go to Da Noi because they have those delicious little fish things, but it was too far and I wasn't sure it was open.

Mooney's calls came to forty-five thousand lire. He got out his wallet and waved it at me, but I knew that this meant, not that he was going to pay, but that I should. I decided at that point that I was going to have to leave Steve standing in the cold at the Piazza Repubblica. There were some sacrifices that had to be made, by some people, all over the world, and this was one – to enable us to go to lunch.

I took Mooney to Marco's, which was very busy, but Marco came himself and turfed some people out so that we could have a corner table. Mooney said he would have whatever I had and I ordered a bottle of their house wine which was very good Carmignano red, straight from the *fattoria*, and *Fettuccine alla Marinara* to start with. While we were waiting we started to discuss what we were going to do with the stud-farm. I drew a plan of the present buildings on a paper tablecloth according to Mooney's instructions. He kept stabbing his finger down on the tablecloth and saying no – here, Raymond, *here* and snatching the biro from me and drawing upside-down various extensions in spidery lines that wrecked my neat imitations of scale drawings. In this way we got the rough outlines of the place down, before the pasta arrived. I studied them and then began to paint the picture of the kind of alterations I wanted to make.

'You want plenty of air, you know.' He squinted down at the scribbles on the napkin. 'I'm against this idea of building them round in a square on three sides.'

I asked him why not. His face creased up as if he were in pain and he looked around the restaurant.

'Air always hangs in an enclosed space. Have you noticed that?'

I objected that it was outside. It depended on where the property was situated. It could provide shelter.

'If it's shelter it needs then you shouldn't have built it there.'

He seized the pen and began to draw a fresh set of rough cubes, free-standing.

'Your northern aspect is cold and cheerless and a southern is no good – hot in summer, d'you see . . . So . . .' His tongue-tip

214

appeared at the side of his mouth, as he squared up the sides of the building upside-down with quick rough strokes of the pen, finally adding the points of the compass with a flourish.

'There you are – east and west is best. That way you get morning and afternoon sun on the windows. Windows on both sides, door, you see, that type of a way at each end or in the middle on each side between the windows. Maximum air and light is what we're aiming for, Raymond. There.'

He looked down at his handiwork with satisfaction.

I raised the problem of prevailing winds on the site. But we were already into the question of ventilation.

'Foul air in a stable is warm air, that's the rule. Give me your hand here now . . .' Roughly he seized my hand and drew it towards him across the table. Instinctively, I drew back as I felt his hot breath like a sudden flame on my skin, as he breathed pure blue smoke over the back of my wrist and relapsed into a fit of coughing. 'Carbonic acid gas . . .' He coughed again, patting his chest. 'You see it is heavier than air at equal temperatures, but when it's heated – as it is when it is given off by the lungs . . .' Another paroxysm. '. . . it's lighter than pure air.'

'So you only have to provide an exit in the roof and . . .'

He smiled.

'Exactly. It will escape by its own inherent lightness. If on the other hand we deny it the opportunity of doing so, what will happen then? Eh?'

He looked at me with the glassy, unseeing eye of the expounder.

'It will condense?' I guessed.

'And then?'

'Depends on your drainage?' I ventured rather frivolously as I looked for the pasta over his shoulder.

'*Con*dense . . .' – the way he said this, the stress falling like a hammer-blow on the word's first syllable, made it sound remarkably like 'Nonsense! – '. . . and descend as vapour running down the inside of the roof pitch and down the walls . . .'

He nodded to himself, grinding his cigarette into the ashtray and picking up the biro the tip of which began to hover in minute circles above the tangle of cancelled yards and stable boxes looking for a space in which to insert the latest design:

'Where it will evaporate in the heat given off from the bodies of the animals and present itself again in due course to the nostrils to be breathed.'

'That is because, as things are at present, the animals are standing in a vacuum,' I countered.

We were off then into draughts, louvres, and air-bricks, and thence into floors and drainage. We canvassed the merits of various types of paving. Granite cubes six inches deep, he insisted, were by far the most durable. When I objected that they would become slippery when worn, he cocked his head on one side:

'No, that's the beauty of them, you re-chisel them, you see Raymond! Good God, you should know this – like they used to at Aldershot. They lasted sixty years there!'

I was determined to have hard-burnt bricks – blue, iron, vitrified, adamantine or clinker – it didn't matter what variety. Preferably from Staffordshire.

'They are very good at first,' he admitted. 'But what you find is it's actually impossible for them to bake the brick equally hard throughout and the fact of the matter is – I know this from experience – when the outer facing is chipped or worn through, this sort of paving wears very rapidly into holes, you know.'

I wanted Etruria bricks with transverse channels cut in them to reduce slipperiness.

He shook his head:

'Stables paved with transverse bricks,' he said, as if articulating a new law of nature, 'are seldom, if *ever*, sweet.'

I was distinctly nettled at this and asked why.

'It stands to sense. They cannot be swept out thoroughly and consequently they retain a portion – however small – of the urine and debris of dung and bedding.'

Peevishly I mapped out a system of circular yards, very self-contained, but all communicating with one another, which would

216

contain different groups of animals. I painted a picture of February mornings at a thoroughly reconstructed Turvey, the horses clattering through the mist for their early morning work-outs, which I thought would appeal to his apparently sentimental attachment to the place, and ordered another bottle of the red. We were both beginning to enjoy this. Mooney had a way with him of listening which was flattering to the speaker. There were all sorts of diminutive sounds of encouragement, while he actually inclined his ear (his good ear, I hadn't thought at the time that he might be deaf at all . . .), like the old His Master's Voice advertisement, towards the speaker, and stared glassily into his wine or at a particular spot on the tablecloth while he grunted, rhythmically, with each pause for breath or emphasis which I made.

It only occurred to me later that he wasn't listening at all.

'And tell me Raymond, what's your pattern of investment for the stock?' he said at last.

He was representing Pequeño Investments now. In fact I realised that one of his secrets was that he was always representing something else.

'Just a mo,' he added, 'splosh time . . .'

He levered himself out of the chair and waddled off with his stiff and open stride. Even his splosh was tactical. As his jacket rose up at the front, I saw that he had tied the trousers round the waist, which were too small for his hanging belly, with one of the spotted silk ties which my mother had given me for my birthday the previous year. It was the red one, of which I was particularly fond, and my retinas retained the glimpse of it I had just caught, long after he had disappeared, the folds of pure silk crushed and twisted into a thin cord stretched tight under the bulge of shirt.

'You know,' I joked, when he came back, 'Franco used to do that. It was one of his favourite tricks with awkward opposition.'

'What?' he asked as he sat down with a sigh.

'Go for a pee,' I said. 'Apparently, he had a very weak bladder, which he converted to a tactical weapon of great delicacy.'

217

'Is that a fact?' said Mooney, stuffing a Nazionali into his mouth.

'That's how he managed to come away with such a lot when he and Hitler had their conference on Hitler's train about Spain coming into the war. I think you've got a similar gift,' I said.

'The moment is not particularly awkward, is it?' he said, as Marco appeared with the pasta. 'In fact, it's propitious . . .' he said, opening his arms to the approaching Marco.

'*Signor? Propizio. Ah si, si . . .*' said Marco, winking at me, and laying the plates down with a quick flourish. He was already looking back towards the counter and easing his way out between backs, well into the next job.

I produced a piece of paper from my pocket.

'Naturally, this is only a rough sketch of how things would go,' I said modestly, 'but I think it gives you some idea.'

It was based on five minutes' calculation at the kitchen table and a single phone call to Sergio in Milan. It was a test for Mooney, because it would show how serious he was, I thought. It developed a scheme, whereby you invested in fashionable stuff one year and then did the real breeding investment the following year, alternating like this so that eventually the profits from the fashionable stuff would begin to pay for more *recherché* breeding activities. These were based on Tesio's theories, and would take at least fifteen years to really develop. I mentioned a few obvious lines in the fashionable stuff, and then some real old chestnuts in the recondite breeding lines.

He smiled at some of the names, repeating them fondly. Then he handed the paper back to me.

'Hmm . . .' he said, beginning to spoon up his pasta, 'interesting, and feasible I think. You've quite a head on your shoulders, Raymond, I can see that . . .'

'I just happen to have been thinking about this for a long time,' I said, pouring him the last splash of the red and holding up the empty fiasco for Marco to see. He nodded from afar and shouted down into the cellar.

The trouble was, I didn't know whether he had swallowed it or not. I looked at his grey hair curling on each side of his forehead like rams' horns, his spectacles with the Sellotape and the magnifying lenses that showed a pair of gigantic, watery, grey-green eyes that seemed to move very slowly with a sudden rapid flick now and again, like a reptile's eyes. How could you tell? The absurdity of the situation never occurred to me at the time – that here I was having lunch with him, as if he were a bank manager. But that is exactly what he was, as far as I was concerned. I had, however, discovered one very useful thing. Mooney loved plans, plans of all description; maps he would squint at for hours, sketches he could always be diverted with if things were difficult, prognoses of every description in schematic form, he would think seriously about from every angle without a trace of self-consciousness. He was a man, like me, only at home in the future. The present, apart from its sensual pleasures, I told myself, was an informal mess, an embarrassment of poverty. The past, an obscure drive, or a set of anchor-weights.

'What could be more agreeable?' I said about nothing in particular, as Marco put the bottle on the table.

Mooney grunted, concentrating on getting hold of the slippery bits of pasta that were trying to elude his fork.

'Little *divel*s,' he said, chewing very rapidly.

'In fact,' I said, 'why don't we go out to Pisa this evening and have a look at my horses. Giuseppe would be very glad to see us, and we could have a very agreeable time.'

The thing to do, I decided, was to furnish the present as richly as possible.

'Yes, we could do that indeed,' he said without enthusiasm.

There was the same difficulty in drawing him out and getting him on your side as there was with my father. I had decided when I was twenty-five, and sharing a flat with Julia in Ladbroke Grove, that it was time to cultivate my father, as a friend, as an equal, and to put an end to all this awe of childhood. Besides my money was beginning to run out, unlike Julia's, who invested hers in various properties, always selling at the right time and getting a good price, so that, even if she didn't make a profit, she always kept on an even keel. I had always kept away, a mixture of rebellion and shame, but Julia went down faithfully every Sunday for lunch to Black Dog Barns, their oast-house smallholding just outside Rochester, and acted as a faithful intermediary for both parties. The parents didn't really understand my attitudes, and Julia helped represent me in at least a faintly intelligible light. After dinner, Pappa and I retired into the library and sat awkwardly side by side on the small leather sofa he had in there. He was talking about the difficulties of maintaining his rose garden, now that he was getting on. He knew, of course, that I was squandering my fund. Julia was quite unable to disguise that from him. What I really wanted was the promise of some more. I sympathised with him about the roses and said I could come down and give him a hand. At this point, he smelt a rat and turned to me with his angular, lean, sharply pointed face.

'Give me a *hand*,' he repeated in a tone of utter contempt.

I stared ahead at the shelves, while he gave me a long look. He wanted me to go into the City, I knew, and he had bred me for this purpose, sending me to his old prep school, putting me down at birth for his public school. I took the same examinations as he did, and failed them, while he was the best classicist of his generation. I had managed to limp into his college at Oxford. He knew me to the bone, I suddenly felt, and I could never get past the contempt, which was strangely like that of a contemporary. I wasn't just a watered-down version of him, I was a poor competitor sitting in the next desk. He had Greek and I didn't. When I tried to appease him by quoting Virgil at the dinner table, he replied with reams of guttural Homer. The timetable at the prep school had only allowed me a limited amount of time for Greek and I had never been very good at it. I got an exhibition on the strength of my Latin, but he had been a scholar in Latin and Greek, a true classicist, who had gone on to do Greats, while I turned, to his disgust, to PPE and gambling.

This all came into my head, as I pressed Mooney to come to Pisa with me. I wanted to show him my horses, to give him the sense that life for me was effortless, and agreeable. I wanted to prove to him that he was not needed, that I was indeed, by a contradiction that was not lost on me, the insouciant amateur he took me for.

The steak arrived and he brightened up. Perhaps it was those years in America, in Venezuela, but the sight of beef seemed to stir something in Mooney's heart. This was another useful piece in the indispensable jigsaw. By now, the wine was beginning to tell, and we were both thoroughly hot under the collar. I judged it was time to move against Don, while Mooney's pores were temporarily open.

'Don's on the board of Pequeño Investments, isn't he?' I enquired.

'Indeed, he is, though a lot of these positions are nominal, as I'm sure you're aware.'

'What's his main function?'

'Security,' said Mooney, keeping his eye on the piece of bleeding steak on his fork, like a tennis player about to strike a crucial lob.

'Isn't he rather expensive?'

Mooney paused with the steak halfway to his mouth.

'I don't now recall what Irving pays him,' he said, 'but he's a useful and an obliging fellow . . . a bit thoughtless, perhaps, at times . . .'

'Yes,' I said, nursing my Chianti between two palms. 'I have noticed. He's the sort of chap you presumably want to keep in the background with some of your clients, I should imagine?'

He huffed and puffed, not really wanting to say anything. He sprayed out one or two unintelligible exclamations between ruminative chews.

I laughed inwardly at what I was about to say:

'You don't really need an extra security man, now that you're over here. I can easily arrange for my Italian friends to take care of that aspect of things.'

I imagined Ettore and Marco kitted up with dark glasses and Smith and Wessons, Sta-Prest jeans and lines of coke and smack in their specially fitted rows of inside pockets. They would be outraged, the two gentlemen trainers.

'Six . . . seven of us, tomorrow,' I said. 'We'll probably need two cars . . .'

'Then let's do it,' said Mooney. 'Let us have two cars, if that's what it takes. Don is coming along. I want him there in case there's any trouble at clorsing . . .'

Time to soft-pedal.

'Of course,' I said. 'D'you like some more?'

He held out his glass.

'Trouble?' I said.

'Misunderstandings . . . difficulties . . .'

'With whom?'

'Well, the Iranians are very tense, Raymond, as I'm sure you're aware. They had to scoot out of that country by any means they could. As a result, they are a mite unprofessional about where they put their clients' money.'

'And then there's Mr Wellcombe,' I said.

'And then there's Mr Wellcombe,' he agreed.

'Who might be accompanied by some of our friends from Cleveland, Ohio,' I said, pushing slightly, knowing that he didn't want to go into this possibility.

'No, no, I'm sure that won't happen. Irving will see to that. No, it's really the unpredictable elements I'm thinking of, you always get a certain amount of leakage about these affairs, and when people get wind of it, they come like flies round the jampot.'

Marco came and twinkled by the side of the table. I ordered *ricotta* and *gorgonzola* and *macedonia* to follow with coffee and grappa.

It was obviously necessary to come at this question from a different direction.

'How did you meet him?' I asked.

After another splosh, Mooney told the story of how he'd come across Don while inspecting an orange grove in California in 1976, acting as a guard for the United Fruit Corporation. He and Irving had been amused by the fact that Don, alert, armed and challenging, was surrounded by orange peel. They had taken him on. It was only afterwards they had realised that he was under the influence of drugs.

'And has he proved valuable?' I asked.

'Well, last year someone tried to push me out of a sixth-floor window of the Flat-Iron building in New York – or at least, I *think* they were – and Don intervened . . .'

'Intervened?'

'Yes . . . he pushed the person out instead . . .'

'How very impressive,' I said, slicing up my *ricotta*. 'What do you mean, you *think* someone was trying to push you?'

'Well we had all just stepped out of the elevator, you know and there was a lot of scuffling and I could feel this fella suddenly start shoving, and Don, well, he reacted with lightning speed, and he had the fella hanging out of the window in a flash.'

'Oh,' I said, 'he didn't fall?'

'No he just dangled a bit, and by jaysus you should have seen the look on your man's kisser . . . Ha . . . ha . . . I'd like to have a home movie of the whole thing, so I could watch it late at night. I would never tire, I swear to you, of the expression on that fella's face.'

'It must have been the coke,' I said.

'I don't know what it was, but he's very quick on the draw is Don, oh yes.' He leaned back and sipped the last of the wine. 'Very quick on the draw.'

This really proved Don wasn't officer material.

'And who was he?'

'Oh,' said Mooney, without thinking, 'a business acquaintance from way back.'

'You mean an enemy?'

'Business is business,' he lifted his shoulders, 'especially in the United States . . . if you're not a gintleman,' he whined in forelock-touching, peasant brogue, 'den a fella has to scrimp and make do wid whativer he can . . . de company you find is de company you keep . . .'

The grappa arrived and Marco, in his plump, wholesome way, left the bottle on the table. The restaurant was nearly empty, I noticed, looking up.

'But let's face it,' I said, in a tone of disinterested concern, 'Don is − even I can see it − a bit unpredictable.'

As I said this, I had a vision of the bedroom door in the flat. I could even see the spots of flaking turquoise paint, spilt on the porcelain handle.

'But very good on his day,' said Mooney, covering his veined nose with one of my clean handkerchiefs and snorting into it. 'There's a lot of waiting around in this business and you can forgive a young, feisty sort of a fella like that if he gets bored now and again.'

I could see that this wasn't going to lead anywhere for now, and that it would be better to pursue some other tack. One last shot perhaps.

'Better watch the drugs though,' I advised. 'Italian law is very harsh about the degeneration of their youth, and, if they raided the flat, we could all be accessories.'

'Tomorrow, we'll all be gone,' said Mooney.

'Monégasque jails are just as bad, I imagine, and their anti-drug laws don't have a lot to choose.'

Mooney looked at me through his magnifying spectacles and a rare smile broke slowly across his face.

'Do I get the impression you haven't taken to our Mr Divine?' he said.

'Let's put it down to managerial anxiety,' I said.

I felt *slightly* rattled as I paid the bill. My back, which was turned towards the table as I chatted to Marco while he rang up the seventy thousand lire and gave me my receipt, felt transparent like a pane of glass. But this was all part of the risks of the game, after all.

Talking constantly over her shoulder to him, Zonda was pushing through the glass door and holding it for Don. I was astonished at her outfit, which was wholly unfamiliar to me. She wore a black hat with a brim, under which she had scraped back her hair, and a small woollen coat, almost like a child's coat, which should have been many sizes too small for her, but mysteriously seemed to fit. She was taking this off, and smiling radiantly at Mooney as she stood over us at the table. Underneath, she had on a heavy-knitwear turquoise sweater with a boat neck that exposed her perfect collar-bones and, when she leaned forward, dipped in the middle to show two swaying brown shadows. A pair of tight red satin pants ran into light brown suede Robin Hood bootees. All of this was new.

'Ah,' said Marco with a sigh, 'the Signorina . . .'

We watched as she patted the chair beside her for Don, who picked up a toothpick from the centre of the table, eased it over into the corner of his mouth, leaving the other hand still in his jerkin pocket, and slipped himself in beside the window. Mooney said something and she looked towards us and threw back her head to laugh as she replied.

'*Que bella*,' breathed Marco, as he came from behind the counter and began to bounce towards the table, where he came to rest, hands on his hips, while he took their order. Zonda's hand shot out and caught him by the forearm. With an exaggerated stagger of helplessness he looked back towards me or some vague audience and bent towards her, as she whispered in his ear. I looked round behind me through the dark half of the room and I could see the shadows of two waiters against the glass panes, watching. The restaurant had closed some time ago, and they were changing tablecloths and folding napkins ready for the evening session. The regular flop of the napkins was broken into by the creak of her chair and the hiss of Zonda's pants. Mooney was talking volubly, issuing staccato remarks from his straightened lips as she and Marco conspired, her hand still on his forearm. Don was staring at them with an expression of anticipation, and when Marco straightened up and said something, he sniggered and stared across at Mooney, who was still talking, while Zonda dropped her hand and made reproachful eyes upwards and then shrugged across at Mooney too. Marco turned away nodding, and then, like a stylised comic, he turned back again to her and made another remark, which set her protesting and the others laughing.

Marco was still laughing when he came back. I could smell his perfume in the half-dark at the counter.

'For the Signorina,' he said putting down the tray and turning to look, '*any*thing, ah? You are a very lucky man, Signor Raymond . . .'

'Marco, that outfit is completely new . . .' I said, rubbing thumb and forefingers together.

He stared, while he reached for the grappa bottle.

'Ma . . .' he said, ignoring the financial point and shaking his head, '*Que bella figura* . . .'

Zonda was sharing Don's Marlboro, taking very deep drags and letting the smoke out in a high spume above their heads and then giving it back to him. Her voice, slightly higher-pitched than usual, flowed above the bass ground of their interjections. I began to approach the table and I could see that her every gesture filled the air like a force-field round the little company and caused some reaction in everyone, even in the stationary Mooney.

She turned to me as I came up to the table.

'. . . doesn't pay the *slightest* attention to me,' I heard her say, as she held her arms out to me. 'Do you darling?'

Stiffly, I evaded them, and I saw the slight moment of hurt, before she recovered.

'You see?' she said, as I sat heavily beside Mooney opposite her. 'What did I tell you?'

'Oh, most ungall*ant*,' said Mooney.

'What did I say?' she said to Don, her arms still spread at shoulder level, one hand plucking his jerkin gently between finger and thumb. This was her element. She loved it, and already she was tyrannical with them, making up little rules which could be broken, so that they didn't have to move or change at all, and by not doing something they broke the rule and then somehow it was slightly coy, or if they did do something, then they acknowledged the rule and then that was something else, just as coy. She reached across and adjusted Mooney's tie.

'No, you don't wear it so high,' she said, 'like *that* . . . you wear it like this . . .'

But then she couldn't get it 'right'.

'Oh, it's a hopeless tie anyway,' she said, theatrically cashing in her chips with the soundless crash of a hand through the air.

'We have a decision to make,' I said, as Marco brought a new round of coffee and grappa.

She was still talking to Don. She *knew* – just *knew* – they would find us here.

'Ahm . . . jest waiting for a layedy . . .' I sang, tapping on the tablecloth with the heel of my empty schooner.

She turned and I saw the enormous blue eyes dancing too much, as she pouted across at me in her matching lipstick.

'How d'you like the colour coordination?' she said in a softer, deeper fashion, and without waiting for a response she took bows. I could now clearly see the rush of the coke in all her compulsive asides, in those dancing eyes that jumped and glittered as if every new phenomenon was a startling drench from a shower nozzle. She was hissing like a drummer on the sideskins, and pressing the bowl of a spoon on the tablecloth, while her neck stiffened in a series of semi-Indian movements back and forth, in time to the rhythm of a song none of us could hear. I wondered how far away or near it was for her. She was raw, I could see, red raw, in the gaps between the bits of theatre. When you got up close, she wasn't continuous at all, but fell apart into consecutive gestures. I could hear her, loudly ignoring herself every time she heard her own voice, and each time one of the little paper kites she was flying took a dive into the ground, turning away and scanning the sky for another.

227

I poured another round of grappa, and realised dimly that I wasn't going to carry on and say what I was going to say, because I had forgotten what it was. It had disappeared somewhere behind my right cheek.

'Might as well,' I said to Mooney. 'Why not?'

'Why not indeed,' he said, taking a Marlboro out of Don's packet.

She leaned back to indicate that she was listening to the conversation of the two Italian women sitting behind her, who had also stayed on, and began to translate non-stop:

'. . . when we went out to visit his mother it was just the same thing on Sunday – yes on Sunday – of course they were all there and they think I am you know beneath them – yes it is true, they all think he has married beneath him and he could have done better for himself than this little Lucchesa – I take no notice of course, I know my worth . . .'

The woman screeched with sudden laughter, and Zonda followed a split second after, a perfect screech.

'. . . and it is much greater than theirs . . .'

The woman stopped. Zonda stopped. The woman slowly turned round and stared. Zonda, shoulders shaking, looked from one to the other of us in turn.

I cleared my throat.

'I was saying that I think we have a decision to make . . .'

'Look at the hair,' said Zonda, staring through the window at a group of figures bent against the wind, and she began to plump her own hair at the back and imitate with absolute perfection the voice of a Florentine just back from the hairdresser's.

'. . . I was horrified at first when I looked in the mirror and saw what he had done – and I'm still not sure, but I like it much better now – one gets used to it, you know . . .'

But she hadn't patience for it, and spun away into another little drama, in which she was a cigarette addict, trembling for a cigarette, and I was a cruel Nazi doctor, torturing her by keeping her off them.

'We either go,' I said, 'or we stay . . .'

'You do . . . you do . . . you *do* . . .' said Zonda, loudly, with her eyes closed.

'No,' I said, 'I didn't say that . . .'

'Honey,' said Don, leaning towards her, but keeping his eyes on me, 'I hate to say this, but I think Ray wants to go . . .'

'He didn't . . . he doesn't . . .' said Zonda, madly, batting her eyelids and lighting another cigarette, 'but anyway . . . bugger him . . . I'm going to . . .'

'I merely thought . . .' I began.

'Well don't luv,' said Zonda, looking poisonously at me. 'It doesn't suit yer . . .'

'I merely thought that it might prove an agreeable close to the afternoon to show these two the horses at Pisa . . .'

'Oh, darling,' said Zonda, the tears glistening in her eyes. 'Isn't he *sweet* . . .' She gave a wriggle, her voice squeaking off the scale into inaudibility. 'He's just such a *sad* little creature . . .'

Calmly, she picked a piece of fluff from my jacket, and left a hot palm for a second against my cheek.

'I'd *love* to go out and see the horses . . . I think it's a *marvellous* idea . . . and you *must* come, both of you . . . Giuseppe and Francesca are *so* nice, they'd love to see you both . . .'

It was too much. Too much the other way, and one could hear it building through the emphases, to some ignominy or other, but Don and Mooney were nodding seriously, much to my surprise, as if they didn't hear this shrieking nonsense.

What marvellous value. She had them both, even Mooney, gaping. He hadn't gone for a splosh for a least five minutes.

I stood up.

'I'll take care of the transport,' I said.

'Wait, *wait* . . .' said Zonda, uncrossing her legs and following me, as I turned in my stiff, almost military fashion, and began to stride off towards the door. It was almost dark in the other half of the restaurant, as she ran into the shadows after me, her knees frou-frouing against one another, in the scarlet pants.

'Raymond, *wait* . . . please . . .' she sobbed in a mad, mock-distress that made me laugh as I turned, and she laughed too, as she threw her arms round my neck and wept two sets of hot tears that ran down my cheek and on to my collar.

Over her shoulder I could see Don shaking his head and blowing with his lips in an O shape.

She was heavy, hanging on me with all her weight, a seismic coke-snigger lifting and rippling up all the way from somewhere near the crotch and ending at the mouth that was pressed against my ear, which instantly blocked with moisture and began to hiss. She was saying something over and over again, as I leaned on her arms to pull them down and away, and I could hear a staccato crackling sound. I looked into the shadows, and gradually, as my eyes became accustomed to the darkness, I could see a waiter dotted here and there, leaning against the empty tables, applauding.

I went to Hertz and rented a new Capri on the plastic. They looked rather scathingly at my licence, which had several endorsements, but didn't say anything. I couldn't get anywhere near the restaurant, so I parked in front of the Metropole by the Arno, and walked up the backstreet, which had become a funnel for the wind.

When I got to the restaurant, I could see the mop of hair at the corner table and I knew what it was. Don was smoking and talking to Marco over by the counter, as he cashed up.

I went over to them.

'She had it?'

'Yeah,' said Don. 'Keeled right over.'

'Where's Mooney?'

'On the phone, down below.'

'Where else?'

'Right,' said Don.

I went over to the table and sat down opposite her, staring at the dark roots of her blonde hair. Her head lay like a dead dahlia in front of me on the tablecloth.

'Darling?' I said, looking back at them as they watched me from the counter.

Marco was making an encouraging, shovelling motion, in the direction of the door.

I whispered to her close to her ear.

'Come on Doll, I've got the car. Time to get out of here . . .'

She grunted, sucking the saliva back into her mouth.

I lifted the heavy head by the hair, and looked at the face of my beloved, as it rose from the damp patch of dribble on Marco's damask tablecloth. It was very pale, the lips flopping, as she breathed through her nose. The eyes tried to open, but they were rolled right up under the lids and I could only see the whites, branched with increasing veins towards the corners.

'Well,' said Mooney as he approached, 'that's that.'

I laid Zonda's head gently down again.

'Young lady gone? I thought she wouldn't keep that lot up for long. Front runner, but couldn't possibly last the sort of pace she was setting . . .'

'What's cooking?' I said, moving round to the same side as Zonda.

'We're picking the Principessa and Habib up tomorrow morning, or more exactly, De Negris is picking them up and bringing them to Via San Gallo.'

'You can't park there, do they know?' I asked, as I got Zonda under the shoulder and began to heave her out of the chair. The two chairs slid together and threatened to crash to the floor as I dragged her limp body away from the table.

'Grab those, will you?' I said to Mooney, who had sat down at the table and had his pocket-book out.

He stared at me, still thinking about his pocket-book, and as Zonda came free of the place, her scarlet-clad legs finally bringing the two chairs crashing down, Mooney started scribbling entries. Don ran and got hold of the legs under the knees and we carried her with little scuffling steps and a lot of exaggerated puffing to the door, which I backed into, in order to open it. But it proved too narrow, and we had to retreat back inside the restaurant.

'This is your bloody coke,' I said over the top of her, as we tried to prop her rubber legs against the vitrine at the entrance.

Don shrugged.

'The booze too, y'know . . .'

I tossed him the car keys.

'You go ahead and open up when we get there,' I said.

'Sure,' said Don.

Worming her legs apart I got my arm under the scarlet crotch. She started flopping around and protesting in moans, even beating on my back with a soft fist or two as I got her up in a doddering fireman's lift, and Don opened the door.

Three or four yards down the windy street, I lurched on a loose rock, and fell sideways and backwards, canting at forty-five degrees for a step or two, as I tried to regain balance, one leg finally doubling backwards underneath me. Our heads cracked together as we walloped down in the wet. Faces, curious, disapproving, but not laughing, appeared at the shop windows on both sides of the street and one person's head appeared amidst the trousers hanging at the entrance to one of the shops. Zonda lay on top of me without a sound, like a huge rag doll. A lady came from the shoe shop with a chair, placing it at a discreet distance from us and retiring. The waiters at Marco's couldn't quite see, but all craned their necks and talked excitedly back, quipping, to the person next to them. Don and I got Zonda up on to the chair, and I sent him back into the restaurant for Mooney and a drink of water. I knew Mooney was writing in his pocket-book, drawing on the tablecloth, or gone for a splosh in the basement, or most probably on the telephone, and would have to be made aware of the situation.

I looked down at Zonda. The rain was running down her grey cheeks out of her plastered hair, one arm flung loosely over the back of the chair, and the legs, bent the same way, still clad in their scarlet, were covered now in great dark patches of wet on the upper thigh. I covered her with her coat, which I found hanging on my arm. I didn't remember unhooking it by the door. It must have been automatic. She threatened to slide off the chair sideways into the road again, and I found that pulling her loose-weave sweater only stretched it and allowed her to crumple further into an incomplete position which demanded resolution on the floor. I crouched helplessly beside her, looking up into her grey face; even the lips were grey, and under the coat she looked resigned and terminal.

'Doll,' I said without conviction, 'come on, this is ridiculous.'

I looked round, fixed on a waiter who had come out into the street to watch, and shrugged.

Then I bent and slapped her face gently and methodically on each side.

She said something, thickly, and raised her hand. The leg on the right moved slightly.

'Doll?' I repeated.

I saw, to my relief, that she was beginning to take her own weight. The spine had imperceptibly straightened, and the legs moved more into the centre of the chair. She was clinging to me, to my arm, to any part of me, and I allowed her to do so, though even then the revulsion mounted and I had to stifle a desire to wrench my arm free of the dirty mudstained fingers that had begun to grasp it. The wind cut off what she was whispering.

I bent closer.

'What? Darling, you passed right out . . .' I said foolishly and then repeated it. 'Darling, you passed out and you are sitting in the street on a chair . . . It's all right, I'm here . . . everybody's here . . .'

The eyes flickered open.

'What do you mean,' she said, with lazy lips, '*every*body's here . . . ?'

'Well . . . Gerrard and Don . . .'

'Never heard of anything so bloody stoopid . . .' she said, 'not in my life, I didn't . . . as this . . .'

She looked around:

'Quite the star, are we not?'

Legs trembling, she stood up and bowed to the faces on either side of the street. I looked just in time to see the face between the trousers withdraw abruptly. She was plumping her hair in the rain and the wind, searching for the slightest bounce in it, and when there wasn't any but a flat, plastered mass, she bounced herself in the manner of a circus performer, and the illusion was given for a moment that her hair had just come from under the dryer. She picked up the chair by the back. Close up, I could see she was panting and woozy.

'Where the chair come from?' she said to me out of the corner of her mouth.

'The lady across the road. Shoe shop.'

'What shoe shop? I can't *see* any shoe shop,' she whispered confidentially, pursing her lips with difficulty and counting with exaggerated care all the shop signs, one finger raised.

'It's over here,' I said, trying to lead her.

'No, no . . .' she said wrathfully. 'You . . .' She threatened and drew away, and then: 'Ah, I have it.'

She walked very slowly to the shop, leaving the woollen coat where it had fallen in the wet, and placed the chair at the entrance to the shop, in the path of all incoming and outgoing customers. A pleasant-looking Italian couple, the man grey-haired and olive-skinned, with aquiline features and a loose, light-coloured mackintosh, and the woman, tall and heavy in her furs, whose whole carriage had the tensile lightness of a good horse, stood back with sensitivity. Waiting for the transaction to gain its natural shape, and come to an end, the woman whispering and lightly placing the hand in which she clutched two navy-blue leather gloves on the man's mackintoshed arm to restrain him, the man nodding and smiling, they stood and exchanged a remark, while Zonda, islanded in front of the chair, stared dumbly and blindly into the interior of the shop, one soaked boot turned over on its side.

The Italians pressed backwards together, the woman drawing him back behind the doorframe, so that Zonda could glimpse the signora who had provided the chair, because she understood at once that this was what was wanted. Zonda's mouth was open and she was staring. Then she looked down at her feet, for a long while.

'*Avanti, Signorina . . .*' said the lady in the doorway, with a slight leading motion of her free arm.

Zonda looked down at her feet again, and up ahead of her, and then, doubtfully, she began to move, carrying the chair with the utmost solemn concentration as if walking a tightrope. The couple pressed against the doorframe and the woman reached out to steady her as she passed at a foundering pace inside the shop. Then the Italian couple stepped out into the street and walked away without a backward look.

I went to the window and stared at the scene inside. Zonda seemed to be holding herself very stiffly, bent slightly forward at the waist. She had placed the chair in front of the counter and kept running her hand, unconsciously, backward through her hair as she talked to the woman. One hand twirled endlessly in a circle in some explanation and the woman nodded several times and then began to laugh cautiously, as Zonda put her hand on her arm and jabbed her thumb back over her shoulder towards the street. She kissed the woman, who stepped back a pace and then tendered her cheek with a tiny smile, holding Zonda under the elbows. She turned to come away, all the expression from the encounter still in her face as she walked towards me down the shop: the eyes dilated and shining, tears running down and staining the now reddening cheeks, the brow furrowed from instinct, and the mouth still open in a broad, strained smile.

When she appeared at the entrance to the shop, this animation had thinned and almost disappeared, as she said:

'What a nice lady. *You* didn't do much . . .'

She put her arms up around my neck and put her wet cheek against my collar.

'What do you mean? I *cushioned* your fall like the gentleman I am.'

'You didn't.' She was laughing.

'I did.'

'It wasn't *deliberate*,' she said, with a child's pause. 'Anyway.'

'So *there*,' I said.

'God, I need a cigarette,' said Zonda, looking round the street as I tried to drape her tiny coat over her shoulders. Quite rightly, she shook it off. Without a word I began to walk briskly towards the restaurant.

'Where're you *going*?' said Zonda. 'You're *leaving* me, you bastard.'

I stopped and turned and did my own gesture of childhood shame, the embarrassed hop from one foot to another and the sound rather like 'Aha'.

'Just going to get . . .'

Zonda looked at me penetratingly across the gust of wind for a moment, her eyes burning blue in the winter light, and said, with a sudden lightness that I knew was meant to save me from myself:

'To get me a cigarette, good.'

But I could never accept that kind of cue. I felt honesty was in order.

'No, actually,' I said, proud of myself, 'just to get the others.'

Zonda didn't reply, but when I turned and carried on, I saw out of the corner of my eye that she was following me doggedly, turning round every now and again to look back, compulsively, at the spot where all this had occurred.

The others were just emerging, coat collars turned up against the wind.

'She OK?' said Don and then: 'You OK, hon?'

We waited as she limped up.

'You OK, hon?' said Don again in a lower voice.

'Yeh,' she breathed comfortably as we grouped in the doorway, 'but *phew* . . .' she rolled her eyes, 'I went right out . . .'

'Missed yurr tip, did ya?' said Mooney, laughing and hunching his shoulders against the cold. The depth of brogue suggested he wanted to get on.

'Well,' I said to him, 'I *was* going to suggest that we went out to Pisa . . .' This was not really a general, unfinished remark at all.

'Well,' said Zonda chokingly, 'don't mind *me* . . .'

She spun and walked off into the wind, the rustle of her large bony knees muted by damp, but still audible.

'Fucking *sod* . . .' she turned and shouted.

Don ran after her and took her by the arm, fishing in his pocket for something.

'Hey, Zonda honey, got something for you . . .'

She looked at him, the poison still in her gaze, and a tiny, interested pout spread into the relief on her face.

'What?' she said, suspiciously.

'Close your eyes . . .' he said.

'*No* . . .' she shouted through gritted teeth and grabbed for the hand that was in his jerkin pocket. '*Give* them to *me* . . .'

They wrestled laughingly, Zonda loosening and smacking Don on the side of the head, Don ducking and weaving and exaggerating the pain of contact, and yet those smacks got heavier and heavier as her giggles grew higher.

'Ah well . . .' said Mooney with a sigh as we started down the street behind them. 'Of course it is quite natural for the young lady to be upset after such an experience . . . quite natural . . .'

I didn't know what this remark meant, but I interpreted it to mean that he would be very happy to go to Pisa.

'She looks alright now,' I said.

They were lighting cigarettes, shielding each other from the wind behind their collars.

I walked behind them with Mooney.

'Well that settles it, then . . .' I said as we drew level at a widening of the pavement. 'We go.'

I leaned over.

'Darling?'

'I don't want to stay at home,' said Zonda, 'that's for sure.'

237

'You can sleep,' I said. 'What could be more agreeable?'

'Raymond,' said Zonda, 'you are a right fucking bastard, aren't you?'

I could see she was recovering her powers.

'Ah, there's only one snag,' said Mooney, looking round behind him. 'How long will it take to go to your friend's?'

'In all, I should say about two hours,' I said.

'I have to make a call,' said Mooney.

'Oh, that's alright,' I said. 'The Bianchis stretch to a phone . . .'

Pisa

We sat in the car while she talked to the one-legged man. She always talked to the one-legged man. He was one of her 'friends'. We both had 'friends' all over the city, and often spent the day moving from one to another, like staging posts in a long circular journey back home. I was impatient of most of hers, because they were street acquaintances, nobodies, non-productive entities: ugly young grocers, one-legged carpark attendants, barmen, cooks, cinema usherettes and the horrors at various boutiques. Mine were superior, I felt: bookmakers, fellow punters, one journalist, one heir to a considerable fortune in the English brewery trade, and several barflies. These categories were not exclusive, of course. But one could have a better time with mine all round.

'One of your "friends",' I said, as Zonda climbed into the car. She was waving, ineffectually, through the back window.

'He didn't see you,' I said.

'He's nice,' said Zonda to Don. 'He used to be in the navy.'

'Yeah? I never met anyone in the Italian navy,' said Don.

'Dirty old lecher,' I said into the mirror. 'He fancies you . . . I wonder what he does at night, when he gets home and takes his ticket machine off . . .'

I continued in this vein for some time, while Mooney's head began to nod and roll around in the front seat by me.

'Hey,' said Don, 'this jeep gotta sound system?'

I couldn't believe he was being tactful.

'I believe it has,' I said, with a brittle formality, and over-Britishness, which I assumed without thinking when in the company of Americans.

'Wanna hear something?'

'What is it?' said Zonda in the back. 'Oh yes . . . is it you?'

'Yep,' said Don, 'it's *all* me . . . piano, drums, vocals, the lot . . .'

'Pass it over,' I said.

'Oh goody,' said Zonda, lighting two Marlboro in her mouth at once.

Don passed the cassette over. 'Various blues' was written in biro on the slip of paper specially provided for titles at the back. Otherwise the tape was blank.

'Very impressive,' I said, slipping it into the machine.

'It's just a demo,' said Don, modestly, to Zonda. 'The quality's not all that hot . . .'

We were waiting at the lights on the Lung'arno. The rain was drumming on the roof, forming rivulets on the car windows. The windscreen wipers seemed very loud, as we waited for the hissing tape to reach something. The people crossing in front of the car bonnet were up to their ankles in running water, lifting their feet high above the surface of the flood, pointlessly, and then putting them down again into three or four inches of informal torrent. I was looking at these people, when a kind of ticking came out of the machine. They were not in time to the rhythm, but there was some significant relationship between the sound and the picture. I looked in the mirror. Don's head was moving like a chicken's crossing a stackyard and he was following the ticking with little hisses that gave out spurts of blue Marlboro smoke in the damp dark air of the car.

'Very good,' I said, as the pedestrians lifted their soaking feet high outside.

Don was laughing, opening his mouth wide and showing the gap between his teeth.

'Hey, no,' he said. 'This is just the intro . . .'

'Shut up Raymond,' said Zonda.

There was a crash of cymbals and a piano clinked in, moving between the major chords of C and G in little runs in the treble and banging dramatically in the bass. The ticking changed to a deeper sort of clicking, and then a voice wandered in over the top, fishing for the pitch, which seemed easily to elude it, and ululated in a depressed, stationary fashion: 'I'd like to take you.' A guitar was being picked industriously in the foreground with occasional changes to the chords of F major and A minor. 'I'd like to take you,' said the voice again, in a dull, hoarse, off-key fashion. And then everything stopped.

I was just about to say: 'Is that all? when the lights changed and I eased off through the puddles. The rain was dancing on the bonnet and kicking up into the lower half of the windscreen in a bubbling fan that made it almost impossible to see. The wipers had swick-swacked for the fifth time, and we were drifting slowly along the quayside with the tape hissing, when there was an almighty thundering, vaguely falsetto scream from the tape:

'WHERE THE SUN DON'T SHIIIIIIINE!'

and everything crashed in behind in a variety of seventh chords. Mooney snapped awake and looked around. The guitar made a brief, mistaken attempt to escape into B flat major, and then settled down into the grim routine of music-box tinkling.

'Great,' said Zonda, clicking her fingers. 'Great rhythm . . .'

'What's that ticking?' I asked.

'That's a drum-box,' said Don. 'Don't you guys know a drum-box?'

'Of course,' said Zonda. 'It's just the upper-class fogey sitting in the front who hasn't ever heard one. . .'

'I thought something had gone wrong with the windscreen-wipers,' I said.

'You lay that down on top when you've got it all worked out,' said Don.

'That one's like a cross between Don Maclean and the guy who made "Veedon Fleece".' said Zonda 'What's his name. . . ?' She snapped her fingers. 'Irish guy.'

'How far to Pisa?' said Mooney suddenly, reaching into the glove compartment.

'This is a hired car,' I said. 'No good looking for maps. I think it's about twenty-five or thirty kilometres.'

'Ah,' said Mooney, 'not so far.'

'Problem?' I said.

'Splosh and call,' he said, 'in that order.'

'I'll let you out when we get on the road. . .' I said.

'That's very civil of you, Raymond,' said Mooney, 'very civil.'

'Think nothing of it,' I said inclining my head and speaking with exaggerated graciousness.

Mooney lit his Nazionali at last, after sitting with it hanging in the corner of his mouth for some time, while the tape went into another hissing silence.

'This next one's acoustic,' said Don.

Three notes quivered out repeatedly, a semitone apart.

'This is more kinda lyrical,' said Don.

The voice came on again, hanging like an ungainly fish, almost a whole tone flat above the picked D major of the guitar's opening chord. It was a saccharine thing, shampoo advert stuff about a girl's shining hair on a beach, the tide washing on the shingle at midnight. The chorus involved a lot of urgency, a switch to E minor, and a lighthouse which flashed, of course, and, in a line that was particularly ludicrous, illuminated 'all this purple world'.

'I don't understand,' I said. 'Purple world?'

Mooney was holding himself in, I could see, so I pulled over and let him out. The marijuana smoke was pouring over the seat and swirling in thick clouds over the dashboard. It followed him out, curling round the top of the doorway as he stumbled into the sheeting grey-green.

'Nuclear, innit,' said Zonda.

'Hey, that's right,' said Don, drawing in his breath sharply, and then holding out the tiny joint.

Zonda shook her head. He held it up higher, and pushed it further towards her.

'You got . . . it . . .' he said as the pent-up blue forces shot out of his nose and mouth in two blue diagonals that gathered in a stationary cloud and then sank below the back seat, bouncing on the window-sills.

Zonda took the joint and inserted a hairpin into the diminutive, soaked, brown end. Outside, I could just see the hang of Mooney's mac through the screen of sleet and a bit of a farmhouse wall. It was very hot in the car. The door seemed to be hanging at an impossible angle, as if it were about to fall off. The drumming of the rain on the roof was demented, as Don switched back into what I hoped was the last verse of 'The Lighthouse', drowning everything and forming a clashing bass which left the final tender guitar chords and the fading tremor of the voice strangely out of tune.

I turned round.

'That reminds me of that Leonard Cohen song in which Jesus lives, apparently, in a "little wooden tower",' I said, hanging an arm over the back seat. 'D'you know I used to be fond of Cohen. We used to live with some hippies in Ladbroke Grove, and one of them used to do this . . .'

I mimed the catching of two strands of long hair from a central parting in my two forefingers and the stowing of it behind the ears, and I bounced in the seat and lowered my voice to a cooling expressionless monotone: 'Cohen is . . . out of sight . . . Man . . . out of sight.'

'Hey, yea,' said Don. 'The Sixties . . .'

'*Lonely* wooden tower. It's the cross innit,' said Zonda, concentrating on the little brown stump.

I realised to my annoyance that I had been addressing Don.

'Lonely,' said Zonda, as she sucked in with a grimace, spitting out the words. 'Not . . . "little" . . .'

'This guy's been out there a helluva long time,' said Don, rubbing off a patch of steam with his sleeve and looking out of the window.

'It's *not* little,' Zonda repeated, breathing out with a long sigh. 'You can tell *you* were never a hippie Raymond . . .'

I could see Mooney straddling and shaking himself in the sleet. He paused for what seemed an interminable moment to do up his flies. Then he ran towards us, looming up holding his hat on with one hand, holding the mac round him with the other.

This happened twice more. Once while Don was in the middle of a syrupy country and western number called 'You Can't Wash Away My Tears' and, then, almost immediately afterwards, just as Don was starting the next song, an adapted twelve-bar blues, in which he impersonated a Chevrolet and his driver Bobby looking for a girl called Gasoline from Texas, Mooney wanted to be let out again. I watched his back receding in the rain, as Don sang against a bank of wailing Nashville Hawaiian and furiously diddling banjos.

> I've had Charlene
> On my back seat
> And Bobby nearly wrecked us
>
> And Marlene
> On my front
> Who told us we were sexist
>
> But we scream and shout
> Cause we can't live without
> Gasoline from Texas!

'I got a buddy on the pedal in this,' said Don with a grin. 'Cute, huh?'

The song went on to lament the decline of the national culture, putting this down to the scarcity of good whores, good drugs, and cheap petrol. At times, in the middle eight bars, one could hear the distant revving of car engines.

'Yeah, y'know, that was *real* hard to get right?' said Don to Zonda.

Zonda was laughing and clicking her fingers again.

'You're *so* talented,' she said.

'I reckon I've got enough to just about make an album,' said Don.

Mooney was panting when he climbed back into the car. I turned Don down, in deference to the grey, soaking figure. I looked across at my own corduroy trousers, which were black with wet for three inches above his dripping shoes.

'Hell fire,' said Mooney, patting his pockets, the sodden Nazionali hanging out of his mouth.

As we cruised slowly through the square, the leaning tower was covered in Japanese tourists, each with a camera. They swarmed everywhere, a figure appearing or disappearing at every balcony, like ants in a Gruyère cheese. I paused and wound the window down. You could hear their shouts as they called to each other from the different levels of the tower, and the sound of their cameras as they shot yards and yards of film. Ragged openings of light appeared in what was otherwise a low, hanging sky, whose lowest rainclouds bumped along just above the top of the tower. Two coaches stood on the verge, their Italian drivers lying across the front seats smoking, and watching the Japanese. The echoes were muffled and intimate across the sodden grass.

I was filling Mooney in about the Bianchis. Giuseppe was the figurehead, a tall handsome man in his late fifties, who had been quite a prominent local fascist in his youth. Giuseppe had had several riding accidents and walked with a stick now. After the first of the accidents, Francesca had taken over the stables, and it was she who really ran things from a discreet position in the rear. He was quite a lad when you got him out, but very proper at home, very much the *padrone*, straight-backed and all that sort of thing.

'Hear that, you two. . .' I said over my shoulder. 'No offering them joints . . .'

'Willco cap. . .' said Don. 'Hey, will ya look at that goddamn thing . . . it's gonna fall over any minute with all them liddle yella fellas all over it . . .'

Zonda drew herself up in the back seat.

'I'm going up it,' she said. 'Come on let's all go . . . it'll wake us up . . .'

Mooney shuddered. Silently I elected to stay, while she and Don got out of the car. Zonda reached for the sky in a sudden movement, revealing a pale gap between the hoisted sweater and the scarlet waistband of the pants. One boot turned in, I noticed idly, as I looked at my watch and told them to hurry up. Don ran with slow controlled strides. He had obviously done some athletics. While Zonda ran in a squelching gleeful patter, everything bouncing from her blonde mop down via the hem of her woollen coat, to the flopping tops of her Robin Hood boots.

I could see Mooney was anxious to get on, and when they reached the bottom of the tower, I got out of the car and shouted and waved. I almost put my hand on my head in a cone-shape with the fingers spread in the 'converge on me' sign of the scouts, but I thought that neither of them, for different reasons, would understand this. I beckoned urgently instead, and they stopped right at the foot of the tower and looked at each other over the heads of a crowd of Japanese that were coming away. I beckoned again vigorously and climbed back in the car.

'This will be interesting,' I said to Mooney, who was staring at a car manual which he had fished out of the glove compartment. Multicoloured diagrams of the transmission and wiring of the Capri flopped on top of one another, as he turned the pages.

Unexpectedly, it was Don who stayed where he was, and Zonda who hesitated, and then, with a tiny gesture of the hands, began to trudge back towards us. He called to her, and she stopped and turned towards him, saying something with head bent against the wind. He shrugged and replied, and Zonda turned and set off back towards us. A confusion of Japanese spilled out of the tower all round them. Don gave a last stare up at the tower and waved his arms despairingly. Zonda was trudging resolutely now, with bent head, while Don began to thread his way, dodging like a footballer through the crowd of chattering Japanese.

'What's the matter?' said Zonda as she came up.

'We haven't really got the time for you to do that, darling,' I said. 'I'm sorry . . .'

'Well why the fuck didn't you . . .' she said, crashing sideways into the back, and groaning, good-humouredly, stretched out on her back.

'What's the problem?' said Don.

'We've really got to get on,' I said, 'otherwise we can't decently go to the Bianchis' . . .'

'Uh, huh,' said Don. 'Shove up, honey . . .'

'Gerrard is wet and cold,' I said, 'and I'm sure he would appreciate some warmth and a drink . . .'

'Sure,' said Don brightly. 'I get it. We can always go see the crazy tower some other time.'

The house communicated with the stables proper via a long path that ran alongside the white wall of a village cemetery and through a small cypress grove. In the summer, the walk was very pleasant, the expectation of seeing the horses lending charm to the undistinguished, rather dry, bitty, landscape. Now, the wind was sweeping into us, chilling to the marrow.

'Where the hell is this?' said Mooney, stumbling along at my side in an effort to keep up with my smart pace. His face was lit, now and again, by a distant flash of lightning from the horizon.

'This is a Godforsaken hole you're takin' me to, Raymond. It reminds me of Ould Oireland,' he said, and laughed, the thud of his feet on the frozen path causing a tremor in his voice.

While we were traversing the copse, I painted a picture for him of the modest start I was making here at the stables, concealing the fact that I belonged to a syndicate. I thought that he might, despite his grandiose background, be more favourably disposed to individual efforts from small beginnings etc.

247

The lights were on in the yards and we encountered Zonda and Don and Giuseppe with the Piedmontese stable girl, looking at Forray, the bay. He was bothered by the thunder and the visit, and sweating up a little, stamping, visibly nervous. Zonda was talking to him like a baby, but he fixed Mooney and me sideways with a bloodshot eye when we entered. Giuseppe was explaining to them about his laziness last season, and his odd gait. The horse ran with his head to one side and this was a sign he didn't want to work, said Giuseppe.

I made formal introductions.

Mooney stood about eight feet in front of the horse, dropping his glance slowly from a point between the ears to the forefeet. Then he moved along the near side of the animal and stood behind him, looking for hip fractures. He walked round the offside then, and finished at the front. Giuseppe looked over at me and raised his eyebrows. Mooney was staring into Forray's face and opening his mouth wide.

He went on to perform a systematic examination of the horse from every aspect. He passed his hand down the front of the near fore-limb, feeling the front of the knee and roughing up the hair for scars. He felt the shank, the fetlock and the coronet bone, and he spent a long time examining the back of the near-side back leg.

Then he asked Giuseppe to press the animal backward two or three times and turn him short and quickly round. He nodded thoughtfully and came over to us.

'So when did he have his accident then?' he asked.

'Some fool ran into his back leg with a horse box, here at Pisa . . .' Giuseppe said.

He was impressed that Mooney had spotted the scar so quickly.

I explained that we had been on the point of selling him last year, because he was so idle. Nothing to do with the accident. He just always seemed to make sixth or seventh place. Then, quite unexpectedly, he had come second in Rome, almost winning indeed. All my money had been on the winner, and to see Forray come galumphing up in the last two furlongs, trying to take this other horse, had been a galling, horrifying sight.

Zonda was laughing.

'He kept jumping up and down and shouting: "No! Get *back*, you stupid animal" . . . it was so funny,' she said to Don.

After that, we had taken him out about four times, but he returned to his own inimitably undistinguished style. The horse's ears flickered at this remark, and he stamped backwards. Probably because he was nervous anyway, but Zonda spoke very loudly, in her best bridge-party accent. In the end, it was hard to tell who was more nervous, her or the horse. But they didn't seem to notice. Mooney was asking Giuseppe a lot of questions about work-rates and feeds and the nature of Italian racetracks.

Zonda came and inexplicably put her arm through mine, as we went to see Dobrovsky. Mooney looked Dobrovsky over very carefully.

'Out of Dobrinska,' said Giuseppe.

'Ah yes,' said Mooney, 'the Dobrowa line . . .'

'You have a good knowledge,' said Giuseppe. 'I didn't expect . . .'

'Ah, come now,' said Mooney, looking at Dobrovsky's teeth. 'Dobrowa was pretty good on his day, you know . . .'

'Dobrovsky is a joke,' I said. 'I was going to call him Satellite . . .'

But Mooney was conferring with Giuseppe about how he was doing, and Zonda dragged me off to see the foal. The Piedmontese stable girl stood by while she kissed me and shivered with delight as the creature came tottering on its splayed legs, an unsteady pyramid. The right leg had a blaze just below the knee I didn't like to look at, because it reminded me of York the year before, and the shattered bone that poked through a similar-shaped blaze. He had been amongst the leaders, poor Hazy Ray, a three-year-old out of Hazel Croft, when he fell. There had been nothing we could do, when we got there, his leg out at this peculiar angle and the compound fracture just where the white blaze was on the front leg. They shot him there and then on the course.

I turned away, and wrenched at Zonda's arm doing so. She looked up at me, startled, but already too captivated by the clattering colt to really notice, as the others came in. The Piedmontese, however, who had once told me I was 'a beautiful man', noticed. She knew what I was thinking. She'd seen me crying afterwards, on the way back to Normandy, where Hazy Ray had been stabled.

She picked up a yard brush and gave a few strokes with it, shaking her head.

Zonda was fussing the colt, with tears in her eyes.

'Oh darling,' she said, suddenly leaping up and putting her arms round me. 'Oh he's so *lovely* . . .' I was backing away, tugging at the crooks of each elbow. I eased away and stood back. She dropped her arms and her eyes welled with two tears, one of which ran immediately down into her drooping mouth and the other stood like a second lens in the eye, making the pupil itself appear to quiver. The toe of one boot rested against the toe of the other. Then the other tear oozed out of the eye and down the side of her nose. She sniffed.

I offered her one of my monogrammed handkerchiefs.

She turned and wiped her sleeve in one crude motion across the whole of her face, looking for Don, sidling round the back of the others as they talked with a strange little backward look. Then she put out her tongue at me, and her shoulders shook with something that was neither laughter nor tears, but some glance at herself. She wiped her face with the same motion and slipped her hand through Don's arm. He bent his head close to her, as he watched the foal.

'Hey,' he said, 'what's up, hon?'

'He's so luvlee . . .' said Zonda, beginning sonorously and sliding right off the scale with a squeak of faked ecstasy.

'He sure is,' said Don, looking back at the foal, 'but they all look the same to me . . .'

Giuseppe had a torch and he shone it on the path on the way back. I found myself trapped in between two parties. Zonda and Don were walking in front and Don was telling Zonda about the 'grassy knoll' theory and the contradictory directions in which shots appeared to have been fired at President Kennedy in Dallas. Behind me, the rays of the torch swung idly up and down.

'Those last days,' Giuseppe was saying, 'what confusion – Salò never worked, how could it, with people like you working your way up the country . . .'

'Aha,' said Mooney, 'not me. I'm Irish. We were neutral, remember.'

'Ah yes, of course. Charming country, Ireland. The Irish have a lot to be thankful to De Valera for.'

'D'you know,' said Mooney, 'I happened to be in a farmhouse in Kilkenny at the breakfast table the day before Dev died. This young man who was having breakfast with us knew he was on the way out, turned out to be one of his aides on holiday from Dublin. And sure enough, the young fella, was he not called to the telephone the moment breakfast was over, still chewing his bacon he was and drinking his last cup of tea? Poor chap had to drop everything and go back to make arrangements for the funeral. The whole country went mad with grief. Buried in the robes of the Carmelites, he was. The pious mathematician.'

But Giuseppe was carrying on a quite separate meditation: 'The dampness of Lake Garda, the Duce never liked it. Hunted from pillar to post, bundled up in different uniforms and disguises, somebody said he looked like a cinema usher, when he was rescued by the Germans. They hardly knew if they'd got the right man . . .'

I turned round. I had never heard him talk about this before.

'. . . and wasn't he wearing a German uniform when the partisans eventually captured him?' I said.

'That's right. Hiding in an armoured car, dressed as a private.'

It suddenly occurred to me, ludicrously, that Mooney was wearing my clothes, and I smiled to myself in the dark as we approached the house.

Behind us, Don and Zonda were discussing the question of instinct.

'Itching,' Giuseppe intervened, turning to Zonda, 'is an unpleasant thing. We have to scratch ... scraaatch ... like this ...'

He curved his hand and ran it theatrically down Zonda's arm. She shivered and stumbled.

'What happens if you can't reach the place?' he asked.

'You rub it against something,' I said.

'Supposing you can't do that,' said Giuseppe.

'I ask Raymond,' said Zonda.

'Exactly,' said Giuseppe. 'This is what the horse does.'

'But how do they ask?'

He spread his arm across the horizon, and in Zonda's eyes I saw a huge pampas spring into existence peopled by herds of horses under a blazing sun.

'There are a group out there grazing. One goes over to the other ...' He took Zonda by the arm. ' "How about scratching me where I itch?" he says. "Show me," says the other one ...'

Giuseppe's hand slid round the back of Zonda's loose-weave top and took a pinch of skin gently between his finger and thumb. Her steps dragged, and she came to a halt. Automatically her head went back and her eyes closed.

' "Here," he says ... "OK," says the other one, "here you are ..." '

Zonda opened her eyes.

'I see,' she said, 'mimicry ...'

'*Not* just mimicry ...' said Giuseppe. 'No it's thought. Horses can think. I can tell you another case. In summer, the air is full of flies and stinging insects ...'

He was pleading with her to grant this, buzzing like a menacing fly and undulating his hand in the air.

'The horses will stand as close together as they can ... hey?'

Zonda thought long and hard.

'Because that way there is less for the insects to bite. They help each other.' He tapped his head. 'You see cows in a field. What are they doing? Just swishing their tails and the fly is gone. Again, you see horses grazing in the summer, how do they stand?'

'Nose to tail,' I said.

'But why?'

Giuseppe passed his hand before Zonda's eyes like a conjurer waking up his somnambulistic assistant.

'To swish the flies from each other's faces. You see they cooperate. They *think*.'

'But it's instinct, isn't it?' said Zonda.

Giuseppe halted theatrically.

'Instinct is just the name we give to what we are not able to explain. I give you another case. I have a horse stabled near the racetrack. There is a bell at the start he can hear from his box. At the stable gate, there is also a bell which he hears. Why is it that the sound of one bell in the distance can make him so excited that he goes off his feed and not the other bell?'

'Doesn't,' said Zonda, stalling, 'do anything to him.'

'Correct. Why?'

'Ah, but that's different,' said Zonda quickly. 'That's association. He connects the one sound with something and not the other.'

'But to do this repeatedly he has to think?'

'Stretching the word,' I said, 'just a *teeny* bit?'

We stood shaking hands, and saying goodbye, declining Giuseppe's invitations to come in and have drinks. Mooney brightened up at the thought of the telephone, but I thought further contact would almost certainly lead to complications. I pleaded Zonda's sleepiness. The main point had been established: Mooney's sense of my qualifications to manage and handle the investments for a stud-farm, and on this front, I thought I couldn't complain, though we had stood close to disaster on several occasions. Fortunately, Giuseppe hadn't asked me outright for the feed bills money. We went round the side of the house, down the shallow, curving slope, to the car. To have tried the pergola steps, even with a light from the house, would not have been wise.

Florence

Most of the way back I was fighting to stay awake, envious of the snoring, whiffling creatures draped around the car: Mooney's head was nodding on to the dashboard, and Zonda and Don lay in separate corners of the back seat. We parked up and straggled back through the empty streets under the arches of the Ospedale at San Marco and round the corner, out of the square. When we got into San Gallo, there was a figure standing in the shadows of Kleenex's doorway in front of the apartment. Zonda fished in my pockets for the keys and let herself and the others in.

'You stood me up,' said Steve.

I came across the road to him, as the lights went on upstairs and illuminated his face.

'This is all very dramatic,' I said. 'It's just like a James Bond movie.'

'It's not funny,' said Steve, offering me a cigarette. 'I've really got to have the cash, Raymond. I've been calling you every hour.'

I told him where we'd been.

'What's the urgency?'

He laughed:

'I'm liquidating my assets.'

'Moonlight flit?'

'That sort of thing.'

'Got an address?'

'No. That won't do,' he said quickly, 'I want it now.'

'Well, naturally,' I said, playing for time, 'if you want it that badly, you must have it right away. Trouble is . . .'

Zonda came to the window above and leaned out smoking a cigarette. She had obviously revived.

'Who's that down there, Raymond?'

'It's Steve, darling, we're just talking . . .'

'Steve, Steve, hi–i . . .' said Zonda, enthusiastically waving. 'Come up . . .'

I seized him by the arm.

'Yes, just come and have a quick one. What could be more agreeable?'

I pushed him ahead of me, playfully manhandling him in through the pitch-black entrance. He tripped up on the steep irregular stairs and kept falling on his hands and cursing. Steve and I were together at Oxford, doing PPE. He spoke in a curious medley of Liverpool and Birmingham to my ear, though he had never been in either of those cities and came from Basingstoke, I believe. He lived with a lugubrious old deb called Perdita over by Santa Croce, and he often needed money for her drugs.

Zonda welcomed us in like long-lost friends. She was vivacious, bright-eyed, and kissed me as if I were a stranger. I looked round. She *had* cleared up. Mooney was on the phone, saying: 'Agreed, we must have ninety-five per cent emission that's what we arranged . . . otherwise the whole thing's off, you know that, we don't want to go chasing moonshine . . .' Don was nowhere to be seen. I went into the kitchen and fixed up two grappas. Peering through the hole, I saw that he was stretched out, in his clothes, prone on the bed. He had claimed his spot for what was left of the night.

Steve was already pouring out his domestic turmoils to Zonda, sitting on top of the stepladder. Things were looking promising. I filled them up and brought the bottle with me. As he talked on the phone, I put a glass in Mooney's hand and poured grappa into it.

'. . . just threw a complete fit,' Steve was saying. 'I don't understand it at all . . . I don't know what I've done . . . I just went out to make a few bets, see a couple of friends and wait for *dear* Raymond, who never showed up, and when I got back . . . completely gone . . . over the hill . . . phh tttt . . .'

'In the *bath*?' said Zonda, putting her hands over her face, knees drawn up on top of the stepladder. 'Oh God . . .'

'Carabinieri, the whole thing . . .' said Steve, slugging the grappa, his voice trembling.

I sat on the steps.

'Perdita,' I said.

'OD,' said Steve, 'in the bath.'

'How original,' I said.

Zonda was furious. The stepladder shook.

'Fucking shurrup you,' she said in her Chip voice, and then, with a strange kind of surprise: 'You *bastard*, how *can* you be so callous?'

'He's right,' said Steve, 'in a way. But, Jesus, what a scene. I couldn't go back there, it was Adriana told me about it, warned me the place was swarming with cops . . .'

Mooney came off the phone and sat on the step next to me. He was still wearing the plastic mac.

I suddenly realised I was quite drunk.

'I never liked her,' I said. 'She was a hideous, destructive old baggage and you're well out of it.'

'We've certainly had some bad times recently,' said Steve, using the wrong kind of past for the deceased.

'Couldn't bloody paint,' I said, writing out a cheque for half a million lire I didn't have. 'Couldn't act, couldn't do a thing, except scream and shout . . .'

'*Raymond*!!!' said Zonda, starting to clamber down from the stepladder. '*You* are disgusting . . .'

'Here you are, my friend,' I said, throwing the cheque at him. 'Here's everything I owe you. Don't try to cash it before the fifteenth.'

'Raymond,' said Zonda, 'I mean it, I'm not putting up with this kind of thing. Whatever she was, Perdita was a *person*.'

I found my mouth leering.

'An *un*person . . .' I said, 'who wore *giovedi d'oggi* clothing quite unsuitable for her baggish body . . .'

'My God,' said Zonda. 'Is this the real you?'

'It would be hypocritical,' I said, 'for me to say anything else. We hated each other, quite cordially. If I threw myself off the top of the Palazzo Vecchio, she would say exactly the same sort of things about me.'

'Don't you have *any* feelings?' said Zonda, wonderingly.

'Not for her.'

'If not for Perdita, you might spare Steve his feelings.'

'Him?' I said. 'He's had this other girl, Adriana, for years, haven't you?'

'Yes,' said Steve, 'but still . . .'

'But still nothing,' I said, trying to rise off the step for some reason, and then sitting down again abruptly.

I looked at Mooney. He was sipping his brandy and writing some figures down on the back of an envelope.

'This is Mr Mooney,' I said, 'business associate. Mr Mooney, this is Steve, whose girlfriend has just killed herself.'

'Be with you in a minute,' said Mooney, jumping up and going to the telephone. He dialled quickly.

'By the way,' he said, 'it occurs to me that we ought to get some more up the front end . . . yes . . . yes . . . another half per cent perhaps, what do you think? That's right, that was exactly my thought . . . Good . . .'

'They're both hopeless people,' said Zonda to Steve, putting her hand out to touch his ginger hair.

'It's alright,' said Steve, stretching the cheque between his fingers with a sigh. 'I'm used to it.'

'Go on anyway,' said Zonda. ' "She had decided on opera . . ." '

'Oh yes,' said Steve, folding the cheque over and carefully putting it in his wallet. 'Well, she had decided that her real *métier* was grand opera, and she started having lessons, it got as far as that.'

I snorted and got up.

Mooney was saying:

'Well we can't do anything about that now, but Henri can fix that in the morning, I'll call him first thing before we leave . . . and perhaps you could talk to him too about the fine tuning . . . yes . . . OK . . . speak to you tomorrow . . . Yes . . . Bye . . .'

He stumbled off into the kitchen. I got up and followed him. He crushed the Nazionali packet that was lying on the table in his hand, and gave an exclamation, pulling a severed cylinder out of it.

'Will you look at that now?' he said, putting the larger half in his mouth.

'I was thinking,' I said, as we sat down at the kitchen table, 'that half a million would make a very modest start. That's all we'd want.'

'Aha,' he said. 'How do you figure that one out?'

'Well,' I said, filling up his glass with grappa, 'have a little touch more . . .'

I could hear Don snoring through the gap in the wall, deep muffled sounds. In the front, Steve was going on and on under a smoke-filled lampshade to Zonda about Perdita's last days.

I pulled the back of his envelope over to me and wrote Year One at the top of it, and then 'Outlay' and 'say 500 million equals £230,000'.

'Look,' I said.

'I'm listening,' said Mooney, socking into his grappa. 'Go on with you, shoot, fire ahead, I'm your man.'

'Well, first we purchase Vada, as I said over lunch . . .'

'Right . . .'

'Plus four mares in foal, four mares to cover – OK . . .'

'Right.'

'Three-year-old fillies . . .'

'Yep . . .'

'And two yearling fillies . . . income nil. Five hundred thousand outlay.'

Then I wrote Year Two. Outlay 144 mil. Income 120 mil.

'You're already in profit in the second year. Modest, it's true, but . . . you have two four-year-olds and two three-year-olds in training . . . you sell two of these to replace with one two-year-old and one three-year-old, repeating this operation every year, so your replacement costs are always that much less . . .'

'Well, you offset maintenance against that, which you haven't counted . . .' he said, pulling the envelope round so that he could have a look at it.

'Steve's off now,' said Zonda.

'Goodbye Steve,' I said in a monotone.

I went to the top of the step and stood there, as Zonda kissed him goodnight. He peeped in round her from the blackness of the stairs and just as he started to wave at me, I turned away.

'It's true, I haven't put any maintenance costs down,' I called back behind me to Mooney, sitting at the kitchen table, 'but those could be covered by the ultimate sale of stock . . .'

Mooney was inclined to see this as bad business, and we sat discussing it in the kitchen until Zonda appeared and went, without a word, past us, nudging me and beckoning me into the bathroom.

I went on discussing the stud-farm with Mooney, until a naked arm appeared at the bathroom door and beckoned me into the long, blue and white checkered space. She was lying in the bath, her hair rather startlingly tied up, her face red with the heat and steam. I sat on the edge of the bath. Her breasts lay flat just under the water. One leg rose in the air perpendicularly, bent at the knee, toes pointed like a ballet dancer's. She was lathering this in the dilettantish manner of soap advertisements.

She looked at me steadily from the water.

'Why are you doing this?'

'Doing what?'

'Oh, please, I'm tired, Raymond,' she said. 'This callous, cruel, indifferent act. It's not like you at all.'

'I'm not aware that I . . .'

260

'Ever since this whole thing started,' said Zonda. 'Ever since that day down there . . .' she reached out and pointed a dripping finger at the floor.

I pretended not to know what she was talking about, but not too much, in case she grew angry, for we had things to discuss. Our low intense voices boomed amongst the tiles.

'But I thought we'd been through all that,' I said with an air of weariness.

'We haven't been through the way you just behaved towards Steve,' she said. 'I was ashamed of you.'

'You don't understand. We were at Oxford together,' I said.

'That doesn't explain anything,' she said. 'The woman is *dead*, Raymond, don't you understand, *dead*? Doesn't that mean anything to you at all, that your friend is suffering a loss?'

'A bit of melodrama does us all good, now and again,' I said. 'But Steve will recover, you don't know him like I do.'

She swept me aside with a wave of the soap.

'Doesn't that disrupt your plans for stables or your stupid obsession with deals and these . . . *crooks*. . . ? No, of course it doesn't – something ordinary and *human* – it doesn't disturb your world for a minute, does it?'

'Well, I notice that you have been taking advantage of it . . .' I said, jerking my thumb in the direction of Don in the bedroom.

Instantly, I regretted saying this. Not because it was cheap, which it was, but because it was tactically incorrect.

But to my surprise, instead of getting even redder in the face than she was, she remained calm.

'What do you expect me to do? Act as hostess for your crazy schemes?'

'Darling,' I said, 'I know you're bored, but it won't be for long, and then we'll be *rich*.'

'You're *mad*,' she said.

'Well, even if I am, and it turns out to be nothing, nothing will be lost,' I said, reasonably. 'One way or the other, it will all be over in a few days, win or lose.'

'Do you really think it's going to be like that?'

'Of course.'

'Do you want to lose me?'

'Of course not.'

'Then call it off, *now*. Let them sink or swim. Don't go to Monte Carlo.'

'Why not?'

'Because, if you do, you'll be losing me.'

'You mean, you're going to run off with Gasoline From Texas?'

Zonda giggled, and dropped her hand in the water.

'Wasn't that *funny*?' she said.

I thought I had her now.

'Well, you did threaten me . . .'

'I was, you know, under the influence . . .'

'In that case, why not come with us for a few days? Treat it as a trip . . .'

'I'm staying here,' said Zonda, standing up and soaping her breasts. There was a red mark round her waist where the hot water had come to, and all below this line was salmon pink. I stared at the water-drops hanging in the curls of her pubic hair.

'What do you mean, losing you?' I said, slightly unsure of how to proceed at this point.

'You're changing,' she announced, handing me the soap. 'You've changed already – do my back will you? – and I can't go with you. Besides, I've got to go and have these test things . . .'

'You're just bored, and you want to swan about with your hysterical shrieking friends Philomena and that Dinky woman . . .'

'That reminds me,' said Zonda, 'leave me some money in the morning, when you go, will you?'

'Hasn't your mother sent anything?'

'No, she's probably forgotten.'

'Well,' I said, doubtfully, 'I need some for expenses.'

'RAYMOND!' shouted Zonda menacingly at the wall.

'Alright alright,' I said. 'There's no need to . . .'

'Look at you,' she said, turning round. 'You're *crouching* – you're actually worried, in case that cheap crook you're harbouring in the kitchen hears you – admit it?'

'Keep still,' I said, 'or I can't do this.'

'Give it to me, then,' she said, angrily, snatching the soap off me and plumping down in the water with a splash that made it ride up over the side of the bath and wet the legs of my trousers.

She clapped a hand over her mouth and squealed. It was as if a third person was present, acting as an audience every now and again. But not always. That was the difficulty. And the anger returned just as swiftly as it had vanished.

'And we have to *live* with them . . .' she said. 'It's incredible . . .'

'Nonsense, you've been enjoying this little interlude,' I said. 'I've seen you . . .'

'Do you really think so?' she said. 'Then you don't know me at all. What else can I do, when it's all so public?'

'Your behaviour at the party, by the strictest standards of social etiquette,' I said smugly, 'left a little to be desired.'

'*Your* behaviour at the party was ten times worse. To start with, you went out and left me with no money to buy the stuff with. You were rude to *everyone*. Don't you understand, what's happening to you? You're so obsessed with this deal business. I shouldn't think some of them will ever speak to you again – and look how rude you were to Sandra and Sidney . . .'

I gave a short laugh.

'Well, they're *your* friends,' I said.

I ducked as she threw the soap and started to splash me with water. 'Fucking sod,' she said. 'What gives you the god-almighty right to *behave* in this way?'

'They are bores,' I said, fanning the flames, as I ran to the far end of the bathroom in my damp, steamy clothes.

'Come *here*, Raymond, I want to *talk* to you.'

'The tone of this conversation would wrong-foot a mountain goat.'

'Never mind about fucking that,' said Zonda in a roar, prompting me instantly to put my finger up over my mouth.

'There you go *again*,' she said. 'That proves it.'

'Proves what?'

'I mean it,' she said, dropping her tone. 'You are changing, you're going *away*, you're *leaving*.'

She stood up, shivering.

I glided in like a butler with a towel, which I draped stylishly over Modom's shoulders. I pulled the plug.

She was shivering, standing in the shallows like a little girl at the beach. The water was being swallowed in stages, lowering half an inch at a time, like the level in a glass when a person gulps at it. I spun on my heel, busy, busy, my squat body working, the steam flattening and damping my hair like a Twenties beau, fetching her blue and white nightdress from the floor, rubbing her up and down, until I hurt her with the towel and she wrenched away. It was no good, she stood there, her eyes welling with tears, as the last swirls of the soapy tide raced over her feet into the vortex of the plughole.

'What's the *matter*?' I said, not without conscious parody.

Her mouth wrinkled into a lying-down 'S' shape.

'What's going to happen to us?' she said, with a sob. 'We're drifting apart . . . it's started already . . . and now you're *going* tomorrow . . .'

I held up the nightdress and she opened the bath towel exposing her pale, blotched, goose-pimpled upper torso. I slipped it over her head as she talked.

'And what did Giuseppe say to you? He said it was *stupid*, didn't he?'

'He said it was a mirror to catch larks and that I must pay attention . . .'

'Well . . . that shows you,' she said, emerging through the neck of the nightdress.

'Never heard the expression before,' I said. 'It must be some Italian archaism. I must look it up in the dictionary.'

'Never mind about the *expression*, Raymond,' she said, one arm stuck through the neck of the nightdress. 'It's what he *meant* that counts . . . and I know what he meant . . . it's all mad and stupid and *somebody* will get hurt. Oh, this *thing*!' she cried. 'Help me *will* you . . .'

I led her arm back through the neck.

'Please,' she said, crying afresh and putting her arms up round my neck, 'please, you don't know *anything* about business, not the first thing, and these people are *sharks* – I don't trust them.'

'*Trust* them,' I said scornfully. 'What's that got to do with it?'

'I know you think I'm stupid,' said Zonda, 'because I don't know where Paraguay is, but I do know you, and I know that this business isn't *good* for you. I tell you it's deforming you. I can't get *near* you any more. You won't even let me . . . look at you, look at you *now* . . .' she cried finally in triumph, as I pulled her arms away from my neck. 'That's what I *mean*, don't you see . . .'

'But *don't you see* . . .' I said, the reflex of quotation operating, as she let me go and climbed out of the bath. She stared at me, mournfully, while her hands disappeared behind her head as she unpinned her hair.

'How *can* you? How can you do this to me?' she said.

'For God's sake, Zonda,' I said sharply, 'I'm only going to the Riviera for a few days. I've asked you to come with me. I *want* you to.'

'I want you here with *me*, while I find out what's the matter with me.'

'It's only a few *tests*, for God's sake. Then you can jump on a train and we can be together. Besides, if things go according to plan, I shall probably be back in time.'

She stumped off up the bathroom and sat down on the lavatory.

'You just don't listen, do you?' she said, the last button pulling very tightly at the hem of the nightdress as she spread her legs. 'Go away, go on, then,' she said. 'See if I care . . . to hell with you, then. . .'

'Oh, *dar*ling,' I said, sitting on the edge of the bath and putting my arms around her. '*Don't* be like that . . .'

'Gerroff,' she yelled, thumping viciously at me with a bunched fist. It was boy and girl again, brother and sister, and there was a built-in desire for defeat in her grimaces, her limp defences, which was designed to show off my strength. I never indulged in this game, which was full of obscure invitations I only partly understood.

We tiptoed out of the bathroom, but Mooney was on the telephone in the front room. It sounded like a report to the Baron, but I couldn't really hear properly, because Zonda was hissing her nothings in my ear. I wanted to go and discuss some more of the details of the stud-farm with him, and I pulled away and let her go into the bedroom.

'I'll be along in a minute,' I said, checking to see if Don was still asleep. He was still face-down. I picked up some blankets from the cupboard.

The bedroom door clicked shut, and I took the inch of grappa left in my glass and sat on the step near the sacks. It wasn't the Baron, it was Drakulič, and they were discussing the timetable of meetings to come with the Brazilians, and which day to fix 'clorsing' from Drakulič's point of view.

I sat, sipping the grappa, listening to Mooney's expert vagueness about dates. Everything he did or said had this quality about it. In fact, most of it seemed to deflect from the subject in hand to casual exhortation on the lines that the details will always work themselves out, so long as the commitment is there. This I believed to be true, so perhaps it was my conversation with Zonda that made me hear it slightly differently. But it had been a long, long day and though my mind was active, it creaked on in a thoughtless way I didn't trust. It seemed an age ago when I'd been doing a translation, a different historical era. How was it possible for time to go so slowly, and for so many non-events to be crammed into it?

When Mooney came off the phone, he was showing signs of

266

fatigue, for the first time since I had met him. Just to look at him made me tired. He slumped down against the sacks of cement, the plastic mac covered in the white dust.

'Well . . .' he sighed, winding the rubber band round his pocket-book and stowing this battered, sweaty volume in his jacket pocket. 'All set for tomorrow.'

I arranged the blankets and improvised a couple of pillows near the sacks.

'D'you know what I could just drink now? A nice cup of strong tea, the brick-red sort . . .'

Taking off his spectacles he went off into a rambling monologue about teas, grabbing my arm as he settled under the blanket:

'. . . Orange Pekoe, that's the one,' he said. 'You don't have any Orange Pekoe, do you Raymond?'

Briefly we discussed waking-up procedures in the morning, and I rang the alarm-call people.

I turned out the light and cleaned my teeth in the bathroom. The cat was not at its station by the chimney-pot. When I came out and said goodnight, he asked me for a match. I threw the box from the kitchen table. I heard him, sighing and muttering and striking the match again and again on the rocky, uneven floor by his blanket, as I clicked the bedroom door shut, and shuffled in the gloom towards the bed. I noted, with approval, as I climbed over them, that Don was still on the outside of the sheets; Zonda rolled on her back, making little movements of the lips, as if she were chewing something unpleasant.

'Been?' she said, blindly feeling for me.

'Just talking,' I whispered.

'Ages . . . cold,' Zonda moaned, patting me round her as if I were a piece of plaster of Paris.

Our breaths began to come in sequence, against the long bass undertow of Don's.

Sometime, the phone rang and I could just hear the uphill and down-dale of Mooney's voice like a dog after sheep at the end of a huge, cropped pasture.

'Goddam phone,' said Don, humping round behind me and pulling the sheets. 'Ain't stopped ringing since we got here. I know,' he said, lifting his head up for a moment, 'where I'd like to stick that goddam phone . . .'

I sat up. I couldn't believe it, but it was time to go.

Part Three

Monaco

The Hôtel du Louvre was a tall narrow box-like building, painted in sea-urchin green, forming, like almost everything else in Monte Carlo, a step between an upper and lower level. The main entrance was up on the Boulevard des Moulins, facing away from the sea, opposite the church of François de Sales, but there was another entrance two floors below, on the opposite side, facing the sea, which gave on to the little Square Winston Churchill with its squat, frog-like bust of the great man, perfect for clients arriving by taxi with heavy luggage or people desperate for easy access to the harbour and casinos. When Mooney spotted this, he livened up and became decisive. He looked around, as we stood in the old-fashioned, plain black-and-white-tiled lobby decorated with aspidistras and provided with a couple of easy chairs and tables near the entrance.

'Two holes to the burrow. Yes, I think this will do us nicely,' he said turning to Irving, as we tendered our passports. He was staring at the lift as he spoke, watching the lit grille sink without stopping through the lobby-floor on its way to the lower exit.

He didn't seem to notice that his room – no. 35 – was a cupboard. Besides the bed, it had a small writing desk, a telephone, a wing chair and a stool and some dark fitted wardrobes and one of those peculiar instruments designed for lodging cases on, a kind of brass toboggan without runners. There was very little room for an occupant. The window looked out on to a yard – a gap in the building, in reality – which was full of mops and bright plastic buckets. The crash of the kitchen could be heard somewhere below.

I had a pleasant double room with a minuscule balcony on the sea side. Very little of the sea was visible, unfortunately, because someone had half-erected a ferro-concrete block of flats or offices which rose from the lower level and just succeeded in blocking the view. Still, one could throw open the windows in the morning and take in the air at least. Irving and Don had another more spacious room on the Boulevard side – no. 29.

Anticipating a siege I went down the end of the Boulevard, which I had already renamed 'Mill Street', and bought a number of useful items: coffee cups, an electric kettle, British Corporation sugar, a filter set, and a large can of Lavazza, my favourite brand of coffee. I suspected we were going to be spending long hours in the Louvre and it looked like the kind of place you could make yourself discreetly at home in. It was four o'clock in the afternoon. Mooney hung his other suit in the wardrobe and got straight on the phone. De Negris was on the phone trying to contact Münzen at the Société Générale. Mooney wanted to get over there right away and use their telex machine. Münzen wasn't there, but would be happy to see him in the morning.

Habib rang from the Mirabeau. He and the Princess wanted us to meet with the representatives of the Venezuelans who were in town. Why didn't we come over to La Coupole, the Mirabeau's gourmet restaurant, and have dinner with them and then we could go to the Casino afterwards? I looked around at the immemorial scene in the cupboard. It was already as if we had been there for weeks. It was too small for all of us to sit, but the lucky few got to loll against the wardrobes. I fetched a couple of chairs from the other rooms. This was obviously going to be the 'engine room' as Mooney called it. All engine rooms looked exactly the same, except this was smaller. The air was already full of the requisite clouds of smoke. Mooney was on the phone, brandishing his Sheaffer and writing lists of figures and scribbling rings round them on the backs of used telex sheets. I hoisted my thigh on the edge of the desk after dishing out the coffee and got out my portable chess set. I hoped the hotel had a decent switchboard. Mooney was trying to get through to something called the Stampa Corporation, to someone called Elmer Moore.

Don was telling Irving about the trip down. With casual sadism, I had arranged for him to ride with Habib and the Principessa in the limousine which De Negris had managed to organise from Livorno while Mooney, Irving and I rode in the Capri. Apparently, Don told me to my enormous satisfaction, they bitched all the way down about the arrangements: the timetable, lunch, the age and size of the car etc. When they arrived, they cheered up a bit, losing no time in taking their eighth-floor suite at the Mirabeau. Mooney broke off waiting for his long-distance call and gently reminded him that they were vital to the enterprise because one peep from her Highness and the Venezuelans would pull out.

Mooney switched on his genial telephone manner.

'Elmer, Gerrard here. Look I just want to confirm some of the details of the proposal with you . . . Yes, with the B of A . . . that's right . . . right . . . an external account . . . that's right . . .'

He broke off the enormous box doodle he was engaged on and put the pen in his ear, wiggling it gently and taking it out every now and then to inspect the end while he nodded and grunted at the telephone.

'Well, we intend to invest . . .'

He was obviously being queried. He corrected himself.

'Are in the process of investing, I should say . . . Yes, that's right . . . *have* invested . . . large ranchlands in the US for the purchase of . . .' He rattled it off, inspecting the end of the pen. 'Soya beans, grain, cattle and hardwood timber . . .'

I was feeling impatient suddenly, my mood faintly for once agreeing with Don's, who was looking more young Dean Martin than ever. I looked around. I was imprisoned with the debtors in this set-up. So far, the Baron seemed to be the only one I had met who belonged to the other side. Once I knew the Princess was

273

only a borrower, she lost her shine, despite what I had said to Zonda. Don was right, she was a prize bitch. I wanted to meet *lenders*, I told myself, bankers, people of substance who controlled things, not out-of-work princesses and penniless ex-racing drivers with cousins in banks. I realised I had to be patient, but it seemed we were dealing with an awful lot of second-rate stuff. The *real* people, the lenders – Ickle, Bisig, and Company – were just Swiss shadows, telephone characters . . . Drakulič was real, but he was just another agent. When were we going to get to meet the real stuff?

'Oh, Elmer, look here, a similar procedure can be adopted for the transaction with the investment bankers, but in that case they would issue the T-bonds . . . Now what I want to know is, is the interest on the T-bonds covered by separate coupons or is it all on one piece of paper? . . . Can you tell me? You'll check back?'

'So anyhow,' Irving was saying in a stage whisper, 'they're running out of time . . . two guys from Romaine truck it out hell for leather all night from California and it arrives at the Desert Inn in the morning . . . there's two scoops of the old banana nut left . . . You should have seen the faces of the food manager and the kitchen staff at the Desert Inn when 350 gallons of the secret Hughes banana nut backs up in a refrigerated truck the size of a condominium . . . Where in hell they going to *put* it. . . ? Next day he eats the ice-cream,' Irving scarcely looked up from his story as Mooney got up and went out for a splosh, 'and he says: "That's great ice-cream, but it's time for a change. From now on, I want . . ." ' Don was beginning to shake helplessly. ' "I want . . . FRENCH VANILLA!" '

They were rolling around, breathless in spasm. I followed Mooney out and waited outside the toilet. When he appeared, I invited him into my room to look at the view from the balcony. We stood staring at the office block, the ferrous cages inside the concrete pillars of which emerged abruptly and shot up like sketches of its future state into the air. All round it stood the beige-washed older buildings of the step below, their balconies hung with geraniums, their shutters still closed for the afternoon siesta.

I looked sidelong at him. What *were* T-bonds, and why did he want them on separate pieces of paper?

Bullishly, he ignored the question:

'It's all coming on very nicely, Raymond . . . veerry nicely . . . tomorrow we'll have a credit line from Münzen all being well – and we'll have a performing bank ready for *clorsing* . . . then all we have to do is post the schedules . . . could have it wrapped up by next week . . .'

'What about Clyde?'

He frowned.

'Well Clyde'll have to come down when we're going into clorsing to be there when we sign the ranch papers . . .'

'If he still exists . . .'

He looked at me.

'Clyde is fine . . . he just sometimes gets cipher stroke . . .'

'Cipher stroke?'

'A joke Raymond. He just gets a bit nervous when he's writing out the noughts . . . But he's a fine man with a lovely home, beautiful wife and charming children . . . and he's doing a great job for us . . .'

He rattled this off with such aplomb that Clyde himself instantly turned into a cipher, a statistic in a bank report. I could hardly hear the voice that wept on the end of the telephone that night.

'Tell me something,' I asked. 'How do you come to know the Principessa and Ickle and all these people . . . the Baron?'

He laughed.

'You mean, Raymond, how does a . . .' He gestured at his crumpled trouser bottoms and the peculiar pointed shoes 'like me get to know these quality names. . . ?'

I demurred, but he was already thinking about the question.

'Let's see. Well Dodie Maxwell put us on to Drakulič and Drakulič had contacts with Ickle . . .'

'Who is Ickle?'

'Very distinguished man,' Mooney puffed. 'Retired now, of course, but he used to be the Chairman of the Swiss National Bank. I think this deal will be his swan-song.'

'Have you met him?'

'Not exactly . . . I've spoken to him on the phone many times . . . I usually deal with Bisig . . .'

'What about the Princess and Habib?'

He jerked his thumb.

'Irving brought them in and they brought the Mauritians and the Venezuelans in.'

'But when we went to Pisa to pick him up, you didn't know Irving . . .'

'I had never *seen* him,' he corrected.

'So even in the Bahamas . . .? But he's a director of your company . . . Pequeño Investments . . .'

'In this world, it depends on what you mean by *know*,' said Mooney.

'And the Baron?'

'He came with Drakulič.'

'And the Brazilians . . .' he mused. 'I brought them in to begin with . . .'

'How did you know them?'

'Met one of them – Jaime – at the Econometrics Conference in Berlin . . .'

'And why Northern Italy?'

'Well you know when Griffiths was shooting *Way Down East* with Clara Bow, the film suddenly got snow and avalanches and scenes of the snowy north in it?'

'Yes. Lillian Gish,' I corrected.

'Well, Griffiths had to go to Canada, so rather than stop shooting, they wrote it into the plot . . . I happened to be in Tuscany, so there didn't seem any reason not to get started there . . . they have *banks* after all . . .' The phone went. He threw his cigarette stub over the balcony. I kept my eyes on it as it floated down against the green of the park until it merged with the grey of the roadway beneath.

Don appeared and said someone was on the phone. Mooney turned to go in.

'And Lillian Gish had to go over the Niagara Falls . . .' I said.

'Nearly, Raymond, nearly . . .' He turned and laughed. 'But you're right, Clara Bow had to do her own stunting out on the frozen icefloes. Let's hope we don't have to go in for any of that sort of caper!'

It was Dodie Maxwell on the phone again. I couldn't understand why, but Mooney never seemed to want to get mixed up with Dodie Maxwell. He was extra polite and charming, but always backing away.

I went out to find another phone, and eventually rang Zonda in Florence from the call-box on Mill Street.

'Doll?'

'Raymond, have you put this place on the market?'

'Oh yes, I meant to . . .'

'Good Christ,' said Zonda. 'You might have told me.'

'Why?'

'Well, these people came to the door . . .'

'Goodness, that was quick. I only told Lanzieri last week . . .'

'Well, you didn't tell *me*, Raymond.'

'I know, I forgot, I'm sorry . . .'

'I opened the door and they said they wanted to look round. I didn't know what they were talking about. They woke me up.'

'So you sent them away?'

'I sent them *packing*. I told them it was a private house and there must be some mistake . . .'

'Well, I'm afraid there'll be others . . .'

'Other mistakes?'

'People.'

'Same thing,' said Zonda bitterly. 'Same damn thing, innit?'

'What's the matter now?' I said, stealing her favourite Bessie Smith line.

But she didn't notice. She was worried. She'd had the results of the tests. It was certain she'd have to go into hospital for a check-up. She didn't know what it was and the doctor didn't know what it was. Should she fly to England? Where would she get the money? Meanwhile, she kept damn well bleeding.

The phone line was crackling with questions, the last of which, 'Well, what have you got to say?', was not rhetorical.

'Why don't you come down here?' I said. 'Time's running out.'

'Too damn right,' said Zonda. There was something peculiar about the way she kept saying 'damn'.

'I mean on the phone. Look, let me give you the number of the hotel, so people calling in with messages for Gerrard can ring us here . . .'

'Bugger him. What about *me?*'

'Look Doll, having committed myself, you know I've got to keep him in my sights . . . and tomorrow we're going to the bank to meet with Münzen. If that goes well, everything will be on its way to closing . . .'

'You're talking like him,' she said triumphantly. 'You're beginning to talk like him.'

'Then I can think about coming back and getting you, Doll . . .'

'I don't want to be *got*. I'm bloody well ill. Don't you understand, Raymond what's come over you? Do I have to scream and shout it? I'm not well, what other expressions can I use?'

In the end, I managed to get her to take down the number of the Louvre and to coax her into a slightly better frame of mind with an exaggerated account of our arrival and the hideousness of the Princess, but it was touch and go, and for a long time I thought she was not going to come round at all. Tonight, I said, we were going to meet with the Venezuelans and we were going to the Casino and tomorrow we would meet with Münzen at the bank.

'It looks as though, at *least* we're going to have a bank,' I said with a sigh of relief.

' "We" this and "we" that ... what's all this "we" stuff, Raymond?' said Zonda.

'It could be you and me,' I said sophistically, 'if Münzen takes the thing on.'

'If you could hear yourself, you sound just like that fucking insurance salesman,' said Zonda, ringing off in disgust.

When I got back everyone was ready to go over to the Mirabeau. My discomfort couldn't really survive the laughter in the lift, and when we came out into the lobby, our steps clipping rhythmically over the black and white tiles, Irving and I in step, swapping quips, it had almost disappeared. We swung out down Mill Street to the end and went down some steps two at a time. It was a beautiful mild evening. Generally it was Mooney, I saw, who set the mood. Tonight he seemed buoyant, cruising along in front with Don, the ram's horns turning everywhere, taking everything in, making a mental note of this and that, his energy flowing back into the group in perceptible waves. When he was up like this, he was almost irresistible. The President out for a walkabout with his aides.

The Princess had booked us a big table at La Coupole. She had 'the Venezuelans' with her. Philippe Jamot and Carlos Bartells. Philippe wore a gold signet ring on his little finger which he played with constantly as he said 'ze' for 'the' and 'kerraces' for the capital of his native land. He was older than he appeared at first, and the black curls bobbed thick and tight all over his skull, which gave him his baby-faced look, were streaked with silver at the sides. Rows of creases, deeply etched in one within the other on either side of the mouth by a lifetime of disappointed anticipation, created a perpetual smile which wasn't actually there. He was drenched in a well-known masculine perfume, which rose in sour clouds from his clothing whenever he moved.

Carlos was shorter than Philippe and essentially blonder. His eyes were of a blue so arresting you could see them from across the room, lodged like chips of broken china in the clay of his cheeks. There was something wrong with Carlos's shoulders which one didn't notice at first. They were not quite symmetrical, and when he walked he listed like a doomed ship, picking up one crocodile shoe slightly higher than the other. The voice was a deeply nasal grunt and he had a habit of waving his arm across from right to left as if brushing aside an invisible curtain of cobwebs to get those blue eyes properly trained on you while he grunted 'No broplep' as if he had a heavy cold. This was a tic, fully developed. He had been in advertising in Hamburg, before breaking horses in Spain. Now they were Venezuelans.

'You see him on TV in Red Square in his old black overcoat,' said Mooney at the far end of the table across a jungle of flowers and napkin cones. 'But don't let that fool you, these Russians are real sly old buzzards . . .'

'I have cancer,' said Carlos crisply, 'but . . . no broplep . . .'

'Chain-smoker, vodka guzzler,' said Irving, 'but these things never impaired his ability to negotiate. You know his greatest weakness?'

He was holding them up to ransom, Philippe, the Princess, Habib, Mooney, all inclined towards him. Don, Carlos and I filled the other end. Carlos pushed his arm across the table in between the individual roses and began fiddling with his yellow graph-paper shirtcuff.

'I know what you're thinking,' said Mooney, 'but he was a good family man. At least when he was . . .'

'Drugs?' said Philippe, moving his hand in a circle.

'Cars . . .' said Mooney, 'fanatical collector of cars . . .'

'No broplep,' said Carlos. 'Look at this . . .'

The button was resisting his fingers. It was jet-black, a swirling bluish milky-silver pattern in the jet.

'Can I help?' I heard myself say.

'Each time Nixon and he had a summit, he took him a new car. In '72 it was a Cadillac, in '73 a Lincoln Continental, and in '74 . . .' sang Irving.

'Yes, what was it in '74? Some smaller thing . . . some

280

up-to-the-minute thing he'd read about in a magazine . . . that's right, it was Car of the Year in *Motor Trend* . . .'

'A Chevrolet Monte Carlo,' said Irving with a smirk, looking round at the view.

'*Ma, boeuf*,' said Philippe, raising his eyebrows at the Princess, who smiled down at him. '*Quelle coincidence* . . .'

'All roads lead to Monaco . . .' said the Princess.

I was staring at the button and Carlos's frantic fingers which worked away squeezing it this way and that into the buttonhole while the hand inside the shirt lifted every now and again, helplessly, like a fish on a dock.

'A Citroën-Maserati speedster and . . .'

'. . . his favourite . . .'

Carlos gave a sigh as the button slipped into the buttonhole and he pushed it through against his forearm. The cuff sprang open at the wrist and Don and I craned forward.

'A 300SL,' said Mooney.

'But when did he ever *drive* them. . . ?' said Habib.

'That's a good question Doctor,' said Mooney.

Everybody agreed it was a good question.

We stared at the wrist. A large dead swelling, a delicate shade of mauve, blossomed on either side of a silver scar.

I was relieved and disgusted at the same time.

'Gee,' said Don, 'that's really something.'

'No broplep,' said Carlos.

'Sure looks like a problem to me,' said Don.

'Shakespeare,' said Carlos to me, presumably as an English-man. 'To be or not to be . . .'

He laughed and pulled at his curtain, his eyes swelling into an exquisite matchless sky blue, perfect middle-distance, without a hint of ultramarine or cobalt. 'No broplep.'

'Nixon didn't get a thing out of him in '74, though,' said Irving, 'despite all the cars . . .'

'Peasant cunning,' said the Princess to Philippe. 'Europeans know nothing about it . . . He would strip you all at cards . . .'

'Now it is . . . *oben*,' said Carlos. He pointed at the back of his neck. 'Finish . . . no broplep . . .'

'You know when the Americans got to his dacha on the Black Sea, they couldn't believe it . . .' said Irving. 'Exterior Plexiglass elevator up and down the cliff and fantastic security . . . whole damn thing . . .'

'Just like San Clemente . . .' said Mooney with a laugh, filling everyone's glass.

'Soon,' said Carlos, 'I start dying.'

I reached for the Margaux '72. I looked at Don.

'Well, I'm starving,' I said.

I was unhappy about my role in this. I was with the wrong group. The action was all at the other end of the table.

'Why not?' said Carlos.

'Nothin' to lose, huh?' said Don.

'I shall retire to my hacienda in Venezuela, take my pistol, and . . .'

He opened his mouth and almost put two fingers in it.

'*Putt* . . .' he said and his hand mimicked the recoil.

The blue eyes thirsted at us across the table.

'In the meantime . . .' I said, 'what will you have to eat?'

I had noticed there was a trace of transatlantic in Zonda's voice on the phone and now, as I watched Don and we listened to the drone of Carlos's biography, it occurred to me he'd probably called her just before me. Carlos was half German and half South American. His father had been a businessman in Hamburg and had married a Venezuelan girl after the war and set up in Caracas. Carlos worked for the government.

I asked what the business was.

'Animal foodstuffs,' said Carlos.

'How very interesting,' I said, but the indifference was a double-take because if Mooney got hold of this . . . I was already watching his face light up as he conjured up a secondary business connection with the stud-farm.

'Not interesting at all,' said Carlos spooning his soup.

'Anything for horses,' I asked.

'We could do anything. Big wholesale warehouse, no broplep,' said Carlos.

'Say, d'you play poker?' said Don, also thinking ahead.

Carlos actually smiled, or rather untwisted his lips.

'I've played.'

'I bet ole nothing-to-lose'd be quite a sandbagger?'

I didn't know what a sandbagger was.

'He slowplays strong hands,' said Don looking sideways at Carlos. He obviously had the trick of untwisting Carlos's lips any time he liked. The next thing, I thought, would be a nudge.

Restless, I slid my chair back and went to the toilet. In the stainless steel mirrors, I stared at the lank, eternally loose, lock of hair over my right temple that had never, since childhood, joined the others, the thickening waist under the grey suit, my pale freckled skin at the wrists. I had been a promising chunky centre-threequarter in the Colts at school, doing the hundred in eleven seconds dead at thirteen. The bow-legs were still there but the thighs – muscular then, fat now – stretched the material of the suit. I remembered the last time with Zonda. When was it? I had touched her breasts on the outside of her blouse, some kind of cream crêpe. The nipples were already large in the draught from something. I heard her sigh in my ears: 'For God's sake Raymond, why d'you always have to start *there*!'

Irving and Mooney were reminiscing when I pushed my way, smiling, between them and stood looking across at the Princess, Habib and Philippe, my eyebrows arched as if expecting someone to do something.

Mooney was in the middle of describing some old deal he and Irving had been involved in.

'Capital flows in '69 really started to get crazy,' he was saying to the Princess. 'The Americans were borrowing Eurodollars in huge quantities, so when they started repaying in '70 and '71, they had a 20 billion dollar deficit and every national bank in Europe had a massive surplus of dollars, so much so everybody in late '71 started thinking revaluation of European currency was inevitable . . .'

'This is what Nixon wanted of course,' said Irving. 'He was stonewalling, trying to force them to revalue so he wouldn't have to touch his own currency.'

'I don't think Nixon gave a damn,' said Mooney. 'Not *then* . . .'

'Not *ever*,' said Habib.

'Of course, we knew of this in my country,' said the Princess, nodding at me. 'Our foreign accounts.'

Mooney looked up.

'Ah Raymond,' he said absently. 'Anyway it meant everybody was scrambling all of a sudden out of the dollar anticipating . . .'

Habib nodded. He clapped his hands together, and gave his high whinny, looking irresistibly like a horse I once knew, a certain Foucon.

' – European exchange revaluations,' he said.

Mooney seemed to have forgotten for a moment that I was his favourite nephew.

'I'm bored with poker stories,' I said suddenly, turning my head away from them towards Don and Carlos, and swinging a limp arm so that it smacked faintly against my suit.

'Little bit highly strung,' said Mooney, getting the message, 'like the sister. Spitting image,' he said.

I settled in between the Princess and Philippe's wan playboy smile opposite Mooney and Irving. Don and Carlos looked up at the other end of the table from grubbing in their hors d'oeuvres, and Don glowered in between the roses.

'Did you just hear that son of a bitch?' I heard him say.

'And where is your friend, Miss Swift?' asked the Princess, blowing a spume of Rothmans vertically out of one corner of her blood-caked mouth. 'I found her an extremely *original* person . . .'

She continued across me for the benefit of Philippe. She was looking scrawnier than ever, great twisted neck-cords and an unmistakably greyish tint to the flesh even in the discreet lights of La Coupole. The waiter splashed out a more than decent Chablis.

'Mr Bosanquet is a person who loves horses. A typical English gentleman amateur.'

Mooney laughed:

'Well, part of him,' he said. 'The Protestant half of the family, you might say . . .'

I explained to the Princess that Zonda had to stay in Florence for a few days for some minor medical check-up.

'So vivacious,' said the Princess to Philippe.

The ghostly marks in Philippe's cheeks filled with the obligatory charming smile that appeared between them at the thought of the charming vivacious young girl. Or perhaps it was at the thought of something else. Or perhaps there was no thought involved. After a few minutes' conversation, it seemed to be the latter.

'But Bosanquet?' said Philippe, 'it is Frurnch is it not?' He sounded exactly like Jacques Cousteau when he said 'Frurnch', except that the 'r' was rolled handsomely, in the Spanish manner.

'Huguenot,' I said.

'*Irish* Huguenot,' said Mooney with a superior smile at me.

This gave us the opportunity to discourse on our family history and our stud-farms in Kilkenny and the West. And Mooney could then drop neatly into the Cumberland Plateau Ranch which we had apparently bought together, conjuring up a picture of shaven lawns and white palings, between which an orderly troop of 'young Mooneys' walked flashing chestnut mares.

'Ah, Tennessee . . .' said Mooney. 'Beautiful country . . . do you know it at all Mr Jabot. . . ?'

Philippe didn't.

'But "Jabot",' I quipped, 'it is . . .' The temptation to do a Cousteau was grave, but I resisted it – 'French isn't it?'

'Not Ja*b*ot,' said Philippe. 'Jamot.'

I felt a pang of regret as he went on to say that his mother had been French. The lace ruff had sprung in my mind, spreading like a fan under his perfect olive-coloured Adam's apple, transforming him with very little effort into a character, or perhaps a lost actor, in the Comédie Française. He faded off the stage, but kept jerking back into the wings every now and again, bobbing about looking for his entrance. Monsieur Jabot.

Mooney was purring as we worked him over: letting him float his biography, and chipping in to upstage at required points. The Princess looked happy enough, glancing occasionally at his face as she listened to us.

Irving and Habib were discussing the effect of the Arab-Jewish problem on interest rates.

Through the roses, I could hear Don:

'There was me, the pro, the bookie who was dealing, and this gambler who played like a monkey . . . down in Cincinnati one time . . . playing "Hold Me Darling" . . .'

I heard him ask Carlos if he had heard of this kind of poker. There was some discussion then about a game called Bedsprings and whether this was the same thing as Hold Me Darling.

The Princess seemed quite uninterested to hear Monsieur Jabot's biography. Hesitatingly, he unfolded its migrant pattern. His mother had come from Tours in the Thirties to Caracas and married his *ranchito* father. I guessed she must have been a Jew. You could live well then. He sensed his audience loss and rapidly switched to describe the fight between the Friedman and Keynesian factions in the government of Venezuela:

'You know it is so irrelevant,' he said down the table. 'Last year, 88 per cent of the return on Venezuela's petroleum industry had to go on servicing the current deficit and its interest, and they are playing party politics. Herrera Campins went to school in Chicago with Friedman. The results are catastrophic . . .' He was pleading with us. 'These fights are irrelevant, they're not appropriate for a developing country like ours. They are the arguments of sophisticated industrialised countries with infra-structures. Meanwhile the cost of purified water in the *avenidas* of Caracas is more than the cost of *benzina*.' He laughed bitterly. '. . . and the hydroelectric potential of the country is enormous. It has *thousands* of rivers. You know what the latest tourist-board slogan is? "Venezuela is proud of its water"!'

The waiters arrived and we tried to take advantage of this to calm him down. Even the Princess fussed with his Chablis. A huge bouillabaisse intervened and several lobsters. A basket of delicate little *croquettes* of all descriptions slid along in between us.

Meanwhile Don was slogging on behind the roses:

'So the pro had a pair of sevens going in . . . the bet was small – five dollars – so he played along. The dealer burned the top card and turned four-six-seven. I called on two court cards. Now – having concealed his triplets – the pro bet the size of the pot – about thirty bucks . . .'

'You know what the Mexicans say – the *Mexicans*!' said Philippe. 'They say: "*Por non finire con il Venezuela . . .*'

He stared at the heaps of fish and yellow corn as a hand ladled them into his dish.

'Well, we are going to do something *about* it . . .' said Mooney in a gentle, fatherly fashion.

'I didn't make a pair on the turn, so I threw in my court cards,' said Don. 'The bookie called, then he dealt. The pro had a full house. He bet fifty bucks. The monkey called. The bookie called . . .'

Philippe picked up his fork and the invisible smile played about his lips until the skin folded like fine paper round his mouth to prove its existence. The Princess laid her hand on his arm lightly.

'That is why Mr Mooney and his friends are here,' she said unctuously, as if Philippe was personally propped up on a set of pillows, dying rapidly in front of our very eyes, as we gathered round the four-poster. 'I know Mr Mooney will be able to help you . . .' She indicated Mooney on her left, the country priest, waiting with his absolution.

'So the final turn card was five,' said Don, 'and that made a bobtail straight in the widow. The pro bet $100. The monkey raised $100. So now we come to it . . .'

Silver tureens were making their rounds. Two more bottles of

Chablis arrived. Hums of satisfaction came from the far end as Habib and Glucksman took tureen and bottle in their hands. There were little murmurs from Glucksman of 'Let me help you to some more of this . . .' He fell silent as he ladled. Mooney was looking at some spiked red snappers in his dish as if they were moon rocks. He was indifferent to this kind of thing. So I noticed was the Princess.

'So now we come to it,' said Don, rubbing his hands. 'The pro raised another $300. The monkey called . . . and whatdyaknow . . . the bookie *tapped*!'

Carlos was saying something I couldn't hear. The waiters converged on them, and Don's flow ceased.

'The difficulty,' said Habib to Irving, 'lies in the Islamic psychology. They don't exist in the world of efficiency and progress. They live in the twelfth century, you see . . .'

Philippe, Mooney and the Princess pecked and smoked while Don picked up the threads again in between.

'Well the pro just smiled and threw his sevens into the deadwood. The bookie, he turned over a pair of sixes which meant he had four of a kind . . . and you know what the monkey said . . .'

'. . . inferiority complexes, megalomania . . . it's the totalitarian conception of the world . . . you can do business with the devil, but not with Allah, you see . . .'

He said: "I *had* to call on a straight . . ." '

They laughed, Don with his reverse sucking noise.

'Very interesting, very funny,' said Carlos sombrely.

The Princess insisted on our walking to the Loews Casino, marching ahead with her desert-eating stride, her blue curls bouncing above Philippe's black and grey frizz. Habib waddled by their side. I fell in step with Irving, while Mooney walked behind with Don and Carlos, engaging the boys in lordly conversation, talking about South America with Carlos, trying to get the measure of him, while Carlos droned on about the potentiality of the oilfields at Maracaibo Lake, and the bitumen workings of the Orinoco:

'You know, in seventy-six when Petroven took over the ownership of the oilfields from nineteen foreign companies, we found a disastrous situation,' said Carlos. 'No one had invested for fifteen years in exploration . . . We now know that we could be richer than we had ever dreamed of, but it is all doomed to be *potential* riches . . . At present levels of technology we can only realise ten per cent of what we have potentially . . . Fifty million barrels a day . . . Meanwhile everything goes to service the foreign debt . . . Venezuela is like a junkie, you know,' said Carlos, 'waiting for its next fix of cash . . .'

'Is it a fact, you don't have the technology to refine the stuff?' said Mooney.

'That's right. Up to now, it has all been refined by foreigners,' said Carlos.

Mooney was nodding. He understood.

Opposite the Loews Casino, on the corner just below the gardens, we passed a small grotto, painted in the usual muddy beige that all fragments of the *belle époque* seem to be daubed in in Monte Carlo, in which a plaster effigy of the young Lady Luck was divesting herself of her last diaphanous scrap of Græco-Roman underwear. In the keystone of the arch pouted a small bas-relief of a satyr's head complete with ram's horns and protruding lips. We crossed the road, a fierce bend in the rally still marked by the tyres of the racing cars, and entered the airless humid racket of slot machines.

The Princess loved roulette, and Don and Carlos and I sat in on some games of blackjack. Mooney was enchanted by the slot machines. He seemed particularly fond of one called 'Golden Incas' which depicted three totems in a line with a triumphant Atahualpa gritting his teeth on top of each one. He was on this machine for most of the night. In vain, the others flashed 'Spun gold' and 'Try Me – Winning Is Easy'. Mooney crouched in the middle of the aisle of clacking machines and peered up at

Atahualpa, a Scotch in one hand and a pile of ten-franc pieces in the other. Irving stood back and took care of Philippe. He played some roulette with the Princess, but he basically wanted to talk. I took over from Irving from time to time, refilling his glass and shouting small-talk. The Princess had the *chef de partie* place her bets. He shouted '*Carrément, Tous les Chevaux!*' and she would signal and he would place the bet. She never looked at the wheel but stalked away carelessly across the plum-coloured sea of holes, pocked with cigarette burns, that stood for a carpet, like a cat pretending to a mouse that it wasn't looking. Some Americans were playing craps very loudly, while their wives looked on and cheered. Ted and Wanda, the Chubb-Lock salesman from Cleveland and his wife, Jacko the failed Catholic priest and peacenik patriot, and his wife Tallulah, the crystallographer, and, standing back watching them, and drinking fruit juice, the massive Jehovah's Witness, Bertha Pentecost, from Dayton, Ohio.

People living outside the capsule. I stared at them. I had already forgotten what so called real people looked and felt like. They were having fun – even the rather sinister Bertha seemed to be enjoying herself. The men were whooping and rolling the dice with the action of parodic slow-motion baseball pitchers, and perspiration was dripping off the big man Ted on to the green baize. Every now and again, Wanda would wipe his brow with a yellow handkerchief. Their first time in Europe. They thought Monaco was great – just like Vegas, only more historic, as they put it. We started buying each other drinks.

'Ah, that was fun hon,' said Ted, as he stood and Wanda mopped him down, while she told Philippe about 'our chairman, Sandy'.

'Oh, old Sandy,' said Ted. 'What a guy.'

'A fine man,' said Wanda, 'with a great love of life.'

'Say that again,' said Ted. 'You know we used to have boats on the lakes . . . you know the Great Lakes . . . and we'd make up weekend parties . . . and old Sandy never missed . . .'

'I'll never forget the time . . .' said Wanda, 'seventy if he was a day, I saw that great long thing hanging down out of his trunks . . .'

'Aw, wasn't *that* bad . . .' said Ted, turning to look around and wink at Jacko and Tallulah. 'You're exaggerating . . .'

'A fine man . . . and a fine Chairman of the Board,' said Wanda.

'Well he sure was . . . with that young girl in the back cabin . . .' said Ted, 'I'll say that . . . but you're exaggerating . . .'

He turned to me, shaking his head.

'Wasn't *that* bad . . . Wanda's right about one thing,' said Ted, solemnly. 'He sure did have a great love of life.'

'You don't happen to know our colleague in Cleveland, do you?' I heard myself asking.

'Who's that?'

'Clyde. Clyde Wellcombe . . .'

'Well, I'll be darned . . .' said Ted. 'Hey, he knows Clyde . . .'

What a dreadful mistake. I watched them devalue as they flocked around, shrinking currency. Why, hey, this calls for a drink. Only known him since third grade. How d'ya come to . . . small world. I looked for Mooney, but he was still doing business with Atahualpa, almost out of sight in the avenues of one-armed bandits.

'Clyde done pretty well in real estate, you know . . .' said Ted.

'You're British aren't you,' said Jacko. 'How come you know Clyde?'

Turning to Philippe, I said modestly:

'Our company has some interest in the area.'

Out of the corner of my eye Mooney appeared and strolled towards us with an empty glass, having disbursed himself of his stack of coins.

'Most enjoyable, Raymond . . .' he said, putting his hand on my shoulder. 'And who are our friends?' he beamed hopefully through his heavy spectacles.

I explained that they knew Clyde. He didn't alter expression but went on beaming. He wanted to know one thing, ducking all their questions about what Clyde was doing for us. When were they going back? When they told him it was not for two weeks, he grew disappointed. He wanted them to take a message, he would be quite frank about it.

It was useful, however, I thought, because it handed on our credibility to Philippe, provided, of course, they hadn't seen Clyde any too recently. That was a risk we would just have to take. Zonda was right, I decided as I examined this line of thought. I was 'one of them'.

Mooney and I said goodnight to them all at the Mirabeau and toiled back up the hill towards the Louvre, arguing about the vexed question of whether you could ever breed steeplechasers.

'You've a number of young horses in a field,' he said, poking at me a cigarette scissored between his brown fingers. 'You watch them. They will run up and down that fence all day, but it'll never enter their head to jump it . . .'

I decided doubt was in order.

'It's not natural to the horse,' he repeated. 'Come to racehorses, now, and look at Austerlitz . . .'

I butted in:

'Well, how do you explain the fact that some flat-racers are better at it than others?'

'Sure it's nothing more than temperament, Raymond . . . If there is one thing I am sure of in this world . . .'

'I know what you are going to say,' I said triumphantly. 'Jumping ability is not inherited?'

'So it isn't . . .'

'Come on,' I said, jeering. 'There must be a way of programming them . . .'

We reached the steps that ran along the side of the Louvre and began climbing.

'I know of not one single case . . .' he said, pausing for breath, '. . . in which the ability to jump has been passed on . . .'

'We've got to get this Mendelism out of the picture,' I said, banging the wall of the hotel with something approaching real passion.

He was intrigued, I could tell. He didn't know what I was going to say next. Neither did I. There was a certain irony in his posture as he silently invited me to explain.

'The Americans have just produced a small cow, about the size of a pig, with a massively increased milk yield,' I told him, 'which takes up nothing like the amount of room and feed that a traditional cow does . . .'

He stopped and looked at me, his spectacles gleaming in the moonlight.

'Who's got the patent?' he asked.

'I don't know whether there is one . . .'

'Already filed,' he said, attacking the last flight with a sigh. 'Got to be. Anyway where were we?'

'Well, the point is quite obvious. The old rules, the old approach to breeding will almost certainly have to yield all the way through, even in horse breeding. *Primarily* there, because that's where the research has been done in the past . . .' We stood on the top of the steps and stared across at the office block on the sea side of the hotel. He was shaking his head.

'It's like the Olympic games,' I said. 'It's a field with a lot of challenges and we want to be in it. Once someone has intervened, they have a basic advantage over their competition. I mean, look at the old rule about Derby-winners, the limited-cycle idea. It has never happened that sire, son, grandson, and great-grandson – four consecutive generations in direct line – have won the Derby, in the whole history of the race. Right?'

'Right . . .' he admitted, throwing his cigarette down the steps as we turned three or four steps from the top and paused again for breath, our voices reverberating between the walls of the narrow staircase.

'This is the modern breeder's challenge. It seems to be an inevitable constraint, but supposing we found a way of breaking it. Think of what advantages we would have. We'd dominate the breeding markets . . .'

I was paraphrasing, with drunken enthusiasm, an article I had recently written for *The European Racehorse*. I wondered if I had gone too far.

Mooney rubbed his chin.

'Research and development,' he said. 'The Turvey Developmental Breeding Centre . . .'

He cheered up.

'Sounds alright,' he said.

'Unit,' I said. 'I prefer unit . . .'

'Whatever . . .' I could hear him saying through the other compartment of the swing doors into the lobby of the hotel. He turned back and waited for me as I trundled like a baby with infantile steps round the turnstile doors into the lobby and joined him. 'I still think it's a long way to genetic engineering, even if what you say is true . . .'

'Is it?' I argued. 'Let's get back to the basic concepts of the breeding of horses . . .'

We picked up the keys.

'Jesus, I never left them, Raymond. Isn't it *you* that keeps on flying all over the place like a filly in the starting box at the Diamond Stakes!'

The lift didn't seem to be working, so we dragged up the stairs.

'Now we know,' I said, panting, 'that the thoroughbred is a selected hybrid . . . and this means that, even if highly selected, each separate characteristic is passed on independently . . .'

Mooney was shaking his head.

'Place is all stairs . . .' he said, struggling manfully with his breathing and stopping every other stride, one knee forward, one hand resting on it. 'I'll just . . . rest here,' he said. 'You go on and I'll see you in the morning.' He laughed. 'It's in me genes, you see, I'm just not made to go over the sticks!'

Purple-faced, he dismissed me, waving me on to bed round the bend in the narrow staircase.

*

The Société Générale de Monaco had a pleasant little conference room with a new chestnut boardroom style table, a white-board, and muslin curtains over a large picture window. Münzen's secretary served us coffee. De Negris and Münzen swapped a few family commonplaces and we got down to business.

I had been doing a lot of typing to prepare the documentation. Mooney took him through the documents. He looked at the bank letter from Kelly, the telexes from Drakulič, copies of the letters from Mooney to all parties on headed Pequeño Investments notepaper, all of which I had typed up retrospectively, just for the sake of the carbon so that his file could look in order. He nodded.

Mooney and Irving Glucksman did the talking. It appeared that the Mauritians and Venezuelans would arrive personally to deposit their countries' promissory notes. Upon receipt of these, he, Münzen, would telex Zurich that they were ready for clorsing. They went through the investor's bank syndication and Ickle's name was bandied about.

Then they came to the collateral security. This transaction was about to be closed, said Mooney. He showed Münzen all the papers relevant, including the original file of Argentinian securities from the Banco Peccaro. And then the Cumberland Plateau Ranch Papers, referring Münzen back to the acknowledgement of this as yet unconcluded transaction in Daniel P. Kelly's New York letter.

Then they came to the financial structure of the deal. Here Mooney was brilliant. He went to the white-board, and slowly produced strings of calculations step by step. The money was Eurodollar on-lent through a chain of banks by Ickle.

'Ickle? You mean, Dr Iklé,' said Münzen. 'Dr Max Iklé.'

That was correct, agreed Mooney, ignoring the correction: Ickle was the sponsor, and Dr Bisig his second-in-command at the Savings and Industrial Bank. The rate of this borrowed money was arbitraged against the rates at which it was lent to the various countries. There were different arrangements for the promissory notes for each country. Then Mooney went into some complicated arrangements with the form of their promissory notes. The emission of the capital sum was to be 95 per cent, interest payments were to take place annually in arrears, and he was asking for a year's interest in advance.

Certain proportions of the borrowed money would be converted into gold and some would be in US Treasury Bonds, to give flexibility in investment.

I could see Münzen pricking up his ears here. He asked some sharp questions about why the emission was so low.

Mooney gave the usual answer. Company fees, and some of the money, would be passed on to the lenders. The notes would be arranged like postdated cheques, falling due at different times.

Münzen said he was surprised that the Brazilians in particular, who had become experienced at negotiating loans over the past ten years or so, were willing to accept such terms. The others, he knew nothing of . . .

'They need the money wherever they can get it from,' said Glucksman, 'and as quickly as possible.'

'And if we don't move fast,' said Mooney, 'this deal will go elsewhere.'

'Everything, of course, will need to be checked by our foreign exchange department – the accreditation and the actual financial structure of the transaction, but given this . . .'

Münzen looked up, and the tension round the table was a visible current shown in a crackling circuit of glances, shorted only by Mooney, who was busy with a geometric doodle.

'Well, it's not going to be easy . . . but I think we shall be able to act for you as your fiduciary bank.'

Breaths were expelled, legs shot out under the table, heads turned, mouths relaxed. We were no longer on the streets. We had a performing bank.

'We want to go over every last detail. The structure is already almost completely in place,' said Mooney, 'and we shall be working overtime to see if we can produce a clorsing date for sometime in the next week or so . . .'

Münzen smiled.

'You'll be lucky, with something as complicated as this, but it could be done if everything falls right for you . . .'

'For *us* . . .' said Mooney, shaking him warmly by the hand.

'I can't deny it will be a feather in our cap,' said Münzen, letting his hand be swung for another few times.

'By the way,' said Mooney, 'would you mind if we used your telex machine to start the ball rolling . . . ?'

Münzen waved us into the foreign exchange office.

Mooney's eyes gleamed when he saw the telex machine. He sent several telexes from the bank, including, I saw, one that was short and to the point:

```
0258102236021 ATTENTION MR CLYDE WELLCOMBE
WE ARE NOW CLOSING PROCEDURES FOR TWO MAJOR TRANS-
ACTIONS.
WE WISH TO EXECUTE THE CONTRACT FOR THE PURCHASE OF
THE TENNESSEE RANCH END NEXT WEEK IN MONACO AND WE
WILL REQUIRE YOUR PRESENCE FOR THIS PURPOSE.
REGARDS
THE PROJECT-FOR-THE-AMERICAS INVESTMENT CORPORA-
TION
ACRY DENT ARB
570215 PP FI I
```

When eventually we emerged from the bank into the washed-down light of Monaco's streets, there was a distinct presence of euphoria amongst the troops. We headed for lunch. We agreed that Münzen was a charming man. A major step forward, as Mooney would put it.

'Looks like we're off the streets at least, Raymond,' said Glucksman at lunch.

'Now we start the serious work,' said Mooney, waving for another round of gin-toniques.

In the bank I had been reminded, or had seen closer up, more

297

continuously, the frail chain of connections which made up this transaction. It was like a huge accumulator. The chain of credit in the Eurodollar market was such that banks were linked in it, without anyone knowing what the source of the money was. One card out of the wall and the thing obviously collapsed. What were the odds it could work? This was the sole question which concerned me at the time. Not what were the chances, but what were the odds. Each bank was like a cell operating on the 'need to know' principle. And what would happen to the promissory notes when they were delivered? The money would be promptly put back into the market, to swell another round of multiplying credit.

I hadn't realised how much the euphoria of the occasion had struck until I phoned Zonda to tell her the good news.

'When are you going to come down?'

'First of all, the people keep coming to see the flat and I have to show them round. Then . . .'

'To hell with them. Next . . .'

'I haven't got the money to pay my fare . . .'

'I'll send you that. Next . . .'

'I have to keep going back to the doctors.'

'Not continuously.'

'What do you know?'

'D'you want to come? Doll, it's fantastic. We've got a *bank*, a performing bank.'

'Sounds like an animal in a circus.'

'It's fantastic . . .' I bubbled on about the Venezuelans and the Americans and the Casino and the Mirabeau and the yachts in the bay.

'I've *finished* the living-room . . .' said Zonda.

'All the more reason to take a break,' I urged.

'You don't care that I've slaved my fingers to the bone on *your* property, do you?'

'Come and see Princess Grace. Anyway, the capital the place realises will be yours to play with . . .'

She wanted to tell me about these prospective buyers . . . how awful they were. She began to go into the details of how they picked their teeth, the way they looked around.

'And by the way,' she said, 'the man has *killed* the cat.'

I didn't like the sound of this at all.

'You're exaggerating,' I said defensively. I didn't want to think about this.

'It's true.'

The way she said this convinced me that she was making it up to paint the blackest state of woe possible.

'Nonsense, I can hear it in your voice . . .'

'It was lying there for several days, and those people next door just went on having their beanfeasts under the pergola.'

'Oh *them*.'

'I spoiled their beanfeasts by telling them about it.'

'And?'

'Now it's gone. The police came. A big fat carabiniere with a moustache got up on the roof and poked it over the edge of the gutter with a stick . . . and the animal people came and interviewed them . . .'

'I know why you don't want to come. You don't have anything to wear . . .'

'You're right. I need some new shoes and a dress . . .'

'I'm sending you the money right away . . . buy *two* dresses . . .'

'Raymond, but you haven't got it . . .'

'By the way, has *he* been calling you?'

'He . . . did . . . yes,' she finished.

'Don't you want to see him, if you don't want to see me?'

'*Ba*stard,' she shouted. 'Ma *d*onnamiesanta . . .'

'Doll,' I said earnestly, 'come down. Do you good a bit of sea air.'

'Conversation with a millionaire or two would do me good.'

'It can be arranged,' I coaxed. I was really confirming her decision.

'I'm fed up with all these people ringing.'

'All serene,' I said. 'Come Friday . . . and I'll meet you at the station . . . in the limousine . . .'

We got on to my mail and the phone calls for me from various creditors.

'Raymond,' said Zonda suddenly, 'isn't there anything else you want to say to me?'

There was a long silence.

'I don't think so . . .' I said slowly.

'I see . . .'

There was a silence. I could hear her breathing and the very faint sound of two people talking in Italian.

'Oh, *that* . . .' I said.

There was another silence.

'You're not *normal*,' she said in a small voice and rang off.

I rang back, putting everything I had into my confessional.

'Doll, I . . . I love you dearly and I am missing you dreadfully and that's why I want you to come so much . . .'

'Pronto?' said a harsh grating voice.

I rang off and kept trying again, but every time I kept getting the Signor in Milano.

In the end I got back to her and repeated my confession of love, but it managed to sound facetious and jaded the second time around.

It fell into a pit of silence.

She was weeping, of course. Long racking sobs, exquisitely timed, that churned my stomach.

The boys came in at that moment, and Don saw immediately my low whispering, my coaxing with pursed lips, from across the room. I saw him smile to himself.

We seemed to take Münzen everywhere with us. He was given the usual promises that he could buy his own bank after this was over etc. We had a lot to do. He was introduced to Philippe and Carlos. I had a lot to do personally. I had to get Jeremy to

300

deliver me some money into my account, because I was still paying for a lot of things. There was the phone bill at the Louvre, the constant lunches and dinners, the Casino every night. I was spending at least £2000 a week on all this. I had to get my cash flow sorted out for at least a couple of weeks. I was getting so desperate I proposed to Don a house game of poker during some of the long periods of waiting which had begun to appear. So Don, De Negris, Irving and I made up a game. I won some from that, sometimes the price of lunch. I was longing to go racing, but there was too much to do 'back at the camp' as Mooney called it.

He began to get agitated about clorsing procedure. He insisted that Michael Casey come from the Isle of Man in order to stand by as a courier for the letter. I was to hire a private plane to fly Monaco-Zurich, and Casey was to take the final letter by hand requesting the money from the Handelsbank Zurich.

At the same time, Eamon Costello kept phoning. He was very excited. He had a hot line to some Arab money, he told Mooney, at six per cent.

'Well Eamon,' said Mooney, 'y'know we've got our own sources all lined up now. The ball's rolling . . .'

Costello insisted. It was too good to miss.

'Let them come. The more the merrier . . .' said Mooney, putting the phone down with a crash as he always did.

Procedure was supposed to be as follows. Münzen and Zurich would nudge each other towards closing, in a ritual mating dance of telexes. Münzen had hypothetical confirmation that the collateral was in place. He had accepted the outfit on this basis, incredibly. The Cumberland Ranch deal was also to close on the same day, thus confirming the collateral. At the moment we were waiting for another hypothetical telex from Zurich, confirming that, if notes were deposited in the fashion our telexes had described, then – subject to all sorts of conditions – they would deposit the money with Münzen. This would be a telex followed by a special courier letter, of confirmation. Meanwhile, by showing Zurich's *hypothetical* telex to the Brazilians, Venezuelans and Mauritians, we would induce them to move from the realms of hypothesis to those of fact, by taking the step of accepting this procedure. Then we would name the day and Zurich would be telexed that the Third-Worlders accepted their terms and were committed to deposit on a certain day. Then Zurich would move from the realms of hypothesis into those of fact. It was at this point in the procedure that Mooney insisted he needed the private plane in order to take the letter irrevocably conveying this information and formally requesting funds from SIB. Confirmation having been achieved on both sides, funds would then be committed irrevocably on closing day.

This was the theory. We had now reached the stage, however, at which collateral had to be confirmed. So Clyde had to make his appearance and the collateral deal had to be signed before any of this could take place. But Mooney wanted to sign this deal when he could show more telexes to give its support credibility. I wondered if the idea was that the collateral was supported by the main transaction which it was supposed to be acting as support of. There were of course the Pequeño Peninsula papers and various supporting documents from the Argentinian government specifying that Pequeño Investments Ltd was a bona fide company with lands and assets in their banks and that Gerrard Mooney was officially a representative of the Argentinian government doing 'agribusiness' on their behalf, but these did not amount to much. The main transaction, in fact, was unsecured. The whole deal seemed to be on the say-so of Drakulič, the Baron, Ickle, Bisig and the other members of the lenders' hierarchy.

We were now at the stage of convincing the various country members of the borrowing group that we had the hypothetical confirmation of availability of funds from Zurich and this was sufficient evidence for them to confirm their willingness to deposit. Each group however, had to be dealt with separately. Nor must the Princess and Habib, who were the links in the chain to the Venezuelans, know what the Brazilians' lending rate was because they would almost certainly want their own cut 'upped'.

We were entering on a tense period. But the euphoria of the Münzen account was confirmed when he rang one morning. Mooney kept saying it was great news. Münzen said, so he told us, that Minsky had rung from Zurich to say that they 'had it on the Committee's agenda'.

'It's all rolling.' Mooney was springing about the office rubbing his hands.

It was a period of intense social activity, and intense boredom. Irving and I were both writing cheques and I had to get him to transfer some more money into my account. I told Jeremy in London that I was selling the apartment, and I asked him for a loan on that basis. I didn't really want to dip into my capital, but there was no other way. I transferred enough money for the trip and a couple of dresses and some shoes into Zonda's Florence account.

There were a few local disputes at the hotel to enliven things. Alphonse the manager wanted us out in the mornings so that the maids could do their work on our rooms. This was alright for most of us, but Mooney wouldn't leave his room, which he insisted on calling the office, for a moment. Then there was a crisis about the telephone. As I had suspected the switchboard wasn't anything like big enough to handle the kind of traffic Mooney was loading it with, and he wanted Alphonse to install a second line. Alphonse just represented a company and couldn't do things like that he said. Mooney was at his most lordly, talking of major countries, major transactions etc. In effect Alphonse gave a Mediterranean shrug and said down his nose, why didn't we all go to the Mirabeau or the Rocabella or somewhere, if we didn't like the facilities.

We got into a routine of morning conference, car maintenance for Don and De Negris, and records of calls, and bookings for me. Someone called Diepgen kept calling with 3,000 used American Post Office vans for Mooney to sell to the Indians in Calcutta.

I kept a notebook on the afternoon poker games. I soon got to know their mannerisms, and what they were worth in cash terms.

De Negris, for example, was a very eager player when he had a good hand, keen to start the betting. 'Whose bet is it?' he said. If, before he acted on his hand, he picked up his column of coins and weighed them in his hand, usually it was a good one. But he saw that I was watching him, and he started to fake this activity. Irving was easy. He usually glanced to the left, just before he raised, calculating to see how many of us were behind him and how many had picked up their money. With Don, it was the toneless 'Luck Be My Lady Tonight!' and he would either light a cigarette and drag on it intensely before betting, which indicated he had a goodish hand, or he would scratch his chin, sometimes unshaven, and say 'Well . . . guess I'll jest have to raise it a bit . . .' when he was bluffing. You could tell when Irving had two pairs because he fitted the odd card in the middle of his hand between them. But when he was going for a flush, he mixed them all up and then squeezed the odd one out. De Negris often asked what cards had gone. This usually meant he had three of a kind and he wanted to know who was going for runs or flushes.

To divert us, Don introduced some Californian variations including Lowball, an inversion of conventional poker in which low cards were high. Once I got used to it, I started winning again on a regular basis.

Every day, both Don and I rang Zonda, each knowing the other was doing it. I could tell by her voice whether I was first or not that day. I was pressing her to come because I wanted her to bring me some money.

Mooney and I elaborated our plans for the stud-farm. I had now formed the idea that we needed an estate – three or four small farms, relatively independent from each other so that if disease broke out, the animals would be protected from each other and we would not lose all our stock at one go. He insisted we must have natural pasturing, moving them seasonally.

'Nearco was bred in the natural way,' said Mooney. 'Just think of it, Raymond . . .' He waved the telex. 'The broodmares are out in the pasture where the long grass has not been cut for the hay.

And we'll want the best upland hay, too, Italian rye grass, timothy, or sweet-scented vernal, none of your cocksfoot or Yorkshire fog! They'll move across that field and in a fortnight, they'll have it stripped. Then what do they do?'

I didn't know. I made a point of not knowing. He had reverted to his Mendelism. He seemed to have forgotten our earlier conversation about research and development.

'They'll tear up the ground with their hoofs to get at the grass roots and they'll try to reach the last green leaves of the horse-chestnuts, and when those are exhausted, what then?'

'They wait for the hay to be brought.'

'Nonsense, man, they stamp nervously up and down at the fence. And if the fence didn't exist, they'd be off to winter pastures.'

Don appeared and said there was someone on the telephone.

'That's how we'll do it.' Mooney turned and put his arm enthusiastically on my shoulder. 'We'll send them south in the winter like old dowagers to live high off the fat of the land . . .' He chuckled. 'That way we'll get Nearcos and Donatellos of our own!'

'Stupid little railway station,' said Zonda.

'Millionaires don't come by train,' I said.

She fished in her bag and gave me a clutch of bills from the apartment. She had left the key of San Gallo with Lanzieri as requested. She told me she thought that the last pair she showed round would buy it.

'Want to bet on it?'

'Same old Raymond,' she said, looking me up and down.

I looked back. She was wearing a pair of Greek sandals with all sorts of strangely aggressive bits of brass on the leather, which exactly imitated the shape of a charioteer's boots.

'I hope you've brought something a little more suitable than those.'

'Suitable for what?' she asked.

'We've entered a phase of pretty high-powered socialising,' I said, already regretting the phrase. I explained about how almost everybody had to be kept away from almost everybody else, yet entertained at the same time.

'Sounds great,' she said absently, looking out of the car window and drinking everything in. I took her on a tour. We drove slowly round the harbour, and up to the Rock. We stood in Palace Square and stared at the sugar candy castle with its red and white striped sentry boxes.

'That's where Princess Grace lives,' I told her.

She frowned at the soldiers with their blue helmets and red-lined trousers.

'Didn't have far to go to her wedding did she?' said Zonda, indicating the Abbey.

'It's the only place where you can't build,' I said, as we got back into the car.

We drove to the top of Pointe St Martin and looked down over Monte Carlo. I pointed out the burgeoning concrete apartment blocks, explaining that Onassis now no longer owned the Société de Bains de Mer, which was the one building company in the place.

'Prince shoved him out in the mid-Sixties in a shareholding gambit. Now it's build, build, build . . . if you've got the cash . . . gone downhill, terribly . . .'

She wrinkled her nose, and sneezed two or three times.

'Whose is the *big* yacht down there?'

'*Atlantis I*? – the blue one . . . ? That's Mavrakis's.'

'Who's he?'

'Your statutory Greek millionaire. You're going to a party on it tonight,' I said casually.

'Whooo,' said Zonda. 'Just what I need. Then I can wear my *other* dress . . .'

She was still truffling around with eyes and nose. I could feel the impact of the place bouncing off her expressions, off the quickly jerking head and wide-angled eyes as she swallowed it all down and chewed the aftertaste. We drove around the Place du Casino.

'Tacky, innit?' she pointed out the crumbling façade.

'Full of yobs and slot machines now,' I said with a sigh. 'You don't even need a tie to go in . . .'

'What, people like you and me, Raymond?'

We laughed.

'Same old Doll,' I said. It had been a week but it was as if we hadn't seen each other for years. She was outraged that I hadn't commented on her dress. The truth was I had not even seen it.

'But Raymond, it's orange. It's meant to be daring.'

'You know I'm not a visual person,' I said. I was anxious to explain the political situation with the borrowers and the lenders before we got back to the Louvre. We sat looking at a cracking gilt cherub on the Casino's corner, while I tried to fill her in on the current state of affairs. The Mavrakis party was unfortunately not only a jaunt. The borrowers had to be kept apart from one another. She was going to be useful, in keeping them happy. I explained the rules of the game. The borrowers when they arrived in town were to be entertained and kept in separate groups so that they shouldn't even know of each other's existence, in case they wanted their rate lowered in relation to some of the others.

'Raymond, for God's sake,' she was shaking me. 'Can't you *see* me? I'm *here*. I've arrived . . .'

It was an irrelevant nuisance, all this talk of my impercipience.

'I could be stark naked, and you wouldn't notice a bloody thing. In fact, I *am* naked, as far as you're concerned. I just have on a pair of objectionable sandals . . . No it's not that I'm naked, it's that you've blotted out the rest of me. What do you see when you look, just a pair of bloody sandals, and you hear my voice as if I were on the telephone, but that's it. I don't have eyes or shoulders, my hair is neither up nor down, and my dress and everything under it, isn't there. There's just a pair of sandals, encasing some vague legs . . .'

307

She snatched up her skirt.

'Look,' she screeched. 'Fuck you!'

She was wearing what appeared to be a green plastic carrier bag, into which holes had been hastily cut with scissors, tied at the waist and the top of the legs with string.

'Extraordinary behaviour,' I recoiled.

'Just the job for a bit of high-powered socialising.'

'But I sent you plenty of money. Surely you could have . . .'

She was beating on the dashboard of the car.

'You're so stupid. I told you I'm bleeding. I don't want to risk staining my nice new orange dress . . . You'd take some notice of it, *then* . . .'

'Very resourceful,' I said, 'to have devised those. Short notice I suppose . . .'

'It's not *ordinary* . . .'

'Sorry, sorry . . . yes, of course . . .'

'Though I'm due for *that* any minute . . .' She dropped her skirt and smoothed it down over her brown thighs.

'You're very brown,' I said, 'for someone who's been showing people round an apartment . . .'

'Julian and Dino have been looking after me,' she said pointedly. 'They took me to San Gimignano and we sat in the sun . . .'

'What is this bleeding?'

'I keep telling you. They don't know . . .'

'Well, if you can hang on till next week, you can buy your own clinic . . .' I took Mooney's line and tried to reapply it.

She made a vigorous Italian gesture.

My eyes focused on her now. 'Alright,' I said, 'you are wearing an orange crêpe paper flower in your hair, which is scraped back and piled up on your head in a manner calculated to fall down from the flower in strings of cultivated untidiness. Your lipstick is pale orange. Your face, however, is grey under the brown. Your dress has what I believe is called a boat neck. It is made of cotton. Your ears have two green stars in the lobes.'

She lit a cigarette and put her arm along the back of the seats. She smiled at me, a full bold smile. She was sweating. The familiar blemish just below the iris of her left eye, a yellowish ridge the colour of egg yolk, made the whole eyeball look like a cockle sitting in its open shell. Beneath the insolent challenge of the nose, the central column of bone was white like a chip of clear rock, whitening the thin pink skin at its base on either side where it rose out of the suggestion of blonde hairs on the top lip which had trapped two beads of sweat, swelling there, crystalline, and actually casting two tiny shadows in the light from the car window. A light sweat glistened at her temples, darkening certain strands of hair at the sides. I stared at the flute of her throat where a pulse was beating.

Her hand reached up into the back of my hair for a moment.

'You see it's foolish to think I'm not aware of you, Doll,' I said.

I turned profile, watching her watching me out of the corner of my eye.

'What colour are my eyes?' she asked.

'It's just there's a maximum future and a minimum future,' I said, 'and one has to decide which one wants.'

'I'm . . .' she started to say, but I cut her short.

'No. Hear me out . . .' I ripped the steering-wheel round with a vehemence that took me by surprise. 'I've changed my attitude towards this caper. It really looks possible for us to win, and if we do, the maximum future will be open for us, do you see, it's not a joke . . . ?'

'I was just going to say: "I'm happy to see you," ' she said softly.

'I know I seem preoccupied, but it's one of those crisis things, that if you don't seize the day,' I said, 'you don't make it . . . Don't you realise what we could do with that money . . . ?'

'It's not the money,' she said, shaking her head and taking her hand away to stub her cigarette on the dashboard ashtray. 'I understand that.'

I put the car away and we got into the lift, at the lower, seaside entrance.

Don got in at the lobby.

'Hi, Zonda,' said Don.

'Hi,' said Zonda.

We stood close together, the three of us, staring minutely at the landings peeling slowly away like soiled slices of Battenberg cake.

'Boss wants you Raymond,' said Don. 'Something's come up.'

Zonda bridled and smiled. She looked at the ceiling.

' "The Boss," ' she mouthed silently.

'Something about a meeting,' said Don. 'Hey baby,' he said as he pulled back the scissor grille. 'How you doing?'

He pushed open the door, but Zonda took my arm and hung back. There was a moment of waiting.

'I'm alright,' said Zonda.

'Well, if nobody wants to go, I guess . . .' said Don and stepped out ahead of us on to the landing.

We walked behind him. He had a little skip in his walk and his feet turned out. He stopped at his and Irving's room.

'He's in the office,' said Don. He pushed open the door to the room. Irving was sitting on the bed in his wide, red braces, reading a book called *Poker: Smart Winning Play*. I put my head in the door.

'It's not going to help, you know,' I said. I gestured behind me. 'New member of the team . . .'

He grimaced, threw the book down and gave Zonda a friendly wave through the door.

'Not with you around,' he said. 'The man's a goddam machine,' he said to her. 'Hi.'

'Don says his nibs is looking for me . . .'

'Gerrard, oh yeah? He wants you to fix something in Nice . . .'

'Oh?'

'Venue for a board meeting . . . he'll tell you. But I would get in there right away. It's been a busy morning.'

Don picked up the book and started flicking through the plays.

'Hey, neat,' he said. 'Diagrams of how to win.'

We went to our room and Zonda fell on to the bed. I showed her the balcony and the view of the concrete block of offices that was going up between us and the sea.

'Welcome to the Louvre,' I said.

'It's like being a picture,' she said, shaking herself. 'God, I'm exhausted.'

'The decadent part of the gallery,' I said. 'Let's say Odilon Redon, *Girl in the Orange Dress*.'

She looked up melodramatically and held out her arms to me.

'Let's just go and see Gerrard first,' I said.

The arms jerked.

'Mmmm . . . ?'

I knelt at the edge of the bed and attempted to give her cold sweaty brow a light peck, but she wrestled me down.

'Come *here* a minute Raymond, for God's sake . . .' she said, in my ear.

For a moment, I felt like someone at a boarding school having a visit.

'I want to *show* you,' I said, itching to pull away.

'What?'

'Things,' I said lamely, in a small voice.

She sighed and slackened her arms, letting them fall with an exaggerated double thump on the coverlet. She stared at the ceiling.

'*Things*,' she said.

'You know,' I said. 'Things *about* . . . here.'

She started laughing at my sudden bout of inarticulacy.

'Well, *I've* got things to show you . . .' she said. 'How would you like to see my new dress and . . . baam bam ba . . . *baaaam*' – she fanfared – 'my *shoes* . . . *two* pairs of new shoes . . .'

'Very becoming, I'm sure . . .' I said.

She propped herself on one elbow with enthusiasm, and motioned to me to open the suitcase. As I stared at my copperplate initials intertwined in the monogram in the leather on the front – RFB: Raymond Francis Bosanquet – I had a

311

sudden stab of *déjà vu* for some institution I had never attended in my life.

She showed me the things. I found them impossible to understand without seeing her in them. They were just flimsy pieces of material as she took them out of the red satin lining of the case, cut in triangles and other shapes. She held one of the dresses under her chin, kneeling back on her heels on top of the coverlet. It was a backless black dress, plain and shaped like a tube.

'Dramatic, eh?' she said, diving and scrabbling in the suitcase to bring out a single black high-heeled shoe.

'And with these . . . it looks really nice,' she said, holding the shoes against the skirt of the dress, 'don't you think?'

'I'll have to get you a cigarette-holder,' I said, still slightly perturbed by the sense of *déjà vu*. A memory that never was. Was she in it, I wondered, as she laughed and pressed the shoe against the material of the skirt as if willing them to be part of the same thing, the same material.

In the end I took her by the hand in to see Mooney. He was sitting at his desk, as he should have been, smoking a cigar. I could see he didn't remember her name.

'Stranger in camp,' he said, nodding.

He took a drag at the cigar.

'Er Raymond, I want to talk to you . . .' He turned the ram's horns. 'I'm sorry, er . . .' he said, looking over his spectacles at her.

'Zonda,' she said.

'Zonda,' he said absently. 'The thing is Minsky's coming down from Zurich. He telexed Münzen this morning. Where have you been?' he said suddenly.

'Escorting this young lady from the railway station,' I answered without a trace of satire. I saw Zonda's eyes grow wide as she looked from one to the other.

'Take that long?' he said.

'I told you she was arriving today . . .'

312

'Well look,' he said, 'I've got these letters for you to run down and do . . .'

I laughed.

'The point is he wants us all to meet in Nice . . .'

'What's got into you?' I said.

'Shape up,' said Mooney. 'We both know what's at stake here . . .'

Zonda's mouth dropped open as she looked from one to the other of us.

'The point is Minsky wants to meet in Nice, where it's most convenient for him. Now I think we may as well have a board meeting, because Casey and Costello will be coming over. At least, find out a hotel that has one of those smart boardrooms and hire it.'

'When for?'

He looked on his desk, and drew the small brown envelope from under the other papers.

'Thursday . . .'

'Afternoon or morning . . . ?' I arched my eyebrows and almost said 'sir'.

'Afternoon. Give us time for lunch. Oh, and find us a gourmet restaurant nearby. I think there's one on the front or something. Book us in there for lunch . . .'

'How many?'

'God knows . . . Er let's say . . .' He counted on his fingers. 'A notional dozen . . .'

'OK.'

'Another thing. The Brazilians are here . . .'

'Aha . . .' I said, looking at Zonda.

'Here's the plan for tonight. We'll all have dinner at the Mirabeau and we'll take the Brazilians to the Casino, first. The old Casino. Then we go on separately to Mavrakis. At Mavrakis, we'll swap over: I want you two and Don to look after the Venezuelans, while Münzen, Irving and I keep the Brazilians with us. Think you can handle that?'

'The Principessa and Habib?' I queried.

'Floating cards,' said Mooney, 'which Irving will pick up.'

'My God,' whined Zonda under her breath, 'I've got to have some clothes . . .'

But she had recovered as we walked away down the corridor.

'Well Raymond, you better run down and get those letters sent, eh?'

'There's no need to be sarcastic,' I said.

'There's every need. To wake you up.'

We walked along the corridor and into our room. I was silent. I wanted to hear what she had to say.

'You're like someone in a dream, Raymond . . .'

'I'm preoccupied, I know, but there's a lot of . . .'

'And in that dream you run about like an office boy . . .'

'I'm looking after my investment.' I hooked my thumb towards the office.

'You're just indulging yourself. Drinking, eating rich food, and pretending that you're mixing with rich people, and pretending that you are rich, when you're not. This whole thing's a farce. If you want to know my opinion . . .'

It would have been easy to say: 'As a matter of fact I don't,' but I didn't.

Instead I found myself, with an earnestness that caught me by surprise, making a speech to her. I maintained that this was what it felt like to know you were at the centre of a historical event.

Zonda looked at me incredulously:

'You call this an event? This is the biggest bloody non-event I've ever come across in my life!'

That was just it, I heard myself maintaining. The sort of things historians write in books didn't include things like this because they were invisible. And yet this was how history was really going on all the time. It had taught me something.

She nodded:

'Me too. Never catch anybody's eye. You never know where they've bin!'

314

No, no. Something I hadn't seen clearly before. The truly historical must include at any given point in time all combinations of probabilities. What we think of as events are just a leak, a drip-feed from the infinitely greater mass of non-events. Didn't she see? Events are just the stuff that becomes visible.

Zonda frowned:

'But Raymond, this tramp you've picked up is simply using you to pay his bills. Who's paying for the hotel and all these meals you've been telling me about?'

'The hotel is really quite reasonable . . .'

'That's not in your favour. What, a dump like this nobody's ever heard of? You should at least be at the Hôtel de Paris . . .'

'How do you know about the Hôtel de . . .'

'Ignoramus little Cockney – ooh! – knows about fancy hotels in Monte Carlo . . .'

She pouted and arched her eybrows. Then her whole face dropped and she threw away that tone.

'Julian told me,' she said. 'They all think you've gone mad you know.'

'Who?'

'All your friends . . . Julian, Noel . . . I'm *hot* . . .'

She was like a vulgar aunt I never had in her mid-fifties, gripped by the change of life, pulling off the little orange scarf she was wearing round her neck and loosening a button here and there, flouncing her skirt up to make a little draught and fanning her face with a telex she had picked out of my hand.

'What do I care?' she said. 'I'm just here for the ride . . .'

'We are all that,' I said, hoping to take back the telex soon.

'Yes, but some of us think we're looking after the carousel,' said Zonda.

'Why are you so hot? It can't be more than twenty degrees.'

'I don't know why I'm so hot . . . don't change the subject,' she said irritably. 'You've changed over from insurance salesman to bank clerk. That's what it is,' she said triumphantly.

We sat facing each other in the bedroom. I felt her energy

slipping, ebbing away in front of me. Her eyes had begun to droop slightly and as I began to speak, they flickered almost unconsciously towards the bed, inspecting the décor of the room and then towards the bed, again.

'Doll, the fact that we have a bank is quite a significant step,' I began rather earnestly.

I began to tell her about Carlos and Philippe, and how we had managed them that night. And the Americans at the Casino. I played upon her sensibilities with my description of Carlos.

'He's not really sinister – it's the name,' she said with a trace of drowsiness. 'It's that terrorist they all want.'

She roused herself and went off into a monologue about her friends and their Italian husbands, playing all the parts herself, sitting up on her chair like someone facing a camera, her hands moving in a continuous run of different gestures. At one point she stood up, ludicrously, laughing at herself, unable to perform, and made three attempts at impersonating the deep voice of Alberto VO5, as she called him, down in the basement of the shop, as he held her in an 'impromptu' extra-marital embrace which had been the culmination of weeks of studied brushing against her breasts and squeezing her arms. She mimed her own rejection of him, pushing against a wall of person, lifting her shoulders to indicate how he was resisting and wrestling her by main force from side to side, bobbing her head to avoid his attempts to kiss her, as she looked him straight in the eye and told him that she wasn't going to stand for this kind of behaviour. Then she slapped his face, honestly, indicating the impact with a sharp expulsion of breath. Now came the punch-line. She pulled down her elastic lips at the corners so that they looked like a weeping clown's and stuttered in his small boy's Italian accent:

'But . . . I *like* you . . . in a *funny* way . . .'

She collapsed into the chair, legs out straight, and sighed with pleasure.

'. . . a *funny* way,' she repeated, staring at her feet as she braced her calves and rested her outstretched legs on her heels.

Half a hour later she was lying with her face down between the pillows, the saliva oozing slowly over her bottom lip and making a small patch of deeper blue in the pale blue sheet beneath her chin.

True to my word, I slipped out, posted the letters and came back with a black and gold Dunhill cigarette-holder which I found in a very English shop on Mill Street: then we went down for a tour of the dress shops.

She wore the black backless number and sat between the Brazilians. There were three of them. Jaime, João and Mr Simonsen. Jaime was about forty-five, an econometrist from the budget office. His eyebrows were bushy and greying. A small dark moustache nestled softly under his brown hook nose. João was from Petrobras, fat, and laughed a lot, slyly. Mr Simonsen was in his sixties, a treasury banker, grey-haired and very reserved.

'You look the part,' I whispered to Zonda.

'What part is it?' she whispered. 'Banker's moll?'

Planted between them with the cigarette-holder going full strength, eyes flashing, head turning, she soon had even Mr Simonsen smiling. She reminded them of their daughters, as she told stories about my horses. Mooney was smiling benignly as he overheard this.

'Of course,' said the Princess from the other side, 'David at Chase Manhattan has been *so* marvellous getting him the clinic and arranging everything . . .'

'If only all Americans were like David Rockefeller,' said Habib. 'It's this Brzezinski that causes all the trouble . . .'

'A Polak,' said Irving, 'completely paranoid about the Soviets. Sullivan on the other hand is a civilised man . . .'

'Yes,' said Habib. 'He read the Shah's mind well . . .'

The Princess snorted.

'He was too soft with the rising from the beginning. The Americans kept telling him to use the steel on them . . .'

'Yeah Brzezinski,' said Irving. 'He's so paranoid, he didn't believe a word of Sullivan's reports, he thought they were just addressed to the peaceniks in the State Department.'

'You know what he did,' said Habib excitedly, working his worry beads over. 'He sent back the Iranian Ambassador in Washington to Iran and told him to stay close to the Shah and report to him every day by telephone . . . He set up his own ambassador!'

'No wonder Sullivan resigned,' said Irving.

The Princess lit another Rothmans and I poured them all slugs of some acceptable though not marvellous Margaux and ordered a bottle of something else.

'You know Khomeini has cancer too,' said the Princess, nodding with satisfaction. 'He is not recovering from a heart disease. He has terminal cancer.'

Then they started talking about Chase Manhattan's involvement in the freezing of the assets.

'Of course he called them in default,' said the Princess, turning to Zonda, who simpered back at her. 'They didn't pay.'

'Who?' said Zonda looking round at me.

'Rockefeller at Chase,' I whispered, 'and the Iranians.'

'Didn't they say it had been stolen from the Iranian people?' said Zonda to the Brazilians. 'I admire their courage . . .'

I prayed the Princess hadn't heard this.

The yawning gulf opened up. Rapidly, I began to develop the Duke of Wellington in the only banking story I knew, the failure of 1825 in which seventy-three banks went bust and brought England to the edge of barter.

'They were within twenty-four hours of it,' I said, looking across at Zonda who, I knew, was well versed in the story. 'They had run out of five- and ten-pound notes and at the last moment they found a block of ancient £1 notes left over in the vault from 1797. They issued these as fast as they could. And, as the Duke of Wellington said about Waterloo . . .'

I handed the punch-line over to her as slowly as I could. I saw her lips begin to curl as she took the cigarette-holder from her mouth.

'It was a damned nice thing...' she croaked the famous words, 'the nearest run thing you ever saw in your life...'

The table broke up with laughter. João had tears in his eyes. Mr Simonsen hadn't heard properly and had to ask eagerly, *sotto voce*, what she had said.

'You can't put the genie back in the bottle,' said Irving. 'It's all very well talking about freezing the assets, but you can't unfreeze the damn things once you done a thing like this...'

'They're not that frozen,' said Mooney. 'At least the interest isn't. All the Iranians and the American suppliers have to do is express their invoices in other currencies than the dollar. The Presidential statement, if you look at the text of it, refers only to the dollar...'

'You mean, they needn't call the Iranians into default if they shift into Deutschmarks, Swiss francs, or sterling...?' I asked, on cue.

'Exactly,' said Mooney. 'They can't get their capital assets but they can at least go on servicing their debts... so the banks don't have to do what Chase did – No, Chase were flying a kite. They didn't need to do that, and that ploy of claiming it took place in London outside American law, sure they're going to lose *that* little gamble...'

'You favour a currency solution,' said the Princess. 'Mr Mooney, that is typical of you. But Mr Rockefeller is right on principle.'

'Like I say, Your Highness,' said Mooney, 'it's bad for the markets to have this needless chain of defaults.'

'It's a mess for everyone except the lawyers...' said Glucksman. 'The acceleration clause on the Chase loan provided that if there's a payment default the entire loan has to be repaid, and this means the other loans fall because there's a knock-on effect, because *they* have acceleration clauses which stipulate that if the borrower is in default with any instalment on the commercial external payment, then the whole loan becomes payable immediately. So the syndicated loan for $310 million to the National Iranian Petroleum Company which they've just negotiated falls as well . . .'

'As I say, they could get round it.'

'But we don't *want* them to get round it Mr Mooney,' said the Princess.

'Well, I am just a simple man of the markets,' said Mooney, lowering his horns with fake humility.

Conversation got round to the latest round of oil price hikes, and I saw it operating like a gigantic cue. The Princess, really working overtime, leaned across the table to João and said:

'These fanatical Arabs are just holding the world up to ransom, don't you agree Mr?'

The Brazilians looked at one another, uneasily.

'Oh, I don't think . . .' said Zonda, who was fortunately drowned in the general buzz of condemnation.

I shook my head. She looked defiant.

'How is it affecting your country?' insisted the Princess, trying again, pushing her elbows forward through the glasses in her attempts to get attention.

'I tell you one thing I don't understand,' said Mooney, expertly deflecting the conversation to Habib. 'Why is it that Sheikh Yamani stays in dollars? I mean since the first price rise, everybody else has multiple currency agreements. And yet the funny thing is OPEC itself puts all its eggs in one basket . . .'

'It is because America has leaned on the Saudi Arabians,' said Habib. 'I'm sure of it.'

'That's right, this secret trade agreement that's just come out,' said Irving. 'The Saudis and the American Treasury have been dealing confidentially, allowing the Saudis to invest in America . . .'

The Brazilians all started talking at once about the energy problem, covering up in front of the Princess the fact – as Mooney said afterwards – that Brazil was actually getting its oil from Iraq, by talking about the development of alternative fuels.

'The alcohol car,' said Jaime, 'is Brazil's answer . . .'

Zonda burst out laughing, held up her claret and said, thickly: 'What, *this* stuff?'

'Ethanol,' said João. 'We can make it from sugar-cane.'

Mooney and Glucksman and Münzen were all ears as this theme expanded.

'This year, as you know, there's been a 400 per cent increase in the price of petrol in our country, and eighty per cent of Brazil's oil is imported,' said Mr Simonsen. 'So we have to do something. Fortunately we have these vast sugar-growing plantations in the south of the country and we have been intensifying our production of alcohol since the first price hike of '73 . . .'

Mooney's eyes were shining greenly.

'How does it work?' said Zonda.

'You just put it in the car,' said João, 'and it goes along . . . putt putt . . .' He clipped his two fingers together like scissors.

Zonda blushed.

'It takes about $360 to convert a car to run on alcohol . . .' said Jaime.

'We have a National Alcohol Programme and Dr Netto has set a target for production for Proalcool of 10.5 billion litres by 1985 . . .'

Mooney whistled. He turned to Irving.

'By jingo,' he said, 'the thing of the future . . .'

'Is production really as large as that?' asked the Princess, accepting defeat for the present.

'Oh yes, everyone's got an alcohol car, they're all the rage in São Paulo where I live,' said Jaime.

They painted a picture of a country in which the rural poor could make it from cassava. Every village could have a still, and have their own alcohol source for village transport.

'There's 25 million tonnes of cassava grown now in Brazil . . .' said Mr Simonsen. 'Oh yes, it is feasible and President Figueiredo has put the Programme on a priority basis, issuing subsidies to companies who are setting out to make alcohol . . .'

'It's *brilliant*,' said Zonda.

'We've got to do it,' said Jaime, 'because we can't afford petrol any more.'

'At the moment, this is the really hot issue in Brazil,' said João, 'because we have a problem. We have a clash between the food-producers and the sugar-cane growers. To put that programme into operation and meet the National Alcohol Board's target, we need a lot more land. Sugar-cane is now grown on 2.6 million hectares. We'll need another 2 million hectares from somewhere if we're to do it by 1985 . . .'

'So there's a big fight going on at the moment . . .'

João laughed.

'It's Brazil. We can't pretend everything's going smoothly, but . . .'

'How efficient is it,' asked Irving, 'in real terms?'

The Princess had to leave. She waved to Habib, rose, and said: 'I shall be interested to find out more when we meet later on tonight.'

They discussed this question, while a ripple of optimism went round the table. Mr Simonsen promised to give Glucksman and Mooney the figures.

Jaime, the econometrist, I saw to my amusement, was the one Zonda went for. This was a feint, because I had seen already that she was attracted to João, the fat one.

Zonda was disappointed in the Old Casino. We passed into the outer room and I got our gin-toniques at the bar. There was a long velvet-covered bench which lined the wall under the high windows and Zonda and João sat on this while Mooney, Glucksman, Münzen, Jaime and Mr Simonsen sat on chairs around the table. Zonda had discovered that Jaime had written a PhD at Yale, and when the waiter arrived with the tray of drinks, she was asking him what it was about. He asked if she knew anything about money and she said no.

He blushed sweetly, and looked down.

'Well, it's . . .' he said, hesitating. 'It's . . .'

Mooney laughed across.

'Spit it out, man!' he said.

'It's on "Endogenous Variables in Efficient Market Models",' said Jaime.

'There's a mouthful,' said Mooney. 'And what does it all boil down to?' He turned to Glucksman. 'These highfalutin fellas, eh, Irving?' He slapped Irving's thigh.

'But it was years ago now . . .' said Jaime. 'I really don't want to discuss it,' he added, as if it were a painful personal problem.

'You know it was translated into Portuguese and published as a book in Brazil,' said João, stirring.

Two drinks later they were arguing about the information market and its role in Efficient Market theory.

'If everything was perfectly arbitraged all the time,' said Jaime passionately, 'then you couldn't have equilibrium at all, because the creation of markets is not itself a costless activity.'

'But,' said Münzen, 'I thought that at any time prices fully reflect all available information . . .'

Zonda and I had begun to behave like people at a tennis final.

'The point is that information costs money . . .' said Irving. 'Right?' to Jaime.

'As we shall see in Nice on Thursday,' said Mooney to Irving under his breath.

'Exactly,' said Jaime. 'Therefore differences of belief are endogenous in the system . . .'

'What does endigenous mean?' said Zonda. João was glad to explain that it was endogenous and that it meant 'created internally', the opposite of 'exogenous'.

'And because of differences of beliefs between traders . . .'

'Nice way of putting it,' said Mooney, sticking a cigarette in his mouth.

'Markets are created which eliminate the differences of beliefs which gave rise to them and cause those markets to disappear. That's it,' said Jaime. 'That's how it happens.'

'Uh, I get it, it's a feedback,' said Irving, 'so therefore you mean prices *can't* reflect at any given time all the available information, otherwise no informed trader would ever get a return on his money. Hey,' he turned to Henri, 'that's neat.'

'It is true,' said Münzen, 'that theorists tend to think the foreign exchange markets are like the stock market, but what is an efficient foreign exchange market?'

'God,' said Zonda, downing her gin, 'I feel like Alice in Wonderland.'

Mooney got up, muttering in my ear:

'What do we need academics for to tell us what we know already?'

'Ladies and Gentlemen,' I said, 'this is not a bar. We have a solemn and noble purpose in this historic place.'

We took our drinks through into the 'kitchen', where the deafening racket of slot machines hit us like a wall behind the velvet drapes. Here they were all round the walls.

'Ugh,' said Zonda.

Mooney's eyes lit up.

'Aha,' he said, 'I wonder if they've got my favourite.'

I could hear Jaime expounding a particular case behind me.

'. . . a storable commodity whose spot price didn't reveal all information because of noise. Traders were left . . .' He began to shout over the clacketing of the slot machines. 'Traders were left with differences in beliefs about the future price, which led to the opening of a futures market . . .'

I turned back, leaving Zonda and João to proceed through into the salon.

'Any of you gentlemen care to play a little poker?' I said casually.

Inside the salon, there was a central table of baccarat and behind it, on the far side of the room, the roulette wheel. I took in the crowd. It was mainly weekending Italians, middle middle, not particularly rich, enjoying some of the fruits of the recent lira hike, and their families, plus one or two older people who were probably institutionalised gamblers.

We made our way behind the mirrors to the *super-privée*, which had a poker game at 2500 fr minimum bet. Glucksman, the ever-faithful Don, Jaime and myself, were rather lost around the huge field of turquoise baize. As a rule I always fold in five-card stud when my first cards don't add up to nineteen. I did a lot of folding. The cards were not running. Jaime seemed to be doing well, but the rest of us were losing, which was just as it should be from the public relations point of view. I was worried about the dealer. He was a thin, rat-like person, French from his accent. Not that I thought he was cheating, but the imperfection of his shuffling tended to upset my probability calculations. On one hand Jaime threw in a pair of aces and those aces turned up near to each other. On the next shuffle a three fell between the queen and the second ace so that they were now separated by two players. I asked for a new deck and complained about the cut. Things however did not run any better for me, or worse for Jaime. In the end, I gave up and came away, putting the twelve thousand or so francs I had lost down to my credibility account.

Zonda and João were sitting it out near the roulette wheel. At her first few goes at roulette, Zonda, who was obsessed with placing her bets in fancy combinations (she seemed particularly fond of *carrée* because she believed it increased her chances), had lost all the float I had given her. She had vowed to win it all back. But now she was ready to give up, I could see. This wasn't quite enough. I thought it better if João saw a little more of our conspicuous consumption, our fearlessness in the face of the odds. Prudence or lack of enthusiasm was the last thing we wanted. Besides, she might just balance some of my losses at cards. I sniffed provocatively:

'Of course, the whole idea of so-called being able to "even up" and redeem a run of bad luck is suspect . . .'

'Why?' she asked.

'Because,' I said, recalling Sir Hiram Maxim, 'how can you know that the "evening up" will take place at the same table? Why not at some other table at some other time?'

Zonda turned to João:

'What is he warbling on about?'

'He means,' said João, 'that runs of luck may be connected with other runs of luck somewhere else and that we shouldn't think that our run of luck begins and ends with us only . . .'

'Correct,' I said, watching carefully her disbelief. 'For example, supposing you do even up tonight or let's suppose you have an abnormal run of luck. How do you know that this run of luck is not an act of evening up to balance a run that has taken place at Ostend, or perhaps took place in faraway China, twenty-four years ago?'

'The cash is mine – so the luck is mine . . .'

She turned to João, protesting. She dug him in the ribs, as I insisted:

'I'm sorry,' I said patronisingly. 'We are all linked together by the great chain of fluctuations which seeks always to return to a zero state . . .'

'And that's your excuse to spoil my pleasure?' she asked João with big eyes. Gallantly, he sprang to her aid, interrogating her as to the numbers she had bet on, offering a system and so on. He informed her that she should bet, not on *chances multiples* as she had been doing, but on *chances simples*, because the amount the bank raked in when zero came up and she had to go into prison was only 1.35 per cent with *chances simples* whereas with the *chances multiples* it was 2.7 per cent . . . He explained that she could still bet *à cheval* if she wanted to. Say, for the sake of argument, 19 and 22, which would give her seventeen times her stake, whereas if she bet on 31–32–34–35, though it looked as if it increased her chances, in fact it only gave her eight times her stake.

We went to the wheel and watched as the little ivory ball skittered on the raised metal edges marking off the numbered compartments. It had enough centrifugal force to jump these obstacles and ran up the bevelled surface at the centre of the wheel before rolling back, agonisingly, and coming finally to rest with a click on the 19.

'*Dix-neuf, rouge, impair et passe*,' shouted the croupier. Zonda's eyes began to shine, and she linked her arm through João's.

326

'Wow,' she breathed, 'you're *good*.'

I stuffed a couple of thousand francs into her crisping outstretched hand behind his back and moved away to get some drinks. I got some drinks from the outer salon and came back in. They were back in the same place.

'That's the problem,' said João. 'Theory and practice.'

'Oh, I *know*,' said Zonda. She had on her Cockney exquisite to accommodate her losses.

I looked around. Mooney was talking out of the side of his mouth to Mr Simonsen, as he fed coins into a one-armed bandit.

'Well, you buy the lands on a long lease, get some good paper in the bank from some Chilean and Bolivian names, then you mortgage the land for capital to push on with the railroad . . . Now, here's where it gets interesting – you go to the towns along the route and you issue bonds for them for stock in our company, you see . . .'

Mr Simonsen was shaking his head:

'Mr Mooney – the days of J. P. Morgan are over . . .'

'What do you mean it's never the same with donkeys?' said Zonda.

'No,' said João. 'It's *different* with donkeys. That's the punchline . . .'

'Raymond,' she sang, waving me over, 'I don't get it. Tell *him*!' She pointed at me.

Mooney was ramming ten-franc pieces into the Atahualpa machine, his cigarette gritted between his teeth as he worked the various silver knobs with both hands:

'That's right, that's the idea, mortgage as you go, then sell the rest of the stock on the prospect of a new link through an improved countryside and then we'll sell the lands at a big advance – we just need these surveys and a bit of leverage down there in Chile – no problem in Bolivia – you know a company called the Fabulosa Mines Consolidated took over the old Fabulosa Tin Company?'

'It is British, and in some difficulties these days I believe,' said Mr Simonsen.

'Well you know what they say,' said Mooney, turning to wink. 'England's difficulty is Ireland's opportunity ... My cousin just happens to work for them – fella by the name of Ramirez O'Hara – so we have somebody on the spot there, no problem at all! – no, you know, smooth our way through the Chilean legislature ... Now this is where you fellas come in, you see, because ...'

'What is this about donkeys?' I said to João and Zonda.

'Oh it's a long story,' said João, resigned.

'No, no, *tell* it to *Ray*mond,' ordered Zonda, leaning over and staring into his eyes.

This was good mileage.

'Better do as she says,' I said in my silly voice.

He looked up at me for a moment, uncertain, and then began to laugh and nod his head. I looked round for Irving, Don and Jaime, steeling myself for the long haul with the donkeys.

'This is fun,' I said.

'Yes,' said João. 'It is a funny story but it is true, which illustrates the Indian mentality, you will see ... It is, you see, the story of a businessman who had been trying for a long time to convince a certain Indian who had a few donkeys that it would be good business for him to expand. The señor explains to him the economic arrangement, you see; donkeys cost a certain amount each and he would lend him the capital. Fodder costs so much, donkey would do so many hours work a day, carrying so much stuff, for which he would pay him a certain fixed price and in a few months he would have enough to pay him back, you will have enough to live on in the meantime and then you will own lots of donkeys and be rich ...'

I looked at Zonda.

'I can just see her somehow, owning a lot of donkeys and being rich ... Go on. There has to be a snag somewhere,' I said, politely.

'The donkeys are the snag!' said Zonda.

'No, no ...' said João earnestly. 'You see I am explaining ... Oh yes, I see.' He laughed, pointing at Zonda. 'You ...' He sighed. 'Oh *no* for such a beautiful ...'

Zonda preened.

'Anyway, let's hear about the donkeys . . . and then I'll get us another drink,' I urged.

'Well, the Indian, he thought for a long time and then he refused. He said, donkeys get sores. They and their packs fall over precipices. Sometimes donkeys don't feel like working. Sometimes *I* don't feel like working. Donkeys have their own ideas about how fast they should go, when and where they should rest, how much they should carry, and what and when they should eat. Your figures sound alright Señor, but I can't accept your offer. You see, it's different with donkeys.'

Zonda was shaking her head.

'So much for economic theory,' I said. 'It's different with donkeys.'

'Exactly, Raymond,' beamed João fatly, holding up a finger. 'There is wisdom in this.'

'You *hear* that, damn it Raymond!' I heard Zonda say, as I turned away to get some more drinks.

I strolled towards the bar, contemplating the example of the Hon. S. R. Beresford, who in 1926 demonstrated to the world the considerable psychological advantage derived from reversing the major gambling systems – the Martingale, the Labouchère, the Boule de Neige, the Paroli – that is, from *de*creasing your stake after a loss and increasing it after a win. You make no attempt to chase your losses. Instead, you resign yourself to losing a small sum daily but with the chance of staking a favourable sequence which will ultimately allow you to break the table or reach the maximum. I put my hand in my pocket, rattled my small change and sighed with Beresfordian satisfaction: I had almost spent everything, and the night was still young.

And how agreeably it had all gone, this opening stage. What splendid people Brazilians were. Such camaraderie. How perfectly they had deflected, for their own reasons of course, the Principessa's attempts to pry into their arrangements with us, with all that marvellous stuff about the alcohol car. Mooney was right, I thought, as I shouldered my way through the crowds at the bar, they were a good deal more civilised than her Venezuelans. However, that didn't tell us anything about who was going to get the better rates.

At first, I thought there had been an accident at the boat, so many ranks of armed police were standing around on the harbour. The car was checked twice before we parked, and we walked towards the huge lit side of the ship through a corridor of them.

'Ah, yes,' I said to Zonda and the Princess, 'the guard of honour.'

This was no joke for the Princess, who could see all too well that they were not presenting arms. At the gangway there was quite a lot of fuss because Zonda got a heel stuck in a crevice and had to take her shoe off. She had on her party gear, which we had bought specially at what she called a 'toffee-nosed boutique', somewhere on Princess Grace Avenue, for a monstrous sum: it was an old-fashioned tinselled dress on a black background with net sleeves and a skirt that finished irresolutely at the ankles. Zonda asked for a pair of scissors, and, humming, slashed at it with ferocity as soon as we got back to the Louvre, taking off the net sleeves altogether and introducing several arbitrary-looking tears up the skirt as far as the upper thigh. She cut enormous jagged holes at the sleeves, slicing into the shoulders, and, turning it round, stared at it for some time.

'Don't you think you've done enough damage?' I said.

'Oh, don't be so square, Raymond,' said Zonda. 'Yeah, gorrit . . .'

She had effectively separated the bodice from the skirt with the exception of three columns of material which were allowed to remain in order to hold the whole frail reconstruction together, cheating, I said later, by putting stitches in all over the place to stop the material running. The effect, when she put it on, was quite extraordinary. Her body floated inside the ruins, as she walked, in a very arresting fashion. 'The hair' was gelled and swept up; lacquered into an arrangement that looked like a tall vase that had fallen into a vat of oil: only on top was dry blonder hair allowed to have existence, sprouting like the flowers in the vase. We had scoured the shops for jewelry and, of course, shoes. She found some very aggressive-looking watch-straps, five of which she wore, and a real Pekinese collar with spikes on it, which to my astonishment fitted her neck. The shoes proved a metaphysical problem, as usual, but she solved her disgust at the plain court shoes by sticking marcasite all over them with superglue. The earrings came from her box – enormous imitation Macedonian cloak-pins, filigreed balls hanging from great curved hooks of brass which looked as if they would tear off the earlobes at any minute. Her full mouth was painted very thinly with a kind of brownish daub which was accompanied by thick orange blusher, and her eye make up was dark and heavy with orange eye-shadow, the effect of which was, I pointed out, intensely displeasing rather than evil or vulgar, as intended. De Negris brought the Livorno limousine to pick us up from the Louvre, and when we got in, the Princess actually had on her tiara. Zonda clapped her hands. The Princess looked more hawkish than ever in a diamante evening gown which fitted round her scrawny frame with the unpredictability of an inadequately filled bolster.

'Is it the real one, or the paste one?' said Zonda at the end of a little cry of delight.

The Princess laughed scornfully.

'I don't have a paste one, Miss Swift,' she said.

Out of the corner of my eye I caught Glucksman, Mooney and the Venezuelans getting into the other car.

'These jewels have survived the desert and many other things with me. I'm sure they will survive here in the capable hands of Mr Cassoudesalle . . .'

Zonda looked blank. I nudged her.

'Rainier's chief of police . . .'

'Nothing much happens in Monte Carlo without his knowing,'

said the Princess happily. She stared at Zonda as we slid off down Mill Street, determined to provoke:

'So this is the new style of English youth,' she said, clutching her diamante bag to her. 'I have read about it in the papers. Kensington was full of people who looked like you dear. The idea seems to be to look as barbaric as you can . . .' She stared ahead. 'I can't think why . . .'

Zonda ground her teeth in the middle of the back seat and made the noise a bull terrier makes when something round, fat, soft and slow-moving comes into view.

After she had got her shoe back on, we moved on up the gangplank, and an usher dressed in naval uniform took our invitations and added them to the pack in his hands. We were taken down some steps into a low salon with a parquet floor. People were distributed in rather tight little groups here and there. The usher asked us to wait until Mooney and company came up and we formed a proper group. Waiters in white coats were circulating with champagne bottles. There was a huge bar at the back of the room, which Zonda had also spotted.

'Raymond,' said Zonda, 'what a terrible bloody cow she is.'

I diverted her towards the drinks on the trays.

'Cocktails,' she breathed. 'Great!'

The waiter took our orders while we stood on the steps and then we were given a nod and the usher took us down to meet Mr Mavrakis, a small bandy-legged man with coils of grey hair, a prominent gold tooth and a conservative business suit matched by toe-capped shoes which had been highly polished. He bowed over the Princess's hand, and she introduced us as 'Mr Mooney, our business associate, and his partners and friends from London'. Zonda tried to offer him her brown-painted nails to kiss but he let her hand sit there softly in his own like a dying pigeon and raised his eyebrows briefly. Then moved on.

Münzen and Habib were already in the group to which I attached myself, and the Princess, holding her champagne high, leant across the group of faces and scrutinised everyone in turn.

I downed as many cocktails as I could, mainly screwdrivers, while the man who introduced himself as Hassan, a New York businessman, and his friend, an American Lieutenant-General called Gurdell, carried on talking about a ten-day course which Hassan had attended somewhere in rural America. He was apparently some kind of graduate from this course and was very pleased with it.

'What does it teach you?' I asked.

'Self-reliance,' said Gurdell.

'You don't look as if you need your confidence boosting,' I said to Hassan.

'Take you out in about thirty seconds you'd never know a thing about it,' said Gurdell confidentially.

I looked at Hassan. I had him down as a delicate, neurasthenically thin Arab.

'The course is called Mantrax,' said the Lieutenant-General. 'Thought it up myself – combination of manta ray, and anthrax, pretty neat huh? Why don't you try it yourself, it's only three thousand bucks a head. You gonna need it in England pretty soon,' said Gurdell.

'Why's that?' I asked.

Gurdell stood back and took a pull on the huge Havana cigar he was gripping with his trigger finger:

'By 1984, civilisation in America will have broken down completely. I founded Mantrax cause the haves're gonna need t'proteckemselves 'gin the havenots. Yo gonna need this over here too way things're goin'.'

'Fantastic,' said Hassan. 'So I have appointed him Lieutenant-General in the Royal Free Afghan Army.'

'Hassan,' said the Princess, cruising in and kissing him, 'how are you, it's been such a long time. Have you seen Reza recently? You know he's in Cairo?'

Hassan said very well, no, and yes, as he was embraced.

'I see,' I said to Gurdell. 'I beg your pardon. I hadn't realised just who I was talking to . . .'

Gurdell triggered me with his Havana, drawing me on one side, and informed me that I was talking to the exiled King Hassan I of Afghanistan.

'And I'm the Queen of bloody Sheba,' said Zonda, shaking his hand and sliding her arm through mine. 'What's cooking over here?'

I introduced her to Lieutenant-General Gurdell and King Hassan.

'Controlled economic disintegration,' said Gurdell, 'a product of the way the United States is being run at the moment. I put it down to this Rockefeller and his Trilateral Commission . . .'

'Now, Hassan, I won't have a word said against David Rockefeller,' said the Princess.

'I tell you this country's gone to the goddam dogs ever since that faggot-face Southern Baptist peanut-farmer got his hands on the presidency. He's soft on communism, why almost the first thing he ever did was give the Panama Canal away. He's screwing the education of American children by organising this new Department of Edu-damn-cation. See him on TV he's encouraging 'bortion and homosexuality, sonofabitch's a bigger goddam menace than all the wops, spades and niggers in the world put *together* destroying the American family with this damn-fool equal rights amendment. Man's filled the White House with faggots and to cap it all now his goddam brother's juicin' it off with the *Libyans* . . .'

'It's much more interesting over *here*,' said Zonda to me, pulling on my arm.

'Well, personally I'm apolitical, jest don't like communists that's all nothing to do with politics . . .' Gurdell was beginning to explain as we excused ourselves and drifted off.

We grabbed a couple of blue cocktails from a passing tray and joined the Mooney group. They had split into twos and each sub-group was pitching remarks at each other.

'Of course they have,' said Mooney, putting his arm round my shoulder. 'Of course they have!'

'Of course who have what?' I said.

334

'The Japanese,' said Mooney. 'Henri is just saying they've been forcefeeding the whole financial system with Government Bonds for years . . .'

Zonda went over to Mrs Mavrakis, who was a tall raven-haired woman with more than a faint moustache, and a huge crop of black hairs sprouting from her jewelled, strapped bodice where it passed tightly beneath the arms. She listened politely while Zonda told her we were English.

'I don't know whether Caroline will come or not,' she said.

Zonda nodded sympathetically.

'They're very upset about the way the Press reported Caroline's wedding.'

'When times are good in Turin,' said the man standing on the other side of Münzen, 'they say industry is taking on new labour.'

'And when times are bad . . . ?' said Henri.

'And when times are bad,' said the man, giving a brief shrug, 'it is always the Agnellis who are doing the sacking.'

'They say he's in Fast-Food,' said Mrs Mavrakis. 'What's wrong with that? People have to start somewhere. Caroline is a modern girl. It's a good business, Rainier knows that. No, I don't think she will come . . .'

A man was standing between them, just behind Mrs Mavrakis's shoulders. He was looking across the room at something.

'Do you think they'll come?' I said to him.

He turned to me.

'*Comment?*' he said.

Mrs Mavrakis waved a hand.

'Security,' she said. 'He doesn't have opinions.'

He moved away, sidling up to a group of waiters who were standing at the side of the room.

Don appeared. I asked him if he'd met Lieutenant-General Gurdell.

'Oh that guy,' Don grinned. 'Tell you something. About five or six years ago the US Treasury seized three thousand machine-guns of his. You wanna know why?'

335

I said I wanted to.

'Because Vesco was trying to buy 'em. And if Vesco was trying to buy 'em, you kin bet your goddam boots ol' Gurdell was sure trying to sell 'em.'

I surveyed the room from the steps. All clients were gathered on the chestnut parquet. It was a ballroom. Along the sides of the walls glittered the lights of the harbour. One of the waiters came towards us with a tray. Zonda and Don went off to the toilet. I descended into the crowd. On the far side of the Mooney group, I could see Carlos and Philippe. As I was passing, Mooney took my arm. He repeated to me that at all costs the Venezuelans must not talk to the Brazilians. Could I help to see they kept apart? Keep my eye on the situation, that type of a way? When I reached Carlos and Philippe they were talking to a tall Greek with a pink-striped shirt on called Demis. Demis was telling them something about a restaurant he had on a beach somewhere in Greece.

I smiled at Carlos. His broken mouth moved slightly.

'Anyway,' said Demis, 'every time we touched glasses . . . I used to give a little cry "Help" – in the end I had the whole restaurant out on the beach looking for this drowning swimmer! . . .'

Carlos said he had a cold. He flourished a very large black handkerchief. He was sweating.

'It comes from the stars,' he said adenoidally.

I asked him what he meant.

He made a fluttering motion with his hand. Small particles fell from the handkerchief.

'The viruses,' he said. 'They are coming from space.' I could hear Gurdell behind me across the room: telling somebody that Chieftain tanks were no good without meticulous maintenance.

Philippe was starting to talk shop, I could see. Habib detached himself from the Mooney group and came over to us. They immediately started talking about rates for the loan. I butted in and asked Habib some questions about the Iran-Iraq war. He looked at Philippe as if to get him to wait a minute while he

336

dealt with this tiresome insect that was crawling on his suit.

'You must understand that it is a war of the Arabs against the Persians – the Semitic Muslims against Zoroastrians . . .'

He was in flight, but I couldn't keep him there for long. I was desperately hoping that Zonda would appear.

'You must realise,' said Habib to all of us, 'that sixty-five per cent of Iraq's population is Shiite, the same as the Iranian regime, and Khomeini has been trying to export revolution to Hussein's Shias . . .'

The Brazilians were wandering on the edge of the Mooney group, looking towards us.

'The Arabs look back to the battle of Qadisiya when the tribesman swept out of Arabia to defeat the Persians and liberated themselves from the Sassanian empire . . .'

The Brazilians were talking to each other and looking round. Where on earth was Zonda? At this moment two doors were flung open at the end of the salon and people began to pass through into the next room. A man standing on Habib's right, in between him and Carlos, stared vacantly at the wall. He coughed and bent down to flick something off his suit, and I could see inside his jacket a leather strap running over his shirt front across his chest.

Zonda arrived just as Habib had got to the Shah's Treaty of Friendship with Hussein.

'We didn't support Iraq's Kurds as a result of this treaty,' Habib was saying, 'and the other thing this treaty did was set the border between Iraq and Iran in the middle of the Shatt-al-Arab waterway.'

We nodded at how sensible this was. I was trying to get Zonda to see the Brazilians who had spotted her, but she was still listening to Habib and looking vaguely at the security man over his right shoulder.

'Now of course since the abrogation of the treaty, there is no way of policing this border . . .'

Don appeared from somewhere. He saw the Brazilians and

took Zonda's arm. She glanced at me briefly over her shoulder as they moved off, jerking her head towards the other group.

'In Khuzestan,' Habib was saying, 'the Iraqis have got their hands on the Ayatollah's . . .'

I watched them go and then turned back.

'Windpipe?' I suggested.

Habib looked askance for a minute.

'Ah, throat you mean?'

'Oilpipe, then . . .' I said, watching Zonda and Don at last start mopping up the Brazilians.

They laughed. The security man stared sullenly.

Carlos and Philippe were not to be put off – they started grilling me, trying to find out first of all where Mooney got his money. I was vague.

'We find Mr Mooney very sympathetic,' said Philippe, 'because he doesn't try to cry wolf and get the rates up . . .'

Was this crying wolf?

'Yeah, no broplep with him,' said Carlos. 'He's not trying to . . .'

'Play hard to get,' I said.

They agreed.

'He's a distinguished financial consultant,' I said, trying to keep the tone up. It seemed they were quite attached to him already. The Mooney magic had worked.

'For someone who has a lot of money,' said Philippe, 'he is . . .'

'Approachable?' I said.

Zonda and Don had the Brazilians in stitches. She was, I could see at a distance, doing her Dolly Parton shimmy inside the dress with a hand on Don's arm. Even Mr Simonsen looked amused.

I let them go off first, while Habib finished his dissertation on the Arabs and the Persians. The Princess was looking round for Habib, unfortunately, and came scurrying over. She didn't want to eat anything, as usual. This was good, because we could also let the Mooney group go too. I looked round. With any luck it meant we could put Gurdell and Hassan between us too. Mooney caught my eye and I inclined my head towards the door to the food. He extended his arms and said something to the whole group. They began to shuffle forward. People were being directed to return via the outside deck and I could see them coming past the window with their plates. The Princess and Habib were asking the Venezuelans how negotiations were going.

'It is slow,' said Philippe, 'but we have faith in Mr Mooney. We think he is trying to help us . . .'

Did they have any idea of the terms of the loan?

'We think the money will be around nine per cent,' said Carlos, 'but we don't know for sure yet.'

The Princess looked at Habib, and then at me.

'The sticking point is not the rate,' said Philippe, 'but the length of time.'

'Which of course affects the rate,' I said.

Habib snorted. He turned back to the Princess.

'The conversation is imbecile,' he said, under his breath.

At last we had begun to move towards the door which led to the food. I could see Zonda hanging on to Don's arm as they began to go down some steps at the end of the room. We were narrowing into a funnel. The walls were lined by white-coated waiters, who stared at us impassively as we approached. A tall red-haired woman with buck teeth brushed against me, in a green dress, drenched in perfume. She had very large feet. On the other side of her, a man who was the spitting image of Omar Sharif was telling someone about the Moscow Olympics.

'The local Russian crowd hated them,' he was saying in French to someone on the other side, 'in the following order: Romanians, Blacks, East Germans . . .'

I wondered if Zonda had spotted Omar. I looked around. She had disappeared with the Brazilians and Don into the food salon. Mooney, Glucksman, Münzen – the banking group were up ahead. Then came Gurdell, King Hassan, and a number of security men. A security man was outside staring in at each window along the side of the room. The windows were shaped like television screens. Occasionally one would lift a radio transmitter to his mouth. The red-head bumped against me again. I saw that she was a man.

The steps gave on to a rear deck that was open, but under a scarlet awning. Waiters were scurrying between tables, standing back to let one another pass in the long aisles between the tables. An usher came and divided the group in front of us up. I dropped back behind the red-head and her beau, a tiny Italian with a polished bald head and a silver suit.

One could relax now a little because the Venezuelans were at a far table. The Mooney group was in the middle. And because of my delaying tactics, we were almost the last people in, on the table nearest the door. Habib had his beads out and was working them over on the tablecloth.

We started talking about whether there was anywhere in the world where there were wild horses.

I mentioned the Camargue.

'Patagonia,' said the red-head, in New York French. 'We came across several herds when we were crossing the Pampas . . . wild and free . . .'

She was called Leslie.

'I used to ride quite a lot when I was a man,' she said.

Carlos was inclined to argue.

'I know those horses,' he said. 'They are not truly wild . . .' He shook his head, the blue remaining steady over the flop of his leathery cheeks and moving head.

Leslie laughed.

'Wild enough for me,' she said, rolling her enormous green eyes, as she lit a cigarette with an onyx lighter.

'No,' said Carlos. 'They are just the untamed descendants of the horses brought by Cortez to the continent.'

A rather shrill argument started up. It depended on what you meant by wild.

'I'm not going to argue with Carlos,' I said to Leslie. 'He used to be a *gaucho*.'

Leslie sucked her bottom lip, following me with her head as I got up. I wanted to check how things were going with Zonda. She was drunk. She lifted her head from Don's shoulder. Her lips were pursed, as for a camera. Her smile wobbled.

I discussed the after-dinner strategy with Don.

'Ah, to hell with it,' said Don. 'There's not much we can do.'

From there I went to Mooney. A swirl of tobacco rolled over his shoulder as I bent my face into it. I told him I would try to keep Habib and the Princess with us, but that they were getting tetchy and I warned him he could have a visitation. In which case, he must not be anywhere near the group with the Brazilians. Zonda and Don were doing a good enough job with them and they should be left to carry on. Then I went back and reported to Don. Zonda looked at me.

'Raymond, come here, *what* are you doing?'

'I'm just trying to coordinate things,' I said, holding her hand.

I told her I had spotted Omar Sharif. She gave a squeal.

'Oh my God,' she cried, 'the most handsome man in the world! Where is he?'

I pointed out where he was sitting.

She immediately began the long climb to her feet. She had forgotten her job.

'I must go and . . .'

I laid a hand on her shoulder.

'Not now. Wait till later.'

'*Dr Zhivago*,' said Zonda. 'Fantastic! My mother's favourite film!'

Don and I raised our eyes at each other.

I looked over at Jaime and João on the other side of Zonda, who were concerned for her. Things looked alright in that department.

'Get his autograph,' said Zonda, 'for me mum!'

She tottered to her feet, evading two politely outstretched Brazilian hands.

'Doll,' I persuaded her, 'there'll be plenty of time afterwards.'

She was adamant, swaying off in the direction of Omar. I sat and talked to Don and the Brazilians. Simonsen was telling us that he thought the Arabs were getting ready to bypass the Euromarket altogether. He said he had it on first-hand authority from the Venezuelan representatives at the recent OPEC meeting that the future long-term strategy was to institute bilateral agreements with specific countries.

'Trips like this are a thing of the past,' he said with a smile.

It sounded like a disturbance in the middle of the tables. Zonda was arguing with a security man who was trying to hustle her off down the aisle. I went down.

'Mamzell,' said the security man.

'For fuck's sake,' said Zonda. 'He's not Omar!'

I asked her how she knew.

Now the security man had his arm under each of our arms.

I explained to him that my friend had merely wanted to express her admiration to Mr Sharif.

'He told me he wasn't!' said Zonda.

'I don't blame him!' I said. 'Quite right in the circumstances!'

'Sit down,' said Don. 'For Christ's sake you're gonna get us all thrown out!'

I realised I was almost as drunk as Zonda was.

'Frightfully sorry,' I said to the security man.

It was an impossible dilemma. We had to use the Princess for social credibility. She and Habib knew who the Brazilians were, and they – she and Habib – could always get at them. But if we could keep them apart long enough, now that Mooney had named the day, then it didn't really matter. There was nothing to stop the Princess ringing their hotel if they really wanted to discuss their rate with them, but since closing day was so close and she and Habib were more interested in the Venezuelans, it was always possible that, with a little social hindrance, their activities would not extend that far.

I saw Habib bobbing up and down, half-standing, looking to see where I had gone. Mooney was visible in the middle of the tables under the awning, the ram's horns lowered at someone amid a cloud of smoke.

Under the awning were spread great molehills of caviare, canapés, little individual portions of *jambon à la crème, coq en pâte*, and individual mussels in *crème*. Sugar baskets sprouted everywhere in the shapes of ships and candelabras.

The Princess was digging into the caviare with Habib at her shoulder.

'It is Persian. The caviare is from our country,' she said to Habib. 'I'm sure of it.'

'Another example of the madness of the so-called "revolution",' said Habib, 'that they allow us to ship out as much caviare as we please . . .'

'By the way, Mr Bosanquet,' said the Princess, pausing to sniff the caviare again on the end of her fork, 'I have heard from the Mauritians. Their people will be coming to town soon for the closing of the transaction . . .'

This was a titbit that Mooney should have.

'The Prime Minister's staff?'

'Naturally . . .'

'I hope we'll be able to get together before they arrive,' said Habib as they moved off.

People were moving round the narrow outside deck with their plates and winding back into the salon, the ballroom. It was possible to drop into a couple of chairs along the way to eat and drink. Waiters were shooting up and down this corridor, their hands full of champagne bottles. Zonda had taken Don's arm and we met the Mooney group reclining here. I told him about the Mauritians getting into town. Mooney and Münzen looked at each other and said it was fine. At this point, a crisis occurred: Carlos and Philippe appeared at the end of the corridor. Since Don was such an expert in handling Carlos, I decided on a bold move and steered him and Zonda towards them and introduced Zonda to them. I looked round. Mooney and Münzen had disappeared.

Zonda was staring at Carlos with great fascination. He tore the curtain and flashed her two pools of blue. A tall man I didn't know was standing between him and Philippe. Waiters were squeezing by the guests in the narrow space, but it was a good site because it was a junction and I was worried about the advent of the Princess and Habib, so at least one could see both ends of the deck. I almost held out my hand to the tall man, who muttered something and shook his head. Philippe turned and looked through him and I realised he was another security man.

Zonda had got some kind of second wind. She was running through a catalogue of the furnishings she had seen on the boat. It was a long expert list of fabrics and where they had come from. She addressed her remarks to Philippe, and I could see by the way she clung to Don that Carlos made her flesh creep. Philippe, however, was another matter. While Don occupied Carlos, they talked about her dress.

But Carlos had fixed her, and even as she talked on her eyes flickered towards him the whole time. I expected the Princess to appear round the corner at the end of the corridor at any moment.

'Then there was Bontoux, Eugene Bontoux . . .' said Philippe.

We were playing that well-known game 'Whatever happened to the great financial swindlers?' and Carlos was describing how the retired manager of LeClerc, Charles Bouchard, had been found dead in Lac Leman in 1977, Zonda staring at him with her mouth open and clinging on to Don's arm, when Mooney, Münzen and the Brazilians appeared on time and began to move down the corridor towards us.

'You remember,' said Philippe to me. 'Bontoux came back to France, did he not, something about a loophole in the law . . .'

'It's a high-risk business . . .' I said, as the other party momentarily disappeared from view in the midst of a company of Greeks. 'I'm bored with this deck. Shall we move on? A little game of cards, perhaps?'

'. . . Something about you can't go to jail in France if your sentence hasn't begun five years after the day it was issued,' Philippe was saying as we began to stroll casually back to where we came in.

'Two things happen to successful swindlers. They all make a run for it sooner or later,' said Carlos, 'or else they kill themselves.'

'There's Vesco,' said Don. 'He had to go to Costa Rica . . .'

'The French go to Canada,' said Philippe to Zonda. 'I know this because my mother told me. She knew Charles Savanagh, you know, the one who swindled the Banque de Lyon. He died there . . .'

Things were going quite well. We were moving reasonably quickly towards the end of the corridor and into the ballroom.

'Ivan Kreuger,' said Carlos, 'the greatest swindler of all time. He killed himself.'

'Yes, Denfert-Rochereau,' said Philippe thoughtfully.

'Eli Black of United Brands in 1975,' said Don.

'And of course Charles Blunt,' I said playing my only swindler card and watching the Mooney party trying to untangle itself from the Greeks.

'Who the hell's he?' said Zonda. 'Raymond, you made that one up!'

'The South Sea Bubble,' I said.

'What happened to him?' asked Don.

'Cut his throat in early 1720,' I said. 'Rather a nice phrase in the newspapers, "Upon some discontent".'

'You know they deserve, if they get caught . . .' said Carlos to Zonda.

I tried to distract him, laughing hollowly:

'Well if they get *caught* . . .' I said.

'What?' said Zonda, swaying drunkenly.

Carlos looked at her and reached out a cancerous arm.

'Hey, take it easy,' said Don.

'No broplep,' said Carlos, 'I only show her. Come . . .'

He took them over to the rail. We leaned over in a line and stared into the blue-blackness.

Carlos slid along the rail and took the shivering Zonda by the arm.

'You know what they did with you in ancient Rome if you killed your father?' he asked, enthusiastically.

'Put you in a sack,' I said laughing, 'and chucked you in the Tiber!'

'Ah yes,' said Carlos. 'But you know what they used to weight you down?'

'Rocks?' said Zonda, hopefully.

Carlos's eyes gleamed and his elbow slid two inches along the rail towards her, his spindly thigh moving into sudden contact with hers through her dress.

'They sewed you in with a monkey and a snake,' he said. 'This in my opinion is the correct punishment for swindlers who get caught.'

'I don't get it,' said Don.

'He means they're parricides,' I said.

Zonda was staring down at the water. Someone opened a porthole and threw out a tray of scraps. Pieces of sopping bread bobbed past down the length of the hull, their progress cut by the flash and roll of fish.

'God, he *really is* a nasty piece of work,' I heard her thrilled whisper to Don as we moved back inside the ballroom.

To my infinite distress, I could hear Mooney's voice ahead of us now in the ballroom. They must have gone round the other way, while we had been at the rail.

As we rounded the corner, he was leaning back, addressing urgently a company which included João, and Jaime, and Mrs Mavrakis. Glucksman had split off with Habib and the Principessa. Mr Simonsen was nowhere to be seen.

'Now the fact of the matter is,' Mooney was saying, 'the Indian of the high Sierras has a lung-development almost one-third greater than the normal human: blood volume four pints more, haemoglobin about double, red corpuscle count up from five to about eight million, and a much slower heart rate . . .'

The Brazilians were looking politely interested, as usual. I looked back at Don, who started steering Zonda. The only thing was to try to slide the Venezuelans past into the gaming room on the lower deck.

We edged along behind the backs of Mooney's listeners:

'. . . My idea is this you see, these fellas can run at eleven to thirteen thousand feet carrying heavy loads – rugged men, in a rugged country – now, properly trained these little dancers could *walk* away with the marathon in the next Olympic Games . . .'

Carlos and Philippe took in this Punch-and-Judy show on their left at a glance, as Zonda and Don followed me down the funnel of backs. To my surprise, they didn't react as Mooney boomed out his pitch:

'. . . Think what a major coup for the Third World this will be. Haven't the Kenyans and Ethiopians done it already? Just the ticket for South America, you know, image-enhancement after all these debts . . . I tell you it will put you people all on the map . . .'

'It's an interesting idea,' murmured Mrs Mavrakis, to Jaime and João.

'Wait for *us*, Raymond,' hissed Zonda. She was glancing behind nervously at Carlos, who was already pressing close to her through the crush, while Mooney got started on the arrangements for the consortium, headed by Pequeño Investments, to train South American Indians for the marathon and ten thousand metres in the next Olympic Games.

As I turned away, I saw that our path was just about to be blocked by the Principessa and Habib, who were strolling up to the edge of the group with Irving and Mavrakis. Mooney's efforts were creating a kind of crossroads. Already I could sense the Principessa's eyes flick automatically towards the Brazilians as João turned round and he and the Venezuelan Carlos acknowledged each other while Carlos scraped by his back. Mooney's fairground barker act had been excessively effective and had formed a knot of people around him. One of the convergences we were trying to avoid was in grave danger of occurring. Our plans stood on the brink of ruin here.

The only action to be taken, I decided, was to form a rough kind of human pen and herd a selected number of key personnel into it, while Don and Zonda continued to get the Venezuelans downstairs into the gaming room.

I decided on a counter-blocking tactic, distracting this new group on its flank and pinning it down, like a section-in-attack in the OTC, thus giving the others the chance to hustle away Carlos and Philippe. It was however impossible to catch Mooney's eye, so busy was he in canvassing for his scheme, so that the Brazilians would have to remain exposed on the edge of the group not five yards from the Principessa who had already begun to bob dangerously up and down in her attempts to find out who was who.

I stood in front of them and held out my arms on both sides in a gesture which invited them to stop strolling and gather round me. I addressed myself to Mr Mavrakis, summarising Mooney's scheme and, as this dried up, launching on a sentence which ended by my saying to my astonishment:

'What people never seem to *quite* take into account is the effect of the business cycle . . .'

'Business cycle?' said Habib suspiciously. He turned to the Principessa. 'What is he talking about?'

She shrugged, still craning ahead.

'You see,' said Mavrakis to Habib, 'in a way, this is just what we have been discussing . . .'

'Yes, but which one?' Habib asked, staring at me. 'There are many.'

I stared back as he lifted a fat finger and buried it in the palm of his other hand. He looked for a minute as if he had forgotten it belonged to him, and was just about to break it off in his impatience:

'You mean the Kitchen cycle, of thirty-nine months?'

I thought I had better shake my head here.

The finger sprang back in the palm like a willow and was bent again.

'The Juglar cycle, then?'

That didn't sound like it to me.

Impatiently he threatened the root of his finger again.

'The Kuznets cycle?'

I shook my head as convincingly as I could.

'I forget the names,' I said. 'I think that's it . . .'

'Twenty years,' he said. 'Based on population changes from generation to generation . . .'

'That's it, that's it!'

He looked at me dubiously.

'And the resultant rise and fall in the *construction of housing*?'

'No, maybe that's not the one,' I said. 'Maybe it's the other one – you know, the . . . K . . . ?'

I snapped my fingers, intending to cut my losses and go back to the Kuznets.

He was disbelieving:

'The Kondratieff?'

'I know there's a lot *said* about it,' I said, 'but I think the Kondratieff is quite a . . . good indicator of . . .'

Mavrakis turned to Habib, and laughed. 'How credulous is youth,' he said.

'The Kondratieff is nonsense,' pronounced Habib, 'because there is no regular time span between the major inventions that are supposed to trigger it. Take the example of the railroad . . .'

I kept him going with the odd interjection while the Principessa detached herself finally and made her play for the Brazilians. Irving was busy handling Mavrakis, who still formed one of the outer walls of the pen. It was still of some use to hold Habib there, I judged, but the Principessa had escaped me through the fence of bodies and was trying to push her way with a combination of sing-song excuse me's and surreptitious violence through the press. Don and Zonda were, presumably, safely in the gaming room with the Venezuelans. I saw finally that Mooney had swept away the Brazilians on the other side of the wall of figures and was whisking them out of the door in the corner. To my relief I noticed that the Principessa's path had been blocked by King Hassan, flanked by two of the Mavrakis daughters, who began saying goodbye to her.

I was suddenly aware in fact that the evening was over. The necessary recondite signals had been given to staff and we were all being discreetly propelled towards the door in the corner of the room. Wraps of all shapes and colours and sizes appeared everywhere in the hands of security men who wielded them like matadors. I heard Habib behind me break off his lecture on the vagaries of the Kondratieff cycle. We turned and began to shuffle towards them. Such a degree of silence prevailed for a moment that I could hear the scrape of feet unaccompanied, on the parquet. Mavrakis had gone, and Irving took over the last of the job with Habib.

Out on the deck, at the head of the gangway, Mr and Mrs Mavrakis stood shaking hands with their guests who streamed down on to the quayside, where a confusion of purring limousines had been driven at different angles towards the boat amongst the capstans, each trying to creep a little nearer than the next. Police patrolled them. Halted, waiting our turn, I felt this was a particularly dangerous moment, as I looked anxiously down on the small army of lackeys that had begun to run to and fro gesticulating and calling up to the undulating wave of distinguished heads that bounced slowly towards them on the gangway. But I could no longer see anyone now from our various groups.

I heard Irving's voice behind me.

'Hey, Ray, that was really something. You really blew my mind back there.'

He was uneasy, I saw, in case I accused him later of not doing his job.

We compared notes. Irving told me that Mooney had managed to get the Brazilians away early before the crush. We stared back up at the boat. Don was waving energetically from the top of the gangplank. I could just see Carlos standing behind Zonda as she turned to say something to Philippe. At the bottom, Habib was gallantly helping the Principessa down the last few steps.

Irving clapped me on the back.

'Looks like we made it.' He nodded toward the harbour.

I smiled, still anxious, my eyes lighting on the figure of De Negris, who was limping towards us, round the curve of the harbour.

'We held the pass,' I said.

Nice

The young men approached, mincing through the traffic at the corner of the Rue Auber and the Boulevard Victor Hugo, in their magenta knee-breeches and blue hose, their buckled shoes and troubadour hats. One of them raised a hand and plucked out of the air the car keys of the young man in the lemon and chrome Bugatti in front of us, who had already got out, and tossed them carelessly to him over the rooftops of moving cars, while the other danced on through the aisles of traffic to collect ours. They leapt into the cars slamming the doors with perfect synchronicity and drove them away in convoy to the carpark. It was the Negresco summit, and Mooney was as keyed up as I had seen him. I was curious too because at last we were going to meet Minsky, who came from the lenders.

Lunch was just up Zonda's street. I had booked the Chanticlere, the gourmet restaurant next door to the Hôtel Negresco. The talk was mainly about the one topic in Nice: the scandal of the ruined Palais de la Méditerranée and the war between the Fratoni faction and someone called Mme le Roux, whose daughter during the share deal for the Casino had been coaxed on to the Fratoni side and had now disappeared, nobody knew where. We sat sipping our drinks and listening to De Negris and Münzen spinning out this story. I was only half taking it in, I was too interested in Minsky, who listened patiently for a minute or two, and then turned to Zonda and began asking her questions about herself. He was an enormous man with big hands and feet, and a German croak. Drakulič, the Baron's agent, on his other side was turned away, listening to Don talking about *Raging Bull*, which had just come out in France. Minsky listened impassively to the tale of the art school, and then my interests in horses and racing. Uncle Mooney and I started doing our horses act. Mooney was telling him about the Arc de Triomphe and my recent successes and then we started reminiscing.

'1938 – remember Raymond – ?'

'Statistically speaking, *yes* . . .' I said. 'Two furlongs out it was – from the rails outwards – Cillas, Cavallino, Nearco, Legend of France, Castel Fusano and a horse called Gubellini . . .'

'Nearco had never seen the whip in his life, but the jockey took a decision at that point when they were all in a bunch and struck him once – '

He paused to down some of the absolutely delicious Cabernet we were drinking.

'The most fateful whip-stroke in racing history . . .'

Minsky and Zonda looked puzzled.

'He flew home to win,' I laughed, 'and it must have been a state of enormous rage and puzzlement at this peculiar event that started him moving at top speed . . .'

'And after that, of course, he became the classic winner that he was . . .' said Mooney. He sighed. 'Ah, that man deserves immortality if ever anyone does, who was he Raymond . . . ?'

I didn't know.

Minsky leaned back with a serene smile and chewed the last of his crab *pâté*. He wiped his mouth with his napkin and folded his hands across his bulging shirt at the front, rolling his shoulders to get some stiffness out of his neck as he did so.

'So,' he croaked to Mooney, 'you are running about Europe with a twenty-year-old girl and a young gambler.'

His eyes were gun-metal blue in the light from the window, and the remark cut a great swathe down the table. Although the lips of the others never stopped moving, all I could hear was the clink of knife and fork against plate. Mooney picked up his glass and held it up to the light. Minsky was nodding slightly as he held Mooney's eyes.

I looked at Zonda.

Then we all started talking at once.

Zonda nudged Minsky, to my astonishment, and said in her best Cockney:

'Hey, less of that, will yer!'

'*What* could be more agreeable?' I warbled.

Mooney was crooning some paean to youth and the future, when the waiters arrived with the second course and the whole moment passed. Minsky leaned back and negotiated with them over his shoulder, sending his chicken back for some minor adjustments, and by the time he sat forward again and addressed us with those amused heavy-lidded eyes, saying nothing however, now the conversation had moved on, Irving had intervened with some hostage or Gulf-War talk.

Mooney looked at his best, I thought. I had tried to spruce him up as much as possible, stealing one of his two suits from the wardrobe in the Louvre and taking it to a twenty-four-hour cleaners and then beginning the fierce campaign to get his hair washed and cut. We had spent a long time at the barbers that morning, the barber visibly gagging as he dumped the greasy curls under the tap and picked and snipped his way round the archaeological site of the scalp and hair arrangement. When he had finished, Mooney, looking very much the disappointed ram, but almost presentable with it, and several years younger, came away wiping his neck with a towel and muttering that he didn't have time for this sort of thing. On the floor round the chair lay a semicircle of blue-grey curls, yellowed at the ends with cigarette smoke.

There was an unaccountable delay after lunch and certain members of the company were beginning to get restive. Coffee and *digestifs* were nothing but cold stains now, in a variety of vessels borne away in discreetly rattling stacks by the final wave of waiters. The bill sat neglected on its saucer to Mooney's left.

Minsky had taken his bib from under his chin, and sat expectantly looking from one person to another. The pairs of conversations amongst board members had begun to break up. Zonda was sitting frozen in thought. I saw Don break off from his discussion with Irving and go over to her. When Mooney still showed no sign of moving, I reminded him gently that we had only booked the boardroom at the Negresco for a certain length of time. He inclined his head graciously. We sat and watched the surge of the Promenade outside, the waiters hovering visibly. Minsky looked at his watch. Mooney still seemed reluctant to move. Finally, when he did, it was only to go for a splosh.

I conferred with Irving. If it was just a question of the bill, then I would handle it. But was there some other reason why Mooney didn't want to move, perhaps? Irving said that we were waiting for Casey.

Mooney had still not reemerged when the manager came over to find out, as politely as possible, if there was a problem with the bill. He was desolated, but his staff were waiting to go off duty. As he was reluctantly retiring, he came face to face with a thin red-haired Irishman, a kind of inflated stable-boy with a sharply pointed nose and freckled complexion, who was doing his best to burst through the phalanx of hovering waiters into the dining-room. They had words, the manager indicating the staff, pantomiming looking at his watch and throwing up his hands, then clicking his fingers and issuing some orders to the diminishing line of figures tailing away towards the kitchen. Then he stood aside ceremoniously to let him stride purposefully across to our table.

Casey laid his briefcase with infinite care on the chair next to him. Then went along the line offering a tremulous hand. I found Mooney on the phone in the usual cubicle next to the kitchen and informed him that Michael Casey had arrived. Mooney set out across the dining-room floor at a foundering trot and immediately they went into conference across the lunch table. He had brought papers for Pequeño Investments. Unbelievably, the company, bought off the shelf in the Isle of Man, had only just received authentication.

A waiter arrived with a silver tray and placed in front of Casey a syllabub, a glass of white wine, and a cup of coffee.

While we watched him deal with these various objects, I asked Mooney beneath my breath about the papers. Was it true that this outfit which had apparently already gone a long way towards acquiring property in America worth millions of dollars was not even registered? No wonder Esclapon had not been able to find it.

'Just a technicality, Raymond.' He looked around the table, nodding benignly at the company, and I could hear little ticks and clicks and groans of approval in his throat.

He explained that it was only a question of the name. They had been registered for quite some time under the old name, but it hadn't been changed. For various reasons they now needed to change it, but they had never had it done. Now our Mr Casey had kindly come all the way from the Isle of Man at his own great personal – here he leaned across and put a veined hand on Michael Casey's arm, who paused from spooning up his syllabub to receive Mooney's almost coquettish smile full against the sunlight – inconvenience, to deliver the right papers and sort the whole thing out, so that they could get on with the job.

Casey pricked up his ears. He resented being told he was paying for himself.

'No rush,' said Mooney silkily. 'No rush at all Michael.'

Casey, who was bolting his dessert and drinking his coffee and smoking his cigarette and sipping his wine all at once, knew now that he was also expected to pay the bill, which the manager had taken away and was amending at another table. He turned to protest, but his eyes bounced off something he saw in Mooney's face, sliding involuntarily towards the figure of the fuming Minsky at the end of the table, and he thought better of it.

I gave Zonda some francs and we left her to look at the town while we all filed into the mock-Georgian boardroom inside the hotel which Mooney had insisted I hire at great expense, because 'it's good for the people getting off the planes, you see . . .' By this, he meant Minsky and Drakulič, who were waiting for us in the lobby. Casey tried to draw Mooney on one side as we passed in. He looked furious, and his jaw was working, as he hissed and shook his head. Mooney made some suitably papal gestures and we passed through into the room, distributing ourselves at random amongst the pads, blotters and carafes of water. I could hear Irving behind me telling some story about what President Assad of Syria's young son said to his father in front of Nixon when he arrived in Damascus in '73.

'Isn't Nixon the one you said on TV is a foreign devil and the friend of the Jews? Now you are having him here. Why?'

Irving was chuckling.

'Now you are having him here,' he repeated across the table to Don for the rhythm of the remark. '*Why?*'

Mooney nodded to me to close the door. Round the table sat Minsky, Glucksman, Don, De Negris and Drakulič, Casey, Münzen, Villanova, Münzen's assistant, and myself.

Mooney made the introductions in his best boardroom manner, referring to me as 'Mr Bosanquet, who is performing sterling service for the Company as our house translator and general secretary in these negotiations . . .'

Don smirked.

'Gentlemen,' said Mooney, squaring his hands round the file which I had spent the night typing up, 'you are all aware of the general purpose of this afternoon's meeting, even though you have not been briefed on any of the particulars. Let me introduce to the Board two representatives of our investment bankers, Mr Minsky the investment analyst, and Mr Drakulič of Window on the World Financial Consultancy from Zurich, and, of course, the representatives of our fiduciary bank, Mr Münzen and Mr Villanova of his foreign exchange department . . .'

'What *is* the purpose?' said Casey, irritably.

Tension rose around the table. Mooney adjusted his spectacles. He looked over them.

'That is a disingenuous remark, Mr Casey, which I could choose to ignore. However, I will not. Is it the Board's wish that I review the general purpose of the meeting before we begin proceedings?'

We all agreed that we knew why we were there.

'Let's get on with it Gerrard,' said Irving.

'Very well,' said Mooney. 'May I say that I appreciate that you have all . . .' he glanced round the table, making a point of smiling at Casey warmly, 'been willing to take time out from busy schedules to discuss the present matters at issue. We have a capital agenda. What I propose to do is to hand you over to Mr Glucksman, first of all, who will brief us on the borrowers in this transaction, then we will hear from Mr Münzen some of the technical projections from the performing bank's point of view, and then' – he nodded to Minsky and Drakulič – 'the Board will hear from the Investment Bankers and their reactions to our proposals. I hope members of the Board will feel free to interrupt as we go along. In this way we may, I hope, have every chance to clarify issues and resolve any differences of opinion we may hold . . .'

Hands shot up immediately. Then Drakulič tried to go out of turn.

'I didn't come all this way to listen to crap like this,' said Casey.

There was a round of clucking and disapproving noises and Mooney asked Irving to make his presentation to the Board.

Irving started.

Irving painted a glowing picture of the investment opportunity that a loan to Brazil presented. He dwelt on the need of the country, as symbolised by the fact that Ernane Gallneas on Labour Day, September 1st, only six weeks previously, that is to say, had given lunch to the top ten American banks and soon afterwards to the European banks . . .

'I know this,' said Minsky. 'I was there . . .'

Irving pointed out that Brazil had been undergoing an 'economic miracle' since the 1960s and '70s, but had been largely financed by external commercial borrowing. The difficulties of the country had to be faced. The rate of inflation was 77 per cent, there was an annual shortfall of around 15 billion which must be met by borrowing. Imports amounted to 18 B, exports generated 15. Debt servicing 11 B. The total debt –

'*Publicised* debt,' Minsky corrected.

'Total publicised debt is 50 billion, planned to reach 55 billion by the end of the year . . .'

'But if all private credits are included, and we know that all restrictions on borrowing by private enterprises were abolished on Dec. 7th last year . . .' said Minsky, 'the actual debt must be nearer to 70 billion . . .'

Tables were passed around from the chair, which I had photocopied before the meeting. We stared at them.

'On the fifteenth of January this year, the finance minister, Sr Karlos Richsbieter, resigned. Why?' said Minsky.

It was a rhetorical question, but it had to be answered.

'Wouldn't you?' said Don. Laughter all round.

Sr Antonio Delfim Netto, who had taken over, was a man of great experience, said Irving, plunging back into his documents, having been finance minister in the Medici administration.

'Never mind the rhetoric . . .' said Casey.

'The upshot of all this was,' said Irving, 'that Brazil still needed to raise another 14½ billion by the end of the year to meet a total need for new or rolled over cash this year of about 15½ billion – 6½ billion to pay off due debts, 7 billion to service the interest on the remainder, perhaps 2 billion to meet the expected deficit in visible trade, transport and service payments. The recent price hike in oil has hit them hard, but we have some interesting information about the creation of alternative energy require-ments . . .' He looked across at Mooney. 'The alcohol car, for example, which required intensive capital investment . . .'

He passed round some more tables.

Irving went on facing up to the Brazilian economy for a bit, and Mooney threw it open for comment.

Minsky weighed in and made a speech which suggested that Irving had presented far too glowing a picture of the economy. The fact was that Delfim Netto, whose concern for foreign opinion verged on the obsessional, was embarking on a desperate gamble. He had announced this year already that monetary correction would not be more than 45 per cent. But there were serious distortions present in the economy, with prices of oil derivatives, grain and wheat, electricity and foreign exchange all being effectively subsidised by the government.

'There is a temptation for the Brazilians,' said Minsky, 'I do not say whether it has been succumbed to, to indulge in index falsification . . .'

He didn't think that Irving should place too much confidence in Delfim Netto, who had already understated the indices for 1973 when he was finance minister in that Medici administration already referred to.

'It's true,' said Drakulič, 'that Petrobras have been able to raise enormous sums on the Eurodollar market under the umbrella of Federal Government guarantees . . .'

'And as for the much publicised alcohol industry,' said Minsky, 'I have some figures from a Harvard survey here which give quite a different, much more pessimistic picture of this industry . . .'

He passed round some tables.

'Figueiredo has indeed given a lot of publicity to this adventure,' he said, 'in an attempt to convince the world that they are pioneering something economically viable, but the survey shows that, even if you assume that a litre of alcohol is directly worth a litre of petrol at the world price of petroleum, since it permits the oil imports to fall by the litre, including the costs of refinery – and, by the way, you can't even make this assumption because the Brazilians are actually mixing alcohol with gasoline, and this reduces your base projections by twenty per cent – anyway, even if we used a one-for-one base projection, it would require a real increase of more than fifty per cent over this year and next in world petroleum prices for a break-even situation for alcohol . . . oil would have to reach $49 a barrel . . .'

Irving was trying to look calm. But the quality of Minsky's information was awesome.

'There is a consumer boom in Brazil at this moment,' said Minsky, 'and so we can see what is happening to this industry as it tries to meet the demand for alcohol-powered cars. The bigger it gets the more we see that it *costs* foreign exchange rather than saves it . . .'

Irving was looking at Mooney as Minsky placed his facts calmly before the Board. Mooney was impassive. Drakulič was beginning to get very uneasy and highly active. There were some sharp exchanges during the remarks about the alcohol industry, but none of us had had time to study the report and all we could do was wait to see where this was all leading. Everybody was alarmed. Minsky had been sent by Ickle to ditch us. Even Casey had swallowed some of his anger, perceiving that Glucksman's cards were of no value whatsoever against Minsky's. Mooney started looking sneakily off at Münzen.

Minsky ceased his flow at this point and Mooney handed it to Henri Münzen.

Münzen pointed out that Brazil had been financed heavily in recent years by American regional bank portfolios which had now, it seemed, reached their country limit and the flood of new lenders had dried up. The huge loans arranged for Brazil by the money-centre banks contained large chunks of finance from these sources. These loans were taken with spreads of less than 1 per cent over the London-offered Interbank rate. With other lenders (Japan, West Germany) out of the market for the moment, at least, as he saw it, Brazil was going to have to accept spreads more in the region of 1½ or maybe even 2 per cent now . . .

This caused quite a flutter round the table. Things seemed to be swinging the other way a little.

Münzen went on to say that pressure was building up for another big devaluation in Brazil as the crawling-peg devaluations lagged behind internal inflation rates. Ever since Delfim Netto had taken over, he had been predicting that the inflation rate was on the point of falling, but it was in fact continuing to rise. It was worrying that the end of the first quarter of 1980 had seen a big dip in the country's currency reserves. It seemed, however, as if the sudden drop had been caused by oil stockpiling. He was glad to say that reserves had risen again in recent months.

'They may end the year at about $5 billion . . .' he finished.

'That is a very thin cushion,' said Minsky.

'With total debt running at the level of at least $4 billion greater in 1981, interest payments will be higher . . .'

This was piety. The argument about spreads had been, I saw, fairly decisive.

'There is another consideration,' said Minsky slowly.

'What is that?' said Mooney. He waved him on from the chair.

'Netto has got his supply of oil this year from Iraq. Iraq is completely in the Soviet fold. My information tells me that Brazil has already signed an agreement with Iraq for the peaceful use of nuclear energy under which Brazil will supply the dictator Saddam Hussein with raw and enriched uranium and with the technology and know-how which Brazil is acquiring through its nuclear agreement with West Germany . . .'

Irving was nodding. Drakulič was nodding.

'Brazil must be financed,' he said. 'It's very important.'

Mooney drove in.

'Gentlemen, my sense of this discussion is that we can agree that the general picture seems to be that Brazil is an accepted credit risk for the kind of long-term loan we are contemplating . . . around the B and three mark I should say . . .'

I looked around. To my surprise, after all this 'facing up' to Brazil's debts, there were nods and signs of assent all round. I had obviously misread the discussion. It seemed to me that the opposite had been established.

Irving was asked to comment now on the case of Venezuela and Mauritius. But here Drakulič swept in.

'Mr Chairman,' he said, agitatedly, 'I fail to understand the financial structure of the deal now being contemplated. The diversifications proposed are very hazardous in my view . . .'

'We'll take this point when we've heard the reports from individuals concerning the countries involved,' said Mooney smartly. It was fairly easy for him to cut this one off, but it was a shot across his bows and Drakulič wanted him to see that things were going to get rough in this sector. His agency alone was responsible for the Brazil money, but he would have nothing to do with the other countries, particularly Venezuela. Primed by the Baron, I remembered. I remembered the Baron's unease about this.

The case of Venezuela proved much more complicated than that of Brazil, and the swings of allegiance were much more difficult to follow.

Irving began by presenting Venezuela as an oil-producing country which could ultimately shoulder its debt, whose economy had been in recession for a long time but which was about to revive due to the measures of the Campins government's restrictive money policy. The government had inherited a massive and unwieldy apparatus of price controls and government subsidies erected by the Perez Accion Democratica administration and were pledged to dismantle it. It was true, said Irving, that oil revenues, despite the '79 price hike, had not been as expected – 39.3 billion bolivars as against the budgeted 44.6 billion, and government projects such as the steel complex at Xulia were being delayed, but nevertheless, these were short-term problems. The long-term prospects looked reasonable, when the short-term difficulties of the Perez years in insane public expenditure were sorted out. The State itself was hidebound. He reported an estimated 2 billion would be required to cover the 1980 budget deficit. The Central Budget Office attached to the Finance Ministry had identified a need for a further 9.3 billion to finance top-priority capital expenditure projects.

'Which is surely very worrying,' said Drakulič.

Irving did some more facing up. Inflation was soaring. In the first quarter of this year, the cost of living had shot up: food, by 37 per cent; clothing 44 per cent; household goods, 21 per cent. But it was a question of identifying whether this was cost-push or demand-pull. It was not clear from his information which.

'But,' he finished, 'as the finance minister himself put it recently, they are and I quote "approaching the end of a long tunnel" . . .'

There were roars of laughter all round the table, led by a hooting Drakulič.

Even Casey laughed at this.

Minsky and Drakulič were caught in a log-jam. Mooney waved Drakulič in.

'I think the point is this,' he said, the smile still sitting in his ghastly cheeks. 'The government has completely lost control of public spending. The fact of the matter is that they have not faced up to the Perez system, as Mr Glucksman has implied – and here I think he is seriously misleading the Board – '

Irving bristled. Mooney waved a calming, chairmanly hand.

'They got cold feet. Campins recently bowed to pressure in Congress when this issue of the Perez indexation of the public sector workers came up. Outside in the streets there was a demonstration of 50,000 workers and the government backed off, afraid to touch the wage bill. The fact is that the country's private sector feels threatened, a symptom of which is the so-called "Maracaibo letter" in which some pretty searching questions were asked of the government's supposed public sector policy, questions which, on the analysis presented so far . . .' Drakulič was finishing with a passionate burst for the tape, 'show no sign of being answered!'

Mooney waved in Münzen to cool things down.

Münzen reported that two months ago in August, nineteen banks under the name of Citicorp had advanced $1.8 billion, repayable over eight years at ⅝ spread for the first five years and ¾ per cent for the remainder.

Whistles and groans all round the table.

'Several of the banks involved in the syndicate,' said Münzen, 'were surprised at these terms after the negotiations had been concluded.'

Minsky wanted to come in here.

'My information tells me that these negotiations were particularly difficult and protracted. One of the difficulties is a serious liquidity crisis in this country . . .'

He went on to describe how the negotiators discovered increasing evidence during the talks that the private sector had been complaining for some months about the government's failure to repay public sector debts and interest obligations on time. By mid-June 1980, he said, the amount of interest and amortisation payments overdue to private contractors had reached the outstanding amount of 11 billion bolivars or $2.6 billion. Drakulič came back in, and attacked Venezuela from another angle.

'I agree the economy is depressed,' he said, 'but look at the current account balance for 1979 . . .' He passed round the tables. 'The depression might well be maintained until 1981, but then there'll be the usual upsurge in imports as they stimulate domestic demand . . . This problem will turn into a severe balance-of-payments crisis . . . I think the difficulty here is that this government is seeking to convert short-term liabilities to medium-term ones . . .'

It was Minsky, as usual, who produced the devastation.

'What the Citicorp negotiators also discovered,' he folded his fat hands across his stomach and crossed his short legs under the table, 'is a problem for *external* creditors as well as domestic ones . . .'

He went on to describe how the Citicorp negotiators had found out that there was a default on the interest for a French firm called GVC-Fesilven. The sums of money were modest, a mere $13 million he said, but the main foreign creditor, Crédit Lyonnais, for GVC-Fesilven, had withdrawn as a result from the syndicate for the 1.8 billion.

'How had the situation arisen?' Minsky raised his eyebrows rhetorically. 'Because borrowing by individual State entities has been allowed to proceed in an entirely haphazard fashion . . .'

He went on relentlessly outlining the appalling nature of Venezuela's foreign debt. At the end of 1979, he said, out of the $21 billion owed to foreign banks, $12.7 billion was due for repayment by the end of 1980 and a further $4.2 billion by the end of 1981.

Minsky smiled.

'At the beginning of last month,' he said wickedly, 'the finance minister, Señor Herrnan Oyarzabal, resigned . . . for personal reasons . . .'

The laughter was intense. Mooney calmed everybody down.

'Gentlemen, I think the important question is the medium-term loan . . . whether we want to accept that this will be the inevitable strategy in any negotiations with the Venezuelans and whether we are willing to take it on . . .'

'I think the point has been very carefully and precisely made by Mr Minsky,' said Drakulič, seizing his chance, 'that Venezuela is a credit risk of unacceptable proportions . . .'

There was a rumble of disagreement.

'All I am hearing at the moment,' said Mooney, pushing his paraphrase in Drakulič's direction, 'is a set of chronic cash-flow problems in the public sector and a state of administrative muddle . . .'

'There is another point,' said Minsky. 'If a long-term loan is contemplated to one of these public-sector entities, the Venezuelans have a ridiculous law on the statute book which says that Congressional approval must be obtained for long-term debts contracted by such public-sector entities . . .'

'This is why they tend to be looking for short-term cash . . .'

'That's right. The negotiations could take for ever . . .'

Mooney swept all these points together in a chairmanly summary which went boldly in the face of the facts presented. They must proceed with caution, but with firmness, he said, but he still didn't take the view that Venezuela's problems presented a clear case of unacceptable credit risk.

Why did he hold out? The stud-farm?

He said there would be an upturn in the economy after this period of monetary restriction was over and demand would rise.

'Of course imports will surge,' said Drakulič, 'and this will lead to a severe balance-of-payments crisis . . . We have to accept this . . .'

'Perhaps,' said Mooney, 'but the country needs long-term capital investment to get on its feet . . .'

'The Venezuelan monetary restriction is not a real financial policy,' said Minsky cynically. 'It's simply an attempt to prevent the "disappearance" of such funds.'

'Don't forget the fact,' said Irving, desperately trying to support Mooney, 'that the government *has* managed to persuade the Bank of the Confederacion de Trabajadores Venezolanos to take on about fifteen per cent of the "wage bill" debt . . .'

'It is obvious that we have a problem here,' said Mooney, 'and all the valuable points that have been made will be taken to heart . . .'

Was Minsky going to offer the threatened ultimatum? Drakulič looked across at him and raised an eyebrow. Mooney sensed it and looked across at Minsky. He asked pointedly if there were any more comments.

Minsky smiled.

'We shall wait, naturally, before offering any further comment to see what the details of any negotiations your company may enter into are . . .'

Mooney passed over to Mauritius, which seemed like light relief. They were stacking their papers into their briefcases. Irving went into his usual routine of facing up to the economic difficulties.

After that they went through the ritual of the Mauritian finances, but it was only a ritual. Minsky led off:

'I'm sure we all have the highest respect for the Prime Minister who has long been regarded as an international statesman with a distinguished record as a negotiator in the field of British post-colonial politics . . .'

Mooney bit his lip. What was coming now?

'But I have it on impeccable sources that the country is highly politically unstable at the present time.'

'The Prime Minister's personal persuasiveness in securing loans for Mauritius is well known,' said Drakulič, putting his oar in, 'but . . .'

'What *are* your sources?' said Casey to Minsky.

'They are high up,' said Minsky. 'A left-wing coup is possible within a year.'

Münzen was beginning to look uncomfortable. Perhaps he knew what was coming. Mooney, however, lowered the depleted horns and stared over his spectacles for a moment, his lower lip hanging, while we took this in.

'I have no idea what sort of arrangement you are contemplating, but I suggest you give this careful consideration in relation to the economic facts . . .' said Minsky.

Mooney said he found this information very interesting, and the Board would take it into very careful consideration.

'I'm sure we all remember 26th June 1974 . . .'

I leaned forward.

'The ID Herstatt collapse,' Irving whispered under his hand.

'It goes without saying that a credit upheaval . . .' Minsky was addressing Henri Münzen now, in his croaking monotone, 'in the Euromarket would certainly not be limited to one bank. The precise exposure of individual banks is information which, at present, is not known to the public; for that reason, even those banks with negligible exposure may come under suspicion . . .'

Mooney began muttering about the provision of acceleration clauses, amortisation etc.

'As I have said on many previous occasions, such things are not a solution. These things can provoke a chain of defaults across the board for the country involved . . .' said Minsky smoothly, returning to his quarry, Münzen. 'No, gentlemen, the fact that a bank taking on a negotiation is merely acting as an agent for another bigger bank will not protect it . . . two-thirds of currency deposits – I need hardly remind you – represent *interbank* deposits . . .'

He stood up, dumping his bulging briefcase on the table in front of him, while he buttoned his jacket. He had a plane to catch.

Mooney made polite noises, and there were murmurs of thanks all round. Minsky nodded and made his exit.

The meeting broke up soon after Minsky had exited after one or two technical discussions between Münzen, Mooney and Glucksman about floating-rate loan contracts.

Mooney and Glucksman seemed well satisfied.

'Well, Raymond,' he patted me on the shoulder, waving his clinking tumbler of Scotch, 'it looks like the green light from Zurich . . .'

'But,' I said, 'but it seemed to me as if he was raising insurmountable objections the whole afternoon . . .'

They laughed.

'Flannel,' said Mooney. He looked at Glucksman. 'All that stuff about the vulnerability of the Euromarket . . .'

'He was saying: "If you want to have a go, have a go . . ." ' said Irving, 'but make sure the spreads are right . . .'

Mooney was laughing about Drakulič. Minsky had ditched him. They'd obviously had an arrangement.

'I think Minsky will go back to Zurich and say to Ickle and Bisig it's OK . . .' said Irving.

'Where's Henri?' said Mooney, wheeling round to look for Münzen. Münzen was in the corner talking urgently to Drakulič, who was about to leave. They came over and Drakulič shook everyone's hand and said he would be in touch.

'Well Henri?' said Mooney.

'It looks alright for Brazil and Venezuela,' said Henri, 'but what are we going to do about Mauritius . . . ?'

'Just imagine the look on the Princess's face when she gets to know about *this*,' said Mooney.

On the sea-front, I found Zonda and a lanky brown French boy with loose clothing sitting on chairs, their shoes dangling in the incoming tide. She was flowing: the wings of her skirt were thrown apart over her crossed legs and the wind was blowing her hair about. After he had been introduced he stood up suddenly, the tide running in over his shoe.

Solemnly, passionately, he raised one clenched fist, the palm outwards, and shouted up the beach:

'Free political action from all totalising paranoia!'

Zonda laughed, entranced. It seemed Luc was a poor little rich boy from somewhere down the coast. He collapsed back on his chair, which started slowly to tilt at a crazy angle as the metal legs began sinking into the wet sand. Lots of mileage in that. He had been telling her about Gramsci and the factory councils. His eyes kept straying to something behind me as he talked.

'But Gramsci was all wrong,' said Luc. 'The group must not be the organic bond uniting hierarchised individuals, it must de-individualise . . .'

I laughed:

'So *that's* why Gramsci was wrong . . .'

'Develop action, thought and desire,' said Luc to Zonda. 'What is not productive is sedentary.'

'And what *is* productive?' I asked.

'Whatever is nomadic.'

There was something fanatical and weightless about his long legs inside the expensive trousers and his ineffably Gallic phizog and the lank quiff *à l'anglaise*.

'Don't think one has to be sad in order to be militant,' he told Zonda tenderly. 'Even though it is the abominable one is fighting against.'

They made me feel tired.

'There are two general laws of the universe . . . One is

371

association – randomly associated units come together to form larger units . . .'

'Isn't he something?' said Zonda.

I hauled her to her feet out of the chair. She started to laugh.

'. . . and the other is the law that those units are not permanent, that sooner or later they will dissolve . . .'

'Wow,' said Zonda, shaking her head. She bent to shoehorn her heel with a finger that she wormed into the damp, sandy aperture. After what seemed like an age, in which they had another couple of intensely desultory exchanges, she stood up and looked at me, cocking one eye against the declining sun.

'Well, how'd it go?' There was a rush about the eyes, a slight bubble in the way she said this.

'Confusing,' I said. 'But *they* seemed to think it was OK . . .'

I searched her face. She didn't explain to Luc, who didn't mind.

Mooney, Don, Irving arrived. De Negris said he had to go back to Ventimiglia and, after Don had failed to persuade him to wait for us, he limped away up the beach.

'Well, young lady . . .' said Mooney, and stared down at her benignly. She introduced her friend Luc. She was surrounded by men in suits. She began to laugh.

'A picture of . . .' said Mooney. His eyes drifted over to a distant coaster on the horizon.

'Decadence?' I stared hard at her, knowing they wouldn't hear me, because I was downwind. 'Overindulgence in narcotic substances?'

Don gave an inconsequential snort behind me. I saw that we were all staring out to sea watching the sun's last rays strike the bridge of the vessel. Zonda was smoking nervously, pushing the smoke out as if she couldn't wait to get it out of her body, and then taking another deep lungful, pressing her lips together, shipping the smoke back into her mouth, jealous of the wind. Luc's leg was jiggling up and down constantly.

'A glimpse of life without fascism,' said Luc, getting to his feet.

'What's the matter?' said Zonda, standing up and facing us all, the water swirling round her ankles.

'You'll catch cold . . .' said Mooney, snapping back, beneficently, from his reverie.

'What are you all waiting for?' she asked.

'Good question,' I said.

Mooney looked at Glucksman. Don stepped forward and took Zonda by the hand, leading her out of the tide. She was giggling, a low nervous giggle, as her wet black shoes emerged from the water. She dropped them off her feet, one by one, saying:

'Luc's coming.'

'We don't have room for Luc,' I said.

'It's cool,' said Luc. He pointed behind me at the brightly painted Toyota jeep which had been hastily wrestled up on to the pavement at an angle, one door hanging open. A gendarme was squatting on his haunches at the back, looking at the number-plate, and another seemed to be leaning at the dashboard.

Luc walked backwards a little way towards it up the beach. He held up two sets of crossed fingers and shook them gently at us, as if scattering a cloud of incense on the intervening sand.

'Whatever is multiple and positive is cool . . .' he said with a dreamy kind of urgency to Zonda. 'Difference has it over uniformity, flows over unities, mobile arrangements over systems . . . You *can* slam the door . . . it's the connection of desire to reality that possesses revolutionary force . . .'

'Jesus Christ,' said Don shaking his head and kicking up a cloud of sand in his anger. 'Where in hell d'you dig *him* up?'

Monte Carlo

The last Board Meeting of Pequeño Investments took place impromptu onstage in the empty lecture hall of Prince Albert's Oceanographic Institute, which Mooney comandeered with one quick peep, the rotating video of the Wonders of the World's Oceans enjoying a hiatus, while the tourists and parties filed by the curtained entrance into the main hall of the museum of natural history. We had just heard by runner (De Negris, who limped panting up the cliff walk and caught us up from behind) that the Principessa and Habib had left town in disgust, and this meant that Philippe and Carlos would almost certainly be looking for us. Mooney was attempting to hold the whole party together, the rams' horns turning from side to side, his face electric with gaiety, a taut expression seen only on the faces of stand-up comedians or certain amphetamine addicts. Zonda, who had recently become one of the latter party, despite all my warnings about the dental impact of such malign substances, responded to him much more instinctively than did his dour Board members. He had not accepted defeat. He had not even acknowledged that such a thing could exist. And he didn't expect that anyone else should at this stage. Meanwhile the irascible Eamon Costello had arrived, said De Negris, with a couple of Australians who had 'a hot line to Arab money'. De Negris said that the lobby of the Louvre was milling with people. The Brazilians were there, Philippe and Carlos (who were in my opinion the people to watch), and Costello and his Australians, all of them equally anxious for an interview with Mr Mooney.

Mooney was sprawled in a brocaded dinner-chair on the stage, smoking and grinding his ash out on the sole of his shoes as he talked. Irving had acquired a cowrie shell from somewhere and sat on the edge of the stage, turning it over and over while he listened to the speeches. When he intervened, his hand gripped it unconsciously. De Negris was crouched in the corner. I sat at the grand piano as if I were about to strike up, and Don and Zonda had drawn up a couple of spectator's loose chairs, and were sitting in the auditorium.

Irving put forward the proposition formally, that we disband the firm. There was no possibility of recovering this operation, he argued, and what was more it was positively dangerous for us to stay around. What we needed was to flit, flee, shazam, take a powder, vamoose, leg it.

'You know?' he said, turning to us. 'Blow town?'

We knew. De Negris the faithful was nodding in the corner.

Closing day had begun well. By ten o'clock in the morning, Münzen had a complete clutch of letters from the Third-Worlders, confirming arrangements for the promissory notes and schedules of payment, even from the Mauritians. No one had had the heart to disclose to the Prime Minister that he had been blocked by Minsky, and two Mauritians appeared at 8.30 a.m. in a helicopter from down the coast with a letter of final confirmation. Mr Simonsen delivered the Brazilian notes. And a little after that, Carlos and Philippe, in the company of the Principessa and Habib, almost bumped into them in the street. Then they all started circulating around, jamming the telephone lines and cluttering the lobbies of various hotels. Not only, however, did no Clyde Wellcombe appear, but by lunchtime Zurich seemed to have dried up on us. Tension rose. Nothing appeared from Bisig. A war broke out between Glucksman and Mooney. People were drinking without getting drunk. We sent to Zurich several times. No reply. In the end, Casey took off from Nice in a Piper I had chartered with the letter of confirmation proving that we actually had the funds committed in the Société Générale de Monaco, but when he arrived, he found, unthinkably, unbelievably, that the Handelsbank was closed – CLOSED – and everyone had gone off home for their coffee and *Apfeltorte*.

The situation had deteriorated rapidly after that. Unavailability in Monte Carlo is a strictly limited commodity, and though for his own sake he had been holding the line for an hour or two, the besieged Münzen could no longer contain the ugly rumours that had started to fly round. It was at this point that we had not exactly fled, but withdrawn from the Louvre to a point of vantage from which to take stock of our position. Mooney was trying seriously to rethink the operation.

'I mean, look, Gerrard,' said Irving, 'I don't want you to feel the rats are deserting the sinking ship.'

'Mr Chairman,' said Don, 'with respect, you are trying to make chicken salad out of chicken shit . . .'

Zonda naturally agreed.

I wanted to hear what Mooney had to say.

He started a long stiffen the sinews and summon up the blood ramble to rally the troops about faint-heartedness. He actually quoted *Henry V* in the process of giving a rigged balance-sheet of the setbacks. Yes, it looked bad. Yes, the negotiations had gone sadly wrong. It was no use pretending, they had to face facts. The facts of the matter were that they had got so close but there had been a hitch, that's all. But look how far they had actually come. They had climbed all the way from the South Col base camp, said Mooney, to assault camp three. They were still only a whisker away from it. They actually had the notes of the Brazilians, for God's sake, in the bank down there and all they had to do was wait and telex Zurich again. What the hell was Drakulič doing?

Someone laughed.

'Drakulič, Gerrard, is over the hills and far away . . .' said Irving, 'where we should be if we had any sense . . .'

We were unanimous that Window on the World Consultancy was not going to help at this stage.

'Alright, alright,' said Mooney, 'but look at it this way. Most of the people who are just nuisance value have pulled out. We've lost the deadwood that's all. There's less for a final cut if we all carry on together . . .'

If we could just hold them all for a day or two while we reestablish contact with Zurich, he said, he was sure that we could put this thing together again. This was only a technical hitch. He was sure that the goodwill was still there on Ickle and Bisig's part.

Irving scoffed at this.

Münzen started off on Irving's side. He wanted out. He thought there was no way, now the date of the negotiations had been surpassed, they could rescue the deal. They would have to start again from scratch and these people were far too impatient. The problem for him was also his superiors. He just couldn't be expected to fool around with the bank's resources any more, he said. But as he spoke, Mooney seized his chance, whittling away with incredible energy at every point, offering schemes to repair the breaches in the fabric of negotiations, and gradually one felt it was possible that Münzen might leave the Irving camp and come over to his.

I came in on the Mooney side arguing that we should consider the probability angle. It might look at the moment as if our run had come to an end and that anything that we tried to do from now on would simply be disastrous, but the maturity of the chances was, as every gambler knew, a false doctrine. No coup can be affected by a coup or a series of coups before it. So it wasn't necessarily getting less probable that we would succeed. While a series was still on, I argued, leaning on the lid of the piano, it is a myth to believe that the probability of its ending increases with every coup. In fact, the *im*probability of a series continuing *de*creases with each successive coup that prolongs it. So what we needed was another coup. Take the roulette wheel. Ten rouge will occur on average once every 1,024 times . . .

'Oh shit,' said Zonda to Don. 'He's off . . .'

There was a lot of shouting. I held up my hand.

378

'Let me finish, please. But the probability *against* a series of ten, which was 1,024:1 before it had begun, is successively reduced in the last nine coups to an even chance of 1:1 . . .'

'Yeah, pretty fancy footwork Raymond,' said Glucksman, 'but c'mon – how many coups do we have left? The fact is we have just lost. The run is *over*.'

I argued that this was simply a matter of opinion. I felt that we should have another go. After all, we could surely do without the Principessa and Habib, I argued. They were just an irrelevant nuisance.

Mooney began to sum up in favour of not pulling out. We still had the Brazilians, he thought. The Mauritian PM would still play, he was confident. It was true that the Venezuelans might not . . .

As he spoke, entering on his peroration, his face was suffused in a bluish green glow and a huge dolphin crossed his features, like the shadow of a cloud, twisting and turning and giving off from the region of his nose a sequence of silver blue bubbles which travelled slowly up his face into his eyebrows while a fanfare drowned his arguments and a deafening voice assured us in French that the ocean's riches were infinite.

The red plush curtain at the doorway was thrust violently aside and tourists began to pour into the room before we could get up from our seats. Mooney stood for a moment on the stage, the smoke from his cigarette outlined in the blue light, silhouetted against the screen, his face imprisoned in a mass of wriggling mackerel, the nose and mouth trying to make their way through the flashing silvery bodies, which were being transferred rapidly from the hold of a ship on to the docks. The shadow of the crane's dangling cord swung briefly across his face and they were dumped on to his shirt front and dwelt upon by a zooming camera, the infinite riches of the ocean. Mooney looked down, mesmerised by his wriggling shirt. Now he looked around in disbelief, and as we began to move towards him, his shirt-buttons metamorphosed into a conveyor belt.

We pushed and shoved our way through the several

coachloads of people bearing a stunned Mooney in our midst and broke out into the aquarium proper, which was a long dim room with the usual rows of tanks along the walls. In the centre of the room stood an octagonal tank with nothing in it, except a few things that looked like pipes and small yacht anchors. The new crowd of tourists had not yet penetrated this inner sanctum; they were still preoccupied with their lecture on the infinite riches of the world's oceans, and we had the place to ourselves apart from the turtles and small grey shark, enormously magnified by the plate glass, that cruised relentlessly back and forth along the walls. Mooney recovered his powers of rhetoric and got into flight again, arguing that it was perfectly possible if we were resolute and stood firm against the forces of dissolution and didn't allow ourselves to be panicked by a few setbacks to save the deal. He leant against the glass of the octagonal free-standing tank and lit another ghostly cigarette. Irving weighed in and said that it was obvious that Zurich were backing out. It had been obvious for some time. This whole thing was a lost cause. How could they possibly recover it now, when Henri couldn't be expected to play ball any more?

Zonda and Don were staring into the tank behind him, when I saw her move back involuntarily.

Irving and Don were challenging Mooney to produce a concrete plan now, instead of trying to whip them up with rhetoric. Well, they could transfer to another bank. He appealed to me for support. Let us cut our losses then. Alright, he admitted the original scheme had been a little ambitious. OK, they could let the Venezuelans go, though we could have a look at what Costello and his Australians had to offer. They could let the Venezuelans go.

'Gerrard,' groaned Irving, 'the point is will they let *us* go . . .'

'Let's stick with the Brazilians and negotiate the original deal that the Baron had wanted with Zurich, then.'

'You don't seem to realise,' said Irving again, 'Zurich are *through*.'

But Mooney was shaking his head in the greenish, smoke-filled light. He was certain that Zurich was not pulling out. This was only a technical hitch, he said. They could move back to Livorno or Pisa or Florence and if it was only a question of another fiduciary bank, he was confident they could . . .

I looked idly at the tank as he talked. A face emerged from one of the plastic pipes littered along its floor. A coarse, gaping face, at once blunt and pointed, with a mouth like the end of a pair of gigantic jump-leads constantly opening and closing to reveal rows of small backward-pointing teeth. The whole tank was full, I saw now, of moray eels, their thick bodies, thicker than a weight-trainer's bicep and ridged with fins, writhing in and out of the pipes and the artfully distributed marine bric-à-brac. They were a metallic grey-blue with an emetic yellowish dapple along the ridge of fins. The pincers of their tapered snouts silently opening and closing, vainly seeking purchase on the featureless curve of the tank glass, they crowded slowly with still eyes one on top of another.

A child ran round the corner at the end of the room, and stood watching these figures grouped round the tank. The argument still going on, we emerged into the crowded Great Hall of the Oceanographic Institute and filed, an urgent, dishevelled procession, between the articulated jawbones of whales, the reddish dried baleen hanging from them like ragged sheets of coconut matting. Mooney paused at the end of the aisle and turned triumphantly to make a point beneath a gigantic skeleton of a fin-whale, which fetched up, so the card read, on the Ligurian coast in 1897 and was donated by the Italians. The body had suffered tremendous gouges on its back from the keels of passing ships . . .

'Tremendous gouges . . .' said Zonda nudging Don, and looking towards a flutter in the crowd. Someone was pushing his way through, grasping at a pair of elbows belonging to different individuals that stood in his way like batwing doors at the end of the room, but the Bavarian coach tour, their solid bodies packed in a circle, their bags on the intervening floorspace, were too intent on listening to their Austrian guide describing the contents of the museum to give way. An arm placed itself between the bodies, an unmistakable arm. It was Carlos struggling through. And behind him I could see the curly head of Philippe. I looked over at Don.

It was time to go.

Mooney was still perorating as we hustled him out of the main entrance and into the *jardin exotique*. He sat on a bench, and lit a cigarette.

'Must think,' he said.

'Don advises we haven't got time to stop here, Gerrard . . .' said Irving.

He looked grey and abstracted, as he rose from the bench. All around him bloomed the early winter shrubs.

We managed to get round to the *ascenseur publique* set in the cliff and stood there inside the lift in a cube which Mooney treated as if it were a small boardroom and continued the discussion as if nothing were happening, while we waited for the big automatic steel doors to roll shut. The Chairman seemed puzzled by the muted and distracted nature of the Board's response. Münzen had gone ashen and was trembling with the strain.

'What's the matter with you all this morning?' he said. 'I know we haven't had our coffee . . .'

We were braced against the sides of the lift, fully expecting the Venezuelans to come round the corner at a run at any minute and sprint for the lift doors towards us.

'What's happening with Eamon Costello?'

Irving took this as his business.

'Well Mr Chairman, Mr Costello, as I said, has arrived in town with a couple more customers . . .'

'Oh yes . . . yes . . . I know that. There was all that scene in Nice, I remember . . .'

'Well, he's pretty sore about that, er, Mr Chairman . . .' said Irving.

We stared out of the open doors at the path.

'Now I think what we can do is this. I want you, Raymond – where's he gone, where's the boy gone?' – I stood on tiptoe and waved my hand from the back of the open lift – 'Ah, there you are – now Raymond, when we get down to the hotel, I want you to get on the phone to Drakulič . . .'

'Mr Mooney, Sir,' said Don. 'With respect what you gotta realise is this here situation is changed. We ain't fooling around here no more in this hotel. Now we are getting out and we are gonna get you out because if we don't, your life, as they say in the movies, ain't worth a plugged nickel . . .'

'It's true, Gerrard,' said Irving urgently. 'You see, these people think that you have been trying to cheat them. They are very angry. We are not dealing with civilised people here and there is danger now to life and limb. I'm sorry . . .' He shrugged with regret.

I listened to the sea pounding at the bottom of the cliffs.

Someone came round the corner and walked towards us. I felt everybody in the lift stiffen.

'This is ridiculous,' said Zonda as we stared out at the ancient, unusually bandy-legged cleaner pushing his cart full of brushes and pails towards us. He started, and raised an arm as the doors rolled shut without warning. As they narrowed to a slit, I caught a glimpse of his curse in the void of which flashed a solitary gold peg.

Mooney stared at the ceiling coordinating the Board's strategy.

'What I want us to do is get this show on the road again. We'll cut our losses and renegotiate the original Brazil deal. Raymond, I want you to get hold of Baron van de Velde. Irving I mean, Irving I want you to go to Zurich and talk to the Baron. Raymond, charter a Learjet and in the meantime find out what happened to – to Casey and the letter. I feel sure that if they only knew what we were doing . . . Don, now Don, I want you to take care of the PR angle with these Venezuelans, you know, calm them down a little . . . and I'll talk to the Mauritians . . .'

Next to me, De Negris began to swear gently.

I asked him what was the matter.

'My *culo* is *fuori* over this,' he said, shaking his head and wiping his spectacles on a handkerchief.

At the bottom of the cliff, we all stepped out, a number of us trying not to be furtive, and went under the tunnel by the hospital, where we knew we could find a taxi.

Mooney seemed to have woken from his boardroom trance.

'The Louvre,' he told the driver.

Who was going with him?

On the corner under the tunnel, there were a lot of raised voices and quick backward glances.

'When you get a cab,' I told Zonda, 'drive to the *bottom* entrance of the hotel, and wait for us there ... Don will show you.'

'Why can't I come with you?'

'Don't worry, Doll, I'll pack your things ...'

'Yes, but ...'

'It's dangerous. It's safer for you to stay with Don and De Negris, while we get him out ...'

'Why do we have to go to the hotel at all ... What's ...'

'Passports and stuff ...' I said as Irving and I piled in, leaving Zonda, Don and De Negris to find another cab and follow on immediately.

'It's more dangerous *here*, Raymond ...' I heard her calling and turning to look up into Don's face as we drew out into the light and shot away down the road and round the quay.

When we arrived at the Louvre, the driver tried to put us down on Mill Street right outside the front door. I got down and asked him to wait. I went up to the Agence des Moulins as if going in and then sidled along the wall to peer in. It was impossible. The Brazilians were seated in the lobby near the front door, Jaime and João playing cards and Mr Simonsen staring at a magazine. We would have to pass them in order to get to the stairs or lift.

I reported this.

'Right, Winston Churchill,' said Mooney to the bewildered driver. 'Let's do it man!'

I explained that he meant that we should go down and round to the Square at the bottom entrance to the hotel and wait there while we went inside and collected some items and then we would want to go to the railway station.

We took the lift to the second floor. On the way, to my horror, it stopped at the lobby floor. We stood behind the scissor grille, taking it in turns to peep through a crack in the frosted doors across the black and white tiles to where the Brazilians, partially hidden by a rubber plant, were slapping down the cards noisily on the little round café table. Mr Simonsen threw down his magazine and looked up. I stood back from the crack and pressed myself against the mirror on the rear wall and shut my eyes tight.

'Look at that, will you,' said Mooney, his eye glued to the crack. 'They're waiting down here like dogs!'

I was still squeezing my eyes tightly shut when the lift moved off to the second floor.

Mooney crashed on to the bed, fumbling for a cigarette.

'Now Raymond,' he said through the cigarette, running through the old pocket-patting routine, 'I want you to get on to . . .'

'Never mind about that now,' I said, 'let's get *out* of here, shall we?'

'Down there, hanging around like a pack of *dogs*!' he repeated. 'Did you see them?'

The phone rang and he began to reach for it, but checked himself and looked towards Irving and me.

'?'

We shook our heads.

'One last try,' he said wrenching himself up. 'I have an idea . . .'

Irving barred the phone threateningly with his hand, while I went to the cupboard full of cartons of rotten milk and old tins of coffee and took down his houndstooth suit trousers and jacket from their hanger, rolling them up into a quick bundle.

'No Gerrard. We've had it. Remember the . . . the dogs down there for Chrissake. We have to . . . No! I tell you . . .'

Irving was still sparring with him and trying to throw his things into a bag when I carried the houndstooth off to our room and quickly packed all Zonda's and my things into one suitcase. I was just kneeling on it and wrestling with the locks when I heard a noise outside. I looked down through the net curtains but could make nothing out over the rim of the balcony, so I stood on the armoire, and craned down. There they were, Zonda and De Negris, just stepping out of their taxi. I couldn't see Don, but I assumed he was there. They had got the bolt-hole right. Unfortunately they hadn't the wit to keep the taxi there and by the time I rushed out on to the balcony and called out to them to stop it, it was already disappearing round the corner. They looked up and waved, their faces, foreshortened, between their feet.

'No!' I shouted uselessly, pointing at the direction in which their taxi had gone.

Zonda turned to De Negris and said something and he looked up and extended his arms helplessly.

I motioned them to get another taxi, and wait. When I got back into the bedroom, Irving was bending over the supine Mooney.

'I don't like the look of this at *all*!' he said.

We looked at him. He was lying on the bed in the same position in which he had been when I left, but he had shut his eyes. Irving removed the burning cigarette from oblivious fingers. His face was waxy and colourless, the pallor yielding to an increasing tinge of green. His breathing was fast.

Irving shook him, muttering, tearing at his tie and collar.

'For Crissakes what a goddam time to choose . . .'

We agreed it was an inconvenient time for a heart attack.

Mooney opened his eyes.

'Pouf,' he said. 'Hot in here, thought I was going to . . .'

We swung his legs to the edge of the bed and got him upright. He was a dead weight, hanging on our shoulders, heaving and panting and giving out deep racking coughs.

'Wouff.' He looked at me, white foam flecked at the corners of an unfamiliar smile. He suddenly seemed to be someone else.

'We're ready to go now,' I said in an unusually loud voice, as if he were deaf.

He was still smiling in a slightly deranged fashion. He staggered as we tried to leave go of his shoulders and looked down at his feet, puzzled.

Irving gave the OK at the door and came back to help as we hauled him out on to the landing. We edged along painfully slowly, Mooney keeping up by leaning more or less continuously against the wall while Irving and I hauled the bags. His hand hissed along the flocked wallpaper behind me.

'Oh my God,' said Irving, turning back. A lift full of suits visibly packed together behind the frosted glass was arriving at our floor. 'Er . . . what's this . . .'

He was trying the doorhandle of a room on our right. I half fell into the gloom after him, Mooney part-slung on my shoulders breathing in loud groans. In the room there was a strong smell of scent. Irving turned back and went to the door which he opened a crack. They were filing past the lighted slit, Carlos and Philippe and some other people on their way to our room, their feet thumping, threateningly synchronised, on the boards of the landing.

'I'm standing on something,' said Mooney out loud.

My eyes were beginning to get a little more accustomed to the gloom. I bent down and moved his feet by tapping them. It felt like silk. I could see the bed now, behind us. An underslip. I rolled it into a ball and threw it onto the vague grey shape of the bed.

'Wondered what the hell it . . .'

Irving had his head out. He dragged the door wide open and

387

we started moving after him. I pushed the listing Mooney out ahead of me into the corridor and turned back to close the door behind me. Caught in the shaft of light, a woman's long horse-face rose blinking from the bed, propped up on shoulder and elbow. She was raising a hand to her hair. I heard her beginning to speak as I closed the door rapidly and softly. I sprang for the lift, bags bumping and scraping the tables and knick-knacks lining the landing walls.

The lift stopped again, of course, at the lobby. I stepped forward to the door and looked through the crack again. Costello and his two Australians were standing at the desk talking to Alphonse, who was turned away trying the telephone. No doubt that had been them a few minutes ago. The Brazilians were still where they were. Mooney lay back against the mirror, his eyes rolling. Irving was wedged panting in the corner with the bags, biting a thumbnail with a green incisor.

'Damn close run thing this,' I said in the voice of the Duke of Wellington. 'Anyone want to take any odds?'

The sweat was springing out of Mooney's forehead in huge opaque thunderdrops. It had already wet the mirror where his head was resting and begun to run down. A drop hung from the fur-covered lobe of his ear and the spikes of his grey hair behind the ears were dark with moisture. A faint colour had returned to his cheeks. As I passed him my handkerchief the lift gave a huge click and began to move, the pointilliste sketch of the lobby through the frosted glass rising into the ceiling. Just as our heads reached the lobby floor, Irving cleared his throat and said aloud:

'Well, looks like you two are on your own from here on in.'

We were alarmed. He was regretful, he shrugged.

'I'll come with you as far as Nice, but then I have a flight booked to New York.'

'You rat!' I mouthed.

Mooney rolled his head on the mirror and looked instantly to me.

'Well young fellermelad!' he said. 'Looks like there's just the two of us!'

I hitched up the bag in response.

We clattered out of the short hall into the sunlight.

Zonda was running towards me.

'For God's sake,' she said, 'where've you . . .'

'Spot of bother with his nibs,' I said. 'He's just had a . . . Got to get him away . . .'

She stood back on the gravel, hands hanging and eloquently opening with incredulity like a rep actress, her body turning with him as she watched Mooney trot past her gingerly with little mincing invalid steps and open the back door of the taxi. She turned back to me.

'Him,' she shouted. 'What the . . . what about *me?*'

I was dodging round, solicitous, looking over her shoulder as his second bent tweed-covered leg lifted from the asphalt and the door of the cream-coloured cab began to close.

'No time Doll,' I said. 'They're after him, Carlos and Philippe . . .'

'Raymond,' she said, 'I can't believe this you bastard. You're *leaving* . . .' She was holding on to me by the elbows.

'Listen,' I said, looking back at the hotel entrance. It stood dark and empty, but at any second I was convinced a pair of crocodile shoes would emerge into the sunlight. I stared into her face, listening to the engine of the taxi change note and the click as Irving opened the front door on the other side of the car and the scrape of his feet on the road and the squeak of the settling suspension as his weight was added to the car.

'Oh Christ!' she said to me wildly and softly. 'I don't believe this. This isn't happening . . .'

I shook her.

'Listen,' I said, 'go to Julia's, OK? Don will look after you, won't you Don . . .' The satire oozed into my voice, as I looked across at him. 'Take her to my sister's flat, Paris. She knows the address . . . OK?'

Irving slammed the front door of the taxi and the engine changed note again. It rolled forward. The back door pushed open and a hand beckoned urgently. I swung Zonda round that little bit more so that I was between her and the taxi now.

She clung to me under the elbows.

'It's all *over*, Raymond, and you are going with *him*! What the . . . You can walk away from this, it's nothing, and you're . . .'

'Doll, please try to under . . . I've got to see this through . . .'

Mooney's voice, restored to its depth, was summoning from the back of the cab.

'They'll be out in a minute,' I said, staring again, fascinated by the dark aperture of the hotel doorway and the crocodile shoes that would be first into the sunlight any minute now. I was pulling myself clear, tearing myself literally out of her hands, lifting my elbows and pulling them away from her puzzled reaching fingers.

'You can't be doing this . . .' she sobbed. 'For God's sake, take me *with* you then! Why not?'

'No room for all of us,' I said. 'You'll be safer . . . Just walk away from here round the corner . . .' I looked at Don who had arrived to hold her.

'Hon . . .' he said holding her back.

I backed my way into the taxi, never taking my eyes off her as she wrenched and stared back, her bottom lip hanging. Behind her the hole of the doorway, still dark.

'Go! go!' shouted Irving, slapping the dashboard.

'Get her away from here!' I shouted to Don. 'They'll be out any minute! De Negris, get her away!'

'Don't worry about a thing!' said Don.

She was wailing and putting up a tremendous fight as he dragged her towards the road.

'See you in Paris!' I shouted, transferring my helpless gaze to the back window as we fled by her flailing, diminishing figure just before I pitched like a leaf onto my side, hurled by the sudden torque on top of the struggling Mooney, our ears filled with the long howl of the tyres, and the pink flaking façade of the corner building at the end of the square wheeled down across the rear windows of the cab like a drawn curtain.

Part Four

Paris

Mooney and I had just met at the Place Gambetta and were standing on the street flapping in the wind. I was holding his airticket, waiting for him to stuff the cash I had just given him into his worn old wallet, when I saw the Venezuelans come up out of the opposite Métro. They stood and looked round for a moment, Philippe hunched down into his trench-coat in regulation fashion as Carlos offered him a light. Their heads came up. Carlos said something out of the corner of his mouth and they immediately split up and started combing the crowds and inspecting the cars in the square. I pressed the ticket on Mooney.

'Holy Mother of, Raymond,' he puffed. 'Don't be so damned impatient will ye!'

I rather enjoyed apologising, in some perverse, time-wasting way, and letting him understand that we, as they say in the movies, had company. He grunted, shoving the ticket-folder in his pocket, and we made as inconspicuous a run for it as we could manage. They would eventually comb the whole square, watching all the major exits. I hustled Mooney along as fast as I could by the arm and the wind almost took our breath away as we turned into the Avenue Père Lachaise, a short street that leads up to the Cemetery. I looked back, as we turned the corner. Unfortunately, Philippe had caught a glimpse of us just as we turned into this road, and I had heard him shouting above the noise of the traffic. He stabbed an index finger towards us. We managed to get to the end of the road but they came round the corner at a run just as we entered the cemetery gates, Carlos in the lead, whose wiry splay-footed harrier style looked good for several miles. I tried sprinting along the gravel under the plane trees, but Mooney immediately fell behind. He couldn't really run at all any more. Ahead of us, someone was standing on the low parapet of a tombstone and addressing a scatter of people on the path. It was a guided tour. I decided to join it, and then hope we could make a break for it at some stage. At least they wouldn't dare to make a move while we were surrounded by people. Mooney looked at me, hesitating with the uncharacteristic air of a dancer about to move off, and we mingled among the crowd, panting and pushing gradually into the centre of the knot of people.

The lecturer was a small bearded figure, who clasped a set of closely inscribed pink filecards which he held in one hand and checked and squared continuously with the other in the cone of thumb and fingers as he talked, reaching for each phrase, his eye resting on a cloud or a branch somewhere above the heads of his audience.

He was just coming to the end of a discourse about Loïe Fuller, the dancer, who to his regret was cinders only. I looked back down the empty leaf-strewn avenue, a flicker of hope rearing as the speaker suddenly skipped down from the parapet and pushed off through the crowd which reverse-ordered around him. We followed him off the avenue and down a little side path between two large ash trees where he briefly indicated the grave of the Silvains, Louis and Louise, who were simultaneously asphyxiated in their own home by the carbon monoxide given off by their domestic stove in 1930.

From there we plunged off among the yew-trees, following our tiny dome-headed leader, the wind filling the plastic macs of our solemn murmuring companions as we stumbled through the heaps of drunken busts, leaning headstones and gaping ivy-clad mausolea, each one of which seemed to conceal a mangy spitting cat, crouching amongst the plastic lilies and broken fragments of stained glass. We were well away from the beaten track now; pausing to acknowledge Bora Linovitch, a clown who invented a scene in which eight *clochards* came into the ring playing harmonicas; penetrating ever deeper into the uncharted interior of the cemetery through the smaller avenues, past La Regia, a female impersonator whose *pièce de résistance* was an imitation of Maurice Chevalier in drag. The main avenues of the cemetery were completely lost to view and I already had no idea where we were. Mooney was sweating and turning from plum to pale yellow as we struck off unpredictably through the damp leaves, stumbling from the grave of one forgotten clown to another, past Footit, inventor of the 'clown blanc', and Chocolat, his drunken assistant, with a nod to Yvette Guilbert, Toulouse-Lautrec's model, whom our little corduroy-clad guide had seen at the Bobino in 1938 – here he cleared his throat and sang in a wavering voice, echoed with discreet enthusiasm by other wavering voices around us, a reedy chorus snatched on the wind which made Mooney and me anxiously scan the path behind us, of 'Il est dix heures!' – and Louis Vigneron – *l'homme canon, messieursdames*! – whose grave, dramatically 'revealed' under a stubborn tummock of grass and dandelion roots, carries a marble replica of the 305 kilogram cannon he lifted on his back; and from the cannon man to Fragson, alias Harry Pot, the son of an English brewer, who was shot by his father.

Here we paused while an *ancien militaire* asked why. I stared at Mooney's face and touched him on the arm: over his forehead the central parting was obscured and the ram's horns had been broken up by the wind, the thick strands of grey-streaked hair blown up into the back of the scalp in swirls sculptured and held in place by grease and dandruff, an arrangement which gave him the air of an animal with its ears flattened in alarm. His mouth was slack, down at the corner. His chest heaved deeply under my raincoat which hung on him, loosely open, bellying helplessly in the wind, its pockets stuffed with miscellaneous papers. I touched him on the arm. He would never have a better chance than this. Now was his chance to make a break. If we left it any longer they would be waiting at the entrances.

I touched him again, and jerked my head. He looked at me once and nodded, then bent double and scuttled away up a slight incline and under some overhanging branches. I turned to watch the scut of mackintosh lift momentarily, its centre vent pulling aside to yield me my last view, engraved forever, of a piece of dried chewing gum adhering to the shiny seat of his houndstooth tweed trousers and my own brogues picking up, picking up, in the long grass, as I listened behind me over my shoulder to the soft snatches of Fragson biography interrupted by the wind:

'*Il voulait faire une tournée qui durerait trois mois . . .*'

'*. . . et le père?*'

'*Il voulait le mettre dans une maison de repos . . . Et ci-devant n'aimait pas . . .*'

'*Puis alors . . . ?*'

'*Et puis alors il a tué son fils. Trois balles.*'

'*Et après?*'

'*Après, monsieur, il le regrettait.*'

I left the tour while we paused at the bust of Charles Davray, a belle époque anarchist songwriter, situated in the middle of the *quartier des milliardaires*. The guide was just conducting the company in a rendition of 'Debout, debout mes révolution-naires . . .' when a tiny woman clad in black and bent almost double burst through the undergrowth, a china bowl in her hands, closely followed by a dozen or so mangy cats.

'Ah, Madame Margot . . .' our guide broke off.

She squinted up at the tour, and raised her hands, like a Greek tragic actress, in a gesture of formal lament:

'*Mais le blanc,*' she declared, '*il a disparu! Qu'est ce qu'il va faire, M. Vincent? Il a toutes ses femmes en bas ici, qu'est-ce qu'il va faire?*'

I looked round. There was no sight of Carlos or Philippe, nor for that matter of Mooney. The cats had penetrated the tour group, arching their scrawny backs, the tails of those who possessed them transformed into quivering umbrella-handles, and had begun the process of rubbing themselves, with a lack of discrimination that was clearly professional, against the legs of anyone they could find, temporarily interrupting the anarchist recital.

I slipped away, tiptoeing across the gravel between the millionaires' graves, and found an exit in the wall into the Rue du Repos and thence I made my way gingerly down the long escarpment of Ménilmontant to République.

I could hear police sirens streets away as I sprang up the Métro steps at Rambuteau. I had been working things out. Of the million or so lire I had got from the San Gallo apartment sale I still had under half left. There was the new racing season to attend to at Glorious Goodwood, York, Ascot. I had to pay Giuseppe, of course. I had all sorts of insurance to pay on the horses. I had the food bills to pay at York and, come to think of it, I still hadn't even paid the vet for poor Hazy Ray. Rag Doll Ltd and the Clapham Bookshop. It really was feasible. Maybe I could approach Pappa or at least the Trust for some 'matching funds'. After all these were sober investments, sound businesses. What could be sounder than a bookshop? Perhaps I could buy some premises. There was an old chemist's for sale on The Pavement. Live above the shop? Maybe they would release some capital on that basis. At any rate we could set up in London and see what we could work out. What could be more agreeable? I sniffed deeply, benevolently, making my way through the throngs at the ailing vegetable stalls in the Rue Rambuteau feeling a degree of pastoral warmth towards these stacks of cartons and cardboard boxes and their cheerless proprietors whose lacklustre shouts I had hated so much in the last few days.

I rounded the corner into Archives. The street was full of police cars with flashing lights. At first I thought it was another bomb, but nothing was shattered. Julia and Noel were standing talking to a group of gendarmes, just outside the entrance to no. 37. Perhaps someone had stolen her car. Whatever it was, was all over. Several of the police were climbing into their cars. Lines of cars were honking systematically, but with a resigned air, as they waited for the street to clear, and people were climbing out and standing by the open doors of their vehicles craning to see not quite what the blockage was, so much as when it would disappear so that they could be on their way.

'What's going on?' I said at my sister's elbow.

'Where have you *been*?' shouted a red-eyed Julia, bending suddenly almost double and covering her face with her two hands as she fell on to me. She had one shoe on and no stockings.

The gendarme caught her from behind and I caught her from the front.

'Woa,' I said. 'Steady up.'

'Monsieur . . . ?' the gendarme started to say as he hauled her off.

Noel intervened, his lip trembling. He gripped me by the arms and faced me. His whole face was working.

'It's Zonda, Raymond. She's . . . They've taken her to Bichât . . .'

I was bewildered.

'Will somebody please tell me . . .'

'Jumped out of the window . . .' said Noel, 'sixth floor. Not much hope I'm afraid . . .'

We drove to the hospital with the gendarme.

On the way it was very difficult to talk because of the noise of the siren. The voices of Julia and Noel sounded like whispers as they strained to tell me things in the police car, but I couldn't find much meaning in them.

Bichât was an enormous building, and they showed us down miles of corridor until we reached the place where they thought she was. Then we had to wait for a time. The gendarme excused himself and wished us good luck. We were shown some seats, opposite a man who kept sighing and vainly inspecting his hands for some feature he had overlooked. Some out-of-date copies of *Nouvel Observateur* and a vase containing blue flowers lay on a small table against a radiator. We sat down, our nostrils flooded with a nauseating mixture of kitchen and ether.

Julia sniffed, and looked over at the flowers.

'Hibiscus, I think,' she said.

I asked them what had happened. Where was Don?

They both started at once. They disagreed as to what had happened. Julia thought she had fallen, whereas Noel was quite confident she had jumped.

Where was Don? I repeated. Then Julia started telling the story in her inimitably disjointed way. She said that Zonda and Don had arrived from Monte Carlo and come to the flat in the middle of the night, looking very much the worse for wear.

'I didn't feel I could put them up,' she said, guiltily. 'Well I had Thierry there and as you know there isn't really room, but Zonda asked me and I still had the keys of the old place so I gave her the keys. She badly wanted to get in touch with you. I told you were at the Hôtel Américain and they went off. Then Zonda came back sometime later in the morning on her own, very upset. She had dispatched Don to find you . . .'

Two people appeared, one obviously a doctor, and shook hands with us. We introduced ourselves. Drs Vivier and Chapellier. I was simply '*un ami*'. They led us into a tiny office and we sat in cane chairs. Behind a glass screen people were moving about and typewriters were clicking. Dr Vivier leant forward. He took a deep breath and shook his head.

'I'm afraid your friend . . . we just couldn't save her, you know?' he said in English.

I heard Julia crumple.

He turned to Dr Chapellier.

'There was very little we could do,' said Dr Chapellier, almost resentfully. 'We took her out of the ambulance and carried her into the building and . . .' She gave an almost imperceptible puff of the lips.

'She was not conscious,' said Dr Vivier.

I wanted to see her. If I insisted, of course. They wondered if it was wise. They hadn't really had time to . . . She was not looking her best.

I insisted I needed to see her now.

'In that case,' said Dr Vivier, 'if you sign a form that you formally identify her, it will remove the necessity of such a thing later.'

They asked us to wait. There was a rapid conference and then Dr Vivier went behind the frosted-glass screen.

I looked across at the others. Noel was looking down at his shoes. Julia put her head on one side and came over to me. She knelt back on her heels with a swish of skirts by my chair and put her arms around my neck, pressing her hot tear-stained cheeks to mine.

'Poor baby,' she whispered.

I assumed this remark was meant for Zonda.

I put my arm round her.

'You and Noel don't have to come,' I said. 'I just want to see her.'

'Don't be silly,' said Julia looking back at Noel. 'Of course we'll come.'

I looked up for a long time without registering the three identical vaccination posters behind the desk. The blue vacant stare of a child receiving health and protection from a needle, repeated along the line.

I asked Julia to carry on. I needed to know everything that had happened.

'She came back in the morning. She was very upset . . . Raymond, are you sure you want to . . .'

I patted her reassuringly.

'Just tell it how it happened,' I said.

Julia sat back on her heels, condemning herself to this strange uncomfortable-looking position near the arm of my chair.

'Well, I couldn't believe it. She told me she had been diagnosed as having cancer . . .'

'Of course, I should have . . . the tests,' I said. 'What kind of cancer?'

'Cervix . . .'

'But she can't . . .' I said, helplessly using the present tense. 'She's only . . . only twenty years of age!'

'She was very angry with you.'

'With me? Why me?'

'Because . . . Oh I'm sorry. I just can't talk about this now . . . it's too . . .'

I looked at Noel, who didn't respond.

'She was furious, Raymond,' said Julia. 'Now she was going to have to go through the whole business of having an operation and chemotherapy and what have you and possibly die after a long and frightful illness and you didn't give a damn. Of course, she didn't know what she was saying. You had abandoned her, she said. She was high as a kite, popping pills the whole time. On automatic pilot really. She said the Italian doctors had refused to commit themselves as to what kind of chances she had. She shouldn't have gone to Monte Carlo at all, you know. I tried my best to calm her down. And then I rang Noel in desperation and he came, didn't you, Noel . . . ?'

'Where was Don all this time?' I asked.

'Disappeared. Never saw him again after the first time . . .'

'But why didn't she *tell* me?'

'She tried to, she said, but you were too obsessed with this thing of yours . . .'

At this point an orderly came in from the corridor carrying a clipboard and a bunch of keys and asked us if we would like to accompany him. The ether smell gave way to stale air, as we threaded our way through bales of used laundry stacked on metal trolleys, and then a sudden shock of fresh air as we pushed through two glass doors at the end of the building and strode across the yard into another building with an identical pair of wooden glass doors. The orderly took us down a few more corridors and then paused briefly for us to catch up before an unmarked door.

'Mind the step,' he said, as he unlocked the door.

I clung to my sister. We stumbled down into a room with a bare flagstone floor. A wooden crucifix was prominent high on the opposite wall between two Gothic mullioned windows. In the middle of the room stood a couple of trestle tables. Two forms lay beneath grey hospital blankets, their unseen limbs and features swelling and transforming the serge material into ridges and depressions like large clay models of landscapes. I put my arm awkwardly across Julia's shoulders. She was weeping loudly. We were motioned back by the orderly. He clearly couldn't remember which was which and had to check beneath both blankets before we could move forward and look. He peeled back the blanket a little way and nodded to me. I let Noel take care of Julia and stepped forward.

This wasn't her, surely. The face was quite different, much wider. Heavily streaked with dirt and plastered with patches of black blood, the hair stood away, as if it had been lacquered, from the dreadful smashed brow. One of the eyelids had lifted, and under its delicately curling blonde lash, I caught a glimpse of upturned bluish eyeball. Instead of her humorous, tip-tilted nose, a thing like a squat button sat in a marsh of scarlet bruising. Under the blocked nostrils a patch of black blood had been inefficiently wiped away, causing a long horizontal smear out onto the cheek the shape of an airforce officer's handlebar moustache. On top of this on the upper lip had oozed, the shade of glistening red housepaint, a coin-shaped leak of fresh blood. The front top teeth, dazzlingly white, were resting out in the faintest of bites on a gashed plum of bottom lip that had puckered and swollen to an unrecognisable size, giving the whole face an expression which I had never seen before, a shocking blandness all her own, as if she were reacting to an impenetrably private, sensual, inward-looking dream. I touched her cheek. She was still warm.

I stared at this alien, faintly Slavic creature without much belief. This didn't seem to be her. The feet lay fallen on their side, at the end of her upright legs, both pointing same way. I stared at the brown disk of the verruca under the sole of her left foot directly beneath the little toe, a blemish I had urged her so many times to have treated, which, far from having the effect of proving any association between this strange wide-faced peasant-looking person and Zonda, mockingly divorced them by coincidence, and proved the opposite.

But I was being asked to identify her as Zonda. I blinked angrily. It was so unfair, slipping away like this and leaving behind this rather coarse-looking simulacrum, not even a proper substitute really, for me to identify dishonestly. I hesitated and looked across at the other blanket. Perhaps there had been some kind of mistake. A mix-up. I even began to ask. A man they dragged out of the Seine, I was told. I hesitated while the clerk paused, his fountain pen poised over the form, the cap held towards me.

In the end, I had no choice. I scratched with someone else's black ink what for me has always been a lie. I identified that person on the trestle with Zonda.

Noel was in the adjoining sitting-room and Julia was in the bedroom itself when Zonda first moved off the bed where she had been lying quietly, apparently asleep, but Julia was already moving round on the other side of the bed picking up a bundle of tights and underwear of hers from where they had been thrown in the corner of the room on the floor to wash them for her. Noel was sitting at the table, reading the Bourse reports in *Le Monde* and trying to find out the new price of an ounce of silver, and she had to pass him at the table when she first stepped up to the window. At exactly the time she first sauntered casually into the sitting-room Julia went out of the door to the bathroom which is adjoining and from which, if you crane your head round the door, you can see a narrow sliver of sitting-room, including the left-hand side of the window, and, separating the rest of the underwear from the tights and balancing the bundle on the edge of the bath, she put a couple of pairs of tights in the sink, ran the hot and cold taps and shook some Calgon which was all she had out of the packet on the shelf above the sink and started washing. Noel looked up as he heard Zonda brushing past the table and nearly said something because she carelessly rucked up the tablecloth as she passed but had just found something in the paper which interested him and it wasn't until a moment later that he exclaimed aloud but still didn't look up because silver had gone up by several points yesterday and he had missed it. They both heard her give a brief sound which Noel described as 'like a grunt of satisfaction' and Julia described as a 'loud gulp'. When he looked up from the paper by what was almost a reflex action he grabbed but she was actually outside in the air in a patch of sunlight, back towards him, the wind catching her hair which was loose, every individual strand of which he could see, and her blouse and rippling it upwards at the waist. He nearly fell out himself in reaching to restrain her and was condemned to watch as she seemed to hang there just below him. There was a brief bellying up of the skirt with zebras on it, legs beginning to cycle slowly towards the end, mercifully over the face he thought. She bounced almost face-down off the roof of a parked car and hit the pavement with a crack that resounded down the street and brought people running out as far as the café on the corner of Blancs-Manteaux.

Julia said she was just through in the bathroom washing the tights when she heard the sound of Zonda's skirt brushing past the tablecloth. She heard Noel say 'Buggeration!' and put her head round the corner to ask what it was and was just about to say and by the way will somebody close the window because of the draught when she heard this funny gulp from the only partially visible Zonda at the window and actually came round the corner hands dripping to get a better view just in time to see the flutter of her garments and Noel diving and grabbing across the table in between and she was no longer there. It wasn't as if she had stood and definitely jumped somehow. It was more as if she had been leaning over and looking at something down below, something on this side down underneath, so that she had to crane to see it and had toppled over. Julia stood there in the middle of the room with Noel blocking out the light at the window and screamed and then there was this terrible noise from the street and then dead silence and Noel turning back into the room and saying 'Oh my God!' and then the noise of people running.

Had she actually seen her looking at something?

No because the wretched doorjamb was in the way and blocked a continuous view to the window. This was a surmise, but that was her sense of it.

Did anyone else see her?

Three more people saw her. Madame Rebstock in the flat opposite whose dining-room commands a perfect view. Madame Andonnet passing by below on the opposite side by the door of the Banque Nationale de Paris who happened to look up. And Monsieur Petitbled who was fixing his TV aerial some way down the street away on the roof opposite. No one on the same side of the street, to see how her head first protruded from the window and give an indication as to intention. Later, I found out that a man had been making a promotional film of the Centre Pompidou from the roof of the Crédit Municipal building at the corner of Archives and Francs-Bourgeois.

What about Madame Rebstock who had the perfect view?

Well, she saw her *at* the window, and she seemed to turn back to say something to someone in the room behind her, and then she was leaning by the window looking down, her hand resting on the right-hand side of the window-door on the catch, but then Madame Rebstock's young son Daniel had distracted her briefly, catching her round the knees as he ran from under the dining-room table, and when she looked up again, Zonda's head, the hair whipped over the face – was already feet below the lead guttering immediately below the window-sill. She was slanting forward, her body positioned slightly behind her.

Then what about the person, Madame Andonnet, who happened to look up just as she was passing the bank?

Well, she looked up for some reason and saw a head appear leaning well out of the attic window above her, a girl's because of the hair dangling round it – it was curious because, at that moment, another head of a person on the balcony beneath had just gone in, and Madame Andonnet was just about to laugh at the effect which was rather like a Dutch weatherclock when she heard the bang of the right-hand window as it crashed back against the roof at the side and the head at the top became a whole body pitching down through the air at an angle, the head thrown well forward, the coloured print skirt up somewhere around the waist.

What about M. Petitbled, fixing his aerial on the roof some way down the street on the opposite side? Had he seen anything which might help to resolve the question?

Well, unlike the others he saw everything – the whole sequence – from where he was mending the aerial about fifty yards away. She was standing at the window when he first saw her and she gave a little look backwards as if speaking to someone in the room – which she certainly wasn't doing, according to Noel and Julia, but it might have been a furtive glance which they didn't see because they weren't looking – and he saw her grasp the window-catch about halfway up as she leaned to support herself as she peered over the edge of the guttering down on to the street. Then she looked up and seemed to close her eyes against the sun but he couldn't be sure, made a gesture anyway like screwing up her eyes and looked down again into the street for about thirty seconds, and then she had been obliged to let go the window-door which had begun to move away from her with her weight – Yes, Julia and Noel and Madame Andonnet had all heard it bang as it flew against the slanting roof tiles after she had disappeared out of the window – and then she had gone down and his view had been cut off by the intervening rooftops.

Did he form any opinion as to whether she had fallen intentionally or accidentally?

No, he couldn't say.

Yes, Julia had forgotten about the window banging. It was after she had stopped scrubbing the tights and came into the room with her hands dripping soapsuds to find Noel blocking the light at the window and she heard the bang of the window-frame against the tiles of the mansard after she had disappeared from view.

And what about the person on the balcony below?

Madame Giraud, who had gone to the balcony to shake a duster out into the street below, had not seen anything at all but she had heard a window bang and clatter above as she was walking away from her balcony back through her dining-room towards her kitchen and then of course she had heard the crash below and ran back to the balcony.

There is a bar across the window, which forms the upper edge of about nine inches of wrought-iron lacework, above the ledge. Anyone stepping out of the window would have to negotiate this barrier.

Was she perhaps standing on the bar or had she partially stepped over it with one foot or wholly with two and was standing on the actual guttering outside? Surely this would tell one something about her intentions in the sense that if she had clambered either upon or over the bar, it was more likely that she intended to jump, but no one had registered her position at all in relation to the bar.

Then what about the young man, Monsieur Fauche, who had been shooting the promotional film of the Beaubourg above the rooftops from the top of the Crédit Municipal building on the corner of Francs-Bourgeois and Archives and who had been panning his camera across the rooftops?

Briefly in the corner of the film one saw her at the window, a vague shape well inside the room, and her right hand and arm begin to move out into the sunlight and then the camera lifted its angle suddenly up over the rooftops until it found and rested on the coloured blues and reds of the Beaubourg building just poking above the rooftops. I sat in M. Fauche's cold garage in Limoges and played the foot or so of film over and over again, freezing each frame and watching the disembodied hand emerge at the end of a length of pink sweater that had come back to me now with the rest of her clothes into the patch of weak sunlight on the window and move towards the lace-curtained french door to – presumably – push it further back and use it as a leverage and support ready for the next sequence of actions but the head, the face which would have told me everything, was in dim shadow behind the other french door of the window, the hand and then the arm moved across the aperture the thumb and fingers opening one could see straining one's eyes at the grain of the film to grip what was going to be the catch halfway up the french door of the window and never quite finishing their action as the camera began to refocus and jerked away upwards in a blur of grey leaded rooftop forms.

'I don't *know* what time it was . . .' said Julia. 'I suppose it could have been four o'clock. She rang the downstairs bell and I let them in and then I went about halfway down the top flight of stairs to meet them. I had my nightdress on. My feet were cold. She came in with Don behind her . . .'

'Wait a minute,' I said. 'You haven't got in the apartment yet. How did they come up the stairs?'

'Well, she came up first and Don came behind, carrying the bags. They were both groaning and she stopped, panting, at the stairwell on the third and then again on the fourth floor . . .'

'I thought you said it was the *fourth* . . .'

'Then too, but I could see their heads and their fingers on the banisters gripping as they came up from the bottom. This is where it really hits you, after the third . . .'

'So they definitely made two stops . . .'

'Yes, they said something I didn't catch . . . then the light went out and I had to go up and press the plunger for them . . . she was swearing as usual . . . I was rather annoyed about that because I had only just moved in here and I didn't particularly want to alienate the neighbours right at the beginning, little did I know . . .'

'Then what . . . ?'

'Well, she came round the corner and slumped against the wall just under the window, just before the last flight of steps with a lot of fuss and theatre – you know the sort of thing . . .'

'What did she have on?'

'Strange question for a man to ask . . . I don't remember – a white dress and a man's black leather jacket over the top of it which I took to be his – white espadrilles which were rather scuffed and dirty, no stockings, and a red ribbon tied in her hair . . .'

'What did she say?'

Julia, who was rather a good mimic but had no awareness of this, paused and looked over at the window:

'Cor fackin' 'ell,' she said with solemn accuracy, and then drew back with an embarrassed smile. 'You know how she talked . . .'

For a moment, I caught a flash in the timbre of the expression, the timing, the whole rhythm of the imitation, the flash of Zonda's presence. The words bore in upon my own saturating rhythms of thought that turned everything they contemplated to their own form of dust. It came for a moment from outside, from the past, like a breeze.

A request to repeat would only bring diminishing returns I knew.

'Go on,' I said non-committally.

'Well, they came in, Don slogging up behind her with the bags, and I made them some coffee on the stove and then we talked. She was very excited, almost raving. Plus it was difficult to believe what had actually been happening when you talked to her. I mean, it all seemed like some kind of fantasy when she told me about what had happened in Monte Carlo at the end and outside the hotel and that. I couldn't believe it. They were both very nervous, even Don. The moment after you had gone, apparently, Carlos and Philippe had caught up with them outside the hotel.

Carlos had a gun and he threatened them in broad daylight. She was really worried because she had to give them my address. At first she tried to give them a false address, but they had actually brought them to Paris with them in a car – what I didn't know of course was that they were waiting around somewhere downstairs at that moment. She gave me the impression they had lost them or they had gone looking for you or whatever. Anyway she wanted to know where you were. So I told her you were at the Hôtel Américain. Then Thierry woke up . . . and I wanted them to be quiet . . .'

'What about Don?'

'He seemed fairly out of it . . . frightfully ugly, don't you think?'

'Young Dean Martin?'

'Not so young . . .' said Julia.

'Well, they needn't have worried,' I said, 'they weren't after them but Monsieur Mooney and me, as long as I was with him . . .'

'I know . . . that's what I tried to explain to her . . . that you were really doing something heroic here . . .'

'Well, I wouldn't go so far as to . . .'

'So anyway, they went off leaving their bags with me . . .'

'How did she seem?'

'Pretty spaced out, but then you couldn't expect much else really after such a nightmare of a journey. She was terribly anxious to get in touch with you and explain that she hadn't had any choice about giving them my address. I really think they would have shot them – '

'I'm sure of it.'

'They both wanted to make phone calls, and I remembered the phone was still on at the old apartment so I gave them the keys and told them to help themselves, you see Thierry can't stand . . .'

'OK, so what happened when she came back?'

'That's just it. They didn't come back.'

'What do you mean? She was here when she . . .'

Julia pulled away a stray hair that was sticking to her cheek and stared intensely at it. Then she tucked it behind her ear, her eyes settling on me again. She laughed uncertainly.

'Seems unbelievably silly after the event – quite funny, really, the way it turned out. They were arrested, you see. Well, we were all arrested.'

'What for?'

I watched the hair starting to uncoil. Julia smiled involuntarily:

'It wasn't anything really, just a misunderstanding. You know what the atmosphere's like at the moment. But she was terribly proud of herself because she'd actually been arrested as a terrorist. As soon as they had arrived, the police had knocked on the door and carted them both off on suspicion. She managed to get a call through here and I had to go down and vouch for her. The police were quite hysterical and even tried to arrest *me*, I ask you, as the owner of the apartment. Apparently they'd been watching it because the neighbours had noticed various comings and goings. Anyway, Thierry came down thank God and vouched for me, and they let her go after a few hours grilling.'

'And Don?'

'Never saw him again. I think they deported him back to Israel, she told me.'

'So then you came back here?'

'Yes.'

'What sort of state was she in then?'

'She was altogether different. Manic. Fantasising about being a terrorist. She kept raving about Silke Maier Witt, as if she knew her personally . . .'

'Who's *she*, for God's sake?'

'Oh haven't you heard? West German. I've got the paper here somewhere. I'll give it to you. It's all over Paris. Had a germ-warfare factory in her flat . . .'

'So what happened *then*?'

'We came back and that was when she started talking so wildly, popping these pills and so forth. She and Don had split, she said.'

'Perforce,' I murmured. But Julia didn't hear me.

'She was incredibly restless and anxious, striding about like some sort of caged animal – thank God Thierry had gone off to the office by then – but eventually she and I managed to have a talk, you know, about this cancer business – '

'What about it?'

'Well, I've told you. She blamed you for the whole thing . . .'

'What *exactly* did she say?'

Julia paused and lit a Kent. She assumed a Maidstone accent.

' "The bastard, the fucking *bastard* did this to me . . ." She said she couldn't get any sense out of those doctors in Florence and she had been desperate to fly home to England to get some decent medical advice. She'd eventually gone down to Monte Carlo, she said, because she was at her wits' end. Poor thing, she couldn't think what to do next. Everything was final . . . she was going to meet Don . . .'

'But I thought you said they'd split up?'

'The situation was confused. Don had told her he would meet her in Italy. He had asked her to go to Fiesole, but she already knew he had some sort of domestic set-up there with an Italian woman.'

'You mean, this is before he was deported?'

'Before?'

'Yes. Did she . . . Is there an address?'

'Try the marble address book.'

'In her things?'

'Yes. He had let this slip, apparently while you were in Florence. Anyway, she got wilder and wilder and got back on this cancer thing. Apparently Don had the stuff and she thought she'd have to go with him – it got a bit melodramatic by this time – I didn't really believe this. I just thought she was trying to touch me, you know – unless I could let her have some money in the meantime so she could find a dealer here, but then at the same time she was waiting for you all along . . .'

'That sounds like surmise . . .'

'Well you couldn't tell, really, she kept saying she would kill you with her own bare hands and all this kind of thing . . . she got really wild but I never quite believed it all – ' Julia smiled. 'Perhaps it's because you're my brother . . .' she said. 'Anyway I did get a bit worried about her because she had this foam in the corner of her mouth and her eyes – her eyes looked really peculiar, you know and she had by then started rambling incoherently and I couldn't make head nor tail of what she was talking about half the time . . .'

'What sort of things . . .'

'Oh I don't know, something about Gauguin and the rectangle. I couldn't make any sense of it . . .'

'Just an argument we once had . . .' I said.

'Well, that was when I called Noel, because you know she's always liked Noel and I thought he could help, you know, calm her down. She was shivering and her teeth were chattering like someone in a fever and I was getting a bit worried about her . . .'

Julia drew deeply on her wholesome Kent, the only cigarettes she has ever smoked, and tried to think.

'She was just like a live wire . . . like someone with St Vitus' dance . . . I put her in the shower and made her wash while we waited for Noel . . . and she washed her hair and put on that old skirt of mine with the zebras on it . . . didn't suit her really at all . . .' She began to weep, shoulders shaking again. 'Sorry I can't help it . . . when I think of how thin she was . . . little stick of a thing, you know Raymond, and those great big eyes of hers . . .'

'And you still think she . . . fell?'

She wiped her eyes.

'Well, I mean she had such a lot to look forward to in fact – ' she looked at me, wincing, as I listed the advantages in having cancer and your boyfriend run out on you – 'No it's true, she was very exercised about you and knowing you were safe and worried about having given them your address through me . . .'

'But you said she *hated* me . . . I can't understand this . . .'

'Yes, because she thought you ran out on her. She wouldn't have been in that position if you hadn't . . .'

'Yes, but I – ' I smiled fatuously, not wanting to acknowledge my embarrassment – 'Surely she could see it was only a temporary situation and we would soon be together again – I mean, I had this chap on my hands who'd just had a heart attack for God's sake, what was I supposed to do just abandon him . . . but that was the idea, that we would be coming back to England again . . . just as soon as . . .'

'Maybe in your head you were, but she didn't *know* any of this . . . this deal business has completely taken you over in the last few months, you have to admit Raymond . . .'

'Yes, I suppose . . .' I said. 'But I still . . .'

'Don't you understand – she felt insecure – she didn't feel you had a future at *all* together . . .'

'So you mean that's why you think she . . . But I thought you said she thought she was going to die and all this melodramatic stuff . . .'

'It wasn't all that melodramatic necessarily,' said Julia. 'It was pretty far on, you know . . .'

'Alright, but . . .'

'Anyway, what I meant was that that's what she *said* . . . She took one look at the future, and it just seemed as though she was going to be an invalid for ever and possibly die in painful circumstances . . . She looked it in the face, the long trail of operations, culminating in a hysterectomy so she could never have any children and then, after that the chemotherapy and the predictable – totally predictable – sinking into skin and bone – and she just thought – as anybody would really – well why not just . . .'

'Well, if she thought that . . . why don't you . . .'

'That's what she *said*,' repeated Julia, 'but at the actual time, everything was much more immediately hopeful – we were waiting for you to come from Charles de Gaulle as we thought – we knew you were seeing him off that morning – and I don't think she could *really* have felt as if it was all over . . . Noel and I told her repeatedly what nonsense she was talking . . . how much we knew you loved her . . . and then she just . . . It shows you can never tell when they're on drugs . . .'

She slumped down in her chair and her eyes filled with tears again.

A single fly was moving in a determined set of trapezoids, covering all the space in the empty dining-room, area after area, settling back after each new area on two bottles of Cuvée du Président, one empty, one barely touched, and a litter of plates in front of us. From upstairs in rooms above the dark narrow Rue au Maire, came the rhythmic crash of the mah-jong pieces and the shouts of the fanatical Chinese players. We had come at Noel's instigation for cous-cous at Ahmar's, but neither of us really had any appetite. I didn't like slumming in Algerian restaurants, but I also wanted Noel's version of what had happened, independently of Julia, before the final sequence. Julia had conveniently dropped out, so conveniently that I couldn't quite decide whether she was being tactful or whether Thierry was being demanding, leaving the boys anyway to have supper together. Noel watched the fly as he spoke:

'Well, Julia telephoned me and told me that Zonda was arrived from Monte Carlo and that it would be nice for us to meet. Perhaps I would like to come over? All this was delivered through clenched teeth in a tone which suggested strongly that she was there in the room and that Julia was in a panic about what to do with her, so I beetled over . . .'

'And what did you find?'

'Well, I could understand why Julia was in such a panic. She was uncontrollable – hyperactive, blaspheming and cursing and making accusations right, left and centre. You know, it was one of those situations where she would turn on you if you said too much and turn on you if you said too little. You couldn't really do anything with her.'

'And what were the accusations about?'

'About you, mainly, and the whole cancer bit . . . Fact is, she blamed it all on you . . .'

'On me? How come?'

He swallowed and licked his lips, his eyes involuntarily following the droning fly.

'Oh, because the doctors had told her it was caused by . . .'

'By what?'

'By having to do with someone who . . .' The fly abruptly ceased its drone and he tore his eyes away. 'Who was uncircumcised.'

'Who *what*?'

'Who didn't care about hygiene beforehand.'

'But, as I said, Noel, this is nonsense – we hardly . . .'

'Well, she was adamant about this and kept repeating it . . .'

So this was what Julia hadn't wanted to talk about at the hospital. I put on my best lawyer's manner:

'Do you think this could have been a motive for what she . . . ? Don't be inhibited Noel, I want to know . . .'

'Well, I don't think this question is quite the same sort of thing at all – I mean, as to what she actually *did* . . . you know already how I see all that . . .'

'Yes, but the question is . . . I'm sorry to play the lawyer here . . . did her attitudes as expressed to you, *predispose* you to think she did what she did voluntarily or not?'

'I can't tell . . . one sees what one sees . . . Why don't we leave this sort of thing to the court, Raymond?'

'Because, Noel dear, the court will be a lottery . . . Tell me why you think she jumped out of that window . . .'

'Because I think everything was too much for her. She was in a vortex. She no longer knew where she was. It was a world she didn't want to be in, because it clearly didn't want her.'

'But that's not true . . .'

'It was true from where *she* was standing. She couldn't see the future at all . . .'

'So she . . .'

'Yes.'

'It doesn't make sense . . .'

'Well, what do *you* think?' said Noel. 'That it was just the drugs? A spur-of-the-moment thing, a mood decision?'

'What I think is that if she jumped, she flipped a mental coin – she wouldn't have done it deliberately, it wasn't a four-square moral decision taken with all her faculties about her. By the way, that reminds me, Julia said she mentioned something in her ravings about Gauguin and the rectangle . . . Did you hear anything like that?'

'I didn't hear anything about that. Yes, she did say at one point: "Let's draw the line and fill it in!" She said something like that a couple of times . . .'

'You heard her say those words?'

'Well,' said Noel, 'you know what I'm like at accents and remembering what people say . . . but, words to that effect – I mean, it sounded financial to me – I thought she was talking about money, not geometry . . .'

'And Gauguin?'

'Who?' said Noel. He shook his head. 'No nothing about painting,' he said. 'For God's sake Raymond, you should have seen her; she didn't know what she was talking about – she was hardly in a state to discuss Western culture with me!'

Florence

Eventually I had to go back to San Gallo and clear out the few things we left and to say my goodbyes to Julian and company, Kleenex opposite and Deaf-Aid and Testucchio and the people at Sotto Hasa. I rang and made arrangements for the refuse people to make a special trip and cart it all away. I bagged up her hundreds of pairs of shoes from the bedroom, her books, the painting gear, and the smock which still lay where she had thrown it over the stepladder under the dry cans of crusted paint and the stiff brushes she had not bothered to put in the spirits. I left the cement sacks and fridge for the incoming people. It was still as if Zonda had gone out shopping or to see her friends. I mean the real Zonda. And that story of Paris, which I found increasingly fantastic and difficult to take seriously, was only that – a story. The old radio still stood on top of the fridge with the knitted interstices of gold thread between the bakelite rays of the sun which was setting stylishly in the bottom left-hand corner like a section of the Japanese flag. The little square red 1920s travelling alarm clock I bought her stood by it. I stood in the kitchen looking out over the chimney immediately in front of me and the spot in the lead guttering at the base of the chimney where the white cat used to curl. Nothing marked this as a spot at all.

Winter was in the air. Immediately in front of me stood the two large terracotta garden pots which Zonda had insisted we lug away from the shop ourselves there and then through the broiling streets and haul upstairs. She had been attracted by the rather crudely moulded fillets of leaves and swags of grapes which chased each other round the rims of these articles. The plants whose names I had never known, sturdy-looking dark-leaved affairs, had wilted and turned yellow, hanging in lifeless strings. The dark soil which had been watered so religiously had turned to a greyish powder of leafmould, empty now except for a few dry sticks that supported nothing.

In the bathroom, the soap she had been the last to use lay in the pale blue mother-of-pearl fish-dish she had bought from San Lorenzo market. I turned it over; between the ribs of the dish and the soap cake lingered a smear of moisture through which two earwigs were busily struggling, their tremulous legs slipping and sliding, as they bolted from the sudden light and scuttled away over the edge of the porcelain. Shampoo bottles stood round on the edge of the bath behind taps flecked with old soap stains. A couple of broderie anglaise blouses and a heavy cotton cardigan which she referred to as her 'cardy' in childish language hung over the bath, their weight bowing down in the middle the primitive line she had erected until their hanging sleeves almost touched the enamel, beneath them a large spider which sat knowingly on the incline of the bath, near to the dry plug-hole. From the Ali Baba laundry basket came a stream of garments – paisley scarves and silk handkerchiefs and brightly coloured underwear which had been so tightly packed down they had braided informally together in long twisted strings – things which were mainly unfamiliar to me as I pulled them out in a stream hand over hand like a conjuror from an enormous hat until they lay in heaps all over the floor, giving off the smell of rancid biscuits, an impossible volume of a past that was not mine. I looked at them, bewildered. I could see that their reverse order had an archaeological significance, but these remnants, even, somewhere near the bottom in a very remote area, a familiar pair of pink stretch pants which, I could not refrain from noticing, still bore a yellow peardrop stain in their white net gusset, carried no charge, connected back with nothing. I bagged them up with the contents of the fridge.

Fiesole

There was just one more thing I had to do.

It was late afternoon, I got a cab out to Fiesole. It took the driver and me quite some time to find the house, tucked away as it was down a steep grass driveway between two very large palm-surrounded villas on the side of a hill overlooking the valley of the Arno. It was a modest house, modern, featureless, tiled patio, shuttered, balcony running round the outside on the ground floor, the garden visibly overgrown. I rang the bell.

For a moment I expected the obviously female figure that showed and hesitated behind the frosted glass to be Zonda. A curtain flicked at the side of the porch. The woman opened the door and stood there. I was introducing myself, going through the rigmarole, when he appeared at the end of the hall. He stood for a moment, then lifted his shades:

'Well, well, son of a gun,' he said cautiously, not advancing from his position deep in the hallway. The woman flattened herself against the wall and even raised herself on her toes.

'It's alright, Don,' I called, 'I am not here for any aggressive purpose!'

'Relax, Morena,' said Don. '*Non ti facce malo . . .*'

He advanced and came out on to the tiled patio. He opened his mouth under the sunglasses and laughed a dry laugh. Over his shoulder I saw Morena slip away down the hall and turn the corner into the house.

'Hey, Ray, kinda surprised me back there. Never thought I'd

be seeing you again. Tell you the truth, thought you was somebody else I'm expecting . . .' He put an arm round my shoulder and laughed as we turned towards the house. 'Guess he won't come when he's expected, though!'

We sat in a cold sunroom on two hard chairs which he fetched, surrounded by boxes. Everything was half-packed, with the exception of a folding card table which stood under the window, across the baize surface of which lay a large backgammon board inlaid with sea creatures at the corners – a starfish and a ray, a sea anemone and a squid, a cuttlefish and some shells. It was open. A couple of dice lay in the inner board, as if they had just been thrown from the cylindrical leather cup, and on the rim the doubling dice had four uppermost.

He apologised for the enormous glass of Chivas Regal. It was all he had. He lit a cigarette and poured himself one. We chinked. Mud in your eye.

'Hey, Ray, so what's new?' he said. He stretched out his legs, crossed them, and placed his hands behind his head and looked across at me with his vacant smile in what was obviously an effort to appear relaxed and casual.

I told him what was new.

He whistled at the Mooney part, but when I came to the Zonda part, he winced and didn't quite know what to do, except fidget as I kept my eyes on his face, shake his head and pour a couple more shots of whisky. I explained that I was still trying to resolve the question of what had probably happened. Would he just talk and let me ask him a few questions – for my own satisfaction, he must understand, nothing official. The inquest would not hear of anything he said to me and having been deported from France to Israel he was not likely to be subpoenaed or anything.

He laughed.

'Well Ray, I can think of one straightaway, if you're gonna git personal like, and the answer's no – '

'No no Don,' I hastened to explain, 'I'm not – it's not that sort of thing I'm interested in – as a matter of fact I had assumed you –

No, it's more the state of mind she was in that interests me . . .'

'Well, didn't anyhow. Never once. Couldn't make it.' He gave me a thick, rueful smile. 'You won. Had her head twisted up every which way over you, my boy, that's how I see it anyhow . . .'

I saw that he knew nothing about the cancer.

Morena came in carrying on her hip a bawling infant wearing a baseball cap and gripping a plastic replica of a Thompson submachine-gun, shushing him and jigging him up and down, while she dumped things on the pile on top of the boxes. He kept his eyes fixed balefully on Don.

'See, Morena and me and Gianfranco – ' He leaned over and caught the child's free hand – 'We're going back to Tel Aviv, pronto, and we have to pack up and get outa here Ray, don't we kid, eh?' He chucked the child's puckering cheek.

I appreciated this, but I just wanted to go over one or two things with him. For example what had happened immediately after Mooney and I had left them outside the Louvre, how did they get to Paris, and what happened then when they had arrived?

Morena said something I didn't catch in rapid Italian, but Don lifted his shoulders and shrugged and told her to wait. She glowered and went out, the child's level of crying rising sharply as she went out of sight through the door into the kitchen.

'Well, they hit the exit just after you left in the cab and they got us into their car. Boy, this Carlos guy had flipped. He was kind of, you know, crazy. They wanted to know where you guys had gone. She tried to pretend you'd gone back to Florence, but that goddam gutless De Negris just couldn't take any more and he just sang – tweet tweet! – and they got the whole bananas – didn't do him any good though – they just left him there – kicked him out on the goddam highway – out through the door – and left him in a big heap down on the sidewalk – anyhow, now they knew you had a sister and they knew you were making for her place so they took us along for the ride and went up to Julia's place and she got the keys off Julia and we went up to the other apartment and then what happened – let me see . . .'

He got up and poured another shot in my glass.

'Oh yeah, I know, they came with us. You know, they weren't such bad guys. But this time, she was really working on them – by this time we was all pretty much, y'know buddy buddy – she made it to the phone while I kept 'em busy, y'know, but then they kind of wanted to know who she was phoning and it all got kinda messy and she had to tell 'em you were at this here Alberto's place because these guys were goin' to blow my goddam brains all over the walls right that minute and so they left and she was trying to phone you and warn you they were maybe on their way – '

'I see. I'm afraid she didn't manage to get through . . . and what happened then?'

'Well, next thing I know there's this knocking on the door and imagine my surprise when it's a bunch of gendarmes – hell I mean they must have been watching us all the way up from Monte Carlo – picked us up as if they knew who they were looking for OK, and so they rode us downtown and boy they really went for us – kept asking did I know this Jan Dekirk guy. Looked at my passport and told me they knew I was this Jewish counter-insurgency agent and all this stuff looking for the Arabs after this Copernic thing, y'know? – boy, I didn't know what the hell they were talking about, y'know?'

'You were separated at that time?'

'Yeah, I never saw her again – no, I lie. I *did* catch a glimpse of her once in a corridor some guy pushing her in front of him past the door of this room I was in, y'know.'

'What were they asking her?'

'I wish I could help ya, Ray – I never saw her again – I guess maybe same as me anyhow then they started on about this Dekirk guy and this Rue Chaillot thing – y'know, showed me photographs of them, him and this German broad, Silky whatsaface . . .'

'Silke Maier Witt – she's a terrorist . . .'

'Yea, that's right – Silky whatever – I didn't know nothing, man, but they just kept on for hours – wanted to know

428

everything about your sister's place – they even made like she had told them things about this Silky, you know? – '

'What kind of things?'

'Things about this conspiracy – they tried it all out on me – said *she'd* admitted it – why didn't I?'

'Admitted what?'

'That she was in on this germ warfare thing – I mean, for Chrissakes Ray, germ warfare? – there was this big sonofabitch kept offering me these goddam cigarettes and this other little one with the moustache kept giving me hell y'know?'

'What is this germ warfare – what are you talking about?'

'Hey, man, I don't know from nuthin' – all I know is they figured we were mixed up in this germ warfare thing with this Silky broad, you know – so they figured we was making like another factory at your sister's place? – Christ, I mean all we had was a few lines of coke, y'know – and there was a little smack in a Cellophane pack. Can you believe that?'

I could readily believe it.

'Anyhow these two jokers kept switching between giving me the hard stuff and giving me goddam yellow cigarettes to smoke tasted like goddam camel shit – excuse my French – and then switching over and the big one giving me the hard stuff and the other one gets all nice and then the big one starts shouting at me . . .'

'She told Julia that they had arrested her on suspicion of being connected with a West German terrorist organisation. I read in a newspaper they were manufacturing an organism called *clostridium botulinum* . . . but then they let her go . . .'

'If you know already, what the hell you ask me for? All I know is they come to me and say "OK, Mr Divine, you free to go back now, we goin' to deport you back to Israel," I goes "Oh *no!*" because this was a goddam disaster for me, uh, can you imagine?'

'Israel?'

'Yeah, I mean I kept trying to get them to drop me off in Italy but these guys jest wouldn't move an inch, man. I had to go to great lengths to get 'em to – I mean they wanted to fly me to Jerusalem and all – I mean, Jeez, Jerusalem, man! – I had to go to great lengths indeed to get them to fly me to Tel Aviv . . .'

'And how . . . did she seem before you were arrested?'

He paused to listen while a fresh outbreak of bawling from Gianfranco broke out somewhere in the depths of the house and the noise of Morena's voice burrowed under his high-pitched cries, cajoling, wheedling and coaxing him into his regulation set of alto sobs.

'Waal, she was *real* stuck on you, boy, was she *jest* – kept talking whole time about Raymond this and Raymond that – goddam it Ray! you couldn't! – '

Morena came in dragging the child. She looked at her watch.

'Yeah, I know honey – ' Don said over his shoulder ' – I know we gotta go – I *know* all that – jest, jest let me kinda deal with one thing at a time huh? Willya? I'll be through here in a second – I just have to tell him somethin' right? Look, honey – '

He sprang out of his chair and grabbed the Chivas Regal bottle by the neck. He placed a hand on one of her upper arms as she talked away at him, and employed the cap of the bottle to brush caressingly against the other.

'Honey, jest listen a minute willya! – Have I ever? No no – ' He placed a finger against his lips for a moment – 'Have I *ever* . . . let you . . . down?'

She slowed the intensity of her speech and looked at him doubtfully as she finished her sentence.

'Have I?'

She stared. He stroked her arms up and down, one with the bottle neck.

'I give you my word, we'll go pack up jest as soon as Ray and I have finished talking, honey, I swear it. Goddam it, what the hell do I want to stay here for and let them get me, huh?'

She nodded finally and trailed the child off back into the house.

He threw himself down on his chair and raised his eyes to the ceiling.

'See how I'm placed here, Ray? – I tell ya she was one hell of a gal – they couldn't find no dope anywhere when they took us in – ya know why? – because she swallowed the goddam packet – '

He laughed at himself and whistled and hooted. He pinched thumb and forefinger an inch wide and then turned it round, miming a rectangle two inches long.

'Straight down . . . Wooo!' He laughed to himself again. 'Attagirl!'

'And this meant?'

'Well, this meant they couldn't get anything on us and that's when they got to using this terrorist idea – that's my idea anyhow . . .'

I now knew the answer to a question that had been puzzling me vaguely. Where had she got the dope from when she was back at Julia's place? She had passed it in her stool in the bathroom.

'I guess . . .' said Don.

He was about to say something but changed his mind, as Morena came in again and he followed her out into the kitchen. I strolled over to the backgammon table and stood in front of it, idly looking down into the garden. Don didn't know anything else, I was pretty sure.

I began to play out the game, as I waited for their argument to grind to a halt in the kitchen, rolling the dice and counting the men off in neat piles. I wanted White to reverse his position over Black. By the time Don came back in, Black had begun to make some poor decisions. He looked over my shoulder.

'About it, Ray,' he said. 'We gotta split. Morena already called you a cab . . .'

I turned and looked at him. He shrugged.

'What do you want me to do now?' I asked in a semi-rhetorical way, but knowing he would take Black's part. The game was poised at its conclusion. White had one man each on his 6, 5 and 2 points. I had rolled 3-2 and used the 2 to bear off his man from the two point.

We stood side by side and stared down at the board.

'Go on,' I prompted.

'With a three you could go from the five to the two point,' he said.

'That only gives me a thirty-six per cent chance of getting off in one throw next time . . . whereas,' I smiled at him and reached forward for the white piece, 'if I move from the six to the three point, I think you'll find that I have a thirty-nine per cent chance.'

'Bluff,' he scoffed.

The cab appeared nosing down the grass drive. I looked at Don, and smiled.

'No, I remember my tables. If you finish the game out, White will probably win now,' I said.

'Same old Ray. Wanna bet?' He showed the gap between his teeth.

We went out on to the patio.

'One last thing. Did she ever say anything to you about being . . . ill?'

He looked at me puzzled as I climbed into the cab and leant on the window sill.

'Sick? No I don't think so Ray. She was one of the best . . . a great kid . . .' He sighed, as the engine started up. 'She had class. She had spunk, y'know, more'n most guys . . .'

I told him to look after himself as the cab moved away.

He waved and lifted the bulge in his pocket where, I assumed, the Rossi lay.

'Don't worry about a thing man, we'll be long gone!'

Morena was dragging him by the arm as we moved away down the drive. He turned, pulled away from her and laughed his Dean Martin laugh, cupping his hands round his mouth.

'Wanna bet?' I heard him shout as we turned under a hanging spray of leaves and he was lost to view.

At the top of the drive, we almost collided with a long-bodied black limousine which was swinging confidently in off the road. The driver, an Arab who was wearing a light tan jacket, cursed and pulled over into the ditch, leaving the car at an angle grossly unsuited to its prestige. I saw an arm and an elbow and a leather-gloved hand in the back of the car extended against the darkened glass of the back window as the well-dressed occupant braced himself against possible collision and retrieved his poise. There was a burst of sharp discussion inside the limousine and then between the driver and the cab-driver, and we pulled out and headed down into the square, the taxi-driver throwing his cigarette violently through the window and continuing for some time to articulate his neglected contribution to this conversation. I looked back to catch the end of the limousine gliding into the drive.

Geneva

The international transit hall at Geneva was a vast desert of static-filled carpet in the middle of which perched a tiny oval-shaped watering hole, a bar so small that the two glossy barmaids in their minuscule aprons, the tall fair and the short dark, scarcely had room to step round one another, but instead were obliged to hold each other lightly as they passed, performing an unpredictable dance of squeezes which they had brought to a fine art, back to back, front to front, back to front, front to back, in the course of their perpetual smiling rotations, clockwise and counterclockwise. Which would it be next? I sat on my high stool, and caught the eye of the bull-necked American two places down.

'Back to back, next time. Care to wager?' I said aloud, translating it into German to increase the chances of including the man between us whose mulish head, to my delight, reproduced exactly the contours of Spearmint's descendants. He was asking for a credit card slip.

The American laughed into his drink. He shook his head repeatedly.

'Come on. Back to back,' I insisted.

The muleheaded man was still waving, but both barmaids were round the other side of the bar.

'You lose. It's front to front,' said the American, pointing up at the mirror hanging on the corner of the wooden fascia. 'I can see.'

'No, no. The other side doesn't count – even in the mirror.'

'Since when?'

We argued the conditions of the bet, while the mulehead grew more and more impatient between us, muttering to himself.

'Want to have a go?' I asked him. 'It's still open. You have four chances. Drinks for the three of us. Split positions don't count.'

He begged my pardon while I stared up at his head. The resemblance was truly remarkable.

'Hey,' said the American.

I shrugged.

'OK,' I suggested, 'let our friend here be the judge.'

At last the tall fair one came round the end of the bar and approached him. We held our breath: the other did not appear. As she leant over to get the credit card slips, her sleeve caught the glass perched on the edge of the sink behind her and knocked it on to the floor.

'Oh *shoot!*' I heard her hiss under her breath as she looked down, dropping her head to kick aside the fragments. Up to then, orders had been taken in French or German and I had assumed the two girls were Swiss.

She put the credit card slip and the pen on the counter, still looking down and kicking surreptitiously.

'So you're English.'

Bunnie, a nineteen-year-old half-French flaxen chestnut expelled from Bedales for arson, sighed at the coarseness of what she thought was my come-on and raised her eyes.

'Please,' she said wearily.

'Do you know,' I said to her with the utmost sincerity, 'you remind me of one of my favourite racemares, Tokamura.'

She looked up and focused on me with her hazel eyes, so pleasingly wide apart.

'Well that's original!' she laughed bitterly as she mopped the counter with a savage sweep. 'I'll say that for you.'

We turned to look up at the clickety-clack of the flight departures. The mulehead gave a cry. His Air India flight to Delhi was boarding.

'So much for the referee,' I murmured to the American. I took out my diary, turned it laterally and picked up the pen from the counter. Across the page, I wrote:

'Could it be that something is causing you unhappiness?'

I swivelled it round towards her. As she glanced down and read it, she was shaking her head ambiguously. Maria, the Swiss-Italian, appeared round the bar. The American tensed as she approached plucking up glasses until they formed a fan in her plump fingers. When I looked down, the diary had been left on the counter and I read upside-down the words:

THIS PERFECTLY *DREARY* JOB!

Bunnie had already turned away, smiling to a customer on the other side, and did not cross Maria. The American blew his cheeks out at the near-miss and took another sock at his beer.

'I absolutely *adore* horses,' said Bunnie wistfully when she returned. 'I used to ride really well.'

I agreed that it was a healthy outdoor occupation. I was just setting up a stud-farm. Looking for new staff. Perhaps she'd like to come on board?

She was still leaning absentmindedly over the counter. Briefly she glanced back over her shoulder as two olive-coloured sets of fingers gripped her arms on each side just above the elbow and the shadowy hardworking Maria passed murmuring in soft protest behind her to take an order at the other end of the bar.

Triumphantly, the American moved up a place next to me, hauling his bulky briefcase up onto his knee.

'That's it. Back to front, I win!' he said, swinging in the meatplate handshake. 'Howdy. Brad Porcaro?'

I opened my mouth, enacting a slow double-take from Bunnie and back:

'You mean . . . *the* Brad Porcaro?'

He simpered.

'Well, I . . .'

He licked his lips, and looked down uncertainly at his half-open briefcase.

'The one who had to cut Howard Hughes's Arbies with a special germ-free stainless-steel knife?'

Brad held up both hands, backing off:

'Hold on a minute. That's . . . you got me mixed up with . . . *Dick* Porcaro . . .' He laughed uneasily. 'Used to be at the Desert Inn? No, we're operating out of the Midwest . . .'

Bunnie inclined her head in a pastoral trance, remembering her first little pony, Skippy.

'No it's just I could help overhearing you mentioning a stud-farm just now, Mr?' said Brad.

I introduced myself, reeling off my assets and breeding connections, my distinguished career as a correspondent of *The European Racehorse*.

Bunnie gave a soft whoop. It seemed she had been at prep school with some remote Bosanquet scion. She set up Brad's beer, another large vodka and tonic for me, and, I noticed, one for herself.

'This is really amazing,' Brad was saying several drinks later as he dug in his briefcase. 'You see, Raymond, my brother and I are in business together. Harold in fact works as a consultant for a subsidiary of Citibank in Chicago . . . and we've been working on setting up a stud-farm for some time now. We have a great little property in mind, but we just can't seem to get the European breeding connections we need. We need an analyst for these markets and it sounds as if you might be just the man we're looking for. Right now the yield slopes for trading in bloodstock, as I'm sure you're aware, are very encouraging . . . As a matter of fact, I'm over here raising some capital for collateral . . .'

He took out a sheaf of brochures and prospectuses from his briefcase and dumped them on the bar.

Bunnie and I looked at each other as Brad bent over to select the first of his brochures. I raised my glass.

'What am I getting myself into?' asked Bunnie.

'Whatever it is, let's *do* it!' I said, clinking her.

Brad laughed weakly.

438

'Hey I'll drink to *that*,' he said, sending his licked thumb and forefinger on their journey to the right page.